BURNING B

Maurice Leitch was b
Antrim and educated in
to writing after working as a teacher in a
country primary school for six years, and
then trying his hand as a BBC radio
producer in Belfast. His first novel,
published in 1965, was *The Liberty Lad*,
which was followed by *Poor Lazarus*,
which won the *Guardian* Fiction Prize. In
the same year he moved to London to
become a producer in the BBC's radio
drama department.

Also by Maurice Leitch

CHINESE WHISPERS
THE HANDS OF CHERYL BOYD

BURNING BRIDGES

Maurice Leitch

ARROW BOOKS

Arrow Books Limited
20 Vauxhall Bridge Road, London SW1V 2SA

An imprint of Random Century Group

London Melbourne Sydney Auckland Johannesburg
and agencies throughout the world

First published in Great Britain by Hutchinson 1989
Arrow edition 1990

Printed and bound in Great Britain by
The Guernsey Press Co Ltd
Guernsey, C.I.

ISBN 0 09 963400 7

For Theo

Acknowledgements

'I'M A LONESOME FUGITIVE'
Author/Composer: Casey Anderson and Liz Anderson
© 1982 Four Star Music Inc.
Reproduced by permission of Acuff Rose Opryland Music
Inc.

'ROSE GARDEN'
Author and Composer: Joe South
© 1975 Lowery Music
Reproduced by permission of Lowery Chappell

'I'LL NEVER GET OUT OF THIS WORLD ALIVE'
Composer/Author: Fred Rose and Hank Williams
© 1952 Milene Music Inc.
Reproduced by permission of Acuff Rose Opryland Music
Inc.

'LOST HIGHWAY'
Author/Composer: Leon Payne
© 1957 Fred Rose Music Inc.
Reproduced by permission of Acuff Rose Opryland Music
Inc.

'APARTMENT No. 9'
Words and music by Johnny Paycheck and Bobby Austin
© 1967 Mayhew Music Co. Ltd. (a Kassner Group
Company)
Reprinted by permission of Kassner Associated Publishers
Ltd, London, England

'MY ARMS STAY OPEN LATE'
Details not known at time of going to press.

'MY HEROES HAVE ALWAYS BEEN COWBOYS'
Details not known at time of going to press.

—ONE—

'Apartment No. 9'

And the sun will never shine,
In apartment number nine ...

The words had risen unbidden to his lips for some reason
the moment he turned in under the high archway and
through the cemetery gates, their squared black bars thicker
than a wrist. That old song of heartbreak – Tammy
Wynette at her most hard done by. He sang the refrain a
second time but if an association was there it managed to
elude him.

There was a hut of sorts just within the gates, and out of
its open window craned the caretaker curious to see what
new lunatic the place had attracted this time. Genuine
mourners seemed a thing of the past. Vandals, winos,
junkies, sniffers of glue, couples – often of the same sex –
with filth in mind, they all trooped past without shame or
decency. But this one didn't seem to belong to that legion
of the damned. A suit – he was wearing a dark suit; and a
hat, some manner of western thing, low-crowned, black, a
silver band. About six foot, hair to the collar, sideburns,
and, when he turned, a flash of metal at the throat, a further
cowboy effect, one of those bootlace ties, a brooch instead
of a knot. He was studying the sign that said CREMATORIUM
but before the old man could call out to him – he was
curious about the accent – this tall and dark stranger strode
off down the path and out of sight in the direction of the
pointing arrow. High-heeled boots as well, the caretaker
noted ...

It was one of those dead London days in August. Dog
days. Not a breath, a sun burning fitfully behind a yellow,
chemical sky, and a hard glaze coating everything you
touched. Late at night tiny jets of that same sticky stuff
came at you from the breathing trees. Everything in the

3

city ached for rain. Now, as he made his way along between leaning tombstones and angels and attendant cherubs missing their limbs, he could feel himself prickling under his clothes. It was something you awoke to each day with the single sheet twisted in a rope.

For the past hour he had been walking steadily, purposefully, having set out early on foot to give himself sufficient leeway to get here, avoiding the Harrow Road and its heat and noise, even if it did lead directly to his destination. Something to be spurned as far as he was concerned, not once did it throw up anything remotely pleasing anywhere on its downward, curving descent to the tangle of underpasses and flyovers where it merged with the Westway.

Sometimes, in softer mood, he would think of creaking farmcarts and hay wains making that slow journey back in the dark – and time – to country villages with names like Harlesden and Neasden or Harrow on the Hill. But how could anyone have ever imagined that places called Kensal Rise or Kensal Green could have turned out to be as they were? This city was full of place names like that, straight from some rural idyll.

When first he came here even the Tube map struck him as somehow magical, not just because of those eight coloured strands holding such a great metropolis so cunningly in their web, but because of the names of the stops threaded along each one. Now he knew better, of course; had no desire to travel to Chorley Wood or Bushey or Arnos Grove or Hainault, or any of those other remote northern outposts, for he knew what he would find there.

Something hard had worked its way into his boot so he sat down at the base of a headstone to shake it out. Facing him, beyond the far boundary wall, loomed a drum, houses high, full of North Thames Gas. The Grand Union Canal was over there, he knew, as well, while at his back, fifty yards off behind another wall, the traffic ground relentlessly along that road he had been so careful to avoid. Far, far overhead above the city, motionless against the sky, hung a silver airship with GOODYEAR on its side. It had been the

4

summer for putting things into the heavens, flocks of balloons that drifted as far as Russia, and now, fat dirigibles advertising things. He had also, on occasions, seen light aircraft trailing messages from the Greater London Council.

He looked at his watch. Ten minutes still in hand. Poor old Lester, he thought, to end up a puff of smoke aloft there with all those balloons. But then, he might have wanted it that way, leaving specific instructions. It was something they had never discussed, oddly enough, because sooner or later, in a pub, it was the sort of thing bound to come up, total strangers happy to talk to you about it.

He had met Lester one afternoon in Safeway in Kilburn High Road. Why they had ventured in there in the first place God only knows. It may well have been the first and last time, for they joined forces in that kind of terror that supermarkets can engender in certain people. The trolleys were bunching up like avenging chariots in the clogged aisles, the cash tills trilled on one continuous, high note while the boys in their red and white uniforms kept screaming out, '*More sliced white, small cottage, crusty!*' On reflection, it must have been just before a public holiday – Easter, or maybe Whit weekend. Panic-buying in the air and bread the first to go.

Anyway, in the middle of all this, he happened on this smallish bloke in a shorty raincoat down on hands and knees trying to put back a pile of tinned stuff he had managed to dislodge. For some reason – again, God alone knows – he knelt to give a hand and this oldish guy, neat as a new pin, flashed a shy smile, saying, 'I only came in for a tin of chunks,' and there was a hint of accent like his own.

He remembered saying something like, 'Me, too,' meaning one purchase, not pineapples, probably a can of Coke, and so they found themselves in the queue for six items or less.

You can tell a lot about people at a check-out and Lester, it was obvious, was one of those who tried too hard to please in life. The girl at the till must have got the impression that they were together for she rang up both items on the same bill. It seemed such a paltry thing, really, that they let it go. Lester, he recalled, insisted on paying. That man had all the old-fashioned virtues.

In the street outside a drink was suggested to redress the balance – he had no change – and it was one of those rare occasions when a certain warmth filled him at the recognition of some instinctive bond between two people from their own tiny, misunderstood part of the world.

'Lester,' said the little old bloke putting out a paw.

'Sonny,' he said, doing likewise, and the friendship was sealed, as simple as that. Surnames were to come much later, as invariably they do.

Looking back, what an odd combination they must have presented. The neat pensioner (well, he had to be) in his rainproof, collar and tie, polished brogues – and himself. The hair was almost certainly longer then, possibly a pony-tail – that Willie Nelson phase? But then, old Lester dyed his own, that was plain; the little Adolphe Menjou moustache, too, unnaturally black as a raven's wing.

Such things, of course, were never referred to. They drank together, talked together, exchanged phone numbers. Lester lived in Willesden, but when Sonny told him he had his own place close to Paddington Rec., a blank look settled on his face. Something about older people made them that way, Sonny had noticed. No matter now long they had been away from the old country they couldn't adapt to the geography of the new. Not that Lester was one of your tedious, tearful Celts. *'Sentiment, yes, but never sentimentality.'* One of his funny little sayings.

Lester, he quickly realised, was shy about calling him by his forename. He could tell it made him embarrassed. It embarrassed him too, sometimes, ringing out in strange company with that strong hint of condescension or even downright derision. People had to get the right degree of affection into it first time, or not at all. Yet it had been so long such a part of him, like a scar or disability, that he accepted he would have to go through life until the gap between his real age and what the name implied became too ridiculous to be tolerated any longer.

But Lester, it appeared, once had an alias himself of sorts, professionally, that is, for he had been a singer in the dance-band era. So he said. And sure enough one night in a pub on St John's Wood Hill he did allow himself to be persuaded to perform. He sang 'The Very Thought Of You', and that high, old-fashioned crooning stilled the place. It was a voice from the past, taking you back to the days of ancient gramophones and valve wirelesses slow to warm up, with names on the dials that no longer existed. When he sat down there were a few tears and much heartfelt applause but he wouldn't do an encore. He seemed distressed.

Then, London being what it is, they drifted apart until one evening he got a phone call from St Mary's in Praed Street. A patient had passed on his name and number to Sister. A terminal case, no next of kin. Would he make an old man's last days happy?

Lester was propped up in bed when he arrived, eyes fixed on the door of the ward as if expecting him, but how could that be? For days he had agonised about going, for places like these were the end of the line as far as he was concerned – in every sense.

He had brought grapes but when he saw those tubes running from Lester's nostrils he knew he would never be able to enjoy them. Lester looked bad – white, shrunken and old in hospital pyjamas. His hands lay flat before him on the blankets as if they didn't belong to him. His hair had reverted to grey and they had shaved off his little moustache. That hurt most of all for some reason.

It was hot in the ward. Even though outside it was high summer not a window was open and he had the feeling the radiators were on. He found it difficult to concentrate sitting there because of all the sights and smells. On the bed next to Lester's was a man arrested in movement, his slippered feet on the floor. He was staring into space and there was no way of knowing how long he had been trying to get himself upright. Now he began to stir in horrible, slow motion until he was swaying a mere matter of feet away. It was hard not to look at him, especially when he began fumbling with his tubes. It was an ear, nose and throat ward; they all seemed to have them. Somehow the man made the disconnection and shuffled off down the ward leaving a bottle behind on his bedside table half-filled with pinkish fluid. *Don't look*, he told himself.

'Lester,' he said, 'how are you? Treating you well, are they? I see they've got a television up there.'

That was where the man with the trailing tubes had been heading. *The Dukes of Hazzard* followed by *Little and Large*.

Lester looked at him sadly without speaking. Then he reached out and took him by the hand. Hot, dry, papery. He could feel the bones and the faraway pulse. Like a baby's.

'I never told you this before. I was nearly famous once.'

He was remembering now, taking deep breaths to get him through what he had to relate.

'It was during the Blitz. You weren't even born. March 8th 1941. The date's important. I was just beginning at the time, a broadcast or two, concerts, even a record, but all back home. Over there, you understand. Then an agent heard the record. Somebody in London picked it up, just like that. By chance. Would I come across on the boat, one night's engagement with one of the top bands? "Snakehips" Johnson's. A society band. He liked my voice. Oh, I was green then, scared too, but I knew I couldn't turn it down. Who would?

'The boat-train got in early. My first time in London. I tramped the streets until I could hardly stand. Then I got scared in case I would be too tired to sing well. They booked me into a hotel near Cambridge Circus, I remember, so I went there and slept. When I woke it was dark, really dark, because of the black-out, you understand. My watch had stopped. I didn't know what to do, so I put on my dinner suit, bow tie, the lot, and dashed downstairs. It was just after nine and I was to be on the stand at half-past. No taxis, all full, not a single one for love nor money. I began to run towards Piccadilly. That's where it was, you see, the Café de Paris. Still is. Most exclusive night-spot in the whole of London. If you could make it there, you could make it anywhere. You do understand that, don't you?'

8

The eyes burned in his head and his grip tightened as if he were afraid he might pull away. Christ, it was hard not to, but Sonny knew there was nothing else for it but to sit through it all, whatever it was. Then Lester began to cough. Something ebbed and flowed in the tubes.

'Here,' he said quickly. 'Have some of this,' pouring out a little water with his free hand. 'Sorry there's nothing stronger.'

Lester put the glass to his lips with a tiny smile. His first. 'Sonny, Sonny,' he murmured. He drank. The spasm passed.

'Well, I got there. It wasn't hard to find. Lots of people in evening dress trying to get in, women in furs, perfume. I had to fight my way through all these toffs. I was desperate, I tell you, and the band was playing. That made me worse. "Oh, Johnny!" I'll never forget it. "Oh, Johnny, Heavens Above" – the big hit of the time. The doorman looked at my letter and I was through.

'I was heading for the stairs; it's well below ground level, you see, the Café de Paris. Safest restaurant in London, they called it. Only it wasn't, as it turned out. Just as I was starting to go down, the first bomb came through the Rialto cinema up above and dropped all the way through to the ballroom below. It's hard to describe. Like an earthquake, I suppose. That's all I felt at the top of the stairs, but down below it was a different matter. It contained the blast, you see.

'Of course I didn't know any of this until afterwards. I was out on the streets by then, along with all the other people. Then they started bringing them up and laying them out on the pavement, all these bodies dressed up to the nines. Just like dolls, shop-window dummies covered in dust. Some of them had their clothes torn off by the blast, quite a few of the women, too. There was one lovely girl, she couldn't have been more than eighteen, and young soldiers and airmen on leave, all lying there side by side. You don't forget things like that. A hundred dead including "Snakehips" Johnson and his tenor sax player. The bomb went off just in front of the bandstand, you see.'

9

It was over. It was, wasn't? The hand in his had relaxed its hold and Lester settled back on his pillows as if he'd just run a long race. Back in time. The mingled scream of car tyres and whooping police sirens came from the television set at the end of the ward.

Then Lester said quietly, 'The luck of the Irish, I suppose you might call it,' and the tears were running down his cheeks. It was a bad moment for Sonny. There was not a lot he could say, after all, that would make much difference after forty-five years.

'Well, take care now, Lester.'

'You, too, Sonny. You, too. Have a stiff one for me.'

And that was the last time he saw old Lester alive.

A couple of days later when he came back during visiting hours the big, freckled Irish Sister took him aside.

'Your friend's no longer with us. Drifted off in his sleep. No pain. Did you know he had the loveliest singing voice? A shy man, but the injections can have that effect, sometimes. He would entertain us for hours towards the end. All the old favourites. A regular John McCormack. But, then, I'm sure you heard him many's the time.'

He nodded in dazed fashion, the notion of it all far too unreal to take in.

'Oh, yes,' the Sister went on, 'he did mention something about records. Most insistent, he was. "Tell him I want him to have my records." I said I'd be sure to pass it on. You could see it was important to him. The cremation's at Kensal Green this coming Friday at noon.'

Oh, lovely, big, uncomplicated nursing Sister, he wanted more than anything at that moment to bury his head between those great, buttressed breasts of hers. True, she smelt of her trade, but in some strange way that seemed more arousing than any perfume.

That was three days ago. Now he was on his way to pay his last respects. He read the etched names as they passed on either side of him. Costa, Lenahan, Vespucci, Riordan, Muscat, Tonelli, O'Brien, Olivera – London's Catholic dead, and then a tiny ghetto of what he took to be Latvians,

10

or possibly Lithuanians. The deeply incised lettering was certainly from a foreign alphabet, and miniatures set into the marble commemorated sad-faced men with heavy moustaches, all of them, curiously enough, young, for some reason. But that, he supposed, was how the relatives wished to remember them.

He continued walking faster, for by now he was becoming worried. The arrows kept pointing him onwards, onwards, but he could see no sign of anything resembling a crematorium; any sort of building, for that matter. He began to hurry, something he had been trying to avoid, but hadn't he read or heard somewhere that this was supposed to be London's largest burying-ground, even outdoing Highgate? And now he was running, he had finally come to it, his built-up heels leaving dents in the gravel.

At one point he noticed a couple of young blacks lurking among the graves. They had stopped whatever they were doing to watch him, two grinning Rastas with the regulation tea cosies on their heads.

One shouted, 'Late for your own funeral, eh, man?' And both laughed in that excessive way of theirs. Yet why was it he was always tempted to grin weakly back like some nervous fool? An even more shaming thought struck him at the picture he must present, for he was holding his hat on his head as he ran, just like a woman.

The laughter seemed to follow him as, bareheaded now, he rounded a bend in the path. Another arrow, but this proved to be the final one, for there it was, his goal, flanked by a grove of suitably sombre trees. He saw two cars and a hearse glittering in the dull sunlight. No people.

As he came up to the building, *Mors Janua Vitae* (whatever that might mean) cut into the brick above the pillared portico, the sound of an electronic organ leaked out into the heavy air. 'Bridge Over Troubled Water.' He found a side-entrance and slipped inside.

He had been right about the music, it *was* on tape, and everything else about the ceremony that followed seemed to share in the same drive for economy. Even the clergyman had no proper robes, just a grey suit and a narrow dog-

11

collar like a junior version of the real thing. He looked about twenty, short hair, rimless spectacles, and he got Lester's name wrong. Christ, Sonny thought, Lester was no Leslie! Leslie was a girl's name or, when shortened, a taxi-driver's name.

There were four other people in the pews. A man and a woman – a hint of disapproving respectability there, he got that from his red neck and her back – and, across the aisle from them, no contact, a big woman in a hat to match, a shade theatrical. At her side a schoolgirl in grey uniform, slumped and unlovable. There was no sign of any coffin.

The young curate stood with head bowed in prayer while the tape wowed into another loop of Simon and Garfunkel. For the first time he noticed what looked like a pair of cupboard doors set waist-high in the far wall, twin brass rails leading straight to them.

Lester had travelled along those tracks, then through those doors, he told himself, *and you missed it*. He sat there on the hard wood full of despair, because he had really tried. Nobody knew how hard he'd tried. He had never stopped trying. And a strange thing happened to him, he felt his cheeks become wet suddenly, and something like a bubble inside struggling vainly to escape. With his gambler's hat clutched to his chest he stood up and left the place then, as the cleric was giving the Benediction. The words 'Holy Ghost' followed him out into the air.

Two wreaths, wilted already in the heat, lay propped against the wall outside. He wanted to stop and read the inscriptions but felt panicky for some reason at the thought of being discovered. The wall, he noticed, was no ordinary wall, for it was covered with names, hundreds of them, each centred in its own little carved stone frame. There were spaces here and there – not many – waiting to be filled. Each dark recess he reckoned to be about the dimension of a shoe box.

But by this time he was well on his way to putting the place and, hopefully, all its upsets far behind him. Yet, as he strode along through the heat, he couldn't get the thought of it out of his head: Lester, or what was left of Lester, reduced to the proportions of a shoe box.

No matter how I struggle an' strive . . .

His voice rose in the air and a few tired-looking rooks flapped listlessly out of a yew tree.

. . . I'll never get out of this world alive.

Then the young clergyman pedalled past without a look or nod of recognition. He wore a fluorescent bandolier and matching cuffs on his trousers and, clipped to the rear carrier, was attached a little brown attaché case. *Off to another quick burning job, eh?*

'Hank Williams for God!'

The bike wavered fractionally then raced on about Its Master's Business, for London was a place full of people pretending to ignore other people.

He continued to sing high and loud. He didn't care any more if he joined those outcasts it's wiser to ignore.

Everything's agin me,
An' it's got me down . . .

He was in full, satisying cry when the first car went past, the disapproving couple in its front seat, ramrod stiff, eyes straight ahead. He held his hat out after their retreating bumpers.

If I jumped in the river,
I'd probably drown . . .

One thing and one thing only was obvious to him; now he was going to get drunk, on a very royal scale indeed. For Lester's sake. Nobody else cared, it seemed, whether he'd lived or died.

But then he heard the second car come up from behind making a steady swishing noise on the gravel. It went past and he saw the big woman's hat filling the rear window. A little way ahead of him the car stopped – it was a red Opel Kadett with a sticker saying MAKE LOVE NOT WAR (SEE DRIVER FOR DETAILS) – the engine running, and as he drew

13

alongside a voice said, 'Would you like a lift back to the house?'

It was the sort of thing you might hear at home, a little bit of the old country, and that accent certainly had a familiar ring to it.

'Why not?' he replied, without committing himself, he felt, and got in beside the driver who looked vaguely middle-eastern. A string of beads dangled from the mirror.

They went past the caretaker's hut, out through the gates, swinging right on to the Harrow Road. At the first set of lights the driver bore left, then headed north in the direction of Willesden. They travelled in silence and soon he began to suffer from that peculiar from of embarrassment that goes with riding in the front of a mini-cab, all this man's personal possessions there within touching distance – it was like an invitation to a burglary – his cassettes, a paperback, his cigarettes and lighter, medallions on his key-ring. There was even a photograph pasted on the dash – it looked like a bearded, religious patriarch. Did they still make those plastic Madonnas? There was a good old fifties number. Remember? *Plastic Ayatollah*, he thought, and the driver caught him smiling to himself. He smiled back and what had seemed a rather sullen face was transformed.

'He was a relative of yours? The departed?'

'No, just a friend.'

'But you are still sad, yes?'

The title on the spine of the paperback read, *Idiomatic English Made Easy*. Christ, he thought, why does it always have to happen to yours truly?

He said, 'He's happier where he is.'

Liar, he thought, remembering that shoe box. Behind him he heard the woman breathe in deeply and a rush of her scent surrounded him. It was that musky, pencil-shavings one, not cheap. He hadn't had a chance to get a half-decent look at her yet, at the schoolgirl daughter either, for that matter.

Ahead of them an Actonian Driving School Metro jerked along in clockwork fashion, too far out for them to pass safely, and he and his own driver stared indulgently at the

14

back of the learner driver's head. It belonged to a black woman who towered above the instructor by her side, or perhaps he was just sinking under the weight of his despair. Good old Actonian, he always had a soft spot for it, just as he had for Number 32 buses or those yellow estate agent signs saying DUTCH & DUTCH, or the crazed graffiti artist who used to sign himself Joseph. *Psychiatry Kills.* Never a misspelling and sprayed in perfect cursive. They were all part of his part of the world, this square mile of the city, as self-contained as if it had a wall around it.

The car, by now, was taking him beyond those confines and, as he looked out at the unfamiliar, as always he wondered to himself how anyone could ever manage to form attachments to places like these. Then the woman said, 'Pull over at the next off-licence, would you?' and the driver smiled knowingly.

'Wine shop, Indian,' he announced a few moments later, beginning to slow. The Actonian finally left them, taking its cargo of hopes up and over the brow of the hill.

'Spirits, beers, ice.' He was reading the sign.

'Just a bottle of something, thanks,' murmured th . woman rummaging in her bag and then *he* turned and said, 'What'll I get?'

They looked directly at one another. It was, really, for the first time. Later, they were to discuss the occasion, as people often do who come together and wonder what they first saw in one another. By then, of course, it's too late, outlines have already begun to soften, personalities to merge. But that was yet some way off and he could still be objective. Make-up a mile thick, hair colour out of a bottle, hat and clothes *totally* wrong. From a different era. Vintage Margaret Lockwood.

She, too, could be objective. Three inches off those locks for a start, ditto the sideboards, or was it sideburns, she never could tell. A grown man got up like a riverboat gambler ... where was the respect in that? Still, he had a nice smile and she had liked the way he'd talked about Lester to the driver.

Her eyes, he decided, were by far her best feature. Dark

brown with more than a hint of passion. But then, he was always reading possible abandon in women's eyes. Mouths, ears, noses, chins, necks, as well, if the truth were known – and that was only the tip of the iceberg, so to speak.

'He liked Scotch, didn't he?' She was holding out a folded tenner.

'Put that away,' he said, liking the way he said it.

'Don't be silly, now.' Her turn again.

The driver began humming softly to himself and you could read the undercurrent there that said, *these crazy peoples, who can ever understand them?*

Then the girl moved forward swiftly, snatching the money. 'I'll take the Tube home,' and she had opened the door and was out on the pavement. The mother gave a heavy sigh, falling back into the seat cushions as if to hide herself and her shame, while he and the driver looked wistfully after those retreating young hips, just a little too tightly encased in school-outfitter's grey flannel for their own safety.

Old Lester had always said, 'Anything beginning with Glen', but he still bought a bottle of Bushmills. It was a compromise. He had a feeling the woman in the car might also like to support the wine of their country for old times sake. This was a sentimental occasion, after all. *'Sentiment, never sentimentality.'* True, Lester, very true, but please allow us to conduct your wake the way we see fit, if you don't mind . . .

Climbing back into the passenger seat he felt as if he were a little drunk already. The car travelled on and he gave it licence to do so, sitting there, relaxed, the untouched whisky bottle safe in its coat of tissue between his feet. Strange how he had never before recognised the political significance of that orange cap. A Protestant whisky for a Protestant people . . .

They were entering a patch of suburbia, detached and semi-detacheds in reddish, not London, brick; heavy trees, high hedges, that stillness that comes from owner-occupation. There were no bus routes here, no parked cars, either; all the husbands had driven them off to their places of business in more congested parts. The driver was slowing, glancing at his *A–Z* broken open before him on the window shelf.

Surely Lester couldn't have lived here. It didn't tally somehow with the picture he carried in his head of a modest flat, above a shop perhaps, one of those dark, piss-smelling entrances with three bell pushes on the door jamb, beside the dry-cleaner's or the Indian newsagent's or the dusty antique shop that never seems to open. He saw him there, resting his little bag of Spar groceries on the step, cautiously looking around, as London pensioners are cautioned to do, before fitting the key into his lock.

The driver closed the *A–Z* and drove on. 'Not far now,' he said.

Then, for some reason, his radio suddenly came alive for the first time. He bore the bursts of static and chopped sentences in a woman's voice for about thirty seconds before slapping the panel hard with the flat of his hand.

'Give you one bloody headache,' the driver said. The noise ceased as abruptly as it had begun and they continued in silence.

He swung the car into yet another avenue – no streets in this neck of the woods, all avenues, roads, drives, rises – and pulled in behind a skip sitting outside a block of purpose-built flats. They sat there for a moment, looking up at the place, one of those blocks put up after the war and already showing its age. You could tell where the bombs had fallen just by charting the positions of such places on London's map. The progress of a whole stick could sometimes be determined by the way a line of council houses ran in a straight path through an otherwise prosperous neighbourhood.

Sometimes he quite amazed himself by the knowledge he had managed to acquire like that, just by keeping his eyes open. People's eyes did overtime here, not like back home. The first thing he'd noticed was the way the eyes were always on the move, always moving. On occasions when he was drunk and travelling home late on the Tube he would hear himself shouting out bitterly, '*Look at me! Look at me,*

17

damn you! Why can't you look at me!' just like any other drunken paddy, for it made you feel as if you were invisible.

That was becoming rarer now, of course. Soon he would be just like all the rest, the way Lester had been towards the end, keeping himself and his eyes to himself. But, for the moment, this moment at least, he was going to cause one last little bit of commotion. He could feel it rising in him like sap.

Thrusting open his door and with the square bottle clasped to his chest, he pulled hard on the handle of the rear door and the big woman came sliding out feet first. He caught a glimpse of stocking-top and what he felt sure must be suspenders. She gazed straight back at him with a look that said, *feast your eyes till your heart's content, it doesn't bother me,* and in return he bowed gravely, hat in hand. The driver was smiling at all of this, so then he leaned in through the open door and serenaded:

> *I don't care if it rains or freezes,*
> *'Long as I got my plastic Jesus,*
> *Sittin' on the dash board of my car.*

And the man with the heavy shaving shadow threw back his head and laughed and laughed.

'What's your name?' he asked him.

'George,' he said. 'George.'

'Sonny.'

And they shook hands across the blue velour of the passenger seat.

Then she said, 'George, come in for a drink,' and he and the woman stood waiting side by side while the other locked the car.

'Sunny by name and sunny by nature, eh?'

'I try, I try.'

'I'm Hazel, by the way.'

And that's how it all started, that strange crazy journey that was to carry them back and forwards in time, both of them. No turning back, just like the words of a song. He felt that, standing there, but for once in his life no words would come. Perhaps there were just far too many; dozens and dozens of duets to fit the bill.

The three of them went into the dark entrance hall. A smell of tom cat and dusty carpeting, a battered reception desk in the gloom; only no one had sat there for an age. When had the decline set in? Had Lester lived through all of it? That tallied, somehow, because of the impression he always gave of knowing better times. But then a lot of old people these days were like that.

Hazel was looking at a piece of paper she had taken from her bag, holding it up to what little light there was in the place and he realised then that she had never been invited back to Lester's place, either. They crossed to the lift, it was the old-fashioned sort with a greased, latticed gate, and went up to the third floor. No one spoke and he cradled the whisky bottle with loving care for it looked as if they might need its services to dispel this gloom. More of it out in the corridor; the smell now was of fish, or perhaps incontinence? He was grateful for Hazel's perfume.

The door of Number 13 was like all the others they had passed. The original panelling had been covered with a sheet of painted hardboard and had a pane of glass above – or *transom*, as he recalled from all those old movies where people seemed to be always listening at, peeking over or climbing through them. But not in this case. This looked like the entrance to a tomb. *For God's sake, brighten up*, he told himself as Hazel rang the bell, *you'd think you were going to somebody's wake.*

He was smiling to himself when the door opened. The disapproving woman from the crematorium stood there. She had removed her hat, gloves and her boxy navy linen jacket and she looked flushed as if she might have been interrupted in the middle of something. Hazel pushed past without a word and he and the driver followed meekly.

'Doreen?' came a voice from a room off to the right. 'Who *is* that?'

'Lester's friends,' announced Hazel, looking boldly around as if nothing could escape her.

The husband came out of the kitchen; he had a brand new pop-up toaster in his hand. Sonny looked at Hazel and then at the two bulging grey plastic sacks in the middle of the carpet, but she was ahead of him. She had already taken in the tell-tale patches on the walls where pictures had once been, the bare mantlepiece and coffee-table, the absence of cushions, lamps and mirrors, everything, in fact, that could fit into one or, in this case, two John Lewis refuse sacks. One of the store's carrier bags lay nearby.

'Are there any glasses left?' Hazel took her hat off and flung it to land on a chair while he and George the driver sank simultaneously on to a pale blue sofa. A delicious thrill was beginning to seep through him as he unwrapped the whisky bottle, because he realised that this big woman with the fierce brown eyes would see them right. She was in the driving-seat, no harm would come to them. She was like that other great bronze female in charge of her chariot high above the traffic swirling around Hyde Park Corner. Despite the ancient joke about her driving abilities, left arm out but turning right, she was a force to be reckoned with and Hazel had that same look about her, not to mention the same hips, breasts, belly, thighs. Christ, he knew where this was taking him, and prudently crossed his legs.

She came out of the kitchen with a clutch of empty tumblers and one full of tap water, and set them down on the bare coffee-table.

'I hope you all take whisky, but this is Lester's day and I never saw him drink anything else.' She looked directly at the other woman. 'You're Doreen. Lester told me about you.'

She made it sound like a condemnation and the woman, sitting close to her husband now on the second settee, rapidly blinked her eyelids several times.

'Trevor,' said the husband. 'I'm Trevor.'

The knot in his tie was as tiny, hard and burnished as a walnut, and his hands, also, for a man of his size seemed surprisingly small. Every button on his suit and waistcoat was fastened despite the heat, his lace-up shoes shone, not a wrinkle on him anywhere from socks to collar. He accepted an almost full glass of whisky but the wife refrained. You could tell he might suffer for his action later.

'To Lester.'

And he and George echoed the big woman's toast with raised glasses.

The mixture was a fierce one and George had to have his back slapped, which somehow lightened the atmosphere. Then they all sat looking at one another, their eyes avoiding the two bulging, plastic sacks, desperate for another such distraction.

'A real gentleman,' Hazel began, and the other woman sniffed. She was rapidly getting her nerve back. 'It was a privilege to know him. He would never hurt nor harm anyone. Anyone,' and again she looked defiantly across the room.

It came to him suddenly that there was more to all of this than he had at first surmised, for he'd assumed that the woman in the navy outfit must be a relative, perhaps even a sister of Lester's, but something wasn't quite right. A distinct rivalry was in the air which had nothing to do with such a theory. Could these two have once shared a claim in that shy little man in the shorty raincoat, perhaps, dare he think it, a *physical* one? He took another swallow to dispel the horrid image that had entered his head, for he was back in the ear, nose and throat ward again, seeing that puny outline under the stretched sheet and the bump no bigger than a marble where the legs began ...

'Poor Lester, he was always his own worst enemy,' sighed Doreen, smoothing down her pleated skirt.

'You surprise me,' countered Hazel. 'He certainly never, *ever* struck me in that way.'

'Oh, yes, he certainly had another side to him. Very few people ever saw it, of course.'

Trevor, the husband, said, 'I never really had the pleasure of meeting him – in the flesh,' and they all turned to look at him. It was the hesitation that did it. Even George, who had been moving his head, Wimbledon fashion, following each deadly lob between the two women, seemed to freeze. Their target unwisely swallowed too deeply from his glass and tears glistened in his eyes. They looked at him without pity.

Hazel flung out a hand heavy with rings. 'Spotless. Not a speck. How many men on their own would keep a place this tidy, eh? That's the sort of thing that tells you a lot about somebody.'

Sitting on the immaculate, tightly upholstered settee and staring into the amber depths of his tumbler, Sonny tried not to take the words too much to heart. It was wiser not to, just as well, bearing in mind the state of his own place.

Again, he thought, poor old Lester, that recurring refrain, is there to be no peace for you, even inside that shoe box of yours, for here they were still picking through your ashes, making judgments based on the number of times a week the Hoover came out. It was a chilling thought that they could still manage to get at you even after you had been reduced to a fine grey dust. He felt a great melancholy suddenly.

Taking up the square bottle with its reassuringly timeless orange and black label, he moved about the room topping up glasses and no one dared deny him, such a look of solemnity had come over him. He even filled the glass for the woman in blue sitting there killjoy fashion beside husband Trevor. A taste for the stuff was coming along nicely there, thank you very much. As for George the mini-cab driver, he was smiling broadly on everyone and everything about him, albeit beginning to tilt a little from the upright.

Hazel was the only one to hold out her glass as if it were her right. She lay back against the cushions of an easy chair, bulky, but perfectly proportioned, and he felt shifty under that scrutiny, bogus, too. It seemed quite obvious that she could tell that he never used or, more to the point, even *owned* a vacuum cleaner. He stood there, bottle in hand. Half had gone already, and a drinker's caution was giving him pause for thought as to how and where they would manage when this one ran out.

'Lester,' he began. 'Lester was somebody it was a privilege to know. I only wish I had got to know him earlier. Some of you did have that privilege.' The repetitions were worrying. He tried to keep his eyes on a point half-way up the facing wall. 'But I did manage to be with him towards the very end.' *Christ, why was he saying all this?* He badly needed another drink, but his glass was too far away.

'I'm pleased about that, that he asked for me to come and be with him in those last moments.' What he was saying was true but it still sounded nauseating, and there was to be more. 'We talked about a lot of things, Lester and me. He told me a lot of things about himself. It made me feel sorry I hadn't met him earlier. That's really all I have to say.' And he walked back to where his drink was sitting on the coffee-table.

Nobody spoke or coughed, even. He had been right, it had been too embarrassing for words. He kept his eyes fixed firmly on the oily swirl in his glass feeling George's spreading presence beside him. There was a fierce smell of garlic, for George was sighing deeply, tragically. The backs of his hands had a dense covering of black hair, something he hadn't noticed before. Then, one of those same hands moved across to take hold of his. He gazed down at this bizarre coupling in amazement.

'To Lester – and Sonny.'

It was Hazel, and when he looked up the hard, quizzical look had gone; in its place one of sentiment, brown eyes swimming ever so slightly and all that new-found warmth directed towards him. Then she said, 'What about a song?' and George cried, 'Yes, yes!' although it was obvious he didn't really understand what was going on.

This time Sonny made sure he held on to his glass as he crossed over to take up a position near one of the heavily curtained windows. He was trying to remember what it was that Lester had given the crowd that night in St John's Wood in that hushed bar, a ballad, an oldie, pre-war almost certainly, not his style, even if he were able miraculously to remember the words.

Instead he sang 'Lost Highway', one of Hank's most plangent laments for misspent youth.

> *Just a deck of cards, and a jug of wine,*
> *And a woman's lies make a life like mine . . .*

23

Eyes closed, he let the song carry him out far beyond the four walls, on and outwards and back in time until he was at one with his hero singing in the back seat of that Cadillac that fateful New Year's Eve in 1953. A legend in his lifetime, dead in the back of a car at twenty-nine. That lanky, hollow-cheeked genius with the shy grin taking his last ride down his own lost highway. The song had just swum up into his head, but it was a good choice for Lester had certainly travelled quite a part of that way himself.

> *Just a lad, nearly twenty-two,*
> *Neither good nor bad, just a kid like you ...*

He felt pierced by a nameless feeling of loss, cheated out of all that suffering. His own voice came back at him and although it wasn't the best acoustic in the world in that room, empty as it was (the short run of tiled tunnel between the Central and Piccadilly lines at Holborn was probably his favourite from his busking days) he felt pleased with it and himself. He sounded 'authentic', the real thing, and for him that was what his sort of singing was all about.

And now he was heading into the last stretch, the words of the song moving towards a conclusion at their own sweet pace, not his,

> *And now I'm lost, too late to pray ...*

when another voice joined in. His eyes were still closed but he knew it could only come from one person. And so, together, they brought the saga of regret to its conclusion in perfect accord – Hazel was harmonising – and the sound they made together, his high nasal tone complemented thrillingly by that rich female voice, sent waves up and down his spine. It was like the best sex, perhaps better than the best sex, but that was something he might be able to put to the test fairly soon, the way his luck seemed to be running.

Opening his eyes he looked across the room to meet hers, and they smiled conspiratorially, while George applauded in wild fashion, Trevor much less so, as was to be expected, and Doreen simply sat there with a little smile on her lips. She felt she had been vindicated because of all that contrition in the words. She even allowed herself one tiny, bird-like sip from the glass in front of her and everyone in the room felt barriers were down at last.

Hazel then sang, 'Great Speckled Bird' without prompting – he came in on the chorus.

> *I'll be joyfully carried to meet Him,*
> *On the wings of that great speckled bird.*

It was one of those rare and majestic moments when he never felt surer of good times ahead rightfully his. To consolidate the mood he went straight into 'Me and Bobby McGee', upping the tempo so that, in that dead man's room, miraculously, the sound of clapping came to be heard; even more miraculous, clapping on the beat. He thought for the first time with regret of his guitar, his old Fender. Yet, old habits die hard, for he could almost feel it in his grip now, as he bounced his way lovingly through Kris Kristofferson's great song to modern-day knights of the road. C-C-C-G. The chords coming back to him like some long-buried but not forgotten alphabet.

From then on they sang turn and turn about and it was as though they were only performing now for each other, the others in the room forgotten, Hazel starting with 'I'm Gonna Be A Country Girl Again' – and she made it sound believable, too, that image of her roving through fields and woods with *'an ole brown dog'* in tow. He saw all of it so clearly, the wind in the hair, roses in the cheeks, the sturdy legs striding over hill and dale like a very young Elizabeth Taylor. He answered in kind with 'Rhinestone Cowboy', for if he could believe in her dream, why shouldn't she see him in his?

Then she sang 'Blue Bayou'; he sang 'Lonesome Fugitive'; she sang '57 Chevrolet' –it was obvious she had a thing about Billie Jo Spears, but who was he to quarrel with that? The mood was distinctly mellow now, they were moving neck and neck down that same road towards sentiment. It was only a matter of time, he felt certain, before they would be duetting on 'Help Me Make It Through The Night'. But then, at that point, George, for some reason of his own, took it into his own head to contribute to the proceedings.

His choice was something they all knew, but coming from George's lips it emerged as, 'My Bunny Lies Over The Ocean', and they all sat there feeling suddenly depressed. Why, Sonny couldn't say, for as voices go it wasn't such a bad one. In fact, the old song took on something of a new and unexpected character, delivered in Camden Town Cypriot, but still he didn't feel like laughing. He could tell Hazel felt the same. It was as if the day, the occasion, had finally caught up with them.

The only light in the room came from a cluster of bare bulbs set in a white and gilt painted wooden wheel high in the ceiling. The shade had been removed – he could guess by whom – but no matter. He was intent suddenly on taking in everything in the room he had missed, as if this were to be his last chance. It was certainly strange. Both windows on the facing wall were hung with heavy blue velvet curtains, drawn; but beyond there would be an additional fall of net to keep out prying eyes, even though they were three storeys up. Oh, that London net, dusty acres of it, one of the things he'd first remarked on when he came here. Only the very rich and the desperately poor felt no need of it; he'd also noticed that on his nocturnal travels.

Lester, he realised, had lived here in this room without benefit or perhaps need of natural light. How many years? Ten, fifteen, twenty? As many again, remembering his story about that bombed ballroom, because would he have gone back home after that? He thought not. He'd worked in a shoe shop, Dolcis, in some dead country town in Armagh; he had mentioned that, hadn't he?

As he sat there, an inch of whisky still in his glass, listening to George's eccentric rendering of the old Scots ballad, he tried to remember something happy about Lester and his life, but couldn't. Nothing would come back to him but that wall of names at the crematorium built out of shoe boxes in stone. Then he remembered, with horror, that Lester had spent half a lifetime handling the real thing, up and down those quaint ladders that shuttle back and forth

26

on their tiny, noiseless wheels, his hands plunging into tissue paper a hundred times or more a day. But perhaps all this was just coming out of his own head like that fragment of a song that had floated up from nowhere, just as he had turned in through the cemetery gates – 'Apartment Number Nine' – where *the sun will never shine*.

He drank his whisky in one fast gulp. That was no coincidence – the number didn't matter – for, as he took a last look around him (yes, it would be his last all right, make no mistake) he realised that *he was in it*.

'I'm afraid I've got to go.' He was on his feet. He looked at Hazel. '*We've* got to go.'

George's song petered out, dying quickly, as he dipped his head towards his glass. He didn't seem put out. He didn't seem put out by anything, George; it was his nature, or perhaps the nature of his profession.

'I think there's something in here that belongs to me.'

Doreen seemed to swell slightly, coming back to the upright. 'Oh?'

'Yes.' Sonny bent down to open the neck of one of the bulging grey sacks. His hand touched something soft, rubbery, that moved internally. It was a pale green hot water bottle and the two on the sofa, that husband and wife team of tomb-robbers, they hadn't even taken the time or had the decency to empty it, so rushed were they at their work. How long had that dead, grey fluid been lying in there? When had Lester last filled it from his little whistling kettle? That, too, was bound to be in here, somewhere. He felt his face heat with rage as he began pulling out each and every one of those pathetic household items. They were all sitting watching him intently but he didn't care. A plastic strainer, a bread board, two blue striped tins marked Tea and Sugar, a bunch of cutlery, an egg beater, one of those things that core apples, an imitation wooden salad bowl, a royal-wedding mug, and at the bottom, more shameful, half-empty packets of foodstuffs and tins, some of them old and valueless to anyone, no matter how desperately scavenging they might be.

'Sorry,' he said, not meaning it. 'Wrong bag.'

27

Something brittle crackled under his foot, a small white measuring spoon, but he still felt none of it had anything to do with Lester any more. It was all just so much junk, destined for some market stall somewhere, to be pawed over by pensioners and poor immigrants.

The second bag held all the portable pieces (bric-à-brac, wasn't that what they called it?) that had been stripped from the room in which they sat – the bedroom, as well, he suspected, for there was a Baby Ben alarm and some old-fashioned lavender sachets of the sort his own mother had favoured. But he had no intention of keeping an inventory; out it all came in a mess on to the carpet.

Doreen began to weep. 'I was his wife for twenty-two years,' she moaned. '*He* left me.' But Sonny just kept on delving deeper and deeper until he found what he was looking for.

They were in a plastic carrier bag, about a dozen old seventy-eights in their original buff and brown Decca covers. He swung them up and out. Their weight was unsuspected, he had forgotten how heavy they could be, those black old devils, but satisfying, too, in a strange way. He no longer felt desperate or despairing, for what he held in his hand meant that Lester's life hadn't been such a complete waste after all.

'Hazel,' he said, in strong clear tones. 'Is there anything here that *you* want?'

She got up from her armchair casting a slow eye over the scatter of debris. 'Only this,' she said, bending to pick up something from the heap and the fine silken material of her skirt went tight over her beautiful big rear end. *I'm in love,* he thought, *there's no doubt about it.*

She had taken a framed photograph, full-face, someone dark-eyed, Latin-looking, in show business; he didn't think it could be Lester, however. There was some handwritten message across the bottom. Hazel carefully dropped it into her carrier bag and looked at him as if to say, *I'm in your hands, big boy.*

'George,' he said. 'Are you fit to drive?'

It was clearly obvious he wasn't, but who cared, all he

could think of was being close to Hazel in the back seat of that Kadett as they sped towards the next phase of their adventure together ...

They all trooped out without a backward look, the room, the two people sitting in it, consigned to oblivion. There would be no talk about either, no recall. There was nothing to recall. He had made certain of that. That was the way it should be. Down they travelled in the clanking, birdcage lift, holding back until they reached the outer air and when they got there the three of them staggered a little. He looked at his watch. It was eight minutes past four.

At the car he waited with infinite patience for George to find his keys. Hazel stood beside him. High in the sky there was a distant whirring noise and a fat, silver fish slowly passed overhead, GOODYEAR written on its side in black script. Only a total clod could fail to ignore such an omen, he told himself. Then the back door swung open and Hazel's magnificent and tightly packed posterior bent within touching distance. But why rush things, he thought. Who was he to go against that message in the sky?

'You Show Me Your Heart (And I'll Show You Mine)'

His real name, the name he started out with, was Wilbur. Wilbur Lyle Dunbar. His mother had been a Lyle before marriage. He had never found out where his first name came from, had never really pressed the issue. From an early age he had disliked the sound, then later its connotation, for by rights he should have ended up a ploughboy or one of those country mechanics spending his life in an inspection pit. In all the films he went to see the oafish sheriff's deputy was almost always called Wilbur, as was the town bully, drunk or psychopath. It seemed his destiny was never to be on the side of the heroes.

But there was a teacher at his school who saved him from his name, a sarcastic man with a grin that never left his face, who ran the two-roomed Primary with a lady infants' teacher just as terrified of him as were the pupils. Master, they all called him, even little Miss Poots, quiet as a mouse, on the further side of the partition which folded across the width of the schoolroom, concertina fashion, when the minister came to hear their catechism.

'You, sonny, roll back the walls of Jericho!' Master Rainey would bawl or, 'Throw wide the heavenly gates, would you, sonny?' He called everyone 'sonny', yet each and every one of them always knew who he meant, even when that heavy patrician head was lowered, or his back turned to them. He liked to stand gazing out of the window at the surrounding countryside, hands in pockets, keeping up a running commentary on what he could see beyond the dusty panes.

'Isn't Nature jest wunnerful? All the little birdies and sheep and moo-cows and horses and pigs and chuckie hens, and, look, if that ain't Farmer Watt about his business up there in the ole Ten Acre. Hello, Farmer Watt, and how are we today? And how does *your* garden grow? Yes, yes, yes, it certainly is a lovely day for all God's creatures. Great to be alive. Makes you want to burst into song. "Each little flower that opens, each little bird that sings, He made their glowing colours, He made their tiny wings ... I'm as corny as Kansas in August" ... Sonny, penmanship time, penmanship time!' And the boy would rise from his place at the front and go to the wooden press and hand out the copybooks (*Procrastination Is The Thief of Time ... Necessity Is The Mother Of Invention*) or it might be the nib-pens, blotters, crayons, compasses, or ink from the stoneware crock. That's how the name stuck, because all the classroom chores started coming his way and those little outside tasks as well, like fetching his ready-rubbed for him from the post-office shop.

'Sonny,' he would say, scratching his balls, 'you know that you're my prize pupil, cream of the crop,' but how did he reward him, that old goat? He made him his errand boy, that's how. That was wrong of him. Especially as about that time it must have become obvious to him – both of them – that a certain musical talent lay dormant there. God knows, little or no sign of such a thing showed itself among the Dunbar connection, but somehow it did struggle towards the light, a frail but persistent shoot. On the way home three or four of them, he recalled, would sing together *a cappella* style. 'Blueberry Hill' and 'Cathy's Clown' drifting out across the pastures. A group was formed, he bought his first guitar, they played a few country dances, the usual dreams were dreamed ...

But that was a long time ago, twenty, twenty-five years. He left school when he was fourteen. Rainey gave him a copy of Henry Wadsworth Longfellow's *Collected Poems* – the schoolmaster's favourite recitation had always been 'Hiawatha', old Gitchee Gumee himself standing there, left hand doing overtime in his pocket.

The day he left school was 18 July 1960, three days before his birthday. It happened to be Ernest Hemingway's, too, something he found out later. Sign of the Crab. When he came to London, a lot later, he found there was much capital to be made out of stuff like that. Girls at parties seemed to pay a lot of attention to such things. He discovered the art of rigging the astrological chart to suit himself. But, despite his expertise, he always seemed to end up with Pisceans, three in a row at one time. Nature's wet blankets. That soft sobbing at your side in the early hours. Not that he treated them badly. If anything he felt he veered towards the *simpatico* – that great word of the time.

All that was off in the future. If anyone had told him all those years ago that he would be scoring consistently every Saturday night into Sunday lunch-time, let alone holding countless middle-class, flat-sharing girls enthralled at parties, he would have laughed long and bitterly.

He remembered one desperate day walking in fields when he succumbed to the unspeakable, one of Farmer Watt's patient young Friesians the object of his lust. Those gentle, swimming, brown eyes turning to him with the merest hint of reproach. Pure Piscean. How could he? But he could, and he had. One of those dark secrets to carry around locked up inside until Judgement Day ... the image he always had, this vast arena, larger if anything than Wembley Stadium, and every seat filled, every place taken, everyone in that multitude silently watching the queue of their relatives snaking out of the tunnel and across the pitch under the lights towards midfield. Right in the centre-spot was the tiered podium where in life athletes used to receive their medals, Gold, Silver, Bronze, but now put to very different use. When it came your turn to mount the steps the lights came on even brighter and a voice over the loud speakers, something like Charlton Heston's, would boom out a list of all your dirty little secrets. No need for any sentence, any moralising, it was punishment enough to have your dear old mother and father, relatives, girlfriends, teachers, drinking pals, employers, the man who sold you your newspapers or milk, standing there watching and listening ...

Where had all this come from, he asked himself, the story of his green young life? They were in the car travelling to a drinking club he knew in Notting Hill. Hazel had asked him how he had got his name. That was it, wasn't it?

'Well, there are two ways of spelling it, with an O or with a U. Take your pick.'

She was looking at him with that half smile of hers, still not quite sure of how to take him.

'At the moment you look more like a U to me.'

'In that case, let me tell you a story. The day I was born, my dear old papa pulled back the curtains of the maternity home and he said to my mother, well, mother, I'll say one thing, the boy has certainly brought the good weather with him.'

'Maternity home?' She laughed. 'I've changed my mind. You're definitely an O.'

And it was then that he started talking about himself in that way, everything – well, not quite *everything* – tumbling out. He wasn't sure whether it had been a right move or not.

Queen's Park, Carlton Vale, The Chippenham pub – his place was nearby but, no, too soon – Harrow Road again, Westbourne Park Station, left, then right into Chepstow Road, past the Villas where little Prince Willie had his nursery school, left again, right . . .

'Here, George! Anywhere here,' and miraculously there was a place just behind a big grey and green German tourist bus.

With Hazel's hand fixed firmly in his, he swept her along the pavement and down a flight of stone steps into a basement area about the size of an average table-cloth. Twin shrubs in tubs, dying at an equal rate, flanked a black-painted door. He pressed the bell and waited. He pressed a second time.

There was a noise above and George looked down on them. *Bring back, bring back, bring back my Bunny to me!* he sang and fell down the steps just as the door opened. A woman in a wool dress too tight for her age and figure stood there. Ignoring George, who had landed up with his back against one of the tubs, she asked, in a carefully polite voice, 'Are you members?'

There was something so terribly distant about her tone, controlled, and yet at the same time disinterested, that Sonny (with an O) thought to himself, here's where everything goes wrong, it was all too good to last, wasn't it? Then he realised with glee that she was more drunk than they were.

'I am, certainly,' he said. 'And these are my guests,' indicating the others with a wave of the hand.

The woman, late forties, blonde, carefully made up except for the lipstick line a little on the high side, studied him for a moment. 'Town or Country?' she enquired and there was gin, most definitely gin, on her breath.

He removed his dark western hat with a flourish. 'Country, Ma'am. Oh, most definitely Country.'

He had to laugh, the joke was such a good one, it seemed to him, and the woman smiled uncertainly, then held the door open. As they filed past, Sonny heard her say to Hazel, 'You haven't been here before, have you, dear?' in soft, sister-to-sister tones.

They went along a short passage – wall-lights, sporting prints – and then through a glass door, stepping down into a low-ceilinged room, longer than it was broad, with a small, semi-circular bar. It was furnished like somebody's living-room, pinkish carpet, assorted armchairs and settees, table lamps and the pictures on the walls were all of dogs or horses. Behind the bar was a woman with a severe haircut, in a man's Viyella shirt, yellow pullover and matching tie. She had her head lowered to a pint of lager she was pulling. Facing her on a high stool was another woman wearing what at one time would be termed a cocktail dress. She also wore a turban-style thing on her head, equally dated. Two men, not so formally dressed, stood on either side staring straight ahead at the upturned bottles. There was nobody else in the place and it was obvious no one had spoken a word for some considerable time. A clock ticked somewhere.

This might have been a mistake after all, thought Sonny,

as he guided Hazel and George to a small grouping of easy chairs. At the bar he ordered a pint of Löwenbrau for himself and two large whiskeys for the others. His last but one tenner left his possession with almost nonchalant ease.

'I think I *have* been here before,' Hazel said when he got back to them. He looked at her. 'When I came to London first I used to know some people who lived around here. Clanricarde Gardens.'

'*My* first place was in Hornton Street. Back of Kensington Church Street.'

'There's a pub called The Windsor Castle?'

'With the tortoise in the garden?'

They laughed and one of the men at the bar turned around. Sonny nodded to him companionably – he suddenly felt on top of things again – and the man swung his head back as if he had been shot. It was their accents of course, mildly irritating at the best of times but, combined with a show of high spirits, positively threatening. Fuck you, too, he thought, fuck you and your pretensions. I've lived among all you lot long enough to know a loser when I see one. But why not show charity – he took Hazel's hand in his, squeezing it anew – it was only that crippling national shyness at work, nothing more.

George laid his own hairy-backed paw on top, as if in blessing. Those were real tears in his eyes. Then Hazel, giggling, slid hers out, slapping it down on the heap. He followed suit and it was George's move. It came after a slow, dawning moment. He did have the most marvellous smile, shedding his years like dead leaves. They were lucky to have met such a fine human being.

'George,' he said. 'Has anyone ever told you you're a fine human being?' Sonny knew he sounded drunk but he wasn't as drunk as he sounded. Hazel looked across the table at him and there was definite fondness there. If further proof were needed he felt it in the strengthening pressure on his right thigh beneath the table.

They all sat there with their thoughts until he said in a corny, sepulchral voice, 'Is there anyone out there?' and they all laughed, even George.

'I'll tell you one thing,' he continued. 'There's not too many live ones in *here*,' and Hazel choked on her Scotch.

He was patting her back, not slapping, he could never, *ever* bring himself to do a thing like that, when the bell started ringing, its peals arriving thick and fast, violent in their impatience. At the sound something seemed to happen to the people at the bar. One of the men hurriedly downed his almost full glass and the woman in the turban thing slid off her stool and headed at speed for the door marked FILLIES. On the other side of the mahogany the horsey one – little crossed riding whips on her tie – looked at the one in the wool dress, but she only shook her head violently and pushed her glass up under the spigot for another refill of Gordon's. Finally, the woman behind the bar laid down her cloth and moved towards the glass door.

Sonny looked at his watch. The time, a minute past the half hour. The pubs were finally out and another effortless connection had been made. He knew that journey all too well. A fast-paced stagger up Church Street, left, then right into the car-park at the back of Mac Fisheries, up some steps, then down into the Tube station, across under the traffic, up, out, a quick breath, thread the throng, another forty yards, left, right – landfall.

The words seemed appropriate, for first into the bar was the one they called Captain Ouzo, not because of his tipple – he drank only beer – but because of his obsession. 'Did you know,' he would tell strangers, 'that the Aegean is the most treacherous sea in the known world? But, oh, what excitement, what a challenge to take a caïque from Patras to Paxos. I've done it, oh, yes, indeed, many, *many* times.'

He talked like that, a big red-headed hulk of a man in a fisherman's smock, faded pink, of the sort advertised on the back pages of *The Times* and *Telegraph*.

He was followed by four other swaying characters, the worse for wear like himself. Sonny knew them only by their nicknames, for it was the custom of that particular pub to hang a label on everyone after two or more visits. The name of this particular game was to keep to a particular conceit. Thus, there were four people at the bar at that moment clamouring for a drink: The Man Who Knew Too Much, The Man From Aunty (he was reputed to have once worked in some capacity for the BBC) and The Man In The Iron Mask. This last had its origin in a dirty neck brace inscribed by all of them and worn to the pub for a good six weeks or more. Inspiration had run out, it seemed, or perhaps it wasn't necessary, when it came to the last person in the group, a tall, ravaged-looking individual in a stained rainproof, simply known as Lawless. That was his real name.

One of the first things Sonny had discovered about pub life in England was that you never, ever asked a man how he earned the price of his pint. The English were funny about income, generally. Everyone lied about money constantly, making out that they were paupers. But, then, perhaps it was merely a middle-class thing. He, of course, had no such scruples – the world was welcome to the state of his finances. Lawless was even more candid, using it as a weapon to belabour the English with their Englishness. He would tell everyone loudly and in great detail about his immediate funds, especially where they had come from.

'I rob books,' he would spit out through ruined teeth. 'I'm a book robber, but only the best, mind you, no rubbish. Nothing under £29.95. Art books are my speciality. Italian Renaissance. This very morning I harvested a nice little crop of cherubs in the Charing Cross Road. This round's on Christina Foyle, she can well afford it!'

He had a combative streak as well, which made people uneasy in his presence, particularly his fellow countrymen. It wasn't the time for displays of national temperament. Tugging the forelock was back in fashion again. They would laugh nervously at his antics but that would only drive him towards deeper and darker behaviour.

'Burn everything English except their coal!' he would yell towards closing time, and the landlord's eyes would twitch. And one night, at his most desperate, 'John Bull has gone bust! The nigger has brought him down!' before being ejected still cursing perfidious Albion.

Sonny tried hard not to look at that line of jutting male buttocks at the bar. The dreaded moment had to come, of course, when one of their owners must turn to blearily scan the room for possible diversion. And what better diversion than the sight of old Sonny with a *woman*. His hand was now on Hazel's thigh, he could trace the beautiful braille of the catch and soft button of her suspender. He had more than a slight erection.

Then Lawless did turn and his voice bit like a whip. 'If it isn't The Man From Laramie!' *Fuck, he had forgotten about that.* Now he was coming over, a full tankard of Guinness in his grasp.

'My friend, I owe you some money, if I'm not mistaken.' That was a surprise all right; but a most welcome one all the same. 'The last time we met, you may remember, you were kind enough to provide me with my taxi fare.'

He didn't remember, but he took the tenner with what he felt was the right amount of delicacy.

Lawless said, 'I'm thinking of throwing a little party. A few close friends. No riff-raff. Expect an invitation.' There was a long silence and his ravaged face softened. One of his hands lay flat on the table. There was extensive grazing across the knuckles and, as a hand, it was one of the most disgusting specimens Sonny had ever seen – an affront that should have been kept hidden from view at all times. He couldn't help thinking of those horrible, dirty fingers with their guitar-picking talons fondling the pink bloom of a Botticelli Venus or a Titian backside, because one of his things was to produce, at some stage, one of his stolen art books and go over its plates gloatingly. 'Ah, my little beauties,' he would sigh. 'I hate to part with but a single one of you, but you do help to pay the rent.'

Winter or summer Lawless wore the same coat, a long and flapping rainproof without a belt, the sort of outfit the James Boys might have worn on their bank-robbing expeditions in those old films. It was reputed to have specially deep pockets sewn into the lining to carry his booty undetected. He sat across from them, a hint of frayed shirt collar buttoned to the neck, his chin stippled with shaving cuts.

'Al Bowlly,' Sonny said. 'Does the name ring any bells?'

Lawless looked at him. 'You know English sport is not my field, my friend.'

'A singer,' said Hazel. 'We *think*. We want to know if he was famous or not.'

George became animated. 'Al Bowlly, Al Bowlly, Al Bowlly,' he murmured, repeating the name until it took on the flavour of a litany, foreign, exotic, even.

'A moment,' said Lawless, rising. He went to the bar, placing a hand on one of the drinker's shoulders. It belonged to The Man Who Knew Too Much. After a moment's serious discussion he returned, dropping down into his seat.

'Quite right. Dance-band vocalist of the thirties. Born, South Africa. Crooner. Guitarist. Reckoned to be the best of his era. Died 1941 in the London Blitz. More?'

'Ask him about another singer. Terry O'Day.'

Lawless shouted, '*Terry O'Day!*' And the man at the bar, a small man with a beard and granny glasses, turned to stare at them. He sipped his drink reflectively for a moment, no more than that, then shook his head, turning away.

Lawless grinned. 'If he doesn't know him, he doesn't exist, your Terry O'Day. Is it for a bet?'

Sonny felt his face go hot. 'Of course he fucking well exists! Why, we – ' He stopped himself in time, glancing at Hazel, but Lawless had intercepted the look.

'Sounds like one of ours, this O'Day character. Is he?'

'No! No!'

Everybody was looking at him now. He felt Hazel's hand take his under the table and a calming coolness seemed to flow between them.

Lawless began unbuttoning his raincoat. 'Are you an art lover, by any chance, my dear? I feel certain you must be. Any friend of Sonny's –' And he produced one of his trophies encased in gleaming cellophane, a coffee-table tome, on its cover two men in armour struggling to hoist a couple of heavyweight nudes on to their horses.

'Rubens. I've had to move on to the Flemish School. I won't break the seal, for obvious reasons, but just look at those skin tones. Would you care for some nice books for Christmas presents? I take orders.'

39

They looked at the composition in silence. The older of the two women – by a hair – wore a narrow bracelet like a snake on her upper arm and her flaxen mane was braided in curiously modern fashion. The back was magnificent, as was the great dimpled backside. Sonny could just imagine Hazel's torso having similar proportions and solidity, although she was dark and these two were very obviously natural blondes.

'The original is in the National. I've studied it on quite a few occasions.'

But Sonny was seeing something else, in place of that mythological abduction scene. It was the smiling man in the photograph again, the one they'd found in the flat, with the dago eyes and the brilliantined hair, across his tuxedo the handwriting *From Al Bowlly To Terry O'Day With Affection* and a date he hadn't been able to make out. Suddenly he felt sick of Lawless and his cronies and, above all, this place. He wanted to be somewhere else where he could remember Lester with a little more dignity. That was a strange word for him, but suddenly it seemed just right for what was missing from his life. He excused himself, got up and walked across the stained pink carpet to a door at the far end of the room.

Beyond were two other doors, one marked COLTS and the second one FILLIES. What must foreigners make of all this shit, he thought. He felt like going into the wrong one, pleading ignorance of the language. Inside, he ran the cold tap vigorously over both wrists while studying his reflection. The mirror's frame, heavily encrusted gilt, looked like a leftover from someone's drawing-room. The water roared in the basin, his wrists ached, but his brain was beginning to slow down. He faced the man in the mirror and waited for revelations, as always.

What are we to do with you, eh? Thirty-nine years old, no visible means of support, future prospects nil, a dreamer, drifting alone in the world. Of course, you do know where you're going to end up, don't you? Dead in a squat.

His own mother used to say, 'dead in a ditch', but then her world had passed on, bless her old-fashioned country

40

ways. Her dearest wish for him to stay back there and get a job in the Metal Box factory on the Derry Road. Fat young wife, kiddies, semi on the housing estate on the edge of the village, new car every two years against depreciation.

All the signs were there. Staring back at his face from the mirror. He would write a song about it.

> Woke up this morning, my Chevy wouldn't go,
> Just like its owner, battery low,
> Bodywork all shot to hell, power and steering too,
> It ain't just cars and trucks, you know, that . . . that . . . that . . .

He needed time to work on it but it would be all right, he had that feeling. He had the title already. 'Depreciation Blues.'

The door behind him opened and one of the men at the bar who had been there when they arrived came in laughing, went directly into the single cubicle and squatted there farting and chuckling to himself behind the locked door as if whatever had happened outside had given him licence to be as coarse as he pleased. Sonny, feeling disgust for the man and his true nature, turned off the taps, quickly dried his hands on the roller towel and went back out into the bar to see what had given cause for so much merriment.

'Over here, *compadre*!' Lawless was sitting at the bar now, holding court. 'Our friend here has kindly bought us all a drink. A man of substance, not to say discrimination. Isn't that so, friend?'

He grinned wolfishly at the businessman who leaned by his side. The man grinned back, raising his full glass to the room. Sonny knew the progression, oh, so well. More drink, more compliments, followed by confessions on the stranger's part, job, wife, children, mortgage, mistress – in that order; tears had been known to appear at this stage, then things would unaccountably start going wrong. The innocent in the suit – that long lunch on expenses had been his downfall – would begin to pick up unsettling undertones, a certain sourness in the atmosphere, which was strange because he'd never felt so relaxed, so at one with the company. They were all his comrades here, they were, weren't they? Seeking

41

reassurance, he might then put his hand out of comradely affection on his companion's shoulder, only to have it brutally wrenched away.

'Don't touch me, you English *cunt*! Do you think you can buy me with a *drink*?'

What had he said, what had he done? Better not ask, friend. Oh, yes, he had witnessed it many times, the rout of the innocents staggering ashen-faced into the rush-hour to catch their 6.05 to Rickmansworth, Epsom, Hassocks or some such place ...

Lawless said, 'Now, that's what I call a nice piece of skin. Italian? Gucci, perhaps?'

The wallet, fat with credit cards, lay carelessly on the counter. The man made some remark meant to indicate modesty, waving his hand about in careless fashion. He wore a gold signet ring with a crest and matching cuff-links, and Sonny saw Lawless's eyes fasten on them. The whole thing was like watching a lamb being led to the abattoir.

The Man Who Knew Too Much said, 'Made in Florence, I shouldn't be surprised. Yes, it has that well-known attention to detail.'

Lawless smiled at him. 'It's only a wallet, friend. We don't need a fucking Reith lecture.'

On the other side of the bar the woman in the yellow pullover stiffened slightly. Lawless said, 'Sorry, Georgie, a slip of the tongue.'

The woman nodded, went back to polishing glasses. Her friend was talking to Hazel at the other end of the bar and Sonny edged closer. He heard the woman in the wool dress say, 'Yes, Christine came in here quite a lot in the old days. Mandy, too, for that matter, but she was never as popular as Christine. I don't know why, now that I think of it, because she was a nice girl, they both were. But Christine was always the favourite.'

Hazel said, 'I shared a flat with her once.'

'Mandy?'

'Christine.'

'Really?'

'Really.'

Hazel laughed, as if remembering, and Sonny felt a strange and ridiculous yearning to have been part of whatever it was she was recalling. He moved up the bar until he was standing close behind her and he put his hands on that firm waist, feeling the construction buried beneath the fabric. A girdle, he suspected, black, almost certainly, and thought of those smiling matrons modelling underwear in the pages of the mail-order catalogue devoted to the fuller figure. Always his favourite section.

He leaned forward, nuzzling Hazel's soft cheek. The blonde behind the bar said, 'I remember *you* now.'

'Oh?'

'Yes, we had a long conversation about music. One singer in particular. Andy Williams? Yes, that was it.'

'Hank,' he contradicted gently.

'You were in a group, weren't you?'

Now it was Hazel's turn to look at him with interest. 'That was a long time ago,' he said, which seemed to satisfy the woman. She had the same lips and mouth as Gloria Grahame and could easily have slipped into one of her rôles as the moll seeking solace in the gin bottle. By his calculation, she must have got through at least six large ones since they got here. Not that he'd ever hold that against any woman, and, anyway, Gloria Grahame had always been one of his all-time favourites. For the life of him he could never understand why the men in her pictures always had to give her such a hard time.

Her lookalike said, 'I like the Irish. So clever with words.'

Yes, thought Sonny, trying not to listen to Lawless weaving his spells around the unfortunate businessman at the far end of the bar.

He and Hazel, heads together, smiled back at the blonde. What she'd said sounded like a compliment but, of course, wasn't, as he'd grown to realise quite quickly over here. The reality was they all despised you, even those guilty liberals with their great love of draught Guinness or the ones with Irish surnames. My God, he had often thought, what about all those sad, invisible fathers rushing like lemmings between the open legs of the English working classes?

43

Or was it the praying mantis who got polished off after the business was done? Nothing left to show for it but a few scales of dead skin – or, in this case, a handle like O'Brien, Flynn or Murphy. Look how many of those were in the phone book, if proof were needed.

'Georgina's from Kildare, originally,' whispered Gloria Grahame, casting a quick glance in her partner's direction. 'Horsey people. Used to own a stud. She cries about it sometimes. How they lost it all, you know.' She sighed. 'I've always been as common as muck. Muriel Burrows from Colliers Wood.'

She attacked the optic behind her again, expertly from long experience, and the clear, oily liquid rose unhurriedly in her glass. By this stage she must be downing pure spirits, it struck him. If he stayed here long enough, it also came to him, he would hear every detail about these two women's lives together. But did he really want that?

'What's the time?' he asked, and the moment it came out he knew he'd said the wrong thing. In the instant the sentimental look fled Muriel's eye – Gloria Grahame turning into Bette Davis at her most baleful.

'Has anyone here got the correct time?' she asked the assembled bar in hard, carrying tones, and everyone turned to look at him, even Captain Ouzo, who was in a corner with George. He had discovered almost telepathically, as is the way in such situations, that George had been born in Larnaka and both were by now firm buddies.

The Man Who Knew Too Much intoned, 'Twenty-seven minutes past five,' and there was silence as everyone seemed to take this in. Emptiness yawned. Each man suddenly saw himself marooned in a deserted bar feeling the coins in his pocket as he calculated just how many more drinks could be spun out to closing time.

Then Lawless spoke. 'My friends, the towels are at this very moment about to come off in The Flag and Archer. I, for one, could certainly go a nice, wet pint of Fuller's best. What say we all adjourn over the road?'

There was a cry of relief from the others and a rapid draining of glasses. The women behind the bar stood straight-faced, side by side, in acceptance of how things were in their little basement world. They would no more have dreamed of showing displeasure at this betrayal than they would have tried to bar Lawless and his cronies earlier when the pub they were now heading for had put them out in the afternoon.

The exodus began. Hazel had the door opened for her by the man who once held down a job at the BBC. Sonny suspected he wanted to look up her legs as she climbed the outer steps but his benevolence still held firm. The others followed – an air of almost coltish jollity about their pushing and jostling – but at the last moment Lawless hung back. Here it comes, thought Sonny.

Almost as an afterthought, Lawless drifted over to the businessman, who was still smiling, his wallet open before him on the bar. All was well in his world, which was exactly why Lawless was about to leave him with a little souvenir. Sonny felt reminded of those printed cards which certain West Ham supporters were reputed to present to their victims after they had been expertly attended to with Stanley knives: Congratulations On Having Met The Firm. Have A Nice Day.

Lawless whispered something to the man and the women behind the counter turned away fastidiously as though from an accident in the street. The man's face went rapidly white, then very slowly red. It was a strange thing to witness; then Lawless joined him at the glass door and they went out together. Lawless had the air and look of one of his famous cherubs, a debauched one, but a cherub, for all that.

'*Greensleeves is my delight*,' he sang softly to himself as they mounted the stone steps to the open air.

On the pavement, Hazel – she was hatless – was surrounded by a group of eager fans. That's what it seemed to Sonny, as his head emerged from the depths. She was holding court to this bunch of swaying, middle-aged schoolboys in Oxfam outfits.

Captain Ouzo, even more purple in the face than usual, clutched his round, black, Greek sailor's cap to his chest in curiously coy fashion. His hair, Sonny noted, was just like the coat of one of those ugly, chocolate-coloured, water dogs, only more ginger. He'd never seen it uncovered before. With his free hand he continued to hold George fast.

'Dear girl,' he was booming, 'don't try to tell me you're not Grecian with eyes like those. It's useless to deny it. And, anyway' – here he shook George playfully – 'the family resemblance is plain for all to see. Plain. All ... ' And he slid slowly to the ground, taking George with him. It was clear now to all of them in the light of day that he was very, *very* drunk indeed,

Lawless bent over him. 'My friend, we have need of this man's services,' he said, managing to prise George out of his embrace, not easy, because he was a big man. The Captain lay looking up at him, his massive curly head resting against the railings, and out of that great body came a sad, little, baby voice.

'Why does your sister deny you, George? I don't understand. Blood is thicker than water. What has she got to be ashamed of? I hate my country.'

'Good man,' said Lawless. 'That's what I love to hear. But we mustn't detain you,' and off he walked, holding up the unsteady George, in the direction of the car. He seemed, for some reason, to know just where it was parked.

'Will he be all right?' asked Hazel, after it became obvious none of them was going to make a move to lift the Captain.

'He's always like this,' lied Sonny. Then, taking his courage in both hands, 'Isn't he, lads?'

The others nodded energetically and Hazel said, 'If he fell he might hurt himself. Seriously. He's very heavy.'

The Man Who Knew Too Much said, 'He *is* on the hefty side, I grant you, but the odds are against someone of his bulk doing any lasting damage to themselves. Believe me, I know. As a matter of fact, I think we would be doing him a favour by letting him rest here like this.'

One of the men who looked like a stick-insect in his flapping blue blazer and ancient flared jeans agreed enthusiastically. 'Yes, yes, he's quite right, you know.'

Sonny loved it when they were like this. Such betrayals always delighted him. He and Lawless certainly had that much in common, except that Lawless got angry when none of them would ever admit to the basic sham of all that much-vaunted pub camaraderie. That was the difference between Lawless and himself, for *he* had given up that particular battle a long time ago.

He had never thought of Lawless in the rôle of crusader before, but then he remembered one night late in somebody's flat and seeing him beat his fists on the floor until the blood ran. 'They have to pay, they have to pay, I tell you, for what they've done. And I want a full, fucking confession. Nothing less will do.' But did he really want to understand Lawless and the nationalistic furies driving him?

'Let's go,' he said to Hazel. 'He'll find his own way to the pub, you'll see,' and they left him there to the tender mercies of passing police or some young black mugger out taking the air. The second seemed the more likely, knowing that area.

At the car Lawless had already settled himself into the front passenger seat. Twisting himself around he pushed open the rear door and Sonny slid in after Hazel. The others stood on the pavement waiting to be allowed in too, but Lawless called out cheerily, 'Full up, chaps. Hackney regulations, I'm afraid.'

Their route took them out into the main east–west rush-hour traffic and George drove unhesitatingly into its flow. He held himself pushed forward in that stiff-limbed way with rapidly blinking eyes that gives the drunk-driver away to anyone in the know. It seemed he, Sonny, was the only one in the car aware of the effect they were having on other drivers for horns blared on a constant, angered note and the cabby with a fare in the back who had been brought to an abrupt halt in the far lane – George's Opel effectively damming both streams – had his window down and was screaming.

'Fucking foreigners!' he yelled. 'Wog! Get back to your fucking donkey cart!' It was amazing how they could always spot a rival in a mini-cab.

Lawless leaned across George who stared straight ahead, expressionless as a sleep-walker.

47

'*Sieg Heil!*' he shouted through the open window and, with forefinger under his nose, shot out his right arm in a Nazi salute. As sharp as ever, he had made the rapid connection between the young man's blond crewcut and the cross of St George stuck on his windscreen. When Sonny first came to London all the taxi-drivers seemed to be elderly Jewish philosophers in cloth caps and mufflers; now, for some reason, the ranks were filling up with young Aryans dressed in Fred Perrys, jeans and trainers, just like this one having a seizure two feet away. His passenger stared across the distance between their vehicles and caught Sonny's eye. He wore a green beret, matching eye shadow, and his cheeks were spangled with glitter dust. He may or may not have been going to a fancy dress party but he blew a kiss to Sonny and, surprising himself, Sonny blew one back. Hazel giggled approvingly.

Then the traffic began to surge and they were heading towards the lights and the green arrow that would allow them into Kensington Church Street. The arrow held fast, their luck holding with it, and in the new quietness, away from the roar of racing engines, Hazel sang, 'You Show Me Your Heart, And I'll Show You Mine', another of those rare oldies. And it seemed the most natural thing in the world to be sitting in the back of a car listening to the woman beside him – a woman of a certain age, as the French might say – giving forth like a happy young girl. He joined in.

Lawless heard them out in silence, then quietly remarked, 'Sonny and Cher, is it?'

George suddenly said, 'Your mother is one great whore,' and they looked at him. When they realised he was thinking of the cab-driver they all had a good laugh, and the sound in that enclosed space seemed to pull him out of his stupor. 'What time is it? Where am I?'

Lawless put an arm about his shoulder. 'You're with friends, we're all freedom fighters here. Up Eoka!'

The car travelled on and, in the mood for introspection, Sonny thought of Lester beached in time in his bombed forties ballroom. Behind him on the window shelf for safe

48

keeping was the carrier bag full of his recordings. And what about Hazel and himself? It would be nice if it turned out they shared the same part of memory's store together. He hoped to be able to remember most if not all of this in the morning – it seemed important – but, with drink and drinking, experience had taught him not to put too much reliance on that.

And that's exactly what did happen. Later, and not just the next morning, either, when he went over in his head the events of that day and part of that night, the sticking point came at that precise place in time when they were in the car and breasting the brow of Kensington Church Street, just where the antique shops begin. He remembered looking out and seeing a stuffed bear holding a round brass tray in its paws. The bear was chained to the window bars and had a red ribbon about its neck. A card on the tray read, *Best Prices Paid For Gold And Silver*. The creature had a most lifelike expression and gazed directly at him as though trying to communicate something of importance which had nothing to do with the printed message.

After the bear there were to be big jumps in time, isolated incidents in sharp detail surrounded by inky oblivion, like holes in a net. Here then was his haul.

One ... The Rose and Crown. It seemed to be late rather than early, for the place was jammed with red-faced regulars. He was sitting close to the wall at a round table with Hazel and there were five, maybe six, pint glasses ringing the wet wood before them. The others, George included, were on their feet, restless, mobile. A powerful feeling of lassitude seemed to have invaded his mind and body. The culprit, he decided, had to be those old depreciation blues back to haunt him again.

Hazel was quiet, as well. She exuded great waves of inner calm, it seemed to him, almost as real to his senses as the scent she was wearing. She said, 'Did you ever go to the Rainbow Room?'

He laughed, remembering.

'I thought you might have,' she went on. 'Everyone in our part of the world did, they did, didn't they? I had a friend, Bernadette, Bernadette Neeson, she was Catholic, and the two of us never missed a single dance. It was our favourite spot. We would start off on foot – no buses, and always, always, we got a lift. Remember the lights, all the coloured lights, hundreds of them? And the sound of the sea? One night we climbed down the rocks in the dark, we must have been both mad, to bathe our feet, two fools sitting there listening to the band. They used to open the windows wide when it got too hot. And Bernadette said, I remember it, she said, "Wouldn't it be lovely to be passing by on a great big ship and seeing all the lights and hearing the music ... one of those liners?" Are you listening?'

Oh yes, oh yes.

'She was like that. She could break your heart with some of the things she used to say. We were going to come to England at the same time, we had it all planned, take a flat together, then her mother died and she was left to bring up the family, five brothers and sisters, all younger than herself. Her father just lay smoking in bed all day.'

She paused. 'The Rainbow Room. It *was* like that, wasn't it?'

'Yes,' he said, lying. 'It was.'

He had only seen it in daylight once. Out of curiosity, he had cycled to the coast one Sunday afternoon. It was summer, but the place looked out of season, a bit of a ruin, until you got closer. There was a concrete flight of steps and he left his bicycle at the foot. The only sounds to be heard were the crying of the seagulls and the slap, slap, slap of a loose rope on the flag-pole at the top. He looked through the windows and saw the dust on the floor, the bare band-stand, the paper decorations hanging in tatters from the ceiling. Haunted, deserted, were the adjectives that came to mind.

'Tell me, tell me, what it was like for you?' She had a hungry look about her now. A change had taken place, brought about by those cruel, old memories. 'We might even have danced with one another. Think of that. I might have asked you in a Ladies' Choice.'

He shook his head. She looked at him.

50

'Why not?'

She was flirting with him now and it felt wonderful. He told her of the night Hammi Hamilton stole all the barometers, fourteen of them, from the posh houses along the Antrim Road. This had nothing to do with the dance-hall, or the cliffs, except perhaps that Hammi was drunk at the time, something he always associated with those Friday nights under the mirrored globe. No one knew why Hammi had done such a thing, beyond the fact he was the worse for wear and the doors of all the houses he passed on his way home from Parkgate stood so invitingly open.

Hazel said, 'We had somebody like that where we lived, too. They never did anyone any real harm, did they?'

No, he agreed. Then he went on to tell of poor Hammi's end, how he was crossing the Wooden Bridge one dark night when he slipped and fell in. His overcoat pockets were weighted down with stout bottles and he stood no chance in that swift and freezing current. He liked to think he felt no pain as he was borne down to the weir, afloat on spread coat tails before that dark brown, liquid ballast did its work.

'Just like the Lady of Shallot,' said Hazel and he kissed her full on the lips – how could he resist? She sat there looking at him, then she took his head between her hands and returned the compliment, but taking her time about it.

'Well,' he said. 'Well, well, *well*,' like some overwhelmed schoolboy.

'Well, indeed,' another voice echoed and, when they looked up, adjusting to the reality of their surroundings, Lawless was standing over them, a twisted grin on his face.

'Isn't romance jest wonderful, folks?' Then, 'Drink up, drink up!' suiting action to his words. That the dark side of his nature had finally surfaced was immediately obvious. 'Let's go, let's go.'

His hands beat a rapid tattoo on the table, a blast of sour breath blowing over them.

'Go where?' asked Sonny in scrupulously polite tones.

'Out of *this* fucking place. Does it matter?'

Sonny looked at the glasses in front of him, then at Hazel and, as if receiving some silent message of support from that quarter, said calmly, 'Don't wait for us. We'll be toddling off just as soon as we've finished our drink. Other plans. Okay?' He surprised himself and Lawless, likewise, looked stunned.

'Come on,' he entreated, lowering his voice. 'If we go now, we'll just be able to get a quick one in across the way.'

'Some other time, Lawless. Another time.'

For a moment he did think things were going to turn ugly but, after a staring match while their temples throbbed, Lawless turned away and walked off quickly towards the door. There were genuine tears of rage in his eyes.

Once more Sonny had that feeling of having fallen into safe hands. Nothing or no one could touch him. Lawless had tried and had failed and, looking about him, he didn't have to be told that there was little or no threat from any of these desperate losers holding out their empties for a chance of the barmaid's eye.

He was seeing all of them suddenly with a cruel, almost anthropological regard. Why hadn't he sussed them in this way before, he asked himself, for the seventies rejects they were. The clothes, the hair. Wide lapels, wider collars. Old men's waistcoats, over old men's shirts, hipster trousers with a flare, mainly culled from War On Want shops, but much of it their own. At least two Frank Zappa lookalikes were there in the throng. Then he noticed a disturbing reflection – a clapped-out Buffalo Bill clone. The resemblance was a little too close for comfort, but quickly he consoled himself. No, no, no way could he ever be confused with *that*. Wasn't his specialness, the reminder of his own uniqueness, sitting right here by his side?

'Shall we be going, then?' she asked.

'What about George?'

'I'll talk to him. Leave it to me,' and, rising in a swirl of perfume, she stalked off across the bar. He watched that sleekly upholstered capable back and thought, *Leave it to me*. Could there be anything more sweet-sounding?

'Now, we can go,' she said when she returned, a little breathlessly.

'George?'

52

'All fixed up.'

He felt slightly guilty at the implication in the words, but his money *had* run out. But not too noticeably, he hoped.

One last look at all those desperate, despairing ones crowding the brass rail. The Man In The Iron Mask, he who was reputed to have broken his neck skiing that time (on the piste, as the others liked referring to it) gave him a stare of drunken misapprehension as he waved, then they were out on the pavement together.

'Run!' he said. 'Run!'

And they went racing off, giggling, hand in hand, like two truants, into the side streets of Kensington, every little mews house they passed in the region of a quarter of a million and rising by the hour. Behind the burglar-proof lattice-work glowed doll's house lamps, sometimes a television screen changing hue, the fragrance of night-scented blooms from the window boxes and hanging baskets engulfing them in waves. *Oh London, London, you are still my oyster. There is much more mileage in you than I thought*, his heart sang. His cowboy boots echoed on the cobbles and he remembered slapping the side of a parked Range Rover with his free hand out of sheer high spirits, one, two, three, as on they clattered to the scene of their next adventure.

The tingle in his palms from that taut and gleaming bodywork was the last thing he recalled before they were whirling in a ballroom together in another and very different part of the city. In between – period and place – was to remain black in his consciousness, almost as if he had run straight into the dark mouth of a tunnel right there in the middle of that mews in W8. Another of those blanks, another of those holes in the net . . .

The band was playing 'The Rose Of Tralee' in waltz time and the two of them, if they had shut their eyes, were back in time twenty years. Hazel wept, remembering, and he felt sentimental along with her.

'Who said you weren't a dancer?'

Moist breath murmured in his ear as he traced the elaborate construction of her underthings. Enough mystery and complexity there, he reckoned, to occupy a man's imagination for an eternity. He was pretty far gone, that was obvious.

They danced and they danced again until the band took a break and they were forced to drop down on to a hard, upholstered bench affair that ran all the way around the hall. There was a balcony-bar at the level of their heads doing a roaring trade. Holding hands, they stared back at the other couples staring at them across the empty expanse of floor; all the single men were downing draught Guinness in the raised section.

'Just like old times, eh?' he said, adding, 'Except for the bar, of course.'

'Yes,' she sighed, whether out of sentiment or exertion, he couldn't quite decide. Her make-up had started to show definite signs of wear and he had no idea what had happened to her hat which had seemed so much a part of her. He was still wearing his own. The fine, smooth base of her neck where the powder had ended had gone cherry red, that same blush he'd remarked in certain women when they made love. The first time he'd looked down on that spreading blood stain covering chest and throat he'd been alarmed, but that had soon turned to something very different. It came to signify the true essence of womanhood, a terrible vulnerability which always turned him to jelly.

Thoughts like that only lead in one direction so, when the band returned and she dragged him on to the floor at the first fusillade from the drums, he wondered if she could feel the way his intentions were turning. What she did was pull him closer until the bump in his trousers pressed against her firm belly. When the quickstep ended, walking back to their place, one of his thighs felt damp.

They sat among the wallflowers again and presently her hand moved under his shirt until her finger probed delicately and expertly, it seemed, the cleft in his buttocks. With an expressionless face he gazed across the floor enjoying the sensation. Even more enjoyable was the thought of all those couples out there eyeing them, oblivious to what was going on behind his back. Those big colleens – they had the look of dazed heifers – planked there beside their red-faced

54

menfolk, how many of them, he wondered, were up to caressing their consort's bare arse at this precise moment with a finely crooked little finger? He rejoiced once more at the thought of his singular good fortune.

The band struck up 'My Little Old Turf Cabin By The Lee', not a number for dancing to, more one to sit out and listen to with heavy, misplaced nostalgia, the sort of home-grown muck he had always despised, but he could feel its sickly sentiments getting through to the woman by his side.

The band – they called themselves a show-band – all well into their forties, milked the mood shamelessly. The saxes wailed an exaggerated two-part, a fiddle waded in and the leader-vocalist, Brendan something or other, from the first two bars had the microphone half-way down his throat. He sported a bottle-green tuxedo and a marmalade-coloured toupée that looked as if it had been fitted back to front. The hands caressing the microphone stand were butcher's hands, raw, red and chapped, and he preceded every announcement with, 'Boys and girls ...' Sonny found the greatest difficulty in looking directly at him.

'And now, boys and girls, we come to the heats of our ever popular talent competition. First prize, a return ticket for two on Aer Lingus to Cork or Dublin, the choice is yours, second prize, record vouchers from the Tara Records Shop worth £50.00, and third prize, two litre-sized bottles of Paddy. The grand finals will take place here in this ballroom on the 22nd of the month ...'

For the first time Sonny noticed the presence of people in the bar at his back who looked even more out of place than themselves – a large woman of operatic proportions in a red velvet dress, a trio of young dancers traditionally cloaked and kilted, an older man with an accordion already strapped across his chest, and a lout dressed, even more loutishly, in comic postcard parody, neckerchief, waistcoat, hat, knee breeches. He carried a varnished blackthorn and looked both drunk and dangerous. Surrounding him was a group of drinkers his own age slapping him on the back and shouting things like, 'Good man yourself, Sean!', 'Up Tipp!' and, 'Show 'em who's boss!'

There was a roll on the drums, a chord from the brass and, to strong cheers from their supporters, the band of hopefuls began to file down from the bar on to the floor.

'Come on,' whispered Sonny and, taking Hazel's hand in his, he pulled her up and raced ahead of the white-haired man with the accordion. The man had a limp and scuttled fast to get there first but Sonny was faster and he didn't care. A great glow had come over him, he felt on fire, yet cold and damped down at the same time. One puff and the blaze within would incinerate this lot. They were all losers, *losers*, and he was on a winning streak.

'Where are you from?' The band-leader was hunkered down to them from the stand. Sonny had a close-up of his bunched privates.

'Mount Olive,' he said, without thinking.

'Mount Olive? Is that Cavan?'

Sonny looked up into the inflamed face, giving nothing but an idiot grin in return.

'What are you two nice people going to sing for us?'

For the first time Hazel betrayed anxiety. He could feel it pass between them like a current. He put his arm about her waist and, squeezing strongly, said, ' "Mansion on the Hill". In D.'

'The old Jim Reeves number?'

No, idiot. Someone else wrote and sang it first. Like everything else worth a damn, but he smiled back in the man's face, as before.

'And the name, folks?'

Hazel came to life. 'Sonny and Hazel,' she announced in clear, strong tones and it sounded like the most natural and enduring partnership in the history of show business. Later, he was to remember the moment. Bells should have rung, but didn't, he was too involved with the way he felt and the voice in his head saying, 'Go! Go! Go!'

Then they were on stage and the band-leader, he was much shorter than he appeared from the floor, introduced them as, 'A husband and wife team from the Land of the Lakes.'

The sound system howled, there was a brief dialogue with the keyboard player who played a chorded intro, and they were singing. It was as easy as that. Never for a moment did it strike him that Hazel might not know the words, just as it hadn't occurred to the man in the badly fitting Crown Topper that they would do anything other than duet together. All of it seemed ordained, a partnership made in heaven.

Their voices came thrillingly back to them from the loudspeakers as Sonny looked out over the heads of the crowd to a point far away in time and space. In imagination, he was paying homage before a simple, speckled slab, a carved stetson at its foot, the name Hank Williams cut into the upright stone. A country graveyard for a country boy like himself. Mount Olive, Alabama. One day he would visit there, he was determined on that ...

They held hands, letting the lyrics travel their course, poor boy, rich girl, never the twain shall meet, all that, but very far from a dirge. Hank's songs were never like that, even the saddest, and this was a sad one all right. The fiddle player swung the tune blues-style, the way it was meant to be played, while the rest of the band filled in. It all seemed so effortless, as if he were merely picking up where he had left off some earlier, forgotten period in his life, where all this was as natural as breathing. He had the feeling that Hazel was with him on that, as well, and when the number ended they were grinning at one another. So was the band, he noticed.

Applause from the crowd, when it came, was grudging and sparse, but Sonny didn't care. He knew these people, expected nothing from them. After all, wasn't he an outsider – they both were – a fact which had been noted the moment they had walked into the place. An element of risk had been involved, but what of it? Tonight, he told himself, he was armour-plated.

He remembered sitting down, his legs feeling weak and he was sweating a lot. Hazel gave him a handkerchief to mop his brow. It was a man's large white linen handkerchief and bore the scent of the contents of her leather bag. That handkerchief and its heady aroma was to be the last definite thing he remembered before waking up in his bed next morning. Alone.

'A Day in the Life of a Fool'

Havergal Court, Number 52, the basement flat next to the tunnel that runs to the strip of communal garden at the back of the block. That was where he lived. Havergal Court. It sounded exclusive. And doubtless had impressed the folks back home when he used to write letters once upon a time. He could imagine his mother showing the neighbours the address at the head of that short sheet of Basildon Bond. But then, everyone's address was like that. Lawless, he recalled, lived in a dump called Montmorency Mansions. All those names culled from Debrett, they had to tell you something about the pretensions of the English ...

But, on that steaming August Saturday, when he opened his eyes around noon and the first thoughts of the day began their painful itch, there was no solicitous body servant hovering at the ready to draw curtains, run a bath or provide tea in a bone china cup and saucer. He'd read about that being the norm once. All the flats had a room, much smaller than the rest, close to the kitchen, to house such a creature. It was a difficult concept to take in, all those men of indeterminate age, women, too, shut away for the night in what could only be termed a box-room and never addressed by their Christian names.

Miriam, his 'lodger', swore her little back bedroom was haunted. She had sensed a presence watching her undress, on more than one occasion, she'd said. He told her to draw her curtains but, no, she insisted, no, it was in the room with her. Miriam, right now, was on an Eighteen-to-Thirties holiday in Corfu and would have just about taken her clothes off for a different 'presence' every night in her hotel room for a week with no qualms whatsoever. He and Miriam rarely saw one another but the place did seem a lot quieter without her.

He lay there staring up at the crusted plaster boss in the

middle of the bedroom ceiling. It had the appearance of a malignant species of fungus inching its way inexorably down towards him, not the prettiest sight to wake to, first thing. Once it might have been, picked out in a lighter, more delicate shade of pink, or, perhaps pale blue, and kept pristine by that presence in the back room with his or her feather duster. He had woken in other rooms in similar flats to this one which had been restored to that former opulence. Brass bed, mahogany wardrobe, Dutch-tiled fireplace, still in use, lamps with globes, a Turkey carpet and the ceiling lovingly highlighted by a steady hand.

For a moment he lay thinking about all the different styles and periods to be found in this one mansion block. If you could just take the roof off, or slice a section through, doll's-house fashion, for a quick peek – what a hotchpotch. Old Jewish Viennese European, Victorian Drawing-Room, Thirties Repro, Country Pine, Festival of Britain (the two gays upstairs), North Circular Furniture Warehouse Flat-pack, Italian Hi-Tech, Matt Black Modern, and, right at the bottom, his own particular mess.

If you really cared to put a name to *that* you'd have to call into use that degraded word, Hippy. For, yes, the mattress *was* on the floor, the bookshelves *did* rest on bricks, the curtains *were* of worn chenille, the poster he had never bothered to pull down *was* one of Jimi Hendrix, and the predominant colour scheme throughout *was* still basically burnt orange and sienna, curiously enough those very hues supposed to signify aggression. Now, why was that? All those peace-loving people – that little portrait of their Bhagwan dangling about their necks – why did they always choose to dress in those same hot shades of the spectrum?

He lay spreadeagled, the thoughts beating on his consciousness like insects on a screen, tiny dive bombers coming in, wave after wave of them. His mouth felt sore and dry and there was a patch of pain about the size of a smallish coin low down on the left-hand side of his forehead. Soon it would begin to spread, he didn't have to be told, when the time came for him to concentrate seriously on the events of the previous night. But, for the moment, those gnats still kept up their buzzing as he lay contemplating his first erection of the day. It seemed to be genuine, for he felt no burning urge to take a piss. The physiology of it intrigued for only a brief space of time before he turned over on his side, taking himself in hand, for it did seem a pity to waste it.

Two feet away on the yellow painted floorboards lay his wallet, watch and a scatter of loose change. There was also a square of folded blue writing-paper only a little larger than a postage stamp. He couldn't remember precisely when and how it had got there, but he had more than a good idea that it must bear a name and telephone number. He tried to visualise the person who must have given him that message but try as he might, to undress, caress, eventually slake himself on the mature body, nothing, no image of lust was forthcoming.

Faced with such a puzzling setback there seemed nothing for it but to fall back on a faithful old standby. She was buried in a dusty pile of *Men Only*s in the far corner, too distant to reach; but then, every intricate detail of that burnished anatomy was imprinted on his memory. Even the prose style of the captions had stayed with him. '*Robinson Crusoe should have been so lucky to have found a girl Friday quite so alluring as our Centre-fold of the Month. Tall and slim and tanned all over by her native rays, Miss Cayman Islands is anyone's dream of tropic bliss. A shapely 38-22-36, she tells us her hobbies are snorkelling, driving fast cars, fine food and wines, and writing poetry of a romantic nature. Yes, indeed, Cindy Delgado-Smith, but who needs poetry on the page when confronted with such a sonnet of shapeliness in the flesh, such lovely, yummy, golden brown flesh at that ...*'

On this occasion he took her from behind, out of pure lust, nothing more, and when it was over, quick, easy, she faded away just as effortlessly, like the last thing on a television screen. The pumping in the blood died, the usual calm followed, but then he felt depressed – much more so than usual, for some reason. The act and the emotion had no connection, he told himself. Once, maybe, when he was younger, but not now. He was like an engineer opening a valve. But if all that were so obviously true, *why the fuck did he now find himself so steeped in this black despair*? Could it be the thought of all those others like himself, all over this city, in similar beds, similar rooms, starting their day the same way? Was there perhaps some deep, cosmic pity about all of that he hadn't reckoned on?

An even more outlandish fancy struck him. Could it be even remotely possible that he was actually experiencing *guilt* at the idea of being *unfaithful*? Could it be? If it was, he thought, then this was much more serious than he had at first realised. He glanced at the folded square of paper on the floor but decided to leave it where it lay for the time being. An attempt meanwhile must be made to rise and face the day.

With legs spread and trembling slightly, he rose like some naked seafarer preparing to ride a bucking deck. The analogy was not so far-fetched. He knew to his cost that if he were foolish enough to close his eyes – just once – a terrible tumbling sensation was certain to overtake him. Trying not to think of washing machines or launderettes, he managed to get his robe on, a blue shorty towelling number. It smelt a bit. In fact, everything did. His nasal passages felt scoured and raw. Some malevolent fairy had hidden his slippers (of course) and he stubbed his toe on a heavy book of some sort, like a dictionary. It was lying on the floor on the far side of the bed. He didn't even attempt to conjecture how it had got there, it certainly wasn't his.

Shakily he made his way out into the long and dark hallway. As he was moving in the direction of the kitchen, the letter flap rattled and he turned to see yet another wad of junk mail fall on to the heap of unopened post growing at the base of the door. The stuff came in triplicate these days, offers to wash your car, mow your non-existent lawn, cook, clean, drive, decorate and mend for you but, above all, buy your flat. He particularly enjoyed the mounting desperation mixed with greed contained in those latter pleas. It meant nothing to Sonny whether a young, childless, professional couple or a Japanese businessman were panting to push ready cash into his hand for the privilege of taking over Number 52 Havergal Court. The truth of the matter was it wasn't in his power to hand the keys over to anyone; he neither owned the place, nor was its lease in his name, but he did enjoy the feeling of being wooed so strenuously by a crowd of young shits in striped shirts.

By this time he was at the kitchen table, first coffee of the day in a mug in front of him. The mug had BOSS printed on its glaze, but the Blue Mountain Blend came from a jar on Miriam's side of the cupboard – his was empty. But then, his need was infinitely greater than hers. A pile of dishes overflowed in the sink, something rank smelt in the plastic orange pedal-bin over in the corner, and the cooker badly needed cleaning, outside as well as in. He made a mental note of these details but nothing more than that. It wasn't that he was a slob, his surroundings *were* important to him – within reason – but a side of him did rebel against Miriam's fanatic regard for the upkeep of her part of the flat. Of course it was a bonus sharing a spotless bathroom and kitchen (when she was here), but he did feel all that scrubbing and tidying constituted an unspoken criticism of his way of life.

There was something more sinister at work there, as well, he convinced himself. Any day now she would begin extending her field of operations – first, it would be the hallway, then the area outside the front door at the foot of the stairs would receive her attention. He had, in fact, seen her rummaging about in the glory-hole they shared with little old Mrs De Soto in Number 51. It was just before she set off for Ipsos. She might, of course, have merely been searching out a suitcase for herself but even so he felt he recognised a quite definite progression, starting with that steady encroachment of territory, to be followed up by the moving in of a boyfriend. '*You don't mind, do you? Clive needs a place for a day or two.*'

On second thoughts, no such conversation would probably take place. There had been a succession of nameless ones in the past – he'd always given them names of his own, for he had never once been introduced. All those Alis, Pedros, Ravis, Tariqs, always foreign students or waiters

63

but, once, the son of a diplomat – a chauffeured limousine with CD plates had waited outside until the early hours – they were just unseen presences he could hear occasionally flushing the toilet, giggling, singing, laughing, reaching a climax. It was hard to mistake that sound, even through the thickness of several walls. One night an Ali had achieved the feat six times. Miriam came continuously like a slow and rolling bout of thunder, with no real perceptible climax. He remembered that night. It was like lying listening to a gathering storm that never broke, punctuated at intervals by single warlike whoops.

But that was all a thing of the past. All those dusky warriors of the small hours over here to learn the language were getting their tuition elsewhere, for Miriam was in the process of changing image. Gone was yesterday's punk, gone were the New Romantic, the existentialist throwback, all in black, the brief butch phase. Once she had been a bike-girl for a steady two months, a messenger, dodging buses and cars on a trail-bike, a satchel full of documents on her rump for business people in a hurry. She would come home after a hard day in the traffic lanes looking and smelling like a stevedore. Not so far-fetched, either, fo' Miriam was a big girl, particularly in the thighs depart-ment. The trail-bike seemed almost featherweight the way she would hump it up the hallway and into her room, for he'd drawn the line about having it stay out in the corridor opposite his own door.

But the bike had been disposed of, along with all the other gear. Now it was tailored jackets and skirts, a belted Burberry and a leather briefcase in oxblood with com-bination lock. She had found herself a new 'post' somewhere off Oxford Street and went to wine bars with colleagues called Mark or Clive or Andrew whom he never ever saw. They would take her home to their own places in areas like Fulham, Wandsworth or Kennington, areas that were 'coming up', just like this one. So, if one of these fine evenings Miriam did bring back a Clive or a Jamie – *needing a place for a day or two*' – as he was expecting, the message was clear. The business of getting him out of his own flat had started in earnest. Two sitting tenants against one, which would soon become three – probably Clive's sister just up from the country. London flat life was like that, a jungle full of predators digging themselves in.

It had always been like that, but much more so now. He saw them on the Tube, those smooth-faced, sweet-smelling young travellers heading to and from their places of business all with but a single thought in mind, how to winkle out some sitting tenant somewhere, some old granny in the basement, some almost forgotten attic dweller, some throwback, back number, like himself. Miriam, he knew for certain, saw him in those terms, but fat, upwardly mobile Miriam hadn't reckoned on one thing – that he had got this place himself by the selfsame methods she was almost certainly contemplating this very moment on her hired beach bed. He could just see her bounding back ready for the fray after a fortnight's sun, sex and positive thinking. The difference, of course, being that it'd taken him a good ten years to get where he was; she would want to be queen bee inside a matter of months.

Patience, that was how the flat had fallen to him. Patience and fortitude. He had seen them come and he had seen them go, a dozen, at least, over the intervening years, transients on that ever-moving escalator of city life. A suicide, two marriages, a breakdown, three drug busts, a couple of unwanted pregnancies – nobody counted abortions – and a camp window-dresser called Peter who had got himself knifed outside Selfridges by a crazed Algerian shop-lifter. Peter had the biggest, best and brightest room at the front and he had moved in by right of succession. After that no one constituted any threat. Dutifully the others paid their rent to him and every month he, in turn, would put a Giro cheque into an envelope and post it off to Bolsover Holdings plc of Cavendish Square.

At one time the place held six bodies, including his own, and the resulting profit kept him nicely in pocket. But he had grown tired of so many alien mattresses and sleeping-bags about the place. People wanted to play guitars – badly, and the wrong kind of music, which was worse – at all hours of the day and night. The toilet seemed to be flushing continuously, double lines of drying underwear festooned the bathroom. And such underwear. One of the great and early disappointments of his young life had been the vicious contrast between the outward appearance and what was revealed only at bedtime. He could write a treatise on that – the young English middle classes and their unconcern about being knocked down and found to be wearing knickers in such a distressed and distressing state. Strangely enough, he had never seen Miriam's. They would have to be on the large side. Like Hazel's, but then Hazel would never, *ever* be seen dead in anything which was holed or frayed or grey with constant washing out. For the first time a flicker of lust centred on those splendid hindquarters ignited briefly, but it came too late, he'd already spent himself elsewhere.

He rose and went to the bathroom to get something for the ache in his head. But, of course, the cabinet was bare, save for the usual collection of old amber prescription bottles, a rusty hairpin or two. Miriam would have something in her room, he told himself. The door was locked, but then he had a key, his little secret. He had five of them, a duplicate for every room in the flat, a precaution, nothing more, for he dreaded the sound of splintering wood. His headache was getting worse by the minute as he trailed back to the bedroom where he kept the ring of keys on top of the wardrobe.

Playing the sleep-walker, he made his way with outstretched arms back along the corridor. Selecting a key at random from the ring he fitted it into the lock first time – *but the door wasn't locked.*

More in wonderment than alarm, he turned the knob and pushed and, what was even more mysterious, the light was on. One of those BIG Japanese paper globes the size of a medicine ball shed a pleasing light on an interior of such charm and, yes, delicacy, that it seemed for a moment that he had, by some fluke of dislocation, stumbled into a room in another flat. The style, if he had to be literary, was vaguely *Cider With Rosie*, perhaps *Mill On The Floss*. There was a young girl's bed, virginal and white, a pine chest, a small chintz-covered armchair, pictures of kittens on the walls and a rug of faded purples and browns. He'd seen similar settings in windows in Liberty's. A faint woodland scent came from a bowl of potpourri on the chest of drawers.

He stood there, barefoot, in his old shortie robe and he could smell himself, as alien as a steer in a drawing-room. How had she managed to keep all this from him, this secret universe he had never once suspected? He thought of Miriam the bike-girl and her machine with its heavy-duty tyres. How could that brutality ever fit in with the nursery innocence of all of this? Could such a transformation perhaps have taken place one day when he was out of the flat? With Clive or Andrew or Jamie giving a helping hand? If they had their way the whole place would eventually look like this, he knew. He saw it all for what it was, this first beachhead in a war of gentrification. No, he vowed, never. Over his dead body. He and shades of Laura Ashley would never, *ever* share the same flat. He was shaking, he needed something quick, something a lot stronger than aspirin.

One thing he did know about Miriam was that she was a pill freak, a haunter of prescription counters. Her handbag – now her briefcase – rattled like a percussion instrument. The only time she had addressed him passionately about anything was the night he had mistaken some nasal remedy for eye drops. She had come running at his scream of pain with a drawer full of antidotes and, treating him, had lectured him fiercely all the while on the respective merits and ingredients of each product. She was like a brusque but good-hearted nursing sister and he would have been content to feel her weight beside him on the bed forever. It was the closest he ever came to fancying Miriam.

Remembering that drawer crammed with bottles, tubes and packets he looked about him and, sure enough, there it was in its place in a little bedside cabinet convenient for any night time emergency. He easily found what he needed, some paracetamol for his head, and some other tablets in a manufacturer's unmarked bottle. But he was familiar with the little beauties. Above the famous Swiss maker's name two tiny, incised eyelids lowered themselves demurely, promising the calm he needed to face whatever the day ahead held.

He shook out an equal number from each bottle – just enough not to be missed – and dropped them into the pocket of his robe, feeling better already. The room seemed a soothing place to be in, suddenly. He could see how pleasant it must be to close the door at the end of the day on all that shabbiness beyond its clean white paint.

He sat on the bed. It felt as taut and well sprung as a trampoline. His hairy thighs looked out of place against its purity, but then he would always be out of place in a room like this; at least, that's the opinion Miriam and her new-found friends would certainly have of him. He could just hear them discussing it – him – with much loud laughter. *How could someone like that, a bogtrotter, basically, when you got right down to it, appreciate the finer points of what was quintessentially English in style, someone, after all –* renewed laughter *– who didn't know his ass from his elbow.*

In the flat above another tenant was switching television channels back and forth for no apparent rhyme or reason. It could well have been a child at play, of course, but he felt it had to be someone older, someone like himself, also in the grip of a private obsession. But he had no real interest in anyone else's concern, not right now, not at this moment, thank you. A one-sided dialogue was running in his head at great speed, so rich and satisfying that he was even prepared to put up with the pain in his brow until it had run its course.

It went something like this . . .

Bizarre as it may seem, this particular paddy just happens to know more about you lot and your so-called 'taste' than you could ever hope to pick up in a lifetime of mindless imitation and pretension. Furthermore (excellent word), *it may or may not interest you to know that, for a period of almost ten years, this laughable emigrant figure made a fat living out of idiots like you and your ridiculous crazes. Ten years spent combing the Welsh marches for pine dressers, pine tables, whatnots, wardrobes, chests, beds, chairs, commodes, bookcases, cradles, churns, hallstands – you name it – and when that ran out, Art Deco, Bakelite, Clarice Cliff pottery, Dinky toys, Parker*

68

pens. Not a period to be particularly proud of – all that plundering of widows' attics to feed your pathetic hunger for nostalgia. Still, you paid through the nose for it, and that was consolation enough ...

He sat there remembering, diatribe forgotten. All those years on the Portobello Road. Everyone was at it, then. Money for old rope (you could even sell *that*, if you had a mind to). Occasionally, he still took a stroll down that way. Many of the old faces were still there, but it was a depressing experience seeing those single-parent girls again in their mittens and leg-warmers and mangy fur coats sitting hunched at their stalls, sad little treasures spread out before them.

He stood up, he had outstayed his visit, but, before switching off the light, he felt drawn across to the chest of drawers, he couldn't help himself. Taking one of the china knobs in his grasp – it felt cold but vaguely erotic – he pulled and the drawer slid smoothly out to reveal a hoard of luxurious silks and satins, all white and pristine, like the bedspread. So much for his theory about middle-class girls and their knickers. These were of the finest water, anyone could see that.

He delved into the slithery depths stirring up a faint aroma of violets. Putting himself into the rôle of voyeur he tried to visualise how these scraps of lace and silk might look stretched over Miriam's pony club haunches. It was a difficult enough feat of the imagination, but nonetheless he felt himself beginning to stiffen for the second time that morning. Then his hand touched something else hard between the layers of softness, a generous replica of his own flesh and blood, only this was cool, smooth and faintly ribbed to the touch. He withdrew the pale, tusk-like object. It felt lighter than it should; Miriam must have taken out the batteries. More to the point, she had left it behind. Not wanted on voyage. Plenty of the real thing where she was going, the slut.

Christ, he felt *really* bad now. Why had he ventured in here in the first place? Well, he knew that, didn't he, for the proof happened to be in his pocket. Reminding himself, he popped a second Valium into his mouth but, of course, couldn't swallow. Then he did a foolish thing. He crunched the tablet into tiny pieces. A bitterness filled his mouth and, running to the tap in the kitchen, he gulped down a good half pint of water. The evil taste still lingered. To think something so foul could bring such sweetness of mood.

He swallowed another of the tablets – whole, this time, with the aid of more water. Then he leaned against the sink prepared to wait for the first, slow, creeping tendrils of chemical ease. He could see one of the pussycat portraits on Miriam's far wall. This particular one had stripes, a ribbon and a bell, and waved a playful paw at him. But, no thanks, no way, for he had the feeling that to stay in there a moment longer would mean other secrets might be revealed to him, perhaps things he had no wish to know about himself. There might be a diary.

It was too soon for the tablets to take hold, he still felt old and frightened and alien. This world, Miriam's world, and that of her friends made him feel a million miles from home. It wasn't a world he wanted any part of. It certainly wasn't Hank's world, or Tammy's or Willie's or Billy-Jo's, even. There were no country songs, thank God, about vibrators. He snapped the light switch off, closed the door, turning the key.

All was now as he'd found it, but not quite – not quite, for after he had another coffee and washed (he didn't dare shave) he went back to his own bedroom and noticed the book still on the floor, the one he had been unable to place. It *was* a dictionary, a fat, blue Concise Oxford. On the flyleaf, he read: *If This Book Should Chance To Roam Don't Delay To Send It Home To – Miriam Lipschitz*, and then an address in Stanmore. The handwriting was that of a schoolgirl – well, he sensed that, although girls' writing seemed always much more mature than a boy's. She called herself Livingstone these days. Ms Miriam C. Livingstone. It was on all the mail. No end, it seemed, to little surprises this morning.

He continued to hold the book open on his lap – it bore her scent, that faint reminder of hedgerows – and, for the first time, he tried to make sense of the past twelve hours.

70

There had to be some clue of sorts here, surely. If he could only manage to deduce how this book came to be lying on his floor like that, then he felt the mists might begin to clear. *Musette: kind of bagpipe; soft pastoral air matching bagpipe's sound.* Fat lot of use that was *Murrain. Infectious disease in cattle.* Worse.

Once in the old days when he'd been stoned he'd gone through the Xs – in slow motion. There were twenty-three in all. It was a favourite of the old acid-head crowd, all those shadows from the past, in their beads and cheesecloth, into 'random-ness'. Could he have been trying to turn the clock back, then, last night? You could play alone, but it was always more fun if there were others with you, all laughing their heads off. No, that was impossible, for Hazel had left him on the doorstep.

The sentence had fallen bomb-like out of the blue. *His* doorstep, not hers. It was coming back to him. The pub, the dance. Had there been a vindaloo between Cricklewood Broadway and their arrival together at his front door? He closed Miriam's school dictionary and placed it on the bed.

They had grappled together, like two teenagers on their first date, oh my God, right outside there on his mat! Little Mrs De Soto, a light sleeper if ever there was one, must have heard all of it ... *A cup of coffee, just one, say you will, ten minutes, five, then. Please, please.* His words came back to him, stinging, red-hot reminders. He couldn't remember if they'd had a curry or not but, my God, the wrestling, the whispered pleas. It was like being sixteen again back home and trying to get Sheena Jenkins to go with him under the old railway bridge. He hadn't been able to manage it then, either, for Christ's sake!

From the wardrobe he took a pair of jeans, a blue and white check shirt, clean socks, trainers. Watch, wallet – replenished from the cigar box behind the row of Jack Kerouacs – keys, and that wad of blue notepaper still unfolded. What if it were blank? But it was as if he were moving underwater now – his brain, as well. He swam gently out into the hallway. There was a long mirror there, but it never received any light. In its dim, mottled reflection

71

he caught a glimpse of someone he vaguely recognised, someone from his past. Sideburns; sleeked-back hair; shirt, pearl-buttoned, big-collared, too snug for today's comfort; Colt .45 belt buckle, flared jeans. Nothing had changed there since 1970.

He kicked aside the latest fall of mail from behind the door. Another of those long buff envelopes with the windows – that made four now. This one had URGENT on it. But who cared? He still felt as though he were in an evenly heated aquarium ...

The climb up the stairs to the street outside made his legs quiver slightly, and at the top he stopped to look back down. There was a *mezuza* fixed to the strip of wall between Mrs De Soto's front door and his own. It had been painted over many, many times. At the moment it was dark cream. There was no way of telling if it had been placed there to protect his flat or hers. Somehow, he didn't think Mrs De Soto was Jewish. More Third World. She played a lot of tango music on her gramophone. It had always intrigued him, that little metal strip fastened up there at head height. One day he intended to prise it away from the wall, make it yield up its secret. But something always stopped him, some uneasiness about the consequences. He couldn't help remembering *The Exorcist*.

The heavy double glass doors swung shut at his back, he was out on the streets once more. At large. He looked at his watch, it was 1.35 on another hot and humid Saturday in London and he had time to kill.

He began walking with no particular destination in mind. It often started off like that, as far as he was concerned, sometimes a whole day spent veering aimlessly across the face of the city as if before a wind no one else but he could sense at his back. Sometimes that same invisible current would send him underground on to a curving Tube line or up to the top deck of a bus. He would get off and on at stops along the way as the urge took him. Today he felt as though a slow-moving *sirocco* was driving him on. At the end of the avenue he allowed himself to bear right before it and he travelled past the modest row of shops, newsagent, butcher, Indian grocer, glazier, launderette, funeral parlour, fish-bar, off licence, all held together as though by invisible bookends. The flats they served continued on either side as far as the eye could travel until the next little trading outpost materialised, perhaps this time a pub at its heart.

Of all these local shops only the glass and mirror establishment, strangely enough, had any real significance for him. He patronised all the others on a regular basis (well, except for J. M. Nodes the undertaker – Economy With Refinement) and never expected or sought any kind of familiarity in return, yet after a single visit to buy a pane – or was it some mirror glass? – at this one shop he felt himself to be an old and valued customer. It was owned by a couple in their forties, Tadzik and Halina, but then the place was always full of other Poles who could have been sleeping partners. They would all take a turn with the T-square and cutter on the big felt-covered table, setting aside their tumblers of wine or beer to do so. He never, ever saw vodka.

'Hallo, Sonny!' would come the call from the open door as he passed by. 'Sonny, my friend, how goes it?' It was the only time his name sounded rich, impressive and somehow mysterious on another's lips.

The shop was more like a club for expatriates, a place for drinking, playing cards, gossiping but, above all, for the exchange of lore on how to beat the system. When they did lapse into English – out of politeness to his presence – the talk would be of conversion grants, VAT returns, sickness benefits, cold-weather payments, ways of jumping the housing and hospital queues, mortgage matters.

Tadzik was a chain-smoking melancholiac with a stained yellow beard. He listened to everything and everybody in silence. Halina, his wife, the converse, was elegant in black from top to toe, witty, outgoing, argumentative, holding court from a high revolving office stool. All money transactions centred on that big, black hide bag of hers, but then that part always seemed unimportant, an afterthought. Sonny liked these people, he liked their style, their warmth, generosity and banter. They seemed to him to possess the better qualities of his own people back home. Those heated discussions about the best ways of soaking the establishment – that wasn't simply a matter of greed, peasant greed, and he knew all about that all right. It seemed to him more a genuine and democratic pooling of information. And the way they looked at you at first meeting, shyly, yet at the same time open to the possibility of intimacy developing very quickly. That was also something to remind him of his own part of the world. Not that he was the type to ever get sentimental when it came to the old folks at home. As far as he was concerned, that's just what it was back there – an old folks' home – and, God, had he been glad to get shot of it, as well as them.

Today, as he passed the shop and looked in, half expecting to hear his name, they were all intently watching something on a portable television placed on the big table. At first he thought it might be some sporting occasion, though why it should be so riveting seemed a mystery – but then, through the glass and on the distant screen, he glimpsed that silver-haired, smiling, world famous celebrity, all in white as usual, gently waving to the four corners of the crowd from his open Popemobile. For the second time in twenty-four hours Sonny felt an acute sense of not belonging. Last night in the dance-hall it hadn't seemed to matter, but this time it did, it really did . . .

His feet took him past the butcher's next door, but then outside the newsagent Priya's he faltered and came to a halt. It was as if his invisible wind had suddenly failed him, leaving him becalmed with nothing better to do than stare at the cards in the window advertising a boy's bicycle, a drop-sided cot, a suede coat, worn once, a set of encyclopaedias, a collection of Matt Monroe records, an electric hotplate (still in the box), a carved African figure, and the telephone number of Christine, New In Town, Busty 'n Black. There was also Georgette, Roxy, Charmaine, Tiffany, Rose (Bracing Massage, Day Or Night), Debbie, Renata, Angel and Beth. In the middle of all these names – for some reason, they seemed appropriate in every case, what one would expect to see over a lighted bell push on a Soho doorway – there was one that surely had strayed there through some terrible mistake. Hazel, he read, Black Leather, Naughty Boys Report, followed by a number.

For a moment the chemicals in his blood seemed to lose any hold they may have had on him. Sweating and trembling he dug deep in his pocket for confirmation of this appalling coincidence. Some grinning deity somewhere had reached down a finger, singling him out for the treatment. *Did you think you could get away with it, then? Well, forget it, sucker.* He found the folded scrap and, opening it, held it up before his eyes. Hazel, he read, and below seven digits. He flattened the paper against the glass beside the card and his pulse rate began slowing as he compared the numbers.

Priya and his buxom young wife were sitting together behind the cash register at the back of the shop. They were grinning out at him, nodding, too, in that maddening way of theirs. Oh, shit, he thought.

He was drawing away from their gaze when there came a muffled roar and a passing gale pushed him back against the glass. A great, black, oiled torso swept past, propelled by thrusting legs.

'Hey!' he yelled, and 'Hey!' a second time, but the roller-skater, naked except for a pair of blue satin shorts, boots and his Walkman, merely stuck up a middle finger as big as a banana. Then he was gone around the corner. My God, thought Sonny, there are some days when it's safer to stay in bed. What he needed were blankets, a hot drink and a soothing hand on his brow.

A drink, however – a real one – might restore the balance. There was a pub, not a favourite, but a pub, on the far side of the recreation grounds. He would head in that direction. At least it would give him a sense of purpose. *Direction. Purpose.* Who was he kidding? He saw the sneer on his own face thrown back at him in J. M. Nodes & Sons' window display. A pair of dark red velvet drapes on a brass pole were pulled across as back-drop to a single spotlit urn set on what looked like a plant stand. That was all. Representing, he supposed, their slogan above the shop front – Economy With Refinement.

He was staring reflectively through the glass at this urn

when his system began taking another turn for the worse for, quite suddenly, what he was seeing was no longer a brass pot on a tripod but the stone shoe box again, *In Memory Of* cut into its face, name yet to be filled in.

Standing there in his jeans and clean Wrangler shirt, it struck him that he must look like anyone else about their business on a Saturday morning. Someone, perhaps, who had just dumped a load of laundry at the washeteria three doors away. A passer-by would simply notice someone quite nondescript standing looking into J. M. Nodes the undertaker's window, but no one would be able to guess what this average joe was seeing right at this moment. For the stand now supported what appeared to be an ordinary supermarket carrier bag – he recognised the Safeway logo. Like the shoe box, it had come back to haunt him. It squatted there in the spotlight, held in place by its contents, a dozen or so heavy old records, all that remained of a dead man and his life. They had been entrusted to him, those records, and he had lost them.

That was what he had been keeping from himself ever since he had woken. Now that it was out and staring him in the face, so to speak, he felt no better about it, merely a dulled hopelessness. Sure, he would make a call or calls, retrace his tracks of last night – that's if he could remember them – but he felt certain of the outcome already.

Where the shops ended he turned right and he was back in flatland once more. On past the bell pushes and intercoms – he remembered the time when those front doors stayed open day and night and you didn't have to wait for some extra-terrestrial voice to ask your name and business before being let in. The burglary rate was higher than ever it had been, however, and it wasn't hard to see why. Anyone could press buttons at random until someone confused, lonely or drunk enough – possibly all three – would release the catch in their apartment above and ... open sesame!

On occasions, coming home from the pub late at night, he had often felt the urge to try such an experiment, not because of any felonious intent, more out of mischief, or perhaps he just needed to hear a voice at that hour. Any voice. The trick was to press all of them in the panel simultaneously and then retreat smartly. Hurrying down the darkened street he would hear a cacophony break out at his back. He'd often felt that that was the true voice of London, that confused sound of people interrupted in the middle of their sleeping, eating, drinking, screwing, quarrelling or putting an end to it all. There was always a weeping woman on the other end, or someone who cried out, 'Come straight up', no matter how late the hour ...

But now it was day and he had problems of his own to contend with. Walking faster he crossed the car-lined road and, avoiding the dog turds that had suddenly increased underfoot as though the pets of the neighbourhood had been no longer able to contain themselves, he entered the park. To his left, behind the hedge, was that area called the Rose Garden, where the mothers gathered with their offspring, spreading themselves and their belongings on the turf between the beds of pink and scarlet floribundae. It was the unofficial no-man's land of the park and, hearing those gales of cruel laughter as he passed, sometimes the hair would stand up on the back of his neck. He was tall enough to be spotted above the bordering hedge and one of the mothers, a dark-eyed, perennially tanned woman with the most corrosive laugh of the lot, seemed to take a delight in causing him to walk faster.

'Howdy, Tex!' she would call out, and once, 'How about a ride, cowboy?'

Yesterday, on his way to the crematorium, he had bent himself almost double like Groucho Marx, but she still had sighted the travelling crown of his hat. Today, bareheaded, he sailed past without comment. Glancing over he could see no sign of her among the tangle of browning bodies. He didn't know whether to feel disappointed or relieved.

At the block of toilets, red brick, and vaguely rustic with their painted barge-boards lining the eaves (he recognised why gays referred to them as 'cottages'), he turned in for a swift crap. Sitting there in the chill, pants about his ankles, he saw the following on the door facing him: 'Thirty-six-year-old wife trained to obey available for photo video work etc. Your flat or hotel overnight stay if required. £35.00 a night. One or more guys – will do most anything of s & m. Mild torture (no lasting marks) meet me at bandstand to discuss. Seven days notice. Can bring photos of her to show you.' There were other messages on the walls of a mainly homosexual nature but this was special. Not a single spelling mistake and the script clerically neat and legible. He wondered if the police had had a hand in it, but even for them it did seem to be carrying entrapment a shade far.

In spite of himself, he couldn't help seeing that couple fleshed out through the power of the words. He – the advertiser – would be much younger, that somehow seemed certain, dark complexioned, a flashy dresser. He distinctly saw white shoes with those little gold chains. The wife would be running to fat, perhaps a drink problem, definitely a heavy smoker, and originally from somewhere up North. Tariq and Denise. Like that couple on the third floor. A great one for aromatic hair preparations and aftershave, his passage could be tracked in and out of the block by scent alone. He had a footballer's oiled perm and a single earring, and he carried a leather wallet dangling from a wrist strap and yes, his shoes were pale, Italian moccasins. She seemed to spend most of her time in the flat. He'd never once seen them out and about together. Denise and Tariq. Could it be them? They must have fallen on hard times to be advertising on the back of a lavatory door.

In certain of his magazines there were pages at the back full of identical wares for sale – or exchange – illustrated with Polaroids, of housewives sprawled unenticingly on the family bedspread. It was the most depressing section of all. Then he thought to himself, no, it was much more likely to be Dick and Dawn, another couple he knew in the block, a couple of lank-haired junkies. But then, Dawn would be like a stick insect without her clothes. Not at all inviting.

Why was he tormenting himself like this, he asked himself, groaning loudly, and the sound came back to him, an almost perfect echo, from a cubicle further along where a drunk must have been sleeping it off. The roar of the flush drowned any further discourse as he made his way hurriedly out and into the light.

To his hard left, over on the cricket pitch, a West Indian team was playing an Asian eleven. Their whites shone dazzlingly bright against the darkness of their skin and every man there, including the umpire, seemed to be taking the game very seriously indeed, the only sounds to be heard the grunts of the bowler followed by the crack of ball on bat. A couple of racing cyclists, equally fanatic, came hissing around the oval track past runners going in a different direction on cinders, and the tennis courts were full of leaping, crouching figures wearing headbands. The place seemed suddenly alive with strenuous activity, making him feel even more of an outcast.

He thought of that wino back there with his feet jammed against the toilet door. They had more in common, it came to him, than all these fitness freaks using up the park's oxygen. His own breathing sounded laboured to his ears, and patches of sweat were beginning to break out under each arm. He felt he had to get away from all of this, it was making him worse instead of better and, despite the heat, he quickened his pace until he was moving like a parody of one of those stringy old long-distance walkers. Past the tea room on its slight elevation, past the southern angled benches where the old sat hunched, faces held up to an invisible sun, past the adventure playground – the noise made him flinch – he jerked onward until he could make out the distant gates. The pub lay just beyond those painted bars.

It was dark, silent and mercifully cool, with only three other customers, all elderly, sitting well apart from one another. He ordered his own pint and sat down. There it squatted on its Budweiser mat in front of him like an object of worship, foam subsiding, a solitary streak of condensation marring the otherwise perfect glass. A pity to have to put it to his lips. He was feeling a little better now, not so jittery, not so doom-laden. Surreptitiously he slipped another of Miriam's pills into his mouth, washing it down with a sip of the beer.

There was a phone at the far end of the bar and, preparing himself for the moment when it seemed right, he took out his precious piece of paper and weighted it down on the wet wood of the table with a tiny heap of silver. Now, he could do this two ways. He could rehearse what he had to say, then do it, or he could wait until he was drunk again. At least there was a choice. Right? No, there wasn't.

Hazel, it's me. Sonny. How are you? Listen, there's a George Hamilton IV concert coming up at Wembley. I could try for tickets. (There was always a George Hamilton IV concert on somewhere.)

He drank deeply, unwisely, and the beer mixed with air filled his stomach too fast. It made his eyes water. *Hazel, it's me. Sonny. Look, about last night* ... This time he sucked on the thin lip of the glass slowly and reflectively, letting the bitter flood down the back of his throat in a controlled way. He was beginning to feel no pain. He sighted on the array of bottles reflected in the mirror behind the bar. Into the frame, shaped by his glass, swam the man of the house transformed to sepia. He had the same moustache he had worn as a fighter pilot, forty years older, that's all. Sonny had noticed the antique alloy propeller on the wall when first he entered the place; also the group aircrew photograph, young pilots in front of a Spitfire. Something to animate the punters. 'Excuse me, but isn't that ...' Yawn, yawn. Then he lowered the glass and the landlord returned to the present except for those hairy handlebars on his upper lip.

Hazel, this is Sonny. Has it occurred to you, I wonder, just what a perfect match our two names do make? Hazel and Sonny. Sonny and Hazel. Take your pick. Okay, I am a little high, I admit, the reason being I needed to screw up the courage to tell you certain things I didn't, couldn't, get around to last night. For instance. Your beautiful breasts and your lovely legs. What I could see of them. Believe me, I'm dying to see more. Does that embarrass you? It shouldn't, because that's only the half of it, or the quarter, or some other fraction of the whole wonderful you. Hazel, I've had a terrible morning and you're the only person I can talk to about it. First of all, there was that thing in Miriam's drawer, then my whole past

*life seemed to pass before my eyes in a shop window – or would have
done if I hadn't dragged myself away in time. Last, but not least, a
vision of hell on the back of a public toilet door. Is it only me, Hazel,
or is this not a sick, sick world we're living in? I mean, do all those
good old numbers we were singing together count for nothing no more?
God knows, I'm no innocent, I've been around, as they say, but there
comes a time when you can't take much more. I have the feeling that's
what's happening to yours truly right now. I mean, old Hank knew
what it was all about, he did, didn't he? 'No matter how I struggle
and strive, I'll never get out of this world alive'* ...

He was singing the words as he left the public house. He
hadn't gone near a phone, yet he felt as though he had
unburdened himself in some way. Perhaps, finally, he had
joined that band of demented ones wandering the streets,
after all. And, as if to put the theory to the test, one of those
same brothers appeared on the same stretch of pavement
as himself, coming towards him. He was pushing a supermarket trolley with one bad wheel, heaped with old clothes
and kitchen ware, broken radios and such like wreckage,
all of it surmounted by a useless tennis racket like a flag of
desperation.

The homeless one came closer, not old by any means, nor
the bottom of the heap by a long chalk. He was wearing
an overcoat buttoned to the neck despite the heat, and
moonboots. At the crucial moment Sonny averted his eyes,
a failure of will, and the stooped figure in the navy melton
coat shuffled past muttering something to himself about
'radiation' or was it 'radiators'? Perhaps there was a connection in the poor sap's mind. Sonny was tempted to catch
him up and thrash the matter out there and then on the
hot pavements. But the moment passed and gradually the
sounds of the defective trolley faded away in the distance.
He continued walking, walking, walking ...

*Hazel, Sonny, again. How was your Saturday? Let me tell you how
I got through mine. Maybe you can make sense of it. First of all I
took a Tube, then a bus, or it might have been the other way round.
The hardest thing, I do know, was to decide on where to go. I could,
of course, have gone in a circle. I've sometimes done just that and,*

for a time, that seemed a sensible proposition, feeling as I did, because ever since we've met, Hazel, that's the way I've been, you see. Like one of those people you spot sometimes just following that endless yellow curve on the Underground map and never getting or going anywhere. Life can be a bit like the Circle Line sometimes. And not a glimpse of light at the end of the tunnel either, eh? Well, except for that solitary stretch between High Street Ken and Gloucester Road. To be frank, there could well be other parts where the sun does shine because I've never been further east than Victoria or St Pancras, but I doubt that. It all looks pretty dark on the map over there to me. Anyway, I do remember I changed at South Ken on to the District Line heading west. Open sky all the way once you've broken clear of Earl's Court. Hazel, I just wish you could have been with me, because there's something I wanted you to see, something special, a little piece of myself no one else knows about ...

So, here I am travelling south, now — I've crossed the river — and the next stop, Kew Gardens, is mine. Yes, Kew. All that grass and trees and exotica under glass. Did you know that the Temperate House was built by an Irishman? And the Palm House, too? But that's not where I'm heading. Not today. Just inside the twin turnstiles, and a little away along past the banked rhododendrons on the right, is a museum, and inside this small botanical museum is what I've come to see.

Let me introduce you to one of my favourite things in London. On the ground floor, in the main chamber, there stands a glass case, square in the centre of the room, and inside that case is a miniature world, spotlit, a piece of history fixed for eternity. The plate on the side reads 'Model Of An Indigo Factory, Nudea, India. Colonial And Indian Exhibition 1886'. It's as if someone had puffed a great cloud of nerve gas over the entire place a century ago and every one of those tiny turbaned figures were frozen in the middle of whatever they were doing. You never saw such industry. Some treading rollers, others working a great wooden press, a dozen more up to their waists in a vat of blue. There's a miniature ox-cart piled high with bundles of raw stuff, a driver hauling on the reins. Three supervisors wearing topees stand about supervising. Nothing changes. They have identical moustaches to the workforce but their skins are much paler. One of them looks as if he might well be white. Of course, it can't all be hard graft — there's a thatched temple and, on a bench in its shade, three labourers, with dyed hands and feet, rest between shifts. It's the strangest thing, but I have to tell you I could stand looking down on that little world under glass for hours on end. I must know every part of it off by heart, the number of times I've been back there. All those details, and so exact in scale. Like the inside of a watch. Do you want to know my particular favourites? A row of miniature shoes laid out on the steps of the temple; a dog lifting his leg against a wall. Oddest of all, a man at the top of a ladder looking down into a darkened room. Just a man on a ladder, but — what's he up to? What does he see? What do you make of it? He keeps coming back to haunt me.

Does any of this make any sense, Hazel? Even if it doesn't, I wanted to tell you about it. Really the reason I returned today is because I always feel relaxed and calm after about ten minutes or so just sitting there. I must say I don't care much for other people doing the same, crazy though that may sound. Anyway, most visitors usually give it a wide berth for some reason, even school-kids, if there's a party of them, which I find harder to understand. But then perhaps they see it as some sort of grown-ups' diversion, the way model railways, even toy soldiers, aren't really for their age-group, but their parents'. They're good at that, the English, they are, aren't they — the construction of such things, ships in bottles, or getting all of the Lord's Prayer on to the back of a postage stamp. Still, I'll never know who he was who put all this together, every inspired particle of it. No name. Not a hint or clue of any sort. Nameless. Sad, don't you think?

That was his own mood, now, as he sat alone in that bright room. He'd run out of things to say. The overhead lights shot reflections off the glass in front of him, a tiny insect hum coming from their fluorescent tubes. There didn't seem much point in continuing to hang around, the old magic wasn't working for him, he couldn't seem to be able to get into that little world today. The tiny figures, the mud-walled buildings, the ox-cart, the dog and the man on the ladder, they had no life about them. They looked as if they never had.

His mouth felt bone dry – because of the pills – so he rose and went outside to where there was a drinking fountain. He played its jet into his open mouth until the water ran icy cold against his gums. Then he popped another pill. Three down. Or was it four? Two to go. His little swimming aids, they would see him through as long as he took care to space them out.

Out of the gardens he stroked his way, through the turnstile and along the peaceful avenues back the way he had come to the station. On the platform, awash with the brutal scent of honeysuckle and the scream of bird song, it was like waiting on some remote country platform, and when a train arrived he climbed in with no care or thought as to its destination. He had a carriage to himself; he laid his cheek against the glass, absorbing the vibration of the ancient rolling stock. The deserted stations, East Acton, Gunnersbury, Kensal Rise – he was on the little used and almost forgotten North London Line – seemed unusually widely spaced. No one got off or on, as far as he could see.

Through the grime of the window he could make out back gardens baking in the heat. Sometimes there were bodies – sometimes, not – strewn gracelessly on the biscuit-coloured grass, oblivious to the passing train. If you were serious about finding out about the English, what they were really like behind the façade, here was the place to start. Their hidden life was here, on their washing lines, in the construction of their garden sheds, in the things they never threw away. He passed allotments – those other private places – where old men worked and watered or lay collapsed in deck chairs as ancient and broken as themselves.

The train curved swaying through the broiling heat. On either side of the embankment West London lay spread-eagled, defenceless, beneath the flight path of the holiday jets. The constant roar of the engines and the fine, dropping mist of their fuel fell like a judgement on the heads of the gardeners. He remembered when he lived in W8, how the incoming 747s would stack directly above his flat roof whenever he wanted to lie out and get a little colour. All weekend long, plane-loads of foreigners staring down at him on his spread towel. Welcome to your first sighting of an authentic London flat-dweller in the flesh, friend . . .

At West Acton two recognisable examples of the species got into the compartment, male and female, both young, less than half his age. The girl wore baggy khaki shorts and a black sports singlet barely disturbed by boyish breasts. Her cropped hair was sulphur-yellow but the tufts in her armpits, Sonny couldn't help noticing, were as dark as her vest.

The boyfriend had his boots up on the seats in no time. He was also smoking vigorously, despite the signs, but then that was to be expected. There he lolled against the cushions, a tattooed arm flung around Blondie's neck, bare torsoed above the sweater knotted about the waist. Sonny knew the type well. Oh, yes. He had only two natural habitats – one was on the football terraces causing mayhem with his mates, the other was roaming the streets and open spaces dragging a half-famished Alsatian behind on a chain. Today found him in neither of those places, so that made him unsure of himself. Dangerous as well, thought Sonny. Probably had a blade tucked down his boot – modelling knives were à la mode – or the sharpened steel comb in the back pocket.

The two young lovers, by now, were biting each others' necks and Sonny made a point of carefully looking away and out of the window at the passing dereliction.

The train seemed to be travelling through an area of 'inner city decay', as the politicians liked to term it. Dear God, he thought, I've had this town up to here, and unwisely popped another pill in his mouth, his last but one. A blast of headbanger music filled the carriage from the couple's transistor and he stood up as the next station came sliding into view. West Hampstead. Why not? He got out and down on to the platform before young Lochinvar back there turned his attention to slashing the seats.

Is there life before death? The phrase floated into his mind and, standing there swaying just a little, he half expected to see the words written across the disappearing tail end of the last carriage, possibly in spray-can script.

Is there life before death? It was a line of graffiti that had originated back home, so he was given to understand. Something Belfast had given to the world, along with Georgie Best, Hurricane Higgins, James Galway – that city of short, dark, driven men.

The city's crest was *Pro Tanto Quid Retribuamus* – For So Much What Can We Give In Return? He remembered seeing that on the side of the old, open-topped, scarlet tram cars. He must have been very young at the time, or perhaps it was only a dream. Never one of his favourite places, Belfast, the people a little too self-consciously abrasive for his liking. But, then, wasn't he a country boy, born and bred, hay seed in his trouser flaps, as the joke would have it? He and Hazel, they were both hicks. It seemed yet another reason why they were made for each other.

His eyes grew misty for a moment as he stood there on that platform. He was feeling a long way from home – wherever that might be.

> *Got those depreciation blues,*
> *Just as low as I can go,*
> *Ain't nothing left for me, 'cept . . . 'cept . .!*

He was unable to finish the line, he would just have to work on it.

For some reason he felt very tired all of a sudden. At the top of the steps leading up to street level his legs seemed to rebel and he hung there for a moment panting, a ringing in his ears, cheek pressed to the defaced paintwork. A few inches away from his face someone had pencilled on the wood of the staircase an inarticulate and poorly-spelled cry of rage against the order of things: *Jimmy Kelly Blaire Peach Fuck Knows How Many More The Fucking Pigs That's Who And For What More Than Two Hundred People Die Are Killed In Police Custardy Every Year The Bastards*. Ancient causes, yesterday's headlines . . .

At some point he looked at his watch, but it had stopped at a little after ten past two. The light in the sky told him it was much later than that, but then why should he care, he wasn't going anywhere.

Still, his feet must have taken him uphill in the direction

86

of Frognal, for out of the debris of the rest of that day and night he managed to salvage the impression that, at some stage, he must have gatecrashed a large, open air party. There were trestle tables on the grass with bottles and food, and the smoke of several barbecues rose straight and true into the branches of mature trees overhanging the edges of a huge communal garden, of the sort usually barred to the likes of him. Fathers and sons played baseball in all the correct, expensive gear, while the women of the family cheered them on. Many of the accents seemed to him to be American and he felt as if he had strayed into a *Saturday Evening Post* cover. But, try as he would to share in all that warm neighbourliness, each time he got close to the wine – there seemed enough for the whole of Hampstead – someone, invariably a woman, would eye him with suspicion.

He found a tree and sat down with his back against its trunk. The scent of crushed grass, earth and bark was very strong; there was also the more pervasive one of hot charcoal and grilling meat. Also, he noted, a distinct whiff of pot was in the air. He may or may not have dozed off but he did have a jolt of consciousness at some stage, for he remembered getting to his feet feeling dazed and, yes, angered, at the extreme lack of hospitality. If this were really a scene from small-town America, he reasoned, his needs would not be ignored in such a fashion. Another dream gone west. These people, despite all their outward show, were just like everybody else in this city, mean of spirit, preoccupied with their own narrow concerns. And, staggering to his feet, he set off looking for the gate, for he had forgotten just how and where he had got in.

The shades of evening were lengthening steadily by now across the grass and the baseball game had long since ended, but there seemed to be much more noise. People were getting seriously drunk, it struck him; every man held a beer can in his fist, and knots of women were shrieking together in an oddly disturbing way. Most of them wore Bermuda shorts, he noted for the first time.

His desperation was by now getting out of hand, for it

seemed to him he had been around the entire area twice without sight or sign of an entrance or an exit. He also desperately needed to have a piss, but nothing would induce him to go behind a tree, despite his contempt for these people and their boorish behaviour. Going back on his tracks he could have sworn he heard one woman say to another, 'I wouldn't let him put it into me, Becky, honey, not if it meant a brand new convertible every single time.'

At that point there came a further vicious turn to the screw, for he began to notice that people, when they were leaving, all without exception headed for their own open patio doors; this great big rectangle of trampled turf being bounded on all its sides by the backs of exceptionally tall houses. He began to stumble along faster and faster looking for a break, an opening to the outside world, but there was none. When a group of children, hard-eyed little Babe Ruths, took to following him, his anxiety knew no bounds. He turned at right angles across the open space and, without thought for the consequences, headed for the first open french windows he came across.

His intention was to push directly through the house to the front door, hoping for a straight line of escape, but beyond the threshold he found himself in a large, expensively furnished room with a television flickering without sound at the further end. A man in a wheelchair was sitting in front of it with his back turned to the garden. At first it seemed he might be asleep but then Sonny heard him mutter, '*Jim'll Fix It*, indeed. Not for me, he fucking well won't.' He was wrestling impotently with a remote control device in his lap, which accounted for the lack of sound.

Sonny stood there, frozen to the spot, watching the white-haired celebrity – he had been decorated by the Queen – performing silently on a fat settee, that great symbol of British cosiness, mouthing platitudes to his millions of viewers sitting at home on *their* settees, watching him on his. There was something terribly deranged about that aspect of the business, it suddenly struck Sonny. The TV personality was also wearing a shiny purple tracksuit zipped open to his navel with enough chains and pendants in the opening to fill a jeweller's window.

'Oh, shit! Shit!' the man in the wheelchair called out – the accent was a well-bred one – and he hurled the gadget he had been abusing into a far corner. It struck a small table with a noise of finality about it. Some crazy reflex made Sonny want to pick the thing up instead of heading for the distant door, but by this time the cripple in the chair had sensed his presence and wheeled about. For a moment they regarded one another like hunter and prey, but there was no sign of fear in the weaker one's eyes.

Instead he said, 'Are you a burglar? You don't look like one,' in calm, almost businesslike tones. It was the first time anyone had addressed Sonny directly that day and it was that fact that stunned him more than the words and their delivery. His mouth felt dry from unuse; the pills also played their part.

'Are you a Yank?' the man went on. 'My daughter-in-law's a Yank. No, I can tell you're not one, despite the get-up.'

Sonny looked at the door, The white-haired man in the chair, as if anticipating his intention, moved the wheels forward slightly. The backs of his hands were mottled brown like gulls' eggs. He wore a woollen dressing-gown, paisley pyjamas buttoned to the neck and slippers with pink new soles.

'She's got one or two nice little treasures upstairs, if you're interested. Second door on the right, master bedroom. This crap's all repro.' He waved a claw dismissively. 'Every stick of mine's in store, the bitch. Well, what are you waiting for? Or, do you want the telly? Take it, take it, be my guest.'

On the screen the credits were rolling over the celebrity's face in cruel close-up. He looked a great deal older than the man in the wheelchair.

'On drugs? Is that it? Her bathroom cabinet's crammed with the stuff. Third door on the right. Help yourself. I said, *help yourself*!'

The voice had risen to a shout and Sonny glanced involuntarily at the open french windows. That made the cripple laugh, an unpleasant sound. You old, upper-class bastard, Sonny thought, don't you know I could crush you like a cockroach where you sit and not a thing would you be able to do about it? But he didn't say those words. His head ached and, instead, he looked down at his hands; they were clenched and shaking.

He made his first move since he had stepped into the room, in the direction of the doorway, but the man in the chair forestalled him with a rapid roll forward across the expensive rugs until he was blocking the exit.

'Oh, dear,' he murmured. 'Oh dear, we *do* seem to have reached something of a dead end.'

The final words seemed to carry more than their fair share of weight as if he was suggesting something much more terminal than mere housebreaking. But, no, thought Sonny, no, I've no intention of playing your sick games, old man in a wheelchair. He moved closer to the man – once he must have been a handsome, sneering devil – and, taking the rubber handles of the chair, began to push it away from the door. The old bloke was much lighter than he had imagined and although there was some resistance, all of it silent, the business was managed easily enough, for the locked wheels rested on one of the rugs, a particularly fine pink and blue Persian.

And so Sonny left him there, shrivelled and bloodless, hunched in his dressing-gown. The wheelchair remained slewed sideways at a humiliating angle and Sonny, as he moved quickly down the hall to the outside air, derived some little consolation from that parting image. But it had been touch and go.

In the street he found a skip and relieved himself against its metal side. All around it was the deadest time of day, as if a bomb had evacuated an entire neighbourhood. He knew, however, what was really going on behind all those tall and elegant house fronts. The only sound to be heard was the gentle hiss he continued to make; the only sign of life, the spreading flood at his feet. When he had finished he felt very tired again. At the end of the street one last look revealed nothing of his existence but that wet streak on the skip, but even that was drying out rapidly. He'd never felt so invisible, or so displaced.

Dear Hazel, he began in his head, but no words were forthcoming, no words could explain or do justice to what was happening to him. He couldn't explain it to himself, didn't even try.

At some stage – the pubs were open – he had a drink, perhaps more than one. He didn't know where he was. There was a lot of noise and a solid crush at the bar, as if it wasn't far off closing-time, but it really wasn't. Joining the throng he found that he couldn't get another drink. It wasn't that he was refused one, it was more a matter of being ignored each time he put forward his glass, like a beggar at someone else's banquet. The people at the bar exuded colossal energy and certainty, it appeared to him. Through a haze he watched the way they ordered and paid as though that simple act was really one of the most stunning expertise and subtlety.

He took to the streets again. It was dark by this time and he literally had no idea where he was. His limbs felt weighted; it was like propelling heavy, lifeless baulks before him and then letting them swing back under their own momentum. He craved desperately some corner where he could curl up unseen; best of all, a still-warm bit of grass to lay himself out on. But the park whistles had long since sounded their melancholy summons. He wanted to howl at the moon, if there was one up there and, of course, if he had, no one would have paid a blind bit of notice. Why should they? The city, on a Saturday night, after all, was full of maddened wolf-men. And there was little or no consolation in knowing something like that, either – the likelihood of a duet being a very remote one. Much more probable would be the spectacle of two fellow creatures tearing into one another tooth and claw over nothing more basic than the dregs in some bottle or the doubtful territory of a bench for the night. But he *did* have a bed to return to, at least he did have that, and all his energies were now directed to the thought of that lumpy old mattress and its familiar red and tan madras cover.

His weariness in mind and body was now so extreme that when eventually, out of the dark, he came upon a brightly lit main road throbbing with traffic – every car seemed to have its radio on full blast and the windows down – he clung to a lamp standard too terrified to move. It must have been the Edgware Road, even though he didn't recognise that at the time, but, instinctively he knew he had to get across. It was as if he were in one of those legendary situations where the hero has to keep on surmounting innumerable obstacles, until finally that river looms up, the one with all the horrors lurking beneath its surface. This was his river of no return, he told himself, except that the final and deadliest of enemies was out there in the open in the shape of all those racing Ford Capris full of potential young killers, a black load, then a white load. He just knew that if he lost his magic power of protection they would imprint him on warm asphalt without compunction, racing gleefully on to whatever disco it was they were heading for.

But then, as he hung there, his arm about the sticky metal of the lamp post, a sudden ringing clamour seemed to sound from inside the very stalk itself and, across the width of the roadway, he saw a little green man light up. It was his guardian angel come to save him, he hadn't been deserted after all, and what power, too, for as though by a miracle all the cars halted at his bidding. The throb of their radios was like one great angry heartbeat and their horsepower revved terrifyingly, but still they had to toe his line. Then his little green friend went out as suddenly as he had appeared and the cars roared away, burning rubber.

Four times the lights changed before he was able to muster enough courage to make the journey. At a staggering run he charged for the distant green cut-out. It seemed to have withdrawn its support for him, flickering with impatience now as if the natty little legs itched to stride quickly away leaving him to his fate. He barely managed to fling himself on to the far pavement before the red warning figure flashed on amidst a roar of car horns, obscenities and coarse laughter. Someone flung an empty beer can at him from an open car window. It was the one they all favoured at the moment, he noted, a Tennent's Super Brew. But in spite of everything he had made it to his own side of that hellish highway, and safety.

Elgin Avenue, that broad and elegant boulevard with the sodium lights dappling the leaves of its massive plane trees, beckoned. Straight as an arrow it led him home, the hero who had overcome everything set before him. And, as in all the best fairy tales, he was in his own bed before midnight. He felt as if he had been travelling for days on end and across every acre and inch of this city.

Last thing he vowed as he took off all his clothes was to sleep around the clock. He didn't dare hope to wake up a new man, that was too much to ask for, and indeed when he did surface late the following afternoon he wasn't feeling all that hot. But, about an hour or two later, en route to the bathroom, something made him idly pick up the latest and newest buff-coloured envelope from the pile of unopened mail in the hall. He might easily have thrown it back down again, too listless to even open it, just like he had done in the past, but some impulse, weird and wonderful, changed his mind for him and when he found and read the offer contained within, that old, almost-forgotten dream of being renewed, of turning a corner and finding new direction, suddenly took on the colour and shape of reality.

—TWO—

'Blanket on the Ground'

'Well? Are you or aren't you going to tell me about it now? The whole thing's been very sudden, you know.'

But all he did was smile that little boy smile of his and lightly take hold of her wrists across the table. 'You've got beautiful hands. Did anyone ever tell you that?' said he, turning them over and examining them attentively. 'One thing I always notice is a woman's hands. Eyes, hands, then dress sense.'

She laughed in spite of herself. 'You've left out a few other items, don't you think?'

He blushed. Oh, he was a rare one and no mistake, but so far she approved of what she'd seen and heard, otherwise why should she be sitting here? Good question, Hazel Kinney...

To be exact, they were in a Little Chef on the A30, about five miles east of Salisbury, the remains of their first meal on the road together in front of them. Her order had been the Scampi Platter and he had asked for the Chicken, 28 and 26 on the menu respectively. Number 38, the Waist Preserver, two burgers served with chives and cottage cheese – she could have dispensed with the bun – seemed a much more sensible choice for her now, for she had decided to travel in trousers.

She had two other pairs with her, more jeans in style and cut but not quite so flattering to the figure. They were stowed with the rest of her stuff in her suitcase, a faithful old Samsonite that had travelled with her everywhere, battered but still unbroken. Just like its owner. From her wilder, younger years she remembered a notorious weekend-case that had caused more than its fair share of comment. The famous Mandy, on one occasion, had even refused to allow it anywhere near her own matching set, not even in the same car boot, as if it might be contagious, for God's sake.

The invitation had been to Cliveden, she recalled, to that famous house on the river and if she and Mandy hadn't had their disagreement over a plaid holdall lacking a zip she might have gone along and, who knows, have become part of history just like the other two. At the time, of course, none of that meant anything to her. It was only much later when the newspapers took up the story and she followed the daily revelations of infamy in high places that it came to her just how innocent then she must have been. To think that once she had shared a flat with two *celebrities*, she, Hazel Kinney, that fresh-faced girl just off the boat, as green as the grass of her native land.

But all of that seemed half a lifetime away. She had to laugh, she really did, thinking about it now. A far cry, certainly, from house parties thrown by the Astors, sitting having Special Of The Day in a Little Chef somewhere in the wilds of Wiltshire. She took a handful of paper napkins from the dispenser on the table, excused herself, and went in search of the toilet.

When she returned three, four, minutes later, war paint restored, there was no sign of her travelling companion or his boyish grin. The table had been cleared and re-set. A moment of panic ensued, for she really knew little or nothing about this man, then she saw something scrawled on one of the fresh napkins. 'I'm on the run, the highway is my home.' Country-freak, she thought, weaving her way through the tables, past the other diners to the outer air and, sure enough, the car park was alive to the sound of Merle Haggard.

Sonny was sitting on the step of the parked camper, a can of beer in his hand, cassette player pumping out its tale of woe, another young life squandered on the road to nowhere.

'Look here, *cowboy*!' She had to call out above the music. 'Exactly where *are* we heading? You still haven't told me, you know.'

He grinned up at her, squinting into the sun. 'Why, west, lady. West. Where else? Don't all roads lead there? For people like us?' The glinting beer can in his hand was lazily aimed towards the stretch of road running away off and upward to the left.

She just looked at him, feeling silly standing there in her maroon silk blouse and french gabardine pleated slacks.

He got to his feet, draining the last inch of foam from his can with satisfaction, before pitching it to land squarely in a metal basket fastened to the fence. *Clunk*. You could tell it was one of those days when everything had to go well for him. He just couldn't miss.

'Come on,' he said.

'Come on *where*?'

In reply he laid a palm on her waist, reaching for her right hand with his left, and began waltzing her about the car park, and she allowed it to happen, just as she'd allowed everything else to take her over since the moment he had phoned and told her to be packed and ready. There was a crazy illogicality to it, she knew; regret, surely, must follow, but it had come at just the right moment, as far as she was concerned. She was so tired, *tired*, of always being the one in control, in charge all the time.

It seemed to her it had been that way ever since she had moved out of the flat in Clanricarde Gardens she'd shared with the two 'celebrities' all those years ago to be with Eric, Ilford Eric, Eric of the Doleful Countenance, as she soon learned to call him. That hadn't lasted, of course; thank God he'd gone back to his old mother and his pigeons, but he always had a way of bringing you down, had Eric Willis, even from a distance, and just recently she had begun to believe across the divide of time, as well.

'*We're on the run, The highway is our home,*' he was singing and she thought to herself, why not, why the hell not? She could feel the outline of his belt buckle pressing against her belly as he held her close. Something else, as well. It was nice to be appreciated and so instantly, too, for she was at an age when she had come to be realistic about such things.

The sun was beating down strongly on the thin silk across her shoulders as they revolved on a patch of tarmac no bigger than a night-club dance floor. Two children stared big-eyed at the strange manifestation from a car across the way, while their father slept in the front seat, his face covered with a newspaper. But who was to say what constituted the stranger sight? A keen sense of the ridiculous was something she always felt came naturally to her and this man with his arms about her and his eyes closed seemed to her to share some of that. It was one of the reasons she'd come along with him. To have a few laughs at the same things, wasn't that what she was so badly in need of?

As for the other thing, 'the other', as they liked to refer to it over here, well, it had been such a long time. She couldn't even remember how long and with whom. She wondered now what it would be like with this one, for it did seem inevitable somehow, didn't it? And, as if to remind her of her compliance in the matter, she felt her own response to that other more direct, more outward expression pressed against her groin, a tiny fluttering, deep inside, allied with the merest wetness in her pants. It seemed to her more than a trifle shocking for such a thing to be happening to her at her age out in the open, and in a public car park, too, so she quickly waltzed Sonny out of viewing range of the two children in the rear of their family Escort and back to the camper.

The music had by now moved decidedly up-tempo, 'Okie from Muskogee'. She told him, 'Time to make a move. That's *if* we're making a move.'

'Oh, we are, we are,' he said. 'Highway is our home,' and opened the far door for her with more of his old-fashioned gallantry.

As she put her foot on the step to climb in, she thought, I just hope it doesn't have to be in the camper, that's all. But once inside, alongside him on the imitation fur covering of the seats, and with that scaled down domesticity at their backs – stove, sink, small refrigerator, a table that folded away, even a wardrobe and two narrow, facing bunks – she felt she already knew the outcome. When she looked in the mirror at what lay behind them in that twelve by six interior, it was like viewing something down the wrong end of a telescope. A smell of hot leatherette from the upholstery filled the space all about them and she felt suddenly drowsy.

Did people stretch out on those things back there on the move, she wondered, then shied away from the thought. Better not push events too soon in that direction...

The rolling landscape began to slide past once more, scents of nature quickly taking the place of the man-made varieties inside the camper. Fat crops ripened steadily in the fields which, to her eyes, seemed more like prairies after the damp scraps of green she remembered from back home. Their great, swelling contours flowed on unimaginable distances, broken only by occasional snub-nosed silos that glittered like giant ammunition, or the solitary copse smoking bluishly in haze. Not a house, not a man, nothing moved out in those well tilled wastes. She understood it was all the fault of the new breed of Euro-farmer and his get-rich-quick agricultural methods, but something told her this had always been a lifeless zone, stones its only harvest. In a moment of fancy she saw herself out there journeying in another time and dimension, just like one of those heroines Thomas Hardy enjoyed tormenting in his books, and coming upon only a solitary stone-breaker in a whole day's wandering. It was a recognisable career, then. All you needed was a hammer and your own pile of rocks and you could be in business.

Then he said, 'Not a lot of life about here, is there?' turning down the music, as if he'd picked up on her wavelength. 'Stonehenge isn't far off. Ever been?'

She told him, no, she'd only ever travelled up the M1 before and once to Brighton.

'I've been to Wales and, yes, north to Blackpool.'

It was the closest they'd come to a conversation since he'd arrived at her place early that morning. All the way the tapes had rolled non-stop, three double sides so far. It was, she supposed, a way of not only passing time on the road, but also of measuring it, as well.

Don Gibson's Greatest Hits took them from the flat in Fulham to the first Service on the M3, then Kitty Wells, 'Queen of Country', carried them to Winchester and now, as they breasted a hill and sighted the spire of Salisbury Cathedral piercing the distant heat haze, Merle Haggard's final track played itself out. She hoped it would be left like that, for she suddenly wanted the countryside and the rushing smells from its fields to reassert themselves and not be coloured by the music of Nashville, Tennessee.

But, behind his dark glasses, Sonny was concentrating on his driving as they hit the city's ring road system. Signposts were rushing at them in clusters as the camper rode the tilting curves.

'Speak now or forever hold your peace!' he called out above the roar of cars and vans. One flashed past with BATHSHEBA BATHROOMS on its side. 'Stonehenge, is it? It's on our way.'

'Oh, we do have a *way*, then, do we?'

He grinned and took the next exit to the right. She noticed how easy it was to spot oncoming signs from their high vantage point. They were almost on a level with lorry drivers. Now she realised why they never seemed to hesitate at junctions, but flowed on effortlessly towards their imposs-ibly distant destinations. She was beginning to feel fluid herself, yes, distinctly so, riding high and relaxed above the lesser breeds in their little cars a good two feet below. A green holidaying Morris rushed by impatiently, the plastic covering the suitcase on its roof-rack was coming undone. It made a noise like rapid pistol fire but the people inside had their sights set on the invisible sea. There was a granny in the back; on the ledge behind her threadbare grey scalp were two tapestry-covered cushions, a dog's rubber bone and a box of Kleenex. It was like looking down on the private disorder of someone else's sitting-room.

The sticker on the Morris's rear window read I LOVE BENBECULA. She'd seen one on a Range Rover earlier that said I LOVE ANATOLIAN SHEPHERD DOGS. All those bright little red hearts. So much love, so much love for small and specialised things. The English were into that in a very big way, weren't they? She was beginning to feel more of an outsider out here than ever before, out here in their heart-land.

The feeling had first struck her in that Motorway Services they had stopped in at Fleet, the first one outside London, with its low-pitched roof nestling among planted birch and conifer. It was a style of architecture she had begun to notice a lot in these parts, chocolate-coloured wood, tile and brick hugging the terrain, never drawing attention to itself, traditional, yet not excessively so, and the people munching inside seemed to favour the same approach with the clothes they wore as if it were important to merge with the landscape – but one where it was always autumn. It was something unexpected, because on the M1 that time heading north, every Granada and Trust House Forte station she'd been in appeared to be overflowing with brightly garbed Asians going to or returning from some family reunion.

Ever since the music had been shut off her brain seemed to be ticking over faster and faster. She wondered if he were affected in much the same way. She looked at him with affection, in his washed-out denim, pearl-buttoned shirt and old jeans. He had those little metal points on the collar, and a leather thong in place of a tie. He did take it all a bit seriously, this western thing, but why not, she thought. Dreams were important to people like themselves; she had her own tucked away, never fear. They were two of a kind, two strangers in a strange land where the people wore camouflage, yet advertised their secret passions on the back windows of their cars.

She thought of Lester, poor little old Lester with his touched-up moustache and those lovely manners of his, a true gentlemen from the tips of his polished brogues to this bald spot. The three of them together, one for all, all for one – now, wouldn't that have been something, the three of them on this trip? Then she choked suddenly and Sonny looked as though he might take his hand off the wheel to slap her on the back and the choking turned to laughter and he said, 'Hey,' and began laughing too.

Oh, she thought, *have you got a surprise coming, brother. Have I got a surprise for you?*

He said, 'Hey,' a second time, dropping his hand to her thigh, and she let it lie there as they drove across a flat and featureless landscape.

The roads all seemed to meet at right angles and there

were signs saying DANGER, TANKS CROSSING, and the earth was torn up and left like that as if one of the iron monsters had travelled that way moments earlier. It wasn't the place to linger, that was the feeling she got; they were only here on sufferance. Keep moving, was the message, and when they got to Stonehenge and saw what it looked like, dropped there like a child's building-set on scorched downland, Hazel wanted to do just that.

Sonny slowed the camper and they approached it warily, this most famous of sights. He drove past, then turned at the next cross-roads, drove back again. Signs directed them to a car park where metal and glass glittered in the sun. At least a dozen tourist buses were berthed side by side like fat submarines. Most were empty but one was full of blue-rinsed heads resting on covered headrests. People were eating and drinking out of the boots of cars and Hazel thought she saw the green Morris with the granny in the back.

A queue of tourists waited patiently in the sun to go into the dark of the tunnel that led under the road and up to the site – mainly Japanese and Americans holding cameras. The English seemed content to stay close to their cars; many were reading newspapers or drinking from Thermos flasks, while the metal legs of their folding chairs sank slowly in the hot asphalt. At night when the place was moonlit and empty, all those little round holes, a puzzle for any extra-terrestrial landing here. For they did say, didn't they, this was where they would touch down, if anywhere?

She felt depressed suddenly. Perhaps there was nothing to stop for in this country, nothing to see; after all, the picture postcards did it so much better. Already she visu-alised the two of them driving, driving, non-stop, two people in transit, like in all those songs he'd been playing. What had she let herself in for when she'd said yes over the phone, just like that?

She thought of her flat; more importantly, her job. They owed her holiday time at the restaurant, certainly, but to take it like that with just three days' notice... Aldo was a sweet man, the sweetest, and he worshipped her, but even he sounded a bit sick, especially now at the height of the tourist season. And what about Natalie, would she really go to her father's place as she'd promised? They were bound to row about her clothes, her hair, her records, her school reports, her friends – the list was an endless one. *Oh, God*, she thought, *God, God*, with a stab of pain, how easily a train of disaster behind her in London might have been started off by this single act of impulse. It was the act of someone half her age, she told herself, the kind of thing she'd thrown herself into regularly and without thought in those early days in Notting Hill. But now was different.

Behind her in the mirror she could make out the camper's strange interior, as unreal as anything out of one of those space ships she'd been imagining earlier. God only knows what lurked in those cupboards and drawers. She'd been aware of all sorts of bangings and collisions as they drove that hinted strongly at domesticity. But did she really want to get into that sort of thing? Again, she thought of her age as some kind of protective shield keeping her free from involvement. She might be travelling in a mobile Wendy House, but that didn't mean she had to play the part of mother...

He said, 'They never let you get up close. Close enough to touch. I bet those old stones give off one hell of a charge.'

She looked at him. 'You never told me you were one of those hippy weirdos.'

'Weird, maybe, but not a hippy. No, sir.'

'Once upon a time?'

'Guilty. But I served my sentence.'

The tourists were coming up out of the tunnel by now on the far side of the road, cameras trained and ready. Three men in uniform directed them gently but firmly into the one-way system that wound about the standing stones. It was like watching sheep being painlessly coerced by three expert collies. With their dark outfits and peaked caps, you couldn't mistake them for anything but a separate and superior breed. She wondered if they had been recruited locally – all had red faces – but perhaps that was due to exposure. It was strange thinking of the three of them locking up, if that were the expression, and cycling home

105

in the dusk of the evening to their wives on the local council estate, because such things did exist out here in this rural paradise, even if they were carefully tucked away out of sight of passing tourists and travellers such as themselves.

She remembered her own village and the row of labourers' cottages she'd been born into. The man next door, also, had a job that entailed wearing a uniform – he was a security guard at the local sewage plant and, of course, behind his back, the joke was the one about who would ever want to steal any of that? Yet he was envied, respected, even admired, because of the uniform and his job which entailed never having to dirty his hands. Another joke. His daughter got a scholarship and became a cookery teacher, and another son Charlie was now a Baptist minister out in Africa.

She and Charlie had done 'it' in McMurray's hay shed before he found his Redeemer, as he put it, down at the Gospel tent. He kept trying to 'save' her after that, after he had already helped her along the path towards transgression. *Oh, Charlie, Charlie, you were my first and, looking back on it now, not the worst by any means.* All she could come up with, in terms of physical recall, was the little ginger ruff he had about his equipment. For his part, he seemed astounded by her own well-formed bush, taking it as some sort of sign that she was exceptionally experienced for her age. *How wrong could you get, poor Charlie, how deluded you were.* Perhaps he still thought of her like that, out there on his remote mission, surrounded by his little black virgins in their cotton frocks, hats and white gloves . . .

'Let's go.'

It seemed a defeat, somehow.

'We can always come back when it's not so busy,' she said, for he seemed to be taking it personally.

'Never is.'

'At night?' He looked at her. 'We could always break in.'

'Hey,' he said, his eyes lighting up. 'Hey.'

'You like the idea?'

'Love it, man,' he said, making a U-turn in a break in the traffic. 'Absolutely *love* it.'

The camper began to pick up speed, travelling as though more than normally weighted along the perfectly straight road. There seemed to be nothing to stop them as far as the eye could see. Sonny held one hand on the wheel while he beat his thigh with the other. 'Wowee,' he kept saying, 'Wowee.' Nobody was being serious, yet the idea of it touched something deep. The system could always be defeated, That's what they both seemed to be agreeing upon, even if all you had at your disposal was the power of imagination.

He said, 'This could well be an old Roman road,' squinting into the glare. 'They built them as the crow flies, you know.' Then, laughing again, 'Sonny and Hazel were here. And the date. What's the date?'

'Fifteenth,' she told him.

'A mark of some kind. On the stones. Why not? Otherwise the bastards just wipe you off the face of the map. The earth, for that matter. Know what I mean?'

She nodded, putting on her sun-glasses. It was too early to get into such serious matters. She wanted to have a few of those laughs first, the ones she'd promised herself. But she knew, in her heart of hearts, the man wasn't born who didn't have a worried side to his nature lurking somewhere. It was only a matter of time before it had to come out, that deep, unhappy desire to be 'understood', and have his uniqueness appreciated.

'Salisbury Plain,' he said. 'One very weird place.' The music seemed to have been forgotten. 'Have a look at the map and you'll see what I mean. Weird, I mean, *really* weird.'

Beyond the glass the brown and yellow landscape curved and dipped in long, slow sweeps to the horizon. Nothing held or halted the eye in its travels in any direction.

Sonny tapped the map spread out in front of him on the padded window ledge. 'See? Just there. Look.' His finger marked their imperceptibly moving position on a patch of white as though the map-maker had suffered a momentary but serious lapse of concentration. 'No roads, no rivers, no villages, nothing. You are now crossing the Gobi Desert of the South.'

And she saw what he meant, how everything stopped, or perhaps just petered out at the edge of that bone-white expanse.

'It used to be all like this, once upon a time. The whole damn country.'

He grinned suddenly. 'Fasten your seatbelts, Mr Spock, we are now entering a different time warp.' And he began to laugh wildly, driving faster and looking, in his dark aviator glasses, like some character out of one of those creepy movies. The strap of webbing separating her breasts, then crossing her stomach, felt as though it were being tightened by someone or something behind her, as the needle in the middle dial on the dashboard crept almost full circle. But then its little arrow-head began to falter and fall back and his hand reached down across between the seats.

'Don't mind me. I'm just a little bit high, that's all. Nothing chemical, you understand, no way, just animal spirits. Must be the company,' and he took off his glasses to prove his sincerity. Or, perhaps, let her see that his eyes were indeed clear of intoxicants.

He began telling her about the forgotten village buried over to the right somewhere. Imber, it was called, and in 1943 the people who lived there had all been expelled from their homes – up to a hundred of them – by the Army, who wanted the place for its own purposes. They never got back. It had to be like one of those western ghost towns, he said, where the doors flap mournfully in the desert wind and those great balls of stuff blow up and down the main street. Every once in a while, Easter usually, the people are allowed to return for a day to see their old houses.

'I don't know if I'd want to do that. If it was me,' she said.

'I do see what you mean,' he replied. 'Still, I wouldn't mind just taking one little look.'

'Another place we're going to have to break into after dark?'

He laughed. 'Stonehenge, maybe, but no way do I fool

108

around with the British Army. Not with this accent.'

'Does any of that ever bother you?' she asked. 'That business back home, I mean?' They were bowling along quite normally now, well within the speed limit.

'Sometimes. Sometimes, when I remember who I am. Where I'm from.'

'Who you are?'

He went on, ignoring the question, concentrating on what he was saying. 'Only when they're giving our lot a bad time of it on the telly, that sort of thing, and the other lot are having it all their own way, as usual. The micks, the paddies. But then again, we're all paddies and micks to them, aren't we? Hey,' he said, laughing, 'are we having a serious discussion here?'

She said, 'Why? It doesn't bother you, does it?'

They looked at one another.

He said, 'With most people, yes, but with you, not, for some reason, Hazel,' and she could tell that he meant it.

Despite what she'd decided earlier about keeping things on a light and easy footing between them there was something reassuring about all of this. Comradely, even. Perhaps it wasn't necessary to have to go through that brittle, bantering stage, after all. Perhaps they had already progressed to the next plateau where they could move together easily and without strain towards friendship, for she felt that she was too fragile at this stage in her life for anything more strenuous than that. He, for his part, might just have his sights set on something a little more physical. She felt she could cope with that, if and when it happened to arise. In the meantime it was nice, the feeling that seemed to have developed between them here in the front of this doll's house on wheels, with the countryside slipping past at just the right speed.

'What do you think of her, then?' He slapped the inside of the door the way someone might pat a dog. 'Great old bus, eh?'

'Is it yours?' she asked, then added, 'You never said.' She hoped she wasn't going to turn into one of those nagging types.

109

'Sure, she's mine. Why don't you climb back in and have a poke around.'

She looked at him and, yes, he had to laugh at the oddness of the expression, if not the idea of her peering into cupboards as, underneath her feet, the road raced backwards at fifty miles an hour.

'How long have you had it?' she persisted, like some polite visitor.

He laughed a second time. 'What day is it today?'

'Monday,' she answered.

'Saw it on Friday, bought it on Saturday. Two whole days. Just like that.'

'So you bought the lot outright?'

'Just like that.'

She was thinking of the curtains which came together, but not quite, behind their heads. They were of the ugliest pattern, texture and shape imaginable, spotted with random daisy heads, mustard and brown, and through their opening she felt sure she could detect more of the same gathered at the windows and on the facing bunk beds. The strip of carpeting in between was cheap green foamback, also stippled with some unrecognisable floral motif. So he doesn't suffer from colour blindness after all, she consoled herself, though why that should concern her was a total mystery.

'This old guy and his missus were all around the world in it. See the stickers on the back window?' She hadn't. 'Not that it's driven into the ground, no way, not this couple. Two dedicated motor-caravaners. But, as he said, time to pull into that last lay-by, put away the road maps for good. I told them she'd be in good hands. Didn't I, baby?' Leaning forward, he planted a kiss on the dashboard. She couldn't help noticing that its padded top was scarred by innumerable cigarette burns.

They passed a collection of deserted army huts, broken windows, weeds, a flagpole without a flag. The sun, full and strong now, outlined it cruelly. There was a lop-sided, rusty children's climbing frame set down in a patch of nettles and she thought of growing up here in this treeless desert. Other peoples' childhoods always seemed strange to her. She found it difficult to describe her own in that huddle of cottages about the mill with farmland all around, the permanent smell of manure from the fields drifting through open doors and windows. It was a sort of half-and-half world, neither one thing nor the other; a rural slum would be the most accurate description, but how could you explain a setting like that to anyone?

About a year ago she'd read somewhere that the young Christine Keeler herself had been brought up in two converted railway carriages in Berkshire, something she had never mentioned to anyone. But then, why should she? She still carried a lot of excess baggage of that sort about with her, herself, from those days. Everything was to do with class then, *everything*, and she'd spent a lot of time trying to be someone and something she was not. Her accent, she knew, still bore the traces. Sonny had mentioned something along those lines when they'd first met, but then, his own delivery had gone through a few changes as well. Poor Sonny, wanting so dreadfully to be American, while in her case her sights had been set much closer to home. Remember that Hermès scarf she'd bought, not to mention the little boxy Chanel number – she'd starved herself for a month to get into that, not to mention paying for the damn thing – and, of course, the pale blue tights and patent pumps with the gold chains across the heels.

She sighed, remembering all that wasted effort, wasted years, for in her heart of hearts she would always be plain, ordinary Hazel Kinney from a little place in the sticks no one had ever heard of. Except for this man at her side. They had that in common. As well as being brought up with only an outside toilet. Together with Christine. That made three of them. And, of course, Lester. Soon the camper would be full.

Which reminded her – when and where would the time be right to tell him about Lester or, to be more accurate, what remained of Lester? She gave a sideways glance at Sonny's profile – those sideburns, wouldn't she just love to get at those with a good sharp razor – but he was still going

111

on about how he had found the camper. The story was getting more lyrical by the second. He made it sound like love at first sight leading to a marriage made in heaven.

There was a park he said, Willesden way, where he remembered people put them up for sale, lines of them waiting under the trees with cardboard notices in the windows. A lot of Australian VWs which had made the overland trip were congregated there, but he had ignored those – the bleached blond surfers who'd driven them there to catch the British summer had really burned the shit out of them. It was the cheapest way to travel, he stated, that's if the engine didn't blow up on you in Nepal or Turkey or crossing the Alps. No, what he had in mind was something looked after, one or, at the most, two careful owners, and when he saw Romany – that was the couple's pet name for their old bus (it was a professionally converted Ford, by the way, none of your DIY crap in somebody's back yard, no way) – he didn't need to look any further. Again he fondled the dashboard, as if beneath all that abused leather-cloth there resided the true, beating heart of the vehicle.

He looked at her. 'Funny how your life can change overnight, just like that. Know what I mean? One day down, the next day up. When I met you first, I was down, Hazel, down. Don't mind having to admit it.'

She said, 'Certainly, you could have fooled me, Sonny,' although, to be truthful, it was a definite strain of melancholy she thought she detected about him that had attracted her in the first place, a vulnerability that hadn't descended as yet to the self-pitying stage. That she couldn't stand in any man. At any price.

Still, she wasn't sure whether this new Sonny with his confident know-how suited her or not. He was going on now about the host of extras that the camper carried, which should have bumped the price up, but hadn't. She lost him in a welter of fittings and fitments the names and function of which meant nothing to her. Why should they? His eyes were gleaming like a child's enumerating the delights of a new and, as yet, unexplored toy, and she reckoned he'd got most of this from the sales pitch of the so-called old couple.

112

He was a retired Plessey engineer, so he said, and she had spent most of her working life in BBC Personnel. The more Hazel heard about the two the more she felt convinced Sonny had been well and truly taken for a ride. Not that that was her concern. However, she couldn't help enquiring, as a footnote, but an important one, to all of this, 'Come into money, then, did we?'

Before replying, he looked at her. 'Yeah, you could put it like that.'

She didn't press the point, she knew she would get everything out of him in her own good time, that's if she continued to care enough to do so.

'How about heading for Devizes?' he said a few moments later as they crested a hill and saw below them a major road, fat, black and glistening, crossing their own pale grey route. A sign which looked important – they all seemed to, for some reason – was glazed by the sun and unreadable.

'Devizes?'

'Sure. Devizes. I've always liked the sound of it. Don't know why. Devizes.' He did seem to enjoy saying it.

'Fine by me,' she answered lazily, eyes closed.

The sun, the southern sun, for she saw it as particular, for some reason, to these rich shires, as though only they were tilted directly into its rays, fell fully on her face through the open window. She had forgotten how good it could be, the sheer, undiluted force of it. The last holiday she had taken abroad – the last holiday – had been to Rimini in 1974. Remembering that hot, soft lash across her belly and upper thighs – there had been a Paolo, she recalled, to oil her back – she thought of her present pale state beneath all these clothes she was wearing. So many straps and layers. She felt armoured. Against what, for God's sake?

At the gilded signpost they turned hard right and began to pick up a distinct traffic flow, milk tankers for the most part, their gleaming metal skins looked as though distended by their liquid loads. Many had wet windscreens and the road soon turned even darker under the effects of recent rain from a storm that must have died as rapidly as it had struck.

Hazel wondered if Sonny might be thinking along the same lines as she was, how they might be able to move ahead of the weather, if they put their minds to it, heading constantly for that next distant patch of blue. It might just be possible. London seemed suddenly very remote, with its yellow polluted dome.

They were now running into a very different terrain from the one they'd been used to, heavily wooded, lush, and with high banks on either side of a wet and twisting road. Glimpses of picturesque cottages, gate lodges and comfortable country seats could be spotted through foliage. On a mossy gate post Hazel read Kitwe Cattery And Boarding Kennels before the lettering blurred and raced past. A little further on she noticed another roadside sign – this one looked makeshift – that said, Breaking Vivas. She puzzled over this, unable to make a connection. Breaking Vivas . . ?

Devizes turned out to be predictable, everyone's idea of a slumbering English market town, prettified and dead at this mid-point in the afternoon. They cruised slowly up its empty, wide main street past baking cars parked at angles on either side, and the Pay and Display machines. The camper's windscreen was to get a border of tickets over the days that followed.

Their exhaust throbbed low and throatily in the stillness. Without exception, the shops appeared closed. Hazel had always assumed it was only back home that everything shut down because of lunch. Did they doze in shuttered rooms, she wondered, stripped of their white coats – it certainly was sultry enough – or were they up to something much less innocent, for another belief of hers had been that such places were hotbeds of wife-swapping and the like. Hot beds.

Sonny caught her smiling to herself. '*High Noon*, eh?' he said.

But on their second slow pass up the main street, they saw a cluster of hippies sprawled out on the stone steps about the market cross. They looked exhausted as though they had dropped down in the nearest patch of shade. As

Sonny went by he raised his hand in a peace salute and a couple of them reciprocated in listless fashion. There were children in the group, ragged little replicas down to the tears in their jeans and the grime on their tiny faces. They stared back, too, with that selfsame look of adult indifference. Hazel had seen them before, on the television. The police, after all, had been harrying their slow column across three counties since summer began but, as close-up as this, they seemed more a spent force than that marauding threat to society the media carried of them.

Sonny said, 'I want to get a paper,' pulling up at a newsagent's which was closed, but there was a rack outside, its contents yellowing in the hot sun. For a moment Hazel felt convinced he was going to help himself – the sort of trick the people hereabouts would just expect of those hippies they had seen earlier – but he grinned at her as if reading her thoughts and made great play of dropping coins from a height into a tin she hadn't noticed before.

Hazel wondered why suddenly he should be so concerned about what was going on in the outside world, then she saw he had another paper, a thick, local one. Folding this carefully he slipped it into the door pocket for later – for himself – while he handed her that morning's *Sun*. 'Only this shit left, I'm afraid,' he said, climbing back in. He grinned. 'Looks as if we're right in the thick of things, folks – where it's all happening.' The headlines had ignored Beirut, Iran or even their own little Ulster and had homed in, instead, on a deserted airfield about ten miles away. Devizes was mentioned as being the nearest town. It seemed the Hippie Convoy had gone to ground on a World War Two stretch of crumbling runway and, reversing that old settler and Indian scenario, had formed their vehicles in a circle to keep out the forces of law and order.

The headline in the *Sun* read UNHAPPY HUNTING GROUNDS, above a picture of a disconsolate group of drop-outs not even bothering to turn away from the camera. They had the look of refugees anywhere at any time in history; indeed, they might easily have passed as made-up extras in any one of a dozen old John Wayne movies.

The other story on page one concerned a boxer who had lost his seven-year fight to live after being in a coma following a knockout in the ring. His family had played recordings of the roar of boxing crowds and even installed a ringside bell beside his bed in an attempt to coax him back to consciousness, but to no avail . . .

'I think we've done Devizes, don't you?'

He put on a Buddy Bare tape – 'Five Hundred Miles From Home' – and made a slow and careful U-turn just outside the famous Tudor coaching inn in the square. As they passed the hippies again one of the women – girls – wearing a tattered damask robe and a man's trilby raised a nicotined middle finger.

'Doesn't care for our music,' laughed Sonny. 'Thinks we're a couple of red-necks.'

He seemed proud of the association, however, breaking into an exaggerated western whine. Hazel let it pass; she was feeling sleepy by now and thinking with envy of those shop people deep in their untroubled siestas.

'Still with me?' The track had run out, he was grinning across at her. 'Why don't you take a nap?' Jerking a thumb over his shoulder towards the rear of the camper.

'I'm fine,' she said. 'Fine. Really.' She must have nodded off.

'Really?' He was laughing at her. 'Just pull a bunk down from the wall. The choice is yours.'

Then she said something foolish. 'What about you?' And felt herself blushing. *This is ridiculous.*

He stared straight ahead at the road beyond the bonnet; it seemed a mere snout, compared with that on a car. Pulling down the sun visor, he said, 'I'll take it nice and easy. Promise. Nothing to disturb your slumbers. Rely on me.'

She took him at his word – why not? – climbing back between the furry seats into the half-light of the interior, even though she knew he was sneaking a look at her rear end as she did so – she'd already put him down as a bum man – but again, why not?

116

The curtains at the rear of the driving area came across easily at her pull and suddenly she was standing as if in her own darkened, private room. There was only a slight vibration, barely noticeable. The effect, she had to admit, was surprisingly restful and when she undid the upholstered back rest the whole contraption slid smoothly forward from the wall to form a decent-sized single bed. From her suitcase she took out her old kaftan with its Moroccan figures and then quickly stripped to her pants as silently and effortlessly as she could. For a moment she balanced there enjoying the experience; the air felt good against her naked skin. A cooling draught from the open driving window found its way under the curtains. She couldn't help feeling just a touch coquettish as well, and a giggle escaped, in spite of her caution, at what a silly cow she could still turn out to be at her age. On the far side of the curtain Sonny laughed too, and dived for the kaftan lying on the bed.

My God, she thought, as she got its soft folds over her head, *here I am just like some silly young honeymooner.*

But now he'd slid in a fresh cassette, a woman singer she couldn't recognise, but something, someone, appropriately lulling. The bed felt harder than she was used to and she thought it better to leave an examination of the sheets until later but, stretching there on top of the covers, her sensation was one of ease, as if she had made a safe landfall. The engine throbbed, the camper rocked imperceptibly, she felt herself drift on its passage. She remembered wondering, but only half-heartedly, whether the back door was secure enough. That old tale about the naked couple being shot out into traffic came to mind. Had that really happened, or had she seen it in a film? The last thing she recalled thinking to herself was that perhaps this *was* a film she was in, after all, she and Sonny, one of those road movies about two people in transit heading for adventures together. And why not? She slept.

Once, when Hazel was younger, she'd stayed overnight with relatives, her first time away from home on her own, and her two city cousins, bewitching and worldly, despite

117

their passion for getting themselves 'saved' at every opportunity, had taken her to the big Billy Graham Crusade at a football stadium in their home town of Belfast. She must have been thirteen or fourteen; it was the very early fifties. Afterwards, the three of them sat up late in her room, a tiny, wallpapered box right at the top of the house, and they were full of what they'd seen and heard, the heat and noise, the two-thousand-strong choir, the fainting supplicants; above all, the amplified voice of the great evangelist himself, the vibrations of which had caused them to wet themselves in a way they'd never experienced before.

When they finally left her to creep back down to their own room, clutching their precious souvenir hymn sheets, she'd lain there unable to sleep for excitement. The night noises of the city seemed unfathomable, coalescing into one deep, low and far-off growl. The strange reflected orange light coming through the skylight in the sloping ceiling was also one she couldn't place. There seemed to be fire at its source, but again distant and diffused. Eventually she must have slept because when she woke up suddenly she was in pitch darkness in a silent tomb. The city centre lights had died down, of course, as had all traffic with them in the early hours, but she was not to know any of that, no one had prepared her. Since then she'd found herself in other strange rooms, on occasions with a sleeping man by her side, but never had there come such a sense of desolation as on that night in the house of her cousins. That was why, when she shot suddenly into wakefulness now, she found herself shouting out, '*Beth!*' then '*Hetty!*' into a similar void.

She lay trembling, as she had done thirty years earlier. A faint smell she couldn't place, vaguely rank, came from nearby. Her fingers touched rough, unexplained fabric. She felt as though she were in a confined space, there was no way of telling its dimensions, but panic convinced her it had to be coffin-like. Then she put her hand out and it dropped until it came to rest against something cold by her side like lino. It *was* linoleum. Now, she knew where she was, because that hideous pattern of brown and interlocking buff squares came back to her.

118

'Sonny,' she murmured in a quiet and questioning tone. Then, 'Get me out of here! *Sonny!*' with no attempt at restraint. She hated to hear such dependence in her voice.

Carefully, like those of a blind person, her arms stretched out above, below, beyond. She got both bare feet on to the chill flooring. *Why was it all so damnably dark?* Then her hand caught in a fold of curtain and an extra dimension suddenly was added to her prison, like a door opening.

Air, cool and refreshing, blew on her cheek and, even more unaccountably, came the smell of new-mown hay. She could see scattered particles of light piercing that backdrop now. They were stars and they hung up out there on the far side of the windscreen. She got the near door open and dropped down into a stubbled field, yelping as her naked soles received its imprint.

'Sonny!' she called into the deep country night. 'You bastard, Sonny, where are you?'

A dog barked far, far away in the distance, but it had nothing to do with her; nothing in this place had, wherever it was. She had been dropped down on to some other planet. Then she heard his laugh, the sound coming from behind and above, and when she turned and looked up in its direction she could make out a shape on the camper's roof.

'I want to go back, Sonny. You hear me? I want to go home.' It was her age speaking, but an element of truth was there, as well.

'This may well be *it*. Right here.' His voice sounded slow and much deeper than she recalled. 'Come on up and see for yourself. I have the feeling that we may just have hit dead-centre. Bull'seye. Forget Stonehenge.' And he slapped the roof with his open palm. The taut metal boomed softly.

She could see him more clearly now, his outline sharpening against the blue-black. She'd forgotten how thickly strewn stars could be. Directly above Sonny's head hung the Plough – it was, wasn't it? – something remembered from her girlhood on those long nights walking home from summer dances. Then, for the first time, she realised he was wearing his dark glasses and her heart sank again.

'Where are we, Sonny? I want to know.'

Once more he struck the roof at his side, but with more of an inviting, patting action this time. 'If you join me, I'll show you. Come on,' and he leaned over, reaching down to her.

Just as she'd suspected, his breath smelled distinctly herbal. 'How did we get here? Why did you let me sleep so long?'

'Hadn't the heart. You looked so lovely. Honestly. Cross my heart and hope to –' and he just managed to save himself from falling at her feet.

'Okay, okay!' she called out hurriedly. 'I'll come up, I'll come up,' for it did seem the only course open.

'Right,' he sighed, stretching out. 'Right. Believe me, you will not regret it.'

To her surprise she found it easier than it looked to make the ascent: the door sill, a leg across on to the bonnet, then up on the shallow dome of the cab and finally to the roof itself. He was still on his back and as she found a place for herself on the slightly moist metal he was murmuring something to the night sky. 'What is the stars? What is the stars?' it sounded like. Raising himself on one elbow, he grinned at her. 'Here, have a little puff.'

She looked at the pale roll-up in his hand. 'Never knew you indulged, Sonny.'

'Just the odd puff. Now and then. Go on, take a drag and we'll star-gaze together.'

She took the joint from him, and sucked cautiously on its soft, damp paper. Even she didn't have to be told the mixture was a rich one, although it had been some considerable time since she'd last tried anything of the sort.

'I thought you guys didn't go in for this. Against your religion, or something.'

He laughed long and richly. 'We cowboys *always* roll our own.' Then, 'Just look up there, would you? How about that for a blanket of blue? Talk to me, Hazel. Talk to me.'

But she wasn't in the mood, she was feeling relaxed now, the cool night air seeking out and finding the secret places of her body under the loose cotton. What had happened to her below, moments earlier, had been merely a nightmare, nothing more. She was no longer that young girl alone in the dark believing in devils. She knew better now and could make sense of things and therefore recover quickly. It happened to be one of the advantages of getting older.

She had the sensation she was drifting in line with her thoughts, suspended between earth and sky. She wanted to savour the moment, only he wouldn't allow her to, for he had started on a talking jag by now. As he babbled she felt her new-found, precious privacy being invaded.

'Air, air, air,' he theorised. 'A cushion of air. Just air, in those four tyres down there. That's all that's keeping us off the ground. You do realise that, don't you? Air, pure and simple. I mean you can't see it, taste it, smell it, even. It really blows the mind. Hazel, baby, we're on our very own Li-Lo in the sky up here. How about just drifting off, you and me? What do you say, just the two of us? Magic carpet time, folks. It's magic carpet time.' And he got to his feet, swaying unsteadily as if the power of the words had indeed taken over.

He's going to fall off and break his stupid neck, she thought to herself, but there was no real compulsion on her part to do a thing about it.

'Shazam! Shazam!' He was calling out now to the heavens, arms outstretched. 'Come on, Hazel, don't just lie there. If we really put our minds to it, we really can get this baby off the ground. Come on, concentrate, concentrate. Mind over matter, mind over matter.'

He began to hum very loudly through his nose, and there was no mistaking the tones of that old sixties love-in drone. Another throw-back, she thought to herself; why do they all have to turn out like this?

'You know something, Sonny,' she said. 'Pardon my French, but you're really so full of shit.'

He stopped his noise. 'Oh, don't say that, Hazel, please don't say that.' There was hurt in his voice and on his face, but whether it was genuine or not she couldn't tell. 'Whatever you do or say, please don't say that.'

He dropped down beside her on the roof. 'Hey, how's about that for a great song title?' And he began to sing the line, 'Whatever you do or say, please, *please*, don't ever say that.'

Hazel felt his arm slide about her waist and with it came a softening in her mood. It was hard not to, the sort of fool he was. After Ilford Eric, frivolity in any man seemed welcome. Eric from Ilford, with his bad back. He would cry out sometimes in the middle of the night with a yell that curdled her blood, the first few times she'd heard it. 'It's givin' me gyp again, Haze.' The English had a certain whining way of expressing themselves at times that made her hate the whole race. 'Rub me back for me, Haze, go on, there's a love. The 'arder the better, that's it, 'arder, 'arder, lower, lower...' She never knew which was worse, the sudden terrifying yell out of the darkness, or the moans of ecstasy that arose from her ministrations – if such a word as ecstasy could ever be applied in Eric's case.

His parents had something he called a 'shally' – it turned out to be a hut on the foreshore at Southend, where the sea never arrived but just lay sullen and unmoving out there beyond the mud flats. It was where they spent their honeymoon. Eric seemed very proud of the family 'shally' and never tired of telling her how privileged she was to have the run of such a retreat.

'Best air in Britain, gel. Ozone,' he would say, breathing in the faint, wind-borne whiff of rotting eggs. Anyone could see the coastline here was one huge tip for the East End of London. The seagulls wheeled and scavenged tirelessly. 'Bet you've nothin' like that in Ireland, eh?'

That was another thing. He could never understand there were two separate, well defined parts to her Ireland and that she came from the more prosperous British part. In fact she owned a blue, royal crested passport while he had none. He talked about 'the bleedin' paddies' when they watched the News together. 'I'd deport the lot of 'em, I would.' She found out later his mother's maiden name was O'Driscoll. Oh, he was a regular prince all right, was Ilford Eric, and she was two months gone on her honeymoon in that 'shally' at Southend. They only did it face to face the one time. On every other occasion Eric was face down having his back pounded for him. ''Arder, 'arder, lower, lower . . .'

'Hazel, talk to me.' Sonny's voice had gone deep again, but with concern now, it seemed. 'You're thinking about the girls, aren't you?'

She looked at him. *Girls?*

'Hetty and Beth,' he went on. 'The one I met in the school uniform, in the mini-cab. That was Beth – or was it Hetty?'

She laughed. *Oh, the fool, the fool.* But his foolishness was of the sweetest kind. Putting her arms about him she kissed him on the mouth and, after a moment of perplexity – she could feel his indecision – he responded passionately. They went over backwards in that mysterious slow motion that always seems to happen at such times, then she felt his hands take advantage of the deep slits in the sides of her kaftan. He was a good kisser, and his touch somehow kept pace with his slow, deep approach. She began to open up for him, but then in the middle of it all she felt she was going to laugh again. Sensing it as well, he began to stiffen. She did laugh then, and, in an attempt to ease the impact, gasped, 'Who's a kinky cowboy, then? Up *here*? On the *roof*?' But the truth of it was that suddenly the whole idea had struck her as just too hilarious for words.

'Look,' she said. 'Later?'

And to show her good faith she took hold of him through the thin fabric of his jeans. She heard his gasp of pleasure – or was it pain? – and thought to herself, for your sake, Hazel, I do hope you're not going to turn out to be one of those cock-teasers you've always despised so much. Really, it doesn't suit someone of your age, you know that, don't you?

She said, 'I'm really starving. Aren't you? Whereabouts are we?'

'Look down there,' he said. 'See those lights?'

Following his outstretched arm – by touch, because of the darkness – she could make out a cluster of illumination, sparse on the outskirts but dense at its centre.

'That's Dorchester,' he announced.

'We've come as far as *that*?' she marvelled.

'It's not so far. I got here about six. Let's hit Dorchester,' and he began climbing down.

She was trying to take in what he'd just said as he disappeared over the rim of the roof. All that time on his own while she slept? Not up here, surely, getting slowly stoned. Surely not. She put it out of her head. *One step at a time, Hazel.* That wise old voice inside her head was making sense again.

The headlights, coming on, froze the field in their glare. Hazel saw a distant hedge in strong detail and, strewn over the mown surface, in between, fresh rolls of hay scattered like great wayward bundles of Weetabix. Sonny steered the camper in a slow wide arc over the bumpy sward as though familiar with all its features. She had an image of him hunkered up there on the roof slowly memorising each height and hollow as the light faded.

'Is it all right to park here?' she asked, although the place did strike her as exceptionally remote. There hadn't been a single other light, as far as she could make out, closer than those in the ancient town far below.

'We don't have to.'

'Oh, no,' she said quickly, for no immediately obvious reason she could think of, 'I'd like to come back here. Will you be able to find it again?'

He laughed. 'This cat's like a cat in the dark, take it from me.' And his eyes, it seemed to her, did gleam in the lights from the dashboard. There was one tiny green and a jewelled red that made the enclosed cab very mysterious and, yes, glamorous, as they rocked over the final few yards of rutted earth leading to the gate. Then they were back on smooth, firm footing again and speeding. The night air streamed through the open window and the road and hedges rushed at them bleached white by the glare of the headlamps.

Sliding down in her seat, Hazel felt like a girl again. The scents and sounds – earlier there had been farm dogs barking across long distances – and the sight of trees and hedgerows in detailed, coral-like close-up as they sped past moved her back once more in time. There had been a man she and her friend Bernadette had trusted to take them home from dances. Arthur Mullholland was his name and he drove an old khaki van with a single seat in the front. They sat beside him on bare metal clinging to each other as they hurtled along the quiet back roads with dimmed lights because Arthur's van had neither tax nor insurance. For years he'd managed to keep going using the label from a Guinness bottle in place of a tax disc. He loved to hear them sing on those night drives. 'Truly Fair' was a great favourite. A Guy Mitchell number. That was all he expected in return, that they sing for him on the way home, one song following another, a medley of all the tunes the band had played that evening. He was a big, bulky man, bald under his cap, in a chocolate-brown suit with old-fashioned wide lapels, who sat at the door and never had been known to get up for a single dance.

She remembered his smell, a mixture of motor oil, sweat and the peppermints he sucked to sweeten his breath – laughably enough. It wasn't unpleasant. In a curious way, it was reassuring, a man's smell, a *real* man's smell. They all seemed to carry it about with them, then, every man she knew, her father included. It came from work, hard, honest work. She realised that much later when she came to London. Now, as she rode through the English country night she almost fancied that the man beside her had something of that same old scent about him. She felt sentimental and, as on those other night drives, she sang for him too. 'Mansion On The Hill' was what she chose. He liked the slow, doleful ballads. She did, as well.

After she'd finished, he said, 'Hey,' in that soft, wondering way of his, squeezing her bare thigh, for she was still wearing her kaftan. The little ruby and its emerald twin embedded in the dash gleamed brightly and beyond the glass the pale road raced at them. Nothing out there beyond this little cave of theirs could touch or interfere with their individual dreams.

'You and me,' he said. 'I've been looking at the local papers. There's plenty of places where we could do a double.

Sonny and Hazel. We're good enough. What do you think? Give it a try?'

'Why not?'

But she wasn't taking it in, she was thinking once more of Arthur Mullholland and his great mechanic's hands on the wheel of his old van as it rattled over roads that only he seemed to know about. She felt sad, then; she didn't have to be told that they would all have disappeared by now, those country back roads, grown over or obliterated by the straight and the new.

'Sonny,' she said. She was about to tell him about old Arthur – it was conceivable they might have run across one another – but she changed her mind and mentioned instead that curious placename she'd spotted just outside Devizes. He pondered for a moment, then he began to laugh.

'What's so funny?' she asked. He really was enjoying it, she could tell. 'Oh, come on, you can share it with me.'

'Breaking Vivas,' he said. 'Don't you get it? Vivas? Vauxhall Vivas? Breaking for parts?'

'Oh, Christ,' she said, 'and I thought it was one of those villages like Little Wallop or Much Wittering or something.'

'Or Breaking Wind?'

She forgave him that, and the camper continued rushing on between high summer hedgerows. The road was falling rapidly now and the first signs of life and lights began to appear as they approached Hardy's old town. Tess in a camper, she thought? A sign raced by – Dorchester Twinned With Bayeux – then they were climbing steeply out of river meadows shrouded in sheets of white mist, because it was a town after all, set on a hill.

They started at the top and cruised to the bottom of the long, straight main street. Not a soul seemed to be abroad and at the foot where there was a river and a low bridge Sonny turned and slowly drove back up again. She made him park outside a shop that sold sporting goods, its windows full of rods and guns and olive green waders, and when they began to walk it seemed as though the few lighted restaurants, too, catered for the sort of people who went in for such traditional pursuits. Couples munched silently at

126

small, candle-lit tables. The men had short, new haircuts and wore dark suits despite the heat, while their blonde companions had taken out that little black number with its single strand of good pearls for its weekly airing. They might have been back in the fifties and, peering in at them there gravely going through the courses, melon boat or prawn cocktail, sirloin or sole, sherry trifle, cheese board followed by Rombout coffee, Hazel felt as though there must have been a dark hole in her life and she was still that girl with her friend watching the Rotary Club swells at their Saturday night function back home in the old Antrim Arms Hotel.

Taking Sonny by the hand – on the journey he had lit up yet another joint and was feeling no pain – she steered him into the town's single Chinese. It was cavernous, dim and empty except for a single young waiter who greeted them in a strong Dorset accent. She didn't even try to imagine what his existence must be like in such a place. There were certain things just too bizarre to bear thinking about. They ordered by numbers, although that accent was too amazing to miss; they had a couple of Tuborg Golds and she insisted on paying. Sonny put up little resistance – he was still aloft and floating, with a grin on his face, the fumes of his roll-up curling upwards like joss to the tasselled lanterns overhead.

She went to the Ladies and, with the door firmly bolted, she washed armpits and between her legs as thoroughly as she could manage at the tiny hand basin because she had no idea what the arrangements back in the camper might be – if any. The mirror framed the face of someone already verging on the unfamiliar. Without its London mask, the one she perfected each morning to armour herself against the day ahead, the skin looked softer, more vulnerable. The old, deep freckles were reasserting themselves; she realised she had caught the sun. Was it fancy or was there more than a hint of that country girl's complexion that men – women, too – remarked upon when she first came to London all those years ago?

She examined her reflected breasts as though they

127

belonged to someone else. Still nothing to complain of in that department. And nobody ever had, except perhaps Doleful Eric who never could stand the full frontal view anyway, preferring to bury his face in a pillow. She thought of those other men who had appreciated what she had on offer. At least no one could ever say she hadn't been able to hold her own in an era that had idolised the charms of Russell, Mansfield, Monroe or Sophia Loren. Tess of the Fuller Figure. She felt like adding something along such lines to the graffiti bordering the mirror. It would be appropriate, something of a tribute, too, to the little bald novelist with the sad eyes and waxed moustache. They'd passed a statue of him at the head of the town, brooding there on a stone about his stories, his little carved dog at his feet. He looked exactly like Lester, she realised, might have been a twin, in fact, displaced by time and space. Lester had appreciated her breasts. Lester, poor dear Lester. He was still travelling with them – in more senses than one.

Right, she said, drawing the kaftan back over her head, *you may not know it yet, but tonight's your big night, Sonny boy*. Her nipples studded the heavy, embroidered cotton and there was a definite flush spreading from the base of her neck. She felt shameless, but didn't care. *You poor sap*, she mouthed to the glass, *you don't know what's about to hit you*.

He was still sitting there, smiling to himself, under the red and gold oriental lampshade when she went back to the table and, at her approach, he rose like a lamb and followed her out into the night.

Somewhere a clock struck the hour and the silence over the old town was deep and unassailable. It all seemed a very long way indeed from the city and the life they both were used to. A weathered stone they passed, close to the great man's statue, reminded them of the exact distance – Hyde Park Corner 123 miles – if they were interested.

Driving back, it was her turn now to put a hand on *his* thigh and she could tell he appreciated it, even though she was careful – well, sly – not to let her touch wander any higher than intended. Of course she had an interest in what he kept in his pants: however did that old myth get started

128

that women weren't? Anyway, she felt confident there would be little or no cause for disappointment. He was still smoking seriously, which had been known to affect performance, but when she took the joint away from him to put to her own lips he didn't seem to notice or care a lot.

'Whatever you do or say, please, *please*, don't ever say that,' he sang softly and repeatedly to himself in melancholy fashion as the camper roared along the honeysuckle-scented lanes. He still couldn't seem to get much further than the title. It was something she found endearing – all those sudden inspirations that never got beyond their initial impetus. Just as long as it's only confined to his song-writing, she thought. Again she felt surprised at all this new-found shamelessness. But then, as Awful Eric was so keen to point out to her when they fought, 'You're a whore, Hazel, that's what you are, deep down you're only a whore.' He pronounced it in the English way, almost as it was spelt . . .

Their camper seemed to find its own way back unerringly, and when the ignition was cut and the lights died it seemed to her that they might well have found the exact spot in the hay field they'd started out from. She liked the idea of that, the wheels resting in their old indentations.

They sat there in the darkness of the cab for a moment, listening to the engine cooling mixed with the mournful sounds of the night, her hand still resting on his washed denim – it had achieved the texture of fine cotton – and presently her fingers slid upwards without scruple until they found the bulge, naturally lying to the left. Naturally. She cupped him carefully, gently, in her own way. He wasn't to know it, of course, but she had always felt strangely unsure when it came to handling those mysterious, hanging objects. Of course, she knew how they – *it* – worked, their – *its* function for giving pleasure, but always there came a moment just before that pleasure began when she realised with surprise just how unnatural and out of place, like some afterthought, the whole apparatus seemed to her.

Often she got the impression that men, too, felt something of the same surprise. When her coaxing fingers finally assured her that all those smoked joints hadn't done any apparent damage or diminution – he was certainly a lot bigger than Eric – she whispered, 'Ever do requests, big boy? How about, "Blanket On The Ground"?'

He gave a sort of moan, half pain, half pleasure, as she relaxed her hold on him. Reaching back through the curtains into the body of the camper, she came upon a rug and a pillow and, taking him by the hand, led him out on to the grass.

He stood swaying there, murmuring, 'Hey?' over and over again to himself as she spread the rug. 'Here,' she said. 'Let me,' because it seemed as though he might be incapable of the next and crucial step.

The boots and jeans were the hardest part, but she managed it and, laughing at her own handiwork – he stood there facing her, white and naked like a great, bemused child, still wearing his cowboy hat – she pulled her own single garment over her head in one rapid movement and he said, 'Hey! Hey! Hey!' his voice rising in appreciation. *You're not so bad yourself, big boy*, she thought, as they made contact on the dewy grass. Then, sinking together on to the spread rug, she prepared to do what came naturally, according to all those songs they'd been singing together about being good to your man.

For his part, he put up no resistance, even entering into the spirit with a few contributions of his own. For a first time, she had no real complaints – her tastes had never been complicated. In fact she was reminded a lot of that other first time with Charlie Orr, but perhaps it was something to do with the smell and feel of mown hay all about and under her bare skin.

When Sonny did come he yelled aloud once with a cry that started off a dog barking on some distant holding. She felt him drain into her and after a moment she faked her own climax expertly, it seemed to her, and why not, she told herself, for there would always be time for the real thing at a later date.

They lay there together, sweat cooling, and over Sonny's naked shoulder she could make out the stars, and although there was no question of the earth having moved for her in

130

that way, it did seem, for one magical moment, that the firmament overhead was indeed shifting slightly, that great inverted dome of velvet sky over Dorset pricked by a myriad tiny gems.

Presently, Sonny rolled on to his back with a groan of contentment. 'I think I'm in love,' he announced, addressing those same stars. She stroked his drying flank.

'I have a surprise for you.'

'You mean there's *more*?' Again he moaned loudly, stretching out arms and legs until he lay spreadeagled on the plaid wool.

'Sonny,' she began very slowly, because it had taken her a long time to get to this point. 'Sonny, do you think – do you really *believe* – we could find a nice place, the *proper* place – to scatter Lester's ashes?'

For a moment she thought he hadn't taken it in properly, his relaxation certainly seemed extreme to her, but then she heard him murmur softly but distinctly, 'If you're saying what I think you're saying, then I *know* I'm in love,' and rolling over on top of her again he began to nuzzle enthusiastically until she cried out, 'No, no, listen to me, you've got to hear me out, I'm being serious! It's not a joke! I mean it, I mean it, Sonny!'

He sighed, shifting his bulk once more.

'Look,' she said, gently seeking out and taking his soft thing between her fingers. She meant it to be a gesture of her sincerity, but perhaps it wasn't such a clever move after all, for, sensing a definite hardening under her touch, she began to talk faster. She talked of the time they'd met, reminding him of what he had told her about how upset he'd been at the crematorium, then seeing all those identical containers like so many anonymous shoe boxes stacked one on top of another.

'But, oh, Sonny,' she cried out, 'they're much smaller than that, the containers, I mean. The ones they give you to take away with you. They're about the size of a –' She didn't know what she was about to say but stopped herself in time because, whatever the comparison, it was bound to sound unseemly.

He said, 'I loved that wee man. I really did, you know,' and there was genuine emotion in his voice.

'I know you did, Sonny. We both did. That's why I claimed him. Nobody else wanted him, you see. And that's why we owe him this.'

It did seem strange to her to be saying such things whilst holding a man's fully erect thing in her hand. Surely it must be a distraction – to both of them – so she hurried on even more swiftly to the important bit about what she had in her suitcase wrapped in tissue paper.

Sonny heard her out in silence and beyond and she began to feel that perhaps, after all, she might have committed some unforgivable breach of behaviour. 'Did I do the wrong thing, then, Sonny?'

'Wrong thing?' he said, clasping the hand that encircled his manhood. Again she had that unreal sensation as she felt the pressure of blood now, from without, as well as within her grasp. 'Wrong thing? Hazel, I can't think of anything I'd like better than to know he's travelling with us, even in a – ' Like herself, he couldn't bring himself to be specific.

'And we *will* look for a place?'

'Of course we will, but sure, haven't we all the time in the world? One thing at a time. Waste not, want not,' and she suffered his attentions gladly for the second time that night under the great dome of Hardy's sky, so much so that the unexpected occurred. This time it was her cry – unfeigned – that set off the distant farm dog.

Afterwards, Sonny murmured, with a hint of self-congratulation in his voice, 'Twice in one night. Not bad, eh?' and she thought to herself, *Oh, Sonny, you fool, you fool, what are we going to do with you?*

Presently they wrapped the blanket around one another as the earth began to cool, for both felt they wanted to prolong the moment for as long as possible out here under the stars on this their first night together. Clinging to each other they were also sensing, too, something of that great silence and vastness in their surroundings that they'd almost forgotten from their childhood in another and distant countryside.

'Hazel,' he murmured.

'Sonny,' she replied and that was all either of them needed to say, it seemed.

'Washed My Face in the Morning Dew'

Sonny dreamed.

He was gliding up an escalator on the Underground and none of the people travelling down to the trains would acknowledge his existence or look him in the eye. For some reason this fact of life was deeply disturbing to him. Every time he thought he detected a glance, no matter how fleeting, the man, woman, child even, would switch his or her gaze hurriedly back to the adverts each with its tiny thumbed-on sticker offering sex – Hayley, Ripe English Blonde, defacing a Dunhill lighter; Zeeta, Tamil Tigress, on a hamburger dripping ketchup. . .

Now he was drifting up Oxford Street against the current, buffeted by parties of French schoolchildren, tourists, innocents up from Essex for the day – the ones who always stand hand-in-hand abreast on the escalators. All had that same preoccupied, glazed look and his despair plumbed even deeper levels. *Oh, boy, are you in trouble*, he tried to tell them, yet still they kept on ignoring him as if he were the unbalanced one, when all the signs of derangement were everywhere obvious.

Outside John Lewis's the blind man with the violin was scraping away, thin white stick hanging from a strap about his neck. The noise he made had always been completely tuneless and grating as far as he was concerned, but suddenly now for the first time it sounded recognisable. A distinctly sinister Arabic whine floated high above the pushing heads. '*Listen! Listen!*' he wanted to call out to them but, of course, they continued to press on regardless of their danger. In a shop window two lazy girls in felt slippers dismembered a model with terrifying callousness and, as he passed, an abandoned motor-cycle in the gutter began talking to itself in strange metallic tones punctuated by bursts of static.

Coming towards him, floating high like a religious banner, he saw the crazed vegan's message linking protein with lust, but *his* warning was mere distraction. He knew nothing, nothing, save his own foolishness, a case of fiddling while Rome went up in flames. As he went past, bespectacled and mild like a clerk, in cap and soiled mac, the temptation to wrest the placard from him with its lists of forbidden foods almost brought his mission to a close. But if he were to be stopped now, who was there to take his place?

He caught a glimpse of himself in a mirror as he went past the Scotch Wool House. The face staring back at him seemed to belong to someone he had once met somewhere, but where? The throb of taped music was getting louder by the second, each shop vying with its neighbour to stun the ear-drums. Great black youths were installed in every doorway wearing the most expensive clothes in stock. They kept calling out to one another in coded language above the funk rock. Couldn't the poor whites stumbling past in all their varying degrees of ugliness not see how terrible a threat they posed to them and their pitiful existence?

He skirted the men selling counterfeit gold chains from suitcases on the pavement, he brushed past the leaflet holders, he ignored the young sharpers peddling life insurance – 'Excuse me, sir, but do you live in London, sir? *Sir?*' The shops and their wares seemed to be getting more and more nightmarish. One was full of china phalluses and realistic looking dog turds and, high in the window, a display of net-stockinged legs jerked in a macabre version of the can-can. People stood staring open-mouthed at the bodyless limbs.

And then he came upon something so terrible in its implications, so unspeakable, that all who saw it must surely cry out in agreement with him that enough was enough. A man in a soiled yellow singlet was selling toy dogs from a baize-covered tray. They were battery operated, these puppies, and as he watched they twitched and fell as if they were new-born and sightless. Presently, one of them managed somehow to crawl to the raised edge of the tray and to drop off, where it spun at the end of its chain, limbs jerking frantically as though in its death throes.

He stood there unable to take his eyes off this horror, yet no one else seemed aware, or concerned at the sight. The shoppers and the sightseers continued to surge past without a second look, the salesman had his hands deep in his swollen money pouch while his look-out hopped about nearby scanning the crowds for police. He felt a choking sensation as though something was biting into his own throat and he tried to cry out to let people know what was happening. The puppy's mechanism was slowing dangerously. *My God – they were choking together!* There, in the middle of one of Europe's biggest and busiest shopping thoroughfares, he was being throttled, and no one was paying the slightest heed. *Help me*, he cried, *help me!*

He awoke in mid cry to find himself on top of a mess of bedding on one of the bunks in the camper, naked except for his bootlace tie which had tightened about his neck. The Brahma bull's head clasp was up under his left ear like a hangman's knot. It felt cold and potentially lethal and, loosening its hold, he shook there for a moment until the bad dream had receded. On the opposite bunk was a mound of bedclothes which gave no indication of life.

His memory of the night before was badly clouded. He remembered the love-making in the open, but beyond that point everything was blank. His head ached and his mouth tasted foul. Then he heard a soft sigh coming from the nest of blankets; a tremor followed and a foot, bare and recognisably alive and well, sought a way to the air. He felt like dropping to his knees to pay homage to that miraculously formed extremity. Wonder of wonders, the nails were even painted a delicate shell-like pink. It all came back to him then – *he was in love!* His protectiveness to that sweet-smelling, slumbering heap knew no bounds and oh, so very carefully, he rose and pulled his jeans on up and over his bare limbs, the denim stiff and slightly damp to the touch.

Outside a dawn mist hung over everything. Spiders' webs were outlined in silver and the distant hedges had receded completely from view. He dropped from the step into wet grass and the shock of it cleared his senses. Then, like Don Gibson in that good old country song of his, he washed his own face in the morning dew. His red spotted bandanna was still in his back pocket and he used it to dry himself. It smelled strongly of pot, he noted, which in turn brought back that dream of his. No doubt about it, that had to be your classic, chemical nightmare, all right, a textbook case if ever there was one.

His bare feet left trails in the short new growth and he wondered if there might be mushrooms. He remembered how they came from nowhere in the dark, disappearing just as mysteriously once the sun got up. His own father would bring home capfuls from his early morning tramps in the fields whenever his sleeplessness got the better of him. His own rest pattern, he'd noticed, had began to alter lately, too. It was funny – or sad – how people seemed to end up like one or other of their parents. In the mirror he saw another little piece of his old man every day. He almost had his jaw, most of his brow and his fleshy ears. At such times, whenever the progression appeared to be accelerating, he felt depressed; not that his old man had been ugly – far from it – but because he felt trapped inside the life he led, which in some odd way had a lot to do with the way he looked. Old family photographs only seemed to strengthen the theory. Not one of those dark-suited Dunbars was ever going to break out of the way things were for them, had been for generations, for it was there in their faces, that doomed family likeness.

When his young brother Drew got married, his mother had sent him such a memento on glossy, deckle-edged art paper along with the customary gobbet of wedding cake inside its tiny white box decorated with silver boots and bells. There they all were on the steps of the old Presbyterian church, the clan, brought together for the camera, the only outsider being the young blonde bride, but then she'd already been absorbed by the tribe. Her blood would be diluted within another six months when the newest Dunbar entered the world. Even if he'd gone to the wedding – he pleaded pressure of work, some joke – he knew the same thing would happen to him too. That was the power they had. No matter how different or apart you might feel inside, the external evidence was there to the contrary, captured in black and white or, in this case, Kodacolor. Of course he knew there were many people who took comfort from family ties but, let's face it, in his case he had only ever felt an unpleasant tightening about the neck whenever the phenomenon showed itself.

Now, as he closely studied the damp grass underfoot for mushrooms – magic or otherwise – he thought of the woman he'd left sleeping back there like a plump and painted Madonna. *You're a lucky man, Sonny, you know that*, he addressed himself. *You have somebody at last who feels the same way as you about things*. It was true, for she had said as much. *With a woman like that at your side, you've every chance of breaking clear for once and for all*. Breaking clear. He liked the sound of it.

Straightening up from his search of the grass, he spread his arms wide, taking in deep gulps of the clean, upland air. Yes, this was his moment all right. The life he'd escaped from, back home, and then lately in that tunnel of a flat, still clawed at him with demands on his nerves. Some taint still lingered, he knew that. His very own name, the name they'd first put on him as a warning of his place in that early world, would always be a reminder of the power they, and it, could exert. And, as for the pull of that more recent stretch of his life, suddenly it came to him that that was no fantastical dream he'd just woken from – that was something that had actually happened to him. Three or, was it four, days ago he had, in fact, not fantasy, actually stumbled along Oxford Street seeing sights and hearing sounds which only he seemed to be able to interpret, a toy dog strangling on a lead, motor-bikes carrying on one-sided conversations, the code contained in the whine of a terrorist's fiddle. He shivered for a moment at the thought of all of that, but then it might only have been the damp morning air bathing his skin ...

Giving up on the mushrooms – he remembered now that they only thrived on grazing land – he headed back towards the camper. Its metal and glass were sheeted in condensation, a myriad tiny bubbles like silver spawn. Entering the darkness of its interior as silent as a thief he felt tempted to rub his hand just once over the side of the door to mar that perfection, but stopped himself in time. Never had he felt so attuned to the world and its natural mysteries as at this precise moment.

And once inside in the rich, fuggy gloom the mood stretched and held and continued to hold as he slid out of his jeans and under the blankets, his hands seeking and quickly finding her. She moaned softly once, welcoming him into her and for the second time he marvelled at the speed of response of her marvellous cunt as it received him.

Now he felt as rampant as that randy old giant himself – the one carved in the chalk across the valley. The mist covered the preposterous nakedness but the giant was there all right, nothing surer, shaking his knobbed club at the killjoys of the world. Yesterday, while Hazel slept, he'd climbed up to crouch on the cooling roof, watching him fade as dusk, then darkness, descended. My God, what a beast, but what power, what beauty, too! As the pot took hold, gradually the distant club changed shape until it was a guitar, quite recognisably so, and realising he was being signalled to across the blue, misty breadth of the valley, he waved back. At the time he remembered being full of gratitude and, as a gesture of reciprocation, he lowered his pants until he also stood there naked, facing the great British Hercules. He had nothing to wave in return – his guitar was stowed away below – but he did manage to muster a partial erection in homage to that other colossally proportioned one.

Now he was demonstrating to his great, watching friend that he could put it to the use for which it was intended,

139

and Hazel matched him in passion until the camper rocked. Lust drove them, and what a beautiful contest it turned out to be. They broke the tapes together, both roaring unrestrainedly, and the first words were his as they lay together tangled and sweaty.

'Photo finish, photo finish.'

They fell asleep after that, until the climbing sun came through a crack in the curtains. He watched her as she moved naked about the small space, making order out of the chaos. False modesty had no place between them any longer and in a rush of affection he dropped to the floor and embraced her, pressing his face into her shaggy bush. The juices they had generated tasted salty and sweet at the same time. Oh, she was so big, so, so *substantial* in everything, he exulted, as his fingers locked about those smooth, slippery haunches. He felt her kiss him on the top of his head, then she laughed as she pulled away.

Lying on the bunk he continued to worship, observing with how much economy and yes, grace, she dressed herself. It seemed to him that the art of striptease wasn't nearly as arousing as its counterpart. The way, for instance, she had of settling herself snugly into her pants, the jut of the breasts, tipped and dark, as if anticipating the touch of the wool of her sweater and, when she turned away, that deep and glistening runnel disappearing between her buttocks. . . .

He was on the point of trying for a rerun, he certainly had no doubts as to his own capabilities, for beneath the blankets he was as stiff as a ramrod again, but then he considered. *Just because our prehistoric friend on the hill up there has been nursing a hard-on since the year dot doesn't mean you've got to go and act the animal, does it? Show a little restraint, friend. Better still, save it for another time, which will be quite soon by the look of things.*

He sang a chorus of 'Rollin' In My Sweet Baby's Arms' just to celebrate this new-found maturity on his part, first song of the day, then he smelt the sickly, sweet whiff of butane followed by the pop of ignition.

'Leave all that, sweetheart,' he called out lazily. 'You're on vacation.'

140

'Just one cup of tea. I can't start the day without a cup of tea.'

'You could well have fooled me, kiddo.'

She laughed with more than a hint of girlish embarrassment.

Bliss, he thought.

Later when they were facing each other across the fold-out table, she with her Brooke Bond and he with the last of the takeaway beer from the night before, he said, 'Just in case I happened to be dreaming last night, do you really have Lester's – ?' He still couldn't bring himself to say the word but he didn't have to, because she rose without a murmur and went to the back of the camper.

Keeping his eyes lowered to his Tuborg – had he been wise to bring up the subject? – he heard the hiss of her suitcase zip and then she returned holding something in both hands. Still without speaking, she placed the object on the table between her cup and his can. Smaller than a cigar box, it didn't seem to have a lid, or opening of any kind, but then, who would dream of checking the contents? There it sat on top of the formica.

'So . . .' he said, already regretting his request. 'So . . .'

The moments passed. Hazel sipped her tea. He felt a great reluctance to touch the thing but knew he had to. He also felt his own incongruity deeply, sitting there in nothing but his underpants and his elephant's hair bracelet. The wood of the box was cheap and not particularly well finished and when he did overcome his qualms it had the feel, as well as look, of something factory-made in bulk. Made In Czechoslovakia, he read on the raw, unsealed under-side. Handling it, the whole thing felt as if it might well be empty into the bargain, he almost said, 'You *are* sure you got the right one?' when he thought, shit, leave it. And Hazel, as though reading his mind, took it from him and carried it back with her to the suitcase.

He said, 'We'll know when the time comes. Where to do the scattering, I mean.'

And she replied softly, 'I know, I know.'

He took another swig from his warm Tuborg. Scatter, he thought, scatter? Dear Christ, *how*!

Hazel rose then and rinsed her red plastic picnic mug at the sink. He was pleased to see that the water supply functioned even though it did emerge as little more than a trickle.

He heard the rattle of a frying pan. 'No, no,' he called out. 'Leave that. Breakfast is my department.'

She looked at him with one of her grins. 'You mean you *cook*, as well?'

It was his turn now to act embarrassed but at the same time he was no fool, for hadn't he realised that one kitchen sink to any woman must seem roughly the same as another? Why exchange that at home for one on the road? It struck him then that he knew practically nothing about this woman's domestic set-up – a slightly worrying concept. But then, he thought to himself, what's the hurry, old buddy, time enough for all of that later. What a very good word that was turning out to be. *Later*. It had all the comfort and warmth of an old and familiar favourite shirt, like his hound's-tooth, black and white Western Wear with the pearl buttons and the arrowed slits. And that was just what he decided to pull on.

'Looking good, big boy,' said Hazel as she took in the full picture – shirt, Levis, handmade cowboy boots – at least, they had been for the previous owner. 'Looking good.'

They climbed forward into the cab and he tickled the cold engine into life. As they bumped slowly out of the field he put the wipers on to fast to clear the screen, manoeuvring the camper, as he did so, to face directly into the distant hillside. The mist had cleared and he waited for her expression to change as she sighted the giant for the first time.

'Sonny,' she said, straight-faced, 'you really didn't have to go to all that trouble, just on my account. You must have been up all night.'

'Wasn't easy,' he replied, equally dead-pan. 'Certainly wasn't easy. Just hope you like it, that's all.'

142

'Oh, I love it, I do. A pity they don't make men on that same scale any more, that's all.'

Stopping the engine he grabbed her and she squealed like a young girl as he rubbed his stubbly beard in her neck. She smelt warm and yeasty. Then she pulled away. 'Look what you've done to my hair,' she complained, but she was smiling as she said it. He watched as she scraped her locks back into a pony-tail and slid on a rubber band, twisted several times, with such dexterity that he felt he could never tire of just looking at how this woman did the simplest of things.

'I'm starving,' she said. 'Must be all this country air.'

'*And* exercise.'

Her neck went dusky red again, but it may have been all those lumberjack kisses he had been handing her.

Once out of the hay field they found themselves on a bare, scrubbed upland road and the air that came streaming through the windows tasted sharp and pure. They saw rabbits in the fields and, once, a pheasant made a spectacular run for it across their path. It almost seemed as if they had returned to some earlier age of innocence and when the descent took on a more serious turn, zig-zagging into dark green tunnels, the sound of countless, invisible springs on either side of the road, Sonny did have the feeling he had travelled this way a long time before. For the first time since they had started out it occurred to him that they might not be too far away from the heart of things, after all. For he saw it like that, a still, calm centre somewhere, just in the same way that he also felt certain he would know it whenever he got there.

The ancient village that gave its name to their giant was as pretty as a picture. The sun was rapidly drying its thatched roofs, and runnels, full to the brim with clear water, ran melodiously alongside every street and alleyway. As yet, no one seemed to be stirring and after they had parked the camper – it did seem an intrusion in such an olde worlde setting – they found a tea-room that had just opened its doors. Two grey-haired, pinafored darlings served them coffee, toast and eggs. He and Hazel sat isolated

143

on their hard Windsor chairs like a couple of awed American tourists; it felt good to be on one's best behaviour for a change after the city, where people pushed and snarled and anticipated the worst.

When they had paid up and were going Sonny noticed a rack of T-shirts hanging alongside the usual picture post-card display. All had a full frontal outline of the Cerne Abbas Giant, knobbed club echoed by that other more arresting image he was famed for. Circumcised, too, he couldn't help noticing for the first time. The two little old ladies didn't bat an eyelid as they noticed him staring. In fact, one of them smiled sweetly across at him as he backed out of the door.

'This is just like something on a chocolate box,' was Hazel's verdict as they strolled past cottages with bull's-eye glass in their windows and doors whose planking looked 'distressed', if he didn't know it was the real thing.

He had done a fair bit of that 'distressing' himself – to various articles of furniture when he was in that line of business. A rogue by the name of Leo – he never asked him his second name – had a lock-up garage off the Portobello Road and it was there that the two of them would lay into the stock with lengths of chain to give that coveted and suitably battered look. Leo had a talent for always finding the right customer until one night he went a little too far and dug up a whole mews in South Kensington for its York Stone paving without consulting the Council, or the residents. Great times, great times . . .

Sonny took Hazel's hand as they wandered past yet another gingerbread house. Hansel and Gretel. His legs were feeling rubbery again. *All your fault, you up there, with your engine of war perpetually at the ready. A thousand years, or thereabouts, affecting the people with that bloody great dong of yours.*

As they climbed into the camper and drove off he almost fancied he could hear a great collective complaining of ancient bed-springs. That was Cerne Abbas, for what it was worth.

The ascent out of the village was as steep as the one they'd come by – he was heading almost due west, judging now

144

by the position of the sun. It bathed the ruins and the ancient lichened walls far below, lovingly, conspiratorially, even. He could see it all framed in the oblong of his driving mirror like a still from a Tourist Board calendar. No place deserved to look as pretty as that, he told himself.

And then at the crest of the hill, steam started coming out from under the bonnet. Hazel noticed it, too, but he said, 'No sweat. We'll just pull in ahead there and fill her up.'

A lay-by had been created by the Council for people to park their cars and study the famous local attraction across the valley. A notice to the effect informed them that this was the best vantage point to view the famous 180-foot high fertility figure cut into the turf more than a millennium ago.

What if, last night, they'd taken Lester's ashes up there in that cigar box and sown him to the wind, standing, the two of them, on that gigantic cut-out? They were certainly both in the mood to go through with it, if such an idea should have taken hold. But then, of course, why should it have, even if they were as high as a couple of kites? It was a foolish thought, nothing surer, for what had their little Lester in common with that monumental piece of ancient British graffiti? He would blush, Sonny recalled, if someone told a dirty joke in his company, or if one of the pub women got a little suggestive towards closing-time, as often they did. No, the time and place for Lester's final resting place would come together later and it made no sense to anticipate or rush that conjunction. . . .

Ahead of them, in the lay-by, sat two other cars. The driver of the white Astra was positioned on a folding picnic chair, binoculars trained on the distant giant, while his wife knitted inside. As Sonny went close to the second car, a metallic silver Mazda, to get water for the radiator, he saw that driver number two, a man in his forties, was asleep behind the wheel. Slumped there with his tie loosened and his mouth agape he looked just like a child, despite the sophisticated car-phone in his lap. His suit jacket hung from a hook on the seat pillar and a sticker on his rear window said, THINK ALUMINIUM. A message such as that could only make Sonny shake his head as he directed water into the radiator.

When he'd finished and wiped the rust from his hands he returned the empty jerry-can to its place and climbed back in. Hazel smiled at him as he fastened his seat belt – hers was still in place – and waited expectantly for them to drive off. For a moment he toyed with the ignition but it was only a blind, for he felt suddenly that he needed time to think – yet, about what, he had no idea. A nameless panic had seized him. In that instant the webbing had tightened its grip on his chest.

'Hang on a tick,' he said, undoing the seat belt and scrambling back into the rear of the camper. There he moved things about as though he were searching for something, but the reality was he needed to steady his nerves. Hanging on to the tiny, circular basin he surveyed himself in the mirror screwed to the wall above the single tap. To gain further respite he twisted the tap, and a trickle of water drummed down on to the curved burnished metal.

What am I doing here? he asked himself. As if the reflection in the glass could come up with some answers. For a terrifying second he thought of opening the back door, stepping down into the roadway and just silently running. But where? Certainly not London. All his boats had been burned back there – bridges, too. It had been the easiest act of arson imaginable. The signing over of the lease, the cashing of the cheque from Bolsover Holdings (they would have given him used notes in a brown paper bag, so eager were they) the clearance of his gear from the flat; he didn't haggle with those so-called friends of his in the trade over a thing, not even the Tiffany lamp with the neck of a swan – everything had taken just a day, two, perhaps three, counting the buying of the camper.

So now he stood looking at himself in a mirror in a lay-by in Dorset with nothing in the world to his name save a guitar, a few clothes, his best cassettes – all the records, as well as the system, had to go – this camper, and in his back pocket, about three grand, maybe a little more. In a matter of days he'd turned into a gypsy. Yes, a gypsy, and one with a finite existence too, because just how long would three grand last?

Unable to help himself any longer he moaned and Hazel called out, 'Sonny?'

Sonny. Even his own name sounded like the name of a loser. Coughing loudly, he turned off the tap and prepared to face up to his responsibilities. For it was he and he alone who had set all of this in motion.

'Be right with you!'

Hazel looked at him as he climbed back into the driving seat. 'Why don't we go to that place you were talking about last night? That gig you saw in the paper. Take a look, that's all.'

She held out the newspaper in question, folded carefully to a square to show where he had ringed an ad in the entertainments section.

He pretended indifference, for what he really craved now was for her to talk him into it.

'Wouldn't you prefer to travel? See all this beautiful countryside?'

She looked at him and, for a moment, he thought she'd rumbled him. 'We can do that on the way, can't we?'

He turned the key in the ignition and the engine caught and fired. 'Let's go!' he called above the roar and he swung the camper out on to the road. Looking down he saw that the man in the company car below was still fast asleep.

'So long, suckers!' he cried through the window, for in that he was also including the sight-seeing couple with their picnic chair and table, their thermos and their guide to the best bed and breakfast places. They were all suckers quite suddenly again, as far as he was concerned, and as he drove, his contempt seemed to grow with each fresh member of the species that they passed.

He sang steadily right through what remained of Dorset and then into Somerset with Hazel joining in occasionally until, without any conscious effort on their part, it appeared that they'd worked out a passable repertoire for themselves.

'Well, are we ready to show these shit-kickers a thing or two tonight, or aren't we?'

'We surely are,' came the reply. 'We surely are.' And throwing back his head he gave a rebel yell at a pensioner painting his gates on the outskirts of Yeovil. Hideaway was the name of his cottage; they had already passed The Bolthole, Moorings and Traveller's Rest.

Around noon Sonny pulled into a pub car park on the A37 to get out of the line of milk tankers that had held him in check for the past twenty miles. The sun kept striking shafts of reflected light off the gleaming hulls in front, straight into his eyes, until finally he'd had enough. The idea of being trapped in that convoy of curdling white stuff any longer made him feel nauseous, but then the previous night's drinking may have had something to do with it.

It was decided they sit out in the beer-garden. A pond with ducks was a feature and there were scattered oak tables with benches attached. They had the place to themselves. The hot, weathered wood felt good to the touch and both closed their eyes tilting up their faces towards the sun as they did so.

Eventually he rose and wandered across to the pub. A sign beside the door read, NO BIKERS, NO SITE CLOTHES. Uh, uh, he thought, one of those, pushing his way in. As expected, the bar was cramped and bijou, every inch of wall surface covered with horse brasses, stuffed fish and vermin in cases, old prints and photographs and rows of hanging, glass-bottomed pewter mugs.

Three couples were at the bar blocking his approach, the women perched cross-legged on stools, the men standing bent slightly because of the low rafters. They were all six-footers – he suspected the women were, as well. Judging by their clothes, the two Range Rovers out in the car-park belonged to them, as well. One of the men had just come to the end of a story, the resultant laughter seemed too loud for such an enclosed space, and Sonny stepped back. Behind him there sounded a yelp and a deep growl and the sleeping pub Labrador, which he hadn't seen until then, bared yellow stumps at him.

The landlord called out, 'Silly boy! Out of it, out of it!' in such furious tones that, for a moment, Sonny thought the words might be meant for him.

One of the head-scarved women slid off her stool to kneel beside the dog. 'Poor, poor Lysander,' she crooned. 'Did the naughty, naughty man step on poor old Lysander's pawsy-wawsy?'

She was giving a sustained flash of long, lean, silken thigh as she cradled the dog's mangy head. Sonny stared, unable to help himself. A hole the size of a fifty-pence piece was situated just below the dusky band of stocking-top.

The men in the pub smiled indulgently down from their great height on the touching scene but the landlord's face, Sonny couldn't help noticing, hadn't changed expression. He, himself, stood there wondering how long it would take before he was offered or served a drink. He was feeling alien again, as though he had missed something on that sign outside that precluded people like himself along with Hell's Angels and yokels in boiler suits.

Then a voice said, 'May I help you?' and it was the landlord's distraught child-bride in a Laura Ashley pinny.

'A pint of best bitter and a vodka and tomato juice.'

He watched her getting into a state over the Bloody Mary. Everyone else did, as well, himself included, but Sonny felt no sympathy. It was like watching an accident; you quickly learned not to get involved. As he carried the drinks outside he overheard the landlord say, 'No need to be quite so heavy with the old Lea and Perrins next time, dearest. All right?'

Hazel enquired, 'Do they do grub, then?' and he heard himself lie despite the blackboard he'd seen inside. Dish of the day was something called Dorset Cobblers, whatever the hell those might be. He'd felt angered by her question; he couldn't figure why, for some reason, until it came to him it was the people in the pub, not Hazel, he was really mad at. Never Hazel.

So, instead of going back and hitting something, even kicking that Labrador properly this time, he went to a swing in the children's section, sat on its worn tyre and, grasping both ropes, gave it a thoroughgoing work-out for about a minute and half. Hazel sat watching as if what he was doing was the most natural thing in the world. Each time the swing flew out and up to its furthest point Sonny could see over the tops of the trees into the distance. Everything looked blue and inviting out there where they were heading. That knob on the skyline, he thought, that must be Glastonbury Tor. Every hippy in England would be heading there, drawn like iron filings to a magnet. The journey might take them days, weeks, even years, but that's where they all ended up.

Well, he decided, if it has to be a choice between joining the love children or those brokers back in the pub, I know which side I'm on every time.

'Hazel!' he called out. 'Your turn!' And she rose and walked across to stand behind him on the grass. He wanted her to share in his feelings and, when she was airborne, he directed her to look north and west across the meadowlands full of fat, grazing Friesians.

'Avalon!' he shouted. 'King Arthur and all that shit!'

She was kicking up her heels and squealing like a young girl as his two-handed shove kept sending her ever higher and higher. Each time he took hold of those solid hips of hers, satisfying and round like the curves of a jug, he could feel himself getting hornier by the second.

But a voice called out, 'Excuse me! Excuse me!' and turning, he saw the landlord watching them. He leant against the door of his pub, arms folded, head to one side, in that familiar stance, one that Sonny seemed to have lived with most of his life. The teacher who first nicknamed him would hold himself in exactly the same way when he had something sarcastic to say. And when this florid Englishman in his buff cords and nautical guernsey enquired, 'Can't you read the sign?' it was as if he were back once more in that one-roomed schoolhouse with its varnished wall-maps of the British Empire, its smell of chalk-dust and drying pee.

'What sign?' he yelled over his shoulder, giving Hazel two more loving thrusts for luck.

'There!' pointed the man. 'There! Are you *blind*?'

Of course there was a sign – This Area For The Use of Patrons' Children Only – but who the fuck cared?

Sonny caught Hazel at the end of her fall, wrestling her gently to a halt. He turned to face the man and Hazel, turning with him, said, 'Don't, Sonny, don't, he's not worth it,' even though he had no intention of any such implied response. The publican must have heard her for he dropped both arms tamely to his sides in a gesture that warmed Sonny's heart. For one tremendous moment he saw himself through two sets of eyes as someone potentially dangerous, not to be trifled with. The image pleased him so much that he felt tempted to take the fantasy a step further, for he was remembering *Five Easy Pieces* and the scene where Jack Nicholson sweeps the crockery to the floor of the diner. The hard-faced waitress in the picture and this arsehole facing him had similar attitudes, it seemed, when it came to serving the public.

He glanced over at the empty glasses on the distant table for a moment, then he said, in a loud voice, 'You're quite right, Hazel, he's not worth it.' And added, 'None of them are,' for he wanted to include that bunch of Big Bangers and their women back in the bar while he was about it. He was thinking of the hole in the stocking. That's the way they were, he told himself. They were, weren't they? On the surface everything about them and their life-style appeared so very plausible, so flawless, but underneath a very different picture presented itself – for those in the know. . . .

Strolling back to the camper to get on the road again, he felt pleased with the way he'd managed to come out of the situation. Still, if he were honest with himself, there was something about that glimpse of long, aristocratic, inner thigh, with the hint of possible sluttishness thrown in, which appealed very strongly indeed. He felt himself hardening again and thought, this *is* a revelation – Sonny Dunbar, Sex Mechanic?

Driving out on to the hot, glittering road – the traffic had eased considerably – in high good spirits, he asked, 'Did you ever see a movie called *Five Easy Pieces*?' And when she said, no, she didn't think she had, how long ago was it, he began recounting for her the plot in the finest detail.

He was still going strong by the time they got to Glastonbury and coming into town, because of his very animation, they almost met with their first accident of the trip. Rounding a bend in one of the ancient narrow streets, he swung sharply into a turning without really taking in its One Way sign and met a large, white American car head-on. At the very last moment he closed his eyes, anticipating the tinkle of broken headlights. Instead, there came a soft, padded collision of bumper on bumper, a mere kiss of metal, if that, but behind in the camper the din of falling kitchenware sounded like the end of everything.

For a moment he sat looking down into the open car – it was a soft top, a Chevrolet or Pontiac, he would have guessed – unable to put the gear stick into reverse. There were two men in the car, a young swarthy individual behind the wheel and an older man wearing dark glasses and a silk, black aviator's jacket. He had on a baseball type cap with gold braid across its peak and clutched a walking stick between his knees. The driver put his hand on the door ready to spring out but the man in the passenger seat shook his head and they both sat back looking up at Sonny sweating high above them behind the glass.

Of course the situation righted itself, he got the camper back on its proper course and the big car swept past with a low and baleful roaring from twin exhausts. The last thing Sonny saw was the back of the second man's head resting against the pale leather upholstery of the front seat. He had his prematurely white hair in a short, fat pigtail which stuck out from a hole in the baseball cap. It seemed one further affectation, that and the personalised number plate PIL 1 below a stamped metal replica of a Confederate flag.

'I wonder who he is?' said Hazel.

'Who he thinks he is, more likely. PIL 1. Probably short for pillock.'

Hazel laughed. They both laughed and he felt much better already.

Glastonbury appeared to be full of exhausted hippies

152

resting from some strenuous mystic endeavour, or perhaps they were gathering what little strength they had left for a fresh onslaught. They lay on benches or hunkered down in doorways, not moving, not speaking, while the residents of the town, ignoring them, went about their centuries old business. It was market day and the streets were thronged with elderly men and women dragging wickerwork 'shoppers'. These seemed to Sonny even more lethal than the great, plaid-covered chariots he'd suffered in the Kilburn High Road. Big, burly, black women had been the ones to watch out for there; down here it was the smiling granny who had licence to maim.

From their refuge on the first floor of the Grail Grill And Coffee Shoppe he and Hazel looked down on the throngs of apple-cheeked pensioners jousting for right of way a storey below. Now he knew why the hippies curled themselves up in corners and doorways – it was to be out of harm's way; why they had that dulled, hungover look about them, as well. Drugs had nothing to do with it. No. They were bemused, that was why, wary, too, for here they had been travelling towards this place of pilgrimage for a very long time – since the sixties, if you wanted to be really fanciful – and when eventually they do manage to make it to their Holy of Holies, what do they find? Certainly not that ancient dropping peace of old Albion, certainly not the stuff of romantic legend and Arthurian myth. What they found was down below right at this moment, the British high-street shopper running in full and anxious tidal spate.

For a weird moment Sonny had a twinge of regret for something he had no part or share in. These crowds with their concerns over kitchen appliances and lawn mowers, school uniforms, car accessories, home-brew kits, cat litter, dog food, package holidays, compact discs, duvets, the Sunday roast – they might as well be from another planet, as far as he was concerned. And, like those hippies, he felt just like a lonely Venusian. But only for an instant, because then it came to him that theorising of that order might easily be having an airing right at this very moment back in that boring pub he used to frequent in leafy London W8.

Stuff like that was for muddled men in bars who got all their insight from the one serious newspaper they loved to carry about with them. Every lunch-time another second-hand editorial. Sonny, he thought, you are well out of that.

He went up to get Hazel another coffee and a second helping of cake. God, he loved watching her eat.

The girl behind the counter was all thumbs, but in a nice, relaxed, giggly sort of way. She had been giving him looks ever since he'd sat down and even though she must have only just left school, he still felt flattered.

He said, 'Another piece of your lovely home-made carrot cake, darlin',' and she blushed and stammered.

''Tisn't ours, sir, we get it sent down from Bath, but it is very good, sir.'

He smiled at her, seeing himself in her china blue eyes already as the glamorous, visiting country star. Without thinking, he'd introduced a twang to his accent. She had baby blonde hair cut in that revived twenties style, bangs at the front, neck shaved as high as the ears like topiary, that young and defenceless nape.

'Do you know a place around here goes by the name of something Magna?' He was pretending ignorance. 'Pub called The George?'

She squealed with delighted recognition. 'Oh, you mean The George And Vulture, sir, at Ditton Magna, sir. Shepton Mallet way.' She leaned forward and he could see the swell of her schoolgirl breasts like two ripening pears. 'Excuse me for enquiring, but are you appearing there, yourself, like? Tonight, sir?'

Shamelessly he replied, 'How did you guess, sweetheart?' taking the tray from her with gentle hands and leaving behind a more than generous tip.

Hazel seemed in pensive mood when he resumed his seat. Had she noticed him at his tricks with young jail-bait yonder? But, no, it didn't seem to be anything like that. She cut neatly into her thick wedge of cake with the edge of her fork, carried it laden to her mouth and, when she withdrew the fork, there were traces of lipstick on the metal. He really did love to watch her eat, he truly did.

Then she dabbed the corners of her mouth with a paper napkin and said, out of the blue, 'My father, *he* was an American. Did I tell you that?'

He said, no, it was certainly news to him, and she sat there looking down at her plate as if she didn't know whether to be sad or sorry that she'd polished off two sizeable portions of such fattening cake. Sonny was wondering why the subject had come up. Perhaps it was because eating dessert that way with a fork seemed a very American thing to do.

'I never knew him,' she said. 'He was a GI – over here. Over there, I mean. Back home. Ireland, I mean.' He waited for more but that seemed to be it.

There didn't seem to be much point in staying on after that and he had paid the bill, so he got up and pulled back his chair for her. She flashed him a smile. Oh, those big, square, capable white teeth, slightly flecked with the red of her lipstick; he could still feel them nibbling his cock, or had that been his imagination? They left arm in arm.

Passing young Blonde Bangs on the way out he winked across at her and for a moment he sensed she might be on the point of asking for an autograph. *Sonny and Hazel, Hazel and Sonny*, he debated on the stairs to the street. *No, Sonny and Hazel, that had to be the arrangement.* It had the right ring to it as if the conjunction had been in place a very long time. Like all the best acts. Husband-and-wife acts, he found himself on the point of thinking, before he took fright. *Easy does it, easy does it, Sonny....*

Four o'clock was striking from the town's church towers as they ambled back to the car park. Pay and Display, again. Past the health food shops and the occult bookstore windows full of tarot packs, astrology charts, ley-line maps and, inside, everything ever published on Stonehenge, Merlin, the Grail, Arthur, the Round Table. The scent of patchouli and joss drifted out into the West Country air and Sonny saw a seminar on Basic Magical Training advertised alongside another poster drawing attention to a forthcoming Witches' Workshop in Chipping Sodbury.

Then they drove out into the depths of the countryside and on a deserted and flinty farm track leading nowhere he brought the camper to a halt. The curtains were still pulled across and in the yellowish, filtered half-light of the interior they fell upon one another without a word being spoken.

Afterwards she had a little weep and, locked in her arms, he lay feeling a touch melancholy himself. Honeymooning must be something along these lines, he couldn't help reflecting, time suddenly slowing down after all the initial excitement. They had found themselves becalmed in the deadest part of the day – why did four o'clock, p.m. as well as a.m., always have the sensation of dying about it? She must have been experiencing some of that, as well, judging by the way she'd been all over him. It was like riding out a storm at sea. That made it sound as if he hadn't enjoyed it. He had, but it was obvious to him that his contribution to the action hadn't been quite so substantial or, as necessary, as last night. But, Sonny, he told himself, you are a lover, always remember that, and to a lover these things are all part of the business. Right? So he kissed her damp eyelids once, twice, and she sighed before sitting up against the cushions and pulling the sheet over her top half.

'Have you got a smoke?' she asked in a little-girl's voice.

'Somewhere,' he said, 'somewhere,' searching about among the clothes on the floor. 'Straight or funny?'

'Straight.'

And he lit up a Marlboro for her before putting it between her lips. It tasted like shit in his own mouth but, then, he couldn't really call himself a serious addict, he only inhaled a little now and then to keep himself in practice for the other thing. With love, he eyed her lying there propped up at the far end of the bed from him like some great, bare-shouldered, cigarette-puffing Earth Mother. Her covered feet fitted under his in what felt like a most natural fashion.

Settling himself even more comfortably, he prepared to listen, for he felt sure she would want to pick up at the point where she'd left off back in the coffee shop, the rest of the story about her father. For, he presumed there was more. He hadn't met a woman yet who hadn't had some hang-up or other when it came to her old man.

'Rhinestone Cowboy'

Crying that way. She hadn't done such a thing since ...
She couldn't remember the last time. The first time, yes,
with Charlie Orr, she'd wept bucketsful. Poor Charlie,
perhaps she'd put him off women for good because of it,
driving him into the arms of the Church. His face, as they
say, had been a picture, just like Sonny's.

Now she turned on a little smile just to reassure Sonny
that everything was all right, that it had been no fault of
his that she had gone all tearful on him. She also moved
her toes about under the sheet, gently nudging his soft parts.
Just how much attention Sonny really needed to keep Sonny
happy, it was still too early to say, but her feelings told her,
like every other man she'd ever known, he had to have it,
the way they seem to need meat and drink.

Hazel Kinney, she thought, dragging on her king-size,
you certainly are one hard-hearted bitch, you know that?
Then she felt like weeping again. Addressing herself by
name in that way, as if it were someone else, always made
her feel sorry for herself, as though it had the power of
turning her into some sort of hopeless case.

Inside, as she continued to smile and smoke, she felt sad,
not only for big Hazel Kinney stretched here on this bunk
bed, but for every other unlovable woman as well, and that
hard and lonely thing they all shared. When did she ever
have a really close friend, for instance, someone to confide
in? She never had, was the answer. All her life men had
been the ones to provide her with whatever it was they
supplied in lieu of friendship, trust. It was true. And right
here and now it was happening to her all over again. She
couldn't help herself. And, as if to prove the point, she
supplied another smile and touch with her big toe. He
grinned back from the far end of the bed, blowing a kiss.
Poor Sonny.

She lay there letting commiseration roll over her like a big, warm and spreading wave, commiseration with her own sex, all those friendless women out there not knowing where it was going to end. The young ones, it came to her, were worst off, nothing in their armoury. She was thinking of that sixteen year old again, the one whose story she didn't want to dwell upon, yet somehow couldn't keep at bay. It was something picked out of the local paper Sonny had bought. If it had been noticed at all by one of the nationals it would have rated maybe three lines, yet to her the episode had the power to disturb, more than any of the mightier horrors she normally came across in the news. The fashionable sport of the moment seemed to be rape, slightly ahead of child abuse, which was for the less valorous. Every park, every stretch of waste ground and railway cutting seemed to have its resident rapist. Desperate cases rubbed themselves against office workers in the Tube or exposed their pathetic equipment in the underpasses. She didn't even bother to count the number of times it had happened to her. She had bought herself a whistle; it also came in handy to blow into the phone at heavy breathers. This summer would go down in her book as the summer of the heavy breather; there seemed to be something in the air, an element of craziness, as if the English suffering under the heat, were reverting to something pagan in their make-up. It was also the silly season of the boxer short, the Filofax, cocktails and the whistling key-ring. Thank God Sonny didn't have the slightest inclination towards any of those ...

The teenage girl in the paper, Mandy Partridge was her name and she came from a housing estate in a remote part of Dorset, had taken out her younger brother's Raleigh Chopper one Saturday afternoon and ridden the thirty-odd miles it took her to reach the M4. At intersection 17 she had climbed up over the railings of the bridge and had jumped down on to the busy westbound stretch of the motorway below. Three cars and a van struck her almost instantly. She was dead when the traffic finally managed to come to a halt. It seemed she'd had a row a week previously with her boyfriend who worked alongside her in a chicken

158

factory. There was a recent photograph taken at a steam-tractor rally. She looked just like any normal sixteen year old, laughing and playing up for the camera. The police said she must have stood on the parapet of the bridge for a good three-quarters of an hour before finally jumping to her death. Motorists in the eastbound lane who saw her must have thought she was larking about, but one man who did come forward was able to corroborate the time.

Hazel closed her eyes. There were some things too cruel to dwell upon, but she kept on seeing that child pedalling determinedly to end her life, on a bicycle much too small for her. She could even visualise the clothes worn for the occasion. Tight, tapered jeans, high heels, a cheap gold chain encircling the thin, bare ankle, top – V-necked and sleeveless – over a clean white bra (first size) and her pants would have come straight out of their wrapping that morning. She would have had to bite through the little plastic price-tag, as one does, before slipping them on and before going downstairs to walk out of the house for ever. And the mother ... the mother getting those clothes back in a parcel a month, maybe more, later, along with one Mickey Mouse digital watch, one charm bracelet, one puzzle ring, one ankle chain. Sign here, please. None of it was in the paper, but imagination provided such details for Hazel with terrifying ease for, at the core of it all, was the thought of her own fifteen-year-old, the one she'd left in London to her own devices.

She thought of her running wild now in Kensington Market, that disreputable *souk*, where all her school friends hung out every chance they got, that incense-smelling maze on three floors, haunted by rich Arab students. Here to study the language, they said, but she knew different. The species never varied, no matter what the place or period. She remembered her own adventures. They were called 'playboys' then, and some of them certainly were very seductive, with manners as well as money, but this latest breed molested you with their eyes whenever you walked past them. She had a sudden, horrific vision of her Natalie laughing, smoking, maybe drinking, too, listening to records in a service flat in Queensway with about five of these expensively smelling jackals. *Why had she turned out to be such a bad mother*, she asked herself. *Why?*

'Have we anything to drink?'

Sonny stirred, dropping a hand beneath his side of the bed and coming up with a bottle and two glasses.

'Geronimo!'

They drank a little and she touched him up again with her toe. The worse she was feeling the more, it seemed, she wanted to please. She was beginning to turn into one of those women she could never stand.

'You were going to tell me about your old man – your dad,' he said. It was he who brought the subject up, not her.

'Was I?'

He looked put out by that, so, relenting, she began telling him about GI Joe, her own private and personal name for the man who had left without trace over forty years earlier. Not even a photograph remained, as far as she could determine; it had taken her mother nearly half that period of time just to admit to the fact that she had been conceived one night after a Christmas hoedown at a US army base close to where they lived.

'I used to be much darker when I was young. My complexion, I mean, and I had this terrible dread he might have been a negro. Can you believe that? Me? At school they used to call everyone Darkie, if your skin happened to be the slightest on the swarthy side. Do you remember that?'

'But surely –'

'I never knew him, I tell you. No one ever mentioned him. His name. Anything.'

'He might still be alive. Did you ever consider that as a possibility?'

'Why should I?'

Oh, Sonny, what a lot you have to learn. His eyes looked a shade pouchy today, spaniel eyes, filling with hurt so fast, really it was best not to take them too literally. Eyes like that in a man, she thought, could only prove to his long-term disadvantage. Dark glasses did have the power of making him into a different person, almost formidable; threatening, even. And with the build he had, he could certainly carry it off if he wanted to.

On the journey down, riding at his side, she felt she could sense a tension, something deep and unresolved, that crackled like live wires touching. Meet my electric boyfriend. What a dumbo she was, really ...

Then they got on to old American comics, the sort that used to arrive wrapped around tinned stuff, cartons of chocolate bars, mittens, scarves and lumberjack shirts in big parcels from the States. Everyone seemed to have relatives over there at the time. Sonny had two uncles who emigrated, both of them to Saskatchewan in Canada, but then they had the same funny papers there as well, didn't they? The Katzenjammer Kids, Blondie and Dagwood, Steve Canyon, Bringing Up Father, Prince Valiant, Little Orphan Annie, Gasoline Alley, Li'l Abner, Dick Tracy, Terry and the Pirates, Alley Oop.

'Let me guess *your* favourite,' said Hazel. 'I bet it was Li'l Abner.'

Sonny laughed, remembering. 'What was the name of that place they all used to live in? Dogpatch, was it? Dogpatch, USA? Well, let me tell you, I grew up in Dogpatch, Ireland. The family next door were pure Yokum, believe me. No, I preferred Bringing Up Father. Those little spats he always wore, and his wife Maggie. Remember her? Looked just like Joe E. Brown. So did he, for that matter. Ah, carefree days ...'

They drank some more. It was Scotch. Now, where had that come from? Then he said, with a soft faraway look in his eyes, 'We could always go out there and look for him, you know. The two of us.'

'Who?' she asked, knowing perfectly well what he was on about.

'I saw this documentary,' he said. 'On television. About this woman reunited with her father. They tracked him down. Somewhere in California, it was. Orange Blossom County. It was very moving, it really was.'

I bet, she thought, *I just bet*.

161

'Nothing's impossible, you know.'

She said, 'There's too much water under the bridge for that, Sonny. Let sleeping dogs lie.'

'Can't put the clock back, eh?'

'Something like that.'

'Out of sight, out of mind? Che sera, sera?'

She looked at him sternly. 'Are you taking the piss?'

'There's a bridle hanging on the wall?'

And she launched herself at him. They wrestled for a bit, laughing, then fell apart, not bothering to cover themselves this time. He had the beginnings of a spare tyre, she noticed, but the rest looked okay in the half-light. Nice, wide shoulders, neat buttocks, better legs than her own. She was glad he wasn't hairy, at least, not excessively so. You could never tell whether you'd ended up with a human hearth-rug or not; the test, they used to say, was whether the eyebrows met in the middle. Backs of the hands were supposed to be another giveaway. Sonny's hands were square, capable, reassuring; they felt cool and dry when they touched her. She enjoyed that part. They went about their business without fuss, as if they knew their route off by heart. Quite inventive, also, she was bound to admit.

Once, she'd known somebody who was in love with his own hands. They were long, fine, pale and tapering with nails exquisitely groomed. He kept on displaying them, as if he couldn't bear having them out of his sight. Of course, he insisted on rolling his own cigarettes, yet how was it he never seemed to get any nicotine stains? He was a struggling writer, a Hungarian, with a perfect English accent, very entertaining and fun to be with, yet she couldn't bear him touching her. It was like having spiders roam all over you. They parted without fuss or any real regret as she recalled. It must have been just prior to meeting Eric that disastrous Bank Holiday Monday on Southend Pier in 1980.

She thought of Natalie again, the two of them together in that council flat of his. It only had the one bedroom and he would never give up his comforts, his old mother having seen to that. That meant that the disgusting old sofa-bed facing the TV would have to be pressed into service and

162

Natalie, despite pretending to be a dedicated slut most of the time these days, would, she knew, be distraught because of it.

Here she was, naked, with a man, similarly undressed, in a lane in the back of beyond somewhere, while the only person in the entire world who meant anything real to her might, for all she knew, be contemplating heading that same way herself. *Why, oh, why, Hazel Kinney, are you such a bad mother?*

'Refill?' she heard her nude companion murmur, and she reached out her glass eagerly and just as eagerly gulped the stinging contents down. It seemed obvious the way the rest of this day and night ahead, too, was taking them. And, feeling as she did, she would most certainly drink to that. Sleep must have overtaken them around about that point because when they came to with a great deal of moaning and groaning and stretching of cramped limbs – *oh, Hazel, you really are too old for all of this* –the light outside seemed to be going.

'What time is it?' she asked.

He put his watch to his ear, then started shaking it furiously. 'The bastard's stopped on me!' he cried, then with panic in his voice, 'Oh Christ, we mustn't be *late*, Hazel!'

'How can we be?' she consoled. 'Look outside. It's about seven. Half-past, at the most. These things never get going until nine or ten.' Sometimes she amazed herself, she really did.

They began to dress, sorting out glad rags and toilet things on the beds like a couple of honeymooners preparing to go out on their first big night together. They kept bumping into one other in the narrow gangway between the bunks, and she also suffered an unaccountable attack of modesty for some reason when it came to laying out fresh underwear.

'Look,' she said finally, 'take the bottle and go behind the wheel while I get changed. I won't be long.'

Feeling a bit drunk she went through the familiar routine which seemed now slightly hilarious to her, given the sur-roundings. The heavy summer scent of her deodorant couldn't quite disguise that other herbal aroma now wafting back from the driver's seat. *Time to get high, high, high, again, folks,* she thought to herself.

'Let me look at you.'

'No, let me look at *you.*'

They were circling each other a trifle unsteadily in the yellow beam of the headlights which Sonny had turned on against the gathering dusk.

'You look terrific, *terrific!*' he cried.

'So do you.'

Laughing like two kids, they continued scrutinising one another with enormous interest, for it was the first time either of them had seen the other like this. Even Hazel had to admit there was something miraculous about their transformation in the glare of the headlamps. Her own perfection appeared to her to be reflected in the brightness of Sonny's eyes – or was that just the grass talking, for she'd had a puff or two, herself, by this time.

He was wearing a fine wool shirt in black and white hounds-tooth with pearl buttons and arrowed slits, tight black jeans, a silver-studded belt and a pair of chestnut-coloured cowboy boots with inch and a half heels. On his head sat the gambler's hat he had sported the first time she'd seen him in the cemetery, and a red bandanna was knotted about his throat. All that could be said to be missing was the horse. She felt like laughing but knew instinctively that that would be the worst thing possible at this time and place. Again she had the feeling of finding herself in a rôle she wasn't quite certain she wanted to take on. She remembered too well all those women back home and the way they were expected to admire the Saturday night grandeur of the man of the house.

Sonny seemed equally approving of her own ensemble. He clapped his hands in appreciation so, dutifully, she spun for him on the flinty laneway, her full, high-waisted skirt flying out to show bare legs as far as the knee above her cowgirl boots. Her blouse was an old Doris Day number she'd held on to over the years. Miraculously, it still fitted.

164

Sonny grabbed her then, for a moment, and they swung together to the beat he generated, more square-dance than jive. He produced a flower from nowhere, out of the hedgerow, most likely, and helped her fasten it in her hair. And what a face he put on too, just as if this was a scene from some movie. She had the Katy Jurado part – her hair was swept back, wet and black for the occasion – while Sonny was Robert Taylor or possibly Rory Calhoun, and they had just walked out on to the verandah for a little air. Mexican music played softly inside. They had met for the first time that evening in somebody's hacienda ...

'Tomorrow, first thing,' announced Sonny, 'I'm gonna have our two names printed across the windshield of this old bus. Put this partnership in black and white – or even colour, if they have it. Why not? Sonny and Hazel.' His hands described a band in the air.

'What do you reckon, huh?'

Was it her imagination or had his accent already undergone a distinct shift westward? She wondered if she herself might be similarly affected. *Say something and find out, Hazel.*

'Right,' she said, putting the dog rose over her ear. 'One final puff and we're on our way.'

He reached her the last of the joint – there were only a couple of drags remaining – and, pouting, she inhaled the last of its magical properties.

'Listen,' Sonny said. 'Do you hear it? Listen.'

'What?' she asked.

'An owl. I haven't heard one of those since ...'

Together they concentrated on the sounds of the evening. The melancholy note of a far-off farm dog reached them; much closer, the sudden squeal of something small and furred meeting its maker. Hazel could smell rich, rising scents all around as if they were on an island set in a living, breathing sea of growing things. She remembered when she was little, lying in bed listening to the corncrakes back home. No other sound was quite like it, and although she knew that such a creature had probably never existed out here in living memory she half believed in miracles for a moment.

'The heart of the heart of the country,' murmured Sonny, as if he could read her mind. 'We may not be so very far away after all, old girl.'

But even though she knew exactly what he meant, something made her nervous of going all the way down that particular road with him.

'Now listen to me, *old boy*,' she said. 'I don't know about you, but I suggest we hit the road.' No longer any question about it, she was beginning now to sound just as western as he did.

On the drive to their mystery destination – 'Our date with destiny' as Sonny now referred to it – because he was in buoyant mood he hummed, joked and, of course, sang, while she allowed the air from the open window to play about her bare arms and face. What he was saying slid past and over her like the passage of the night air.

'Once I heard this man say, "Sure, I shaved Stevie Wonder," to this other bloke. The two of them got off the bus together at that point – it *was* on a bus – and I didn't hear any more. Yet, it always stayed with me, that, I don't know why. Certain things do. "Sure, I shaved Stevie Wonder." Are you like that?'

She smiled, wondering how long she could manage this without speaking.

He said, 'He may have been his regular barber, yet I have to admit he didn't look like it, a little old cockney with a drip at his nose, a cloth cap and one of those long, white, silk scarves. They all had them once. Funny that, because your toffs went in for them, as well. Still do. Night out at Covent Garden or the Albert Hall? Weird old country, this. Weird, man, undoubtedly weird.'

The Dragon And Vulture, *not* The George And Vulture, like its name, didn't look quite right, somehow. From the outside it appeared more like an assemblage of disused farm buildings than the country pub they were expecting, as far removed from that perfect specimen of the breed they'd stopped at earlier as both of them could imagine. A rusty flap appended to the main sign did say PETS, PINTS, PUTTING, but that was either a joke or a short-lived mistake on someone's part.

Piles of far-gone rustic implements littered the open spaces about the collection of low structures. Hazel recognised several of the tools that farmers still worked with back home which, over here, were revered as folk objects. They drove carefully past an up-ended cart, a tangle of ancient harness, tepees of forks, flails and broken rakes, assorted churns, barrels and buckets. On the remains of a threshing machine someone had painted CAR PARK THIS 'A WAY complete with arrow and, underneath, in denser script, AT OWNERS RISK OF THEFT, DAMAGE OR ACTS OF GOD. Sonny looked at Hazel and she smiled back at him as if determined on reserving judgement.

'Bloody hell,' he said, a moment later, as they turned into a large field filled with cars and vans, even one or two lorries and tractors. Without exception, all looked candidates for the breaker's yard, but they did have tax discs, so must have driven here on the public road.

'Remember what we were talking about earlier? Dog-patch? I think we've just found it.'

'Thought you loved that sort of thing, Sonny.'

'Sure, I do, but who *are* these people? I mean, what must they *look* like?'

Laughing at his worried expression, she climbed down on to the baked ground. A smell of barbecuing hung in the air and a far-off, muffled bass beat came throbbing from the direction of the main buildings.

'Listen,' she said. ' "Wild Side Of Life"?'

'No,' he said. ' "Ring Of Fire".'

'Clever old you,' she said and meant it, too.

'Before we go in . . .' Sonny hesitated.

He really is nervous, she thought, look at him quaking like a great child, all dressed up in his party clothes. Taking his hand, it seemed the proper thing to do in the circumstances, she murmured, 'Big, deep breath now.'

The unseen band finished its set, and they heard a round of applause breaking distantly.

'Great crowd,' she said brightly.

167

'Hazel ...' He was glancing about him at the ranks of clapped-out vehicles. Quite a number, she noticed, had CB aerials, a proportion of which sported fake fur tails. They dangled in the still air, possibly like their owners' equipment after a night out in this place, Hazel couldn't help thinking, a little maliciously. 'What if ...?'

'What if what, Sonny?'

He was beginning to sound like someone living up to his own name. 'Well, I mean, it may be okay to dress the way we are, back in London, but down here ... what do you think? In the sticks?'

'Don't be crazy,' she insisted. 'What did that paper say? Go on, tell me. Tell me.'

'Hitch Up And Hike Down To The Dragon And Vulture For The Best In Country Sounds East Of Nashville.' He coughed with embarrassment.

'Well, then, what's worrying you? Let's go in and enjoy ourselves.'

He still looked only half convinced.

They made their way through the cars towards the lights and the sound of music which had started up again. Someone was singing, a young girl, high, nasal, mournful – 'There Goes My Everything', not one of Hazel's all-time favourites.

'Wait until they hear a *real* singer, eh?' said Sonny.

She squeezed his arm, savouring the reassuring bulge of biceps under his shirt sleeve. It had been a long time since she'd had a proper man to walk by her side. The feeling was a good one and already that other almost-forgotten, old quickening inside, an anticipation and confidence in her own attractiveness, had also started its slow upward rise.

'Kiss me,' she commanded, pulling him gently but firmly towards the opening of a dark shed. Docile, he complied, and as they moved into their clinch she saw over his shoulder in the shadows the great white American car they'd almost collided with in Glastonbury. She recognised the unusual number plate, but, also, the set of animal horns crowning the radiator grille. On fat, white-walled tyres the thing crouched there in the gloom, as if watching them. Something about its bulk seemed threatening, she didn't quite know why and, realising that Sonny hadn't spotted it, she manoeuvred him back out of the archway and on to the cobbles of the yard.

'Look at that,' she said, indicating a wooden and metal object, making doubly sure of his distraction. 'Isn't that an old butter churn?' Not that there was anything intrinsically fascinating, as far as she was concerned, about old farming relics. Her own virginity might have been taken in a hay shed but that was no reason to get nostalgic, was it? Yet, she still couldn't help enquiring casually, as if it was an irrelevance, 'Tell me, where did *you* do it for the first time, Sonny?'

'*It?*'

'*It*. You know.'

He'd stopped and was gazing up into the blue blackness. Stars were out, millions of them, a fact she would never have taken note of back in the city, even if they had been visible. 'In an air raid shelter. With a townie cousin of mine. Big girl called Rachel McConkey. Wore a hat on Sundays and sang in a church choir, but that didn't stop her. I remember she sucked a peppermint all through it.'

He stopped there, which seemed a shame, for she loved it when he talked that way, the words coming out in short, reflective instalments. She would much rather be lying in the dark cosiness of the camper right now listening to another chapter of the Sonny Dunbar life story than out here. There was something more than a touch ridiculous about the situation, standing dressed up like this in such an odd neck of the woods, preparing to go into what looked like a barn full of hicks and country weirdos.

The last part she only suspected, but a moment later it appeared that her instincts hadn't let her down. The man at the door – he was sitting just inside at a small table which was bare except for a brace of pearl-handled revolvers (they had to be replicas, Hazel thought) – said, 'Welcome, strangers. Travelled far?'

He wore the full western regalia, hat, plaid shirt, bandanna and a sheriff's star pinned to his chest. His age might

169

have been fiftyish, perhaps more, and his demeanour was as serious as a bank manager's, if it hadn't been for the outfit he was wearing.

Sonny said, 'Just about as far as you can get. All the way across the Great Pond.' He made an illustrative flying gesture in the air with his right hand. 'This is Hazel, and my handle happens to be Sonny. You may have heard of us? Sonny and Hazel?'

The man studied them for a moment. 'Sonny and Hazel. Hazel and Sonny. Does have a familiar ring to it, I have to say. But then, I'm no expert, I just take care of the law side of things around these parts.'

Sonny smiled back at him, a respectful, honest-Injun sort of smile. 'You'll get no trouble from this good lady and yours truly. Singing is the only thing we know. Isn't that so, honey?'

Hazel looked at him. Behind his wide smile, far back in the eyes, was a beseeching look that said, *don't fail me, please, not now.* Playing her part, she replied demurely, 'That's no word of a lie, sweetheart.'

The make-believe law-man, evidently satisfied as to their credentials, pointed to a door at the end of the short passage. They could hear the slurred whine of a steel guitar and a rumble of crowd noise beyond its wood panel. 'Have a good time, now, folks. And welcome to the Mendips Mescaleros Country Music Club.' Very adroitly he stamped both of them on the wrists with a little rubber die.

When they reached the far door Hazel looked back. The man at the table sat there composed, business-like, staring straight ahead. There was something the matter with one of his legs – the right – she noticed. The boot looked thickened; it was also reinforced with a steel calliper. Sometimes she worried herself, she really did, she was forever finding defects in things and people.

Sonny whispered, 'Didn't I tell you it would be easy?' squeezing her hand and as she glanced at him in disbelief, recalling his panic outside earlier, he pushed on the door, and the heat, smoke and noise met them head on.

They had entered a high-ceilinged barn of a place, fitted

out with tables, bentwood chairs, a long curving bar, and on a small stage, a combo – four men and a girl vocalist – well into 'Please Help Me I'm Falling'. Some further attempt at authenticity had also been intended, for there was a gallery with balustrading, inviting fight scenes, as was the suspended wagon wheel converted to electricity, and the several ornate mirrors behind the bar advertising Jack Daniels, Old Crow and other lesser-known brands of bourbon. As for the customers, they too looked as though they had come straight from a small-budget western's casting department. Hazel had always suspected the English, as a race, to be unhealthily obsessed with dressing up – their mainland after all was bursting with Morris dancers, *Doctor Who* fanatics, English Civil War Societies, not to mention all the countless undercover transvestites, as well as the amateur dramatic and operatic companies – but fetishism on such a single-minded scale as this made her feel distinctly nervous.

Sonny, on the other hand, seemed to be in his seventh heaven. He kept glancing about him with delighted approval. Steering her towards an empty table close to the band he embarrassed her by joining in loudly with the singer's final chorus.

Hazel didn't care to admit it to herself but things did look as if she might be stuck with the singing, bar-room drunk for the evening. Looking about her she was easily able to pick out most of the other cameo parts on display. There were several gamblers, dressed in undertaker black, assorted cowpunchers and miners, greenhorns, farmhands, quite a few gunslingers and, on the feminine side, a regular bevy of dance-hall girls, rouged, painted and mascara'd to the nines. Subtle variations were also present, like the lonely men along the bar staring down into their beer, hunched and preparing to be even more miserable as the night wore on, the ones who always requested songs about divorce. She couldn't quite be certain whether these were merely playing parts or not; they could so easily have been for real.

Sonny said, slapping his thigh, 'Are we in hillbilly heaven, or am I dreaming? Wake me if I am.'

171

She smiled back at him, which was sufficient, for she knew that he expected no answer, the mood he was in. For the first time she wasn't totally certain if she could rely on him as she had done up to now.

'Bring the good lady and myself two large whiskeys. And keep the change, honey.' Sonny laid a hand on the young waitress's bare arm. Naturally she had to be half undressed in keeping with the standards of the place, skimpy bodice, short, black satin skirt, fishnets, stiletto-heeled patent shoes. Hazel, with her incurably beady eye, also noted she had a tattooed butterfly on her right shoulder and hadn't shaved her armpits. Her hair, too, had streaks of green and orange as if she had walked under a painter's ladder. These were details which somehow were reassuring in their ordinariness, compared with the detailed perfection Hazel could see all about her.

Sonny seemed reluctant to let the waitress go. 'Weren't you that girl back in Glastonbury – in the coffee-shop? You served us this afternoon.'

The young, rural punkette shook her chemically damaged locks. 'You're mistaken, sir. I be from Frome way.'

She went off through the tables with her tray under her arm. It might well have been a school satchel the way she carried it and those fledgling legs of hers, too, barely able to fill out the contours of her stockings. Hazel couldn't help herself: she was thinking of Natalie again.

'I could have sworn she was that other kid,' brooded Sonny.

'They all look the same at her age. At *our* age,' she said. 'Don't let it bother you.'

'It doesn't. I don't. Oh, hell, let's drink up.' That glitter was back in his eyes again.

She said, 'Excuse me, I have to head for the ladies' room – or should that be the cowgirls'?'

He threw back his head, laughing excessively. Several people glanced across at the sound as she picked her way between the tables heading for the door that said TOILETS. She sensed eyes evaluating every detail of her walk. It was

172

like being back in time at one of those dire, backwoods dances everyone used to go to, mainly to sharpen their considerable talents for small-mindedness. Now, she said to herself, *they can't harm you, Hazel Kinney*, as she'd done then; *they can't touch you for not looking the way they do*. But by the time she'd reached the distant door and gone through, her skin felt hot and tightly stretched.

The mirror neither confirmed nor denied the sensation. She was all alone in there – it was a normal ladies' room, scented, pink, white – and so took her time renewing her make-up. The pulse in her throat went back to normal; the natural flush in her cheeks was artificially restored. It was a moment to be savoured, as always, but then one of the dance-hall girls arrived, moving in determined fashion towards the nearest cubicle, locking herself in with a single, angry bang of the bolt.

Hazel gathered up her stuff and prepared to leave. She heard the woman behind the door address herself to its painted surface.

'See if I care, Derek – high and mighty – Foster, just see if I care, you great Dorset pudden.' Then she began sobbing and Hazel thought, what would any of us do if we hadn't got a ladies' room to retreat to?

There was a pay-phone outside – even cowpokes, she supposed, had to dial taxis when they were too pissed to drive – but it was hidden away in a very dark corner. She wondered whether there might also be one of those Durex machines somewhere about the place as well: Buy One And Stop One. She looked at the telephone in its perforated, metal cowl. It did seem singularly untouched by vandals. Tomorrow, she thought, I'll ring tomorrow. Tomorrow, definitely . . .

The band was playing 'Orange Blossom Special' when she got back, the crowd urging the solo guitar on faster and faster with whoops, yells and boot stamping. The young player – he had thinning blond hair, sideburns and a pitted complexion – didn't look as if he was up to it. Crescents of sweat showed under his arms and his eyes were closed more in prayer, it seemed to Hazel, than inspiration. She just

173

stood inside the door a little way waiting for the insanity to run its course. Even the lonely ones at the bar had swung about on their stools and were howling in unison. She could see Sonny at the table, head thrown back, hollering with the best of them. He looked as much a part of the place and its citizenry as anyone there.

It was the nature of the enthusiasm she couldn't go along with. That sort of thing, and on such a scale, tended to make her uneasy. Just one, give me just one fed-up face, one cynic, she told herself, otherwise I'm really out on my own here among the zombies. Her own date seemed to be included in that.

And then she got what she asked for. Sitting with his back to a pillar, out of the way of things, flanked by a couple of equally unimpressed customers, was a man dressed in what looked like a black frock-coat. And that seemed to be the only concession he had bothered to make to the place, for it was open at the neck revealing an ordinary, yellow T-shirt. He also wore a baseball type hat with braid on the brim. He looked familiar, somehow, as did the thick and silvery mane falling almost to his shoulders. The last time she had seen hair like that, it had been fashioned into a healthy plait. For, indeed, it was the man in the big white American car, the one they had nearly collided with earlier that day, the one she'd also seen in the darkness of the shed outside.

Something of that same forbidding quality she felt she'd detected there in that great, crouching bulk on four white-walled tyres appeared also to find an echo in its owner. Even in the uncertain light it was obvious he had the torso and upper arms of a body-builder. Coats like the one he was wearing, she knew, had to be specially tailored to cope with such measurements, or else came from High And Mighty. The nickname seemed apt, even though she hadn't yet seen him on his feet.

But, then, as she watched the man and his two companions – a couple of hired hands, nothing more; either of them might well have been the one behind the wheel of the car – another name came into her head. Raymond Burr,

174

she thought. He's taken on the Raymond Burr part. For, if you forgot the T-shirt and the baseball hat with the gold, all the other attributes seemed in place. She wasn't close enough to double-check on the eyes but she did vaguely remember the way they had stared at her earlier, heavy, hooded, an out-and-out baddy's eyes. *Oh, Hazel, Hazel, get a grip on yourself, girl, the man's nothing more than some backwoods poser indulging himself, no different from any of this lot around here. Can't you see that?* But she couldn't, not completely, not a hundred per cent.

She went back to the table; it was on the far side of the room from where the big man held court. She felt certain Sonny hadn't seen him yet.

'Well, well, *well*,' Sonny greeted her. 'Have I got news for you?' His thumbs were hooked in his armpits and his chair tilted back at an angle. 'They're putting us on after the interval. Visiting celebrities. Recording stars in our own right.'

'*Celebrities? Recording stars?* Oh, Sonny,' she moaned.

He came forward on his chair putting his hands over hers. 'I told them we cut a disc in Nashville. Small company, of course. An independent. Johnny Cash said he liked it a lot. Oh, don't worry. Have you heard *this* mob? Call themselves The Prairie Dogs. For Christ's sake, they're awful! There's another group on the bill, The Denver Boot Band. They're bound to be just as dire. Don't worry.'

He squeezed her fists together and she sat there trapped by his certainty. He looked a lot more youthful suddenly than she remembered. They've cast me opposite the spoilt, young whippersnapper son in the picture, she thought, the one with his head stuffed full of impossible, even dangerous schemes. But if this is Robert Wagner grinning at me now across this table, where does that leave me?

Certainly she didn't relish running foul of one of the dance-hall girls, as the Ann Blyth character always seemed to do. Little Miss Wholesome getting socked one or going over backwards into a convenient horse-trough ...

'Some joker called Pilgrim seems to be the boss around here. Everything has to get his say so. So they asked him

175

and – geronimo – we're on. Just like that.'

He waved a hand and made instant eye contact with the waitress. Two fingers, Hazel presumed, meant the same again.

She took a swallow from the almost full glass in front of her. 'This Pilgrim,' she suggested tentatively. 'Is he around?'

'So they say. Likes to lie low, was the impression.'

'Yes,' she murmured, for it was as though she were able to foretell events which were about to overtake them. They'd lived a charmed life up to now, the two of them, in their travelling Wendy House. She wanted to say to him, *let's get out of here, please, Sonny, right now. Look at these people. They're not our sort of people, we don't need them, we don't need anyone, come to think of it, especially a collection of losers like this bunch. Sonny, the two of us, we spent our lives trying to keep ahead of the losers, because they always pull you down and back to their own speed and level. We both know that, we do, don't we?* Her internal eloquence knew no bounds but that was where it stayed, locked up inside, as she continued sipping her drink. Less than twenty-four hours ago, less even than that, she could have said all of it, but now she couldn't, just as she was unable to tell him she'd always hated the taste of whiskey.

With all the inevitability that she'd dreaded she heard him say, 'Hold everything until I go and get the guitar. They said I could plug it into their amp and speakers. We'll wipe the floor with them, you'll see. Wait and see,' and he was off weaving through the tables and already smiling all about him that way she'd often seen celebrities do, attuned and expectant as they are to recognition.

Wait and see, she thought. There didn't seem to be any alternative, so she sat there on her own doing just that. The excited atmosphere that had come to a head during 'Orange Blossom Special' had died down and an air of depressed inactivity seemed to have taken its place. The solitary drinkers at the bar had once more turned their backs on the world, while most of the supporting cast about the room looked as though they had forgotten not only their lines, but their place in the script, as well.

Just as she'd noted the disfiguring callipers on the doorman's leg earlier, now she registered something else, the fact that there were very few young people present; the average age seemed to be around her own, or a little over. Whether that was a comforting thought, she couldn't quite make up her mind. That no one, as yet, had given her the eye – something she expected only as a formality – she put down to a serious blood-cell deficiency in the men present, even though most of those were dressed as John Wayne look-a-likes. But, then, she couldn't help being a little cynical about that sort of thing. Young Christine K. who, despite her waif-like looks, had known more about men than anyone she'd ever met, always said it was the slightly effeminate ones who were the real experts in bed. She and Mandy would have had hysterics at this lot, Hazel told herself. *Oh, where are you now, girls, where are you now?*

Sonny said, 'I'm here,' and she couldn't help laughing. But Sonny was so preoccupied with imminent stardom that he didn't even notice. He positioned the guitar in its green, padded plastic cover on a free chair beside his own as lovingly as if it were some swaddled infant, then he looked at his watch.

'Around about ten-thirty, the guy said. When we're on. Exciting stuff, eh?' He was giving off a renewed blast of aftershave, overlaid with something minty like mouthwash.

Across the room something was taking place, something that seemed to be mildly exciting people. Ripples of interest were spreading from a couple of men, younger than most, who seemed to be arm-wrestling. They had long greasy hair bound about their brows, Indian fashion, heavy moustaches, and they looked more like bikers or minor Hell's Angels with their leather waistcoats next to naked, tattooed flesh than true western devotees. Hazel couldn't help wondering whether Raymond Burr approved of this sort of thing or not.

Sonny said, 'So, it's "Heartaches By The Number", "Me And Bobby McGee", "My Arms Stay Open Late" – that's yours – then I'll do my tribute to Hank Williams, and for an encore I thought we'd give them "Rose Garden". I've got it all down here,' and he showed her the back of an envelope. His handwriting was as neat and tiny as any girl's, Hazel noticed.

'I could always tape it to the back of the guitar, but it isn't hard to remember, is it?' And he went through the list again, tapping off each title on the pale lilac paper. The colour, like the penmanship, didn't fit with the picture she'd built up in her head of him. Poor Sonny, she found herself thinking, you and I may well have reached that fork in the road where the good things start coming to an end.

The sentiment was a deeply cynical one, far too hard-edged, it struck her, to find its way into any of those songs she was shortly to perform. '*My arms stay open late, so you'll come home.*' Only a man could have written that. She saw him clearly, someone fat, balding, perpetually tanned, perhaps a little fringe of beard and lots of Indian jewellery – those bluish stones. Semi-reclining beside a pool, wrestling with his muse, while girls in bikinis and high heels brought him refreshing drinks and the phone, on a tray. He was called Burt or Lou or Sol ...

The arm-wrestlers – they were laughing uproariously and seemed to be the only people in the place seriously enjoying themselves – had now opposition at the next table from two women. This couple, butch and denim-clad, a blonde and a chalk-faced brunette, were locked in stalemate, forearms intertwined. It seemed to be a much more serious affair with the two of them, and Hazel didn't want to see the outcome.

'Don't start without me,' she said, rising suddenly, and Sonny smiled up at her abstractedly. He was carefully tearing the edges of his envelope all around as if he'd changed his mind about taping it to the curve of his guitar.

Once more she took her way towards the dim, bluish sign over the far curtained doorway, but although she felt drawn in the direction of the man in the baseball hat she held to a detour. The barest glance from those eyes, she had convinced herself, would be able to pierce her to the quick.

At the restaurant where she worked back in London, a man, a regular, had the same ability to make her feel undressed whenever he looked up at her from his plate. The same table was reserved for him on a thrice-weekly basis. It directly faced her cashier's box, where she worked the register behind glass, and she could find no protection from the man's stare. It was quite obvious to her what his secret intentions towards her were, but he never made the slightest move in that direction, even at the end of the meal when he rose to present his bill. He was around her own age, always beautifully turned out, and he had an unusual silver snake ring on the little finger of his left hand. Both his hands trembled slightly whenever he paid – by cash, and almost always the same amount. Main course, sweet, coffee, half carafe of house wine – the meal rarely varied. Aldo seemed to know more about him than anyone else in the place but she was careful never to mention the subject.

In her little black number and single strand of pearls she sat on her stool punching the keys of the old Sweda, looking out over the lowered heads of the diners. That was her place and she knew it and she'd kept it that way without change or threat all those years. Yet, a matter of mere days ago – she'd lost track of how many – hadn't she decided to break with all of that and take to the road like some green-as-grass teenager? For what? Romance on the run? It sounded like one of those songs she'd been listening to non-stop. She wondered whether they did, after all, have an effect akin to softening of the brain.

At the curtained doorway she took a quick backward look around the place. If any proof were needed as to what a strict diet of country and western could do to you, it had to be out there at all those tables, she told herself. Then she pulled back the heavy dark folds – they smelled of cigarette smoke and cheap scent – and found herself once more in the badly lighted corridor leading to the toilets. There, she headed for the phone-booth and, piling up her coins on the metal in readiness, she dialled home. Some sort of irrational urge must have made her try her own number first, even though she knew no one could, or would, be there. Perhaps she needed the idea of throwing out a line first, without hope of connection, just to prepare for the real thing, a call to the council flat in Ealing where Eric would be sprawled in front of the television.

She looked at her watch – the John Player snooker would still be running – and was about to cut off the call when the receiver was lifted and, stunned, she pushed in her money, and a young male voice in her own living-room enquired in bored tones, 'Yeah? Who is it?'

She said, 'Could I speak to Natalie, please?' trying to keep the panic out of her voice.

There was some sort of thump-thump music reverberating in the background and laughter as well, but she held her worst fears in abeyance until she had spoken to their main cause.

Then the voice on the other end said, with a certain politeness, 'Hold on, I'll just get her,' and the noise in her home became suddenly amplified as if in mockery of her state. The singer on the record was now screaming what sounded like '*annihilation*', or it might have been '*violation*', over and over again.

Hazel stared at the mesh of sound-proofing a foot away from her face, glad there was no mirror to reflect the true state of her feelings. But what *were* her feelings? Their real impact would only strike in the instant she put the receiver down. She was as certain of that as she was certain of the fact that the moment of her reckoning had at last arrived. Her chickens had finally come home to roost. *Oh, Hazel, Hazel, why, why have you been such a bad mother to your only child?*

'Hello,' said a voice but, although young and female, it wasn't her daughter's voice. 'Natalie isn't here at the moment. She's gone for some takeaway. Is there a message?'

'No, I'll call back later,' was her feeble response and she returned the receiver to its cradle. Then she made her way back to the ladies' room and, like that other desperate woman earlier, locked herself in one of the scented cubicles. But weeping wasn't for her. The situation seemed much too hopeless to be resolved or even reduced in any way by something so simple. Instead, she sat there peeing – she

180

hadn't realised she needed to go, yet it was amazing how long it lasted – and, after wiping herself, went through the suddenly very complicated ritual of dressing the lower part of her body. How long would she be able to keep this going, she wondered.

At the mirror she found she couldn't draw a lipstick across her mouth in a matching line. *I know what you look like*, she mouthed to herself in the peach-tinted glass. *Pissed*. She wasn't, of course, despite the considerable intake, for she had the impression she'd kept pace with Sonny, and Scotch, at that, for Christ's sake! But who was counting? As far as she was concerned, the only course open to her, it seemed, was to proceed steadily in the same direction. Nothing could be done until morning. Nothing. If she kept repeating that to herself, while dulling her senses, she might just be able to keep her terrors in check until she was in a position to do something about them. Which, in brutal terms, meant catching the first train or bus back home.

She put away her make-up in her bag and, wiping off an errant streak of lipstick, prepared to go back inside again to an unsuspecting Sonny. As she was leaving, two Dolly Parton look-alikes came breasting past her and she heard one of them say to her clone, 'Don't thee take the piss out of I. Had he any call to talk to me that way? Had he? You were there, you heard him, Jeanine, so don't defend him, not if you value our friendship.'

But Jeanine was heading for the nearest basin and as the door closed on the two, the unmistakable sound of a female puking, in that curiously inhibited way, reached Hazel on her re-entry to hillbilly hell.

'A Legend in My Time'

Sonny sat wondering what the great Hank would have done in this situation. For the truth of the matter was he had now the deepest, most terrifying misgivings about what he had let himself in for.

The answer to his question, of course, lay there on the table in front of him, for, taking advantage of Hazel's absence he had set up another double round. He looked at the still-life of water jug and glasses arranged on the wet wood before him. The most amazing precision and artistry, it seemed to him, had to have gone into such a grouping. Like a snowflake, he thought, that same one-off perfection, a snowflake, or one of those random patterns formed at the shake of a kaleidoscope. He'd forgotten he used to have such a gadget when he was younger. It did seem a sophisticated sort of plaything for a kid growing up in the Ulster back-woods to own. So where the fuck did that come from? His mother's side of the family. Had to be. The Dunbar connection wouldn't know a kaleidoscope from a kazoo – or a kangaroo.

For the ninth or tenth time he took out his oblong of paper and scanned the titles he had carefully written there, but no help was to be found in that quarter. The list still looked like jottings in some esoteric language. Sanskrit? Swahili? Serbo-Croat? He groaned loudly at the way his brain seemed to be functioning, then he took another sub-stantial drink. *Hank, Hank, was it like this for you, too? Another country boy awaiting his turn to be found out?* The biography on his hero was a slim one, but it was all there in the songs. Forget the booze, the painkillers, the bad marriage, the lack of serious management, the acclaim which never seemed quite real or lasting enough – the true anguish was in the songs, always the songs.

182

No matter how I try to survive,
I'll never get out of this world alive....

Too paralysed to interfere in any way now with the grouping on the table before him he sat hunched there, glass in hand, a solitary and pathetic figure, for that was how he saw himself. Then someone, obviously with no feelings for art, took the matter out of his hands by slapping down an almost full tankard of pale beer and froth in the middle of the composition.

'Hi, there, I'm Hoss. Tanktop over there tells me you want to plug into our amp. Our pleasure. Shake.'

A beefy paw grabbed Sonny's free hand, pumping it energetically. Below the knuckles, in faded indigo print Sonny could make out the word LOVE. He didn't have to be told what was spelled out across the other fist. Perhaps he was left-handed, this Hoss character, because surely HATE had to be the more appropriate of the matching sentiments, the last word to reflect upon before its tattooed message exploded in your face and you woke up in Casualty. But, for the moment, at least, this arm-wrestling bear exuded nothing but good will.

'Tell me, man, did you ever work with Dottie West? That woman gives me goose-pimples, I tell you. I have a video of her in concert and it's nearly played bare. I'd drink a pint of that woman's piss, straight up, I would,' and Sonny watched in a mixture of fascination and horror as he put the beer mug to his bearded lips and downed half the frothy mixture.

'Dottie?' he heard himself croak. 'Only once. I mean, I caught her act down in Florida. She's never off the road. Has her own show.'

The big man in the leather waistcoat covered with badges growled, 'Let anyone say one word against that woman's sweet voice and I'll fucking well pulverise them. I've all her albums. Even the ones she did with that cunt Kenny Rogers.'

Sonny said, 'She's greatly admired in the business, I'll tell you that. There's talk of a film. Jane Fonda, I believe.'
Careful, Sonny, don't press your luck.

The man called Hoss stared at him out of bloodshot eyes. He groaned. 'I suppose we'll have to wait another two, three, fucking years before we even see it over here. You don't know what it's like, man, in this neck of the woods. Fucking Pitsville.'

Sonny smiled understandingly. 'We're all good old country boys at heart, that's what's important. Roots, my friend, roots.' Settled back on the rear legs of his chair, he began picking his teeth with a spent match. 'Tell me, what sort of music do you and your friends over there go in for, friend?'

He could see the three of them on the far side of the room. An even greater space seemed to have been cleared for them and their antics. Tanktop, it would appear, was now pouring beer into the cleavage of one of the girls in the group – the brunette – in a steady, sustained stream. He looked rapt, as did both girls, as if it was part of some serious scientific experiment, or perhaps a cookery demonstration of some kind. Take one pint of lager and one motor-cycle slut. . . .

'Rock-a-billy, mostly, with some truckin' numbers thrown in. Tanktop does a terrific version of "Convoy". Everybody's still fucking CB crazy down here. You got a call-sign yourself, Sonny?'

Sonny looked at him. 'To tell you the truth, Hoss,' he said in his most mellifluous, elder statesman's voice, 'as far as most of the people I do business with are concerned, CB is yesterday's news. We all had them a few years back, I grant you. But the beat does move on. Car-phones, yes, but not CB. Nein. Niet. Not any more. Different beat, different drummer. But I guess that's the name of the game back in the li'l ole US of A.'

Again he felt he might well be tempting fate a little, but this big gorilla opposite appeared to be an eager acolyte. He sighed now and Sonny watched fascinated as the mat of chest hair facing him rippled as if activated by some seismic force.

'Nobody appreciates a fucking thing you ever do in this country, I tell you, man. Fans? Forget it. Bet you've got a lot of fans, though. I can tell you do. 'Course, as a group, we're still only semi-pro. The Tank and me, we work in a Kwik-Fit in Swindon. He does suspensions, I'm the exhaust king. I mean, look at these hands, man, then take a look at your own.' He certainly had a point, but then any hand had to appear lilywhite and decadent alongside such a brutalised specimen.

'Anyway' – another sigh and again the hairy pelt convulsed – 'we'll be on soon and then it's your own good self and your good lady.' He rose swaying slightly. A look of definite affection was directed towards Sonny, who grinned back. It came to him for the first time that this man was a great deal more drunk than he was.

'Vaya con Dios,' he heard himself say. 'May the bird of paradise fly up your nose.'

The giant with the tattoos smiled at that, then his expression changed. 'Listen,' he said, leaning closer. Sonny's face was suddenly three inches away from the matted chest of a King Kong who dismembered cars for a living with his bare hands. I'm for it now, he couldn't help thinking, now I pay for being a smart-arse. But the man called Hoss had only the sweetest of intentions, it seemed. 'There's someone who wants to meet you very much,' he said. 'A real fan.'

Sonny smiled his modest celebrity smile, the one that takes years of practice to get just right. 'Why not? Is he around?'

The big man laughed. 'Oh, he's around all right. Just *owns* the fucking place, that's all.' Then, still laughing, he grabbed Sonny's wrist, turning it over on the beer-ringed table. Laying his own mighty forearm alongside, he indicated identical violet markings on their skin. Sonny remembered the man at the door with his little junior stamp outfit. 'Has his brand on every fucking thing. See. Pilgrim. That's his name,' and sure enough the initial P stood out clearly against the pale flesh. 'But a really great bloke. Throws terrific parties, too. One tonight, after the show. You're invited. All the booze you can get down you. Not to mention wall-to-wall nooky.'

Unable to help himself, Sonny enquired innocently,

'Nooky? Is that one of your quaint old English expressions?'

The swaying king of the exhausts said, 'You'll know it when it comes up to you and bites you in the leg.' And, suddenly leering, he struck Sonny what was meant to be a playful pat on the shoulder.

Sonny smiled back, wincing in spite of himself.

'You're on after we do "Chantilly Lace". Remember that. Then the Tank will plug you in. Man, this is going to be one night to remember, I can feel it, and afterwards we'll all get stoned out of our mother-fucking minds.' He put two enormous fingers to his lips, inhaling, then crossing his eyes in a parody of ecstasy. Not a pretty sight. 'You indulge yourself, Sonny.'

Now, this was tricky. Sonny's natural instinct was to welcome any such proposal; he'd never before, on principle, ever refused the opportunity of getting high from any source. But, and it was a very big but, he did have a certain image to sustain. That old outlaw style was now very much a thing of the past. Wrecking hotel bedrooms in a haze of drink and drugs was deeply unfashionable. These days your average country star was more likely to be caught under the covers with a Gideon Bible than a bottle and a bird.

So, taking a deep breath and chancing his arm, Sonny said, 'Who am I to throw the first stone, friend? Or be the first to get stoned, for that matter?'

It sounded good, if a little enigmatic, but the big man did seem to buy it. Slapping his tree trunk of a thigh, he laughed uproariously. 'I gotta tell that to the Tank, man, I really do. Ace, man. Fucking ace,' and he went lurching off back through the tables, still roaring.

Hazel came back shortly after that in a scented haze and he greeted her with, 'Guess what? We're invited to a party.'

She looked at him and it seemed to him she'd never appeared more stunning, like some great, freshly painted and powdered craft. Images of water and flotation, for some reason, crept into mind, a swan, a figurehead, Cleopatra's barge at full stretch. The finest looking creature in the whole damn place was by his side at his table and no one else's.

'Seems we're to be the guests of honour, too. What do you think about that, eh?'

'They haven't heard us sing yet.'

'Oh, Christ, Hazel, why do you have to say things like that?'

'We must talk, Sonny,' she said. 'Really.'

Why couldn't she take things one step at a time the way he was doing? It was like getting to the top of an impossibly high peak, wasn't it, but only impossible if you looked up or down. Then when you got there you said, did I do that?

Leaning across the table, he gave her hand a squeeze. It felt cold to the touch. 'Hey,' he said, 'hey, we're on our holidays, kiddo. Remember?' Then, taking a gamble, he added, 'We can walk out of here any old time we want to. Nobody owes nobody nothing, and you remember that. We're as free as the air. Now, listen, listen ... I've given this a lot of thought. The way I see it is this. You and me, we're never going to fit in over here, let's face it, I mean, *really* fit in. At the same time, we won't be going back over there, either, 'cause it seems to me the two of us didn't exactly hit it off too well in that place, either. Notice I didn't say "home", Hazel. Notice that. Because home is just a word, that's all it is. People like us, we carry it about with us wherever we go. Like a little old snail does, but not on our backs. To be more precise about it – here.' He patted himself in the breast area, while keeping his eyes on those other sweet pectorals just across from him. His hand reached out to take her hand. It felt much warmer already.

'Leaving all that aside, though, what are our options? Everybody has options. They do, you know. Let's just lay them out on the table, in a manner of speaking. One, you go under without trace, just another expat, tugging the forelock to the last. Or – you cause a ripple or two. Make a stir, a fuss, maybe even a name for yourself. Take the fight to *them*, Hazel, to *them*.'

There was a pause. The Clampettes, that's what they called themselves, Sonny had found out earlier, were now impatiently signalling for Hoss and Tank, the remaining complement of the Denver Boot Band, to join them on stage.

Hazel said, 'This is what this is all about, is it? Fighting back? Against this lot? The English?'

Sonny looked at her. 'It's a start,' he said. 'That's all I'm saying.'

'You're all mixed up inside, Sonny, and I can't help you.' Another icicle to the heart.

He grinned at her. 'That's me, all right. But only you and me know that. Okay?'

In spite of herself, she forced a little wintry smile. 'I've got to ring Natalie. I've already tried once, but I can't get through.'

So, that's what's bugging her, he thought, that young piece of jail bait in the school uniform. Natalie. He'd been trying to remember the name and now it had been provided for him he must hold on to it. Natalie? Natalie Wood? Right.

He said, 'After we've done our stuff here we'll find a phone and we'll give it top priority.'

'There's one here,' she said.

'Better still.' He had both her hands in his and every particle of sincerity he could muster was flowing across the table. *What an out and out cunt you're turning out to be, Sonny.*

Deep in the corner of his left breast pocket was a hard little pellet; he could feel it. It was the last remaining pill he had filched from Miriam's bedside cabinet. It went into his mouth, carefully with sleight of hand, washed down with watered Teachers.

Absent friends, he silently toasted, thinking of Miriam's face when she got back to the flat with her suntan and holiday snaps and souvenirs to discover what he'd done, that he'd gone and sold out the lease over her head. But, then, hadn't he only been living up to expectations? Sooner or later, in Miriam's book, he was bound to revert to that image she always cherished of him, treacherous, shiftless, like all his nationality.

For an instant he saw himself in a new light, the new Sonny, hard, avenging, ruthless, the one who did it to them, before they had a chance to do it to you. But he thought, who's kidding who? The truth is, whether you were fucked

188

up back there in the land of perpetual rain, or over here by living too long amongst this lot, the bottom line is you're still fucked up. Hazel recognises it – she just said so – so why can't you?

He was beginning to enjoy the dialogue running in his head. It was as if there were two of him in there. Could the pill be that quick off the mark? Yeah, he thought, that little old white baby *is* a sprinter, after all. I can feel it, I can surely feel it. Keep up the good work, friend, and help me make it through the night. . . .

After that things got a trifle blurred, with quite a few blanks in there as well. It was as though he were now astride something with a will of its own. Alternately he kept reining in this mettlesome steed, then allowing it its head. Whatever the outcome, he hoped Hazel would come along for the ride but, for the most part, he wasn't too perturbed by that. Certain trips are better made alone and he kept seeing himself at some little distance as though observing the progress of someone involved in a fascinating journey which for the moment, at least, hadn't yet revealed its true meaning or destination.

Hoss, Tank and the two tambourine-wielding backing singers were by this time heavily into their set. Sonny found it hard to judge whether they were any good or not, the amplification being so excessive. His sinuses were popping with the noise as he sat there, a half-smile on his face. His gaze he kept carefully fixed on a set of antlers someone had hung over the stage. A strip of tinsel fluttered there from one of the tines; it could have been there since the previous Christmas, or the one before that; earlier, even. It came to him that he'd stumbled across a very eerie place indeed, somewhere normal people didn't frequent, or even know about. He couldn't be certain whether he fitted in this place or not but, for the moment, at least, he felt he could live with it.

'Are you okay?'

It was Hazel, leaning across and looking concerned. She mouthed the words because of the noise and he smiled back at her for the same reason.

The wraparound din ceased suddenly and in the ensuing silence the voice of Hoss was announcing, 'And, now at this time, it's my privilege to introduce a couple of visiting celebrities to our own little western club. They're over here presently on vacation, I understand, but I'm sure we can persuade these good people to step up and oblige us with a selection of some of their hits. How about a strong country welcome for Sonny and Hazel, folks! *Sonny and Hazel!*'

The throb in Sonny's head from the music hadn't quite abated, his arteries seemed still to be carrying the rhythms of the number just completed. He wanted more than anything to continue to sit looking up at the animal horns growing out of the wall above the stage. Buffalo, buck, bison? He'd heard the announcement, of course, his own name as well, but any connection between himself and that message from the stage made no sense to him. He sat there feeling the drag of the chemicals in his system. They also spoke softly to him, telling him not to get involved, but to rely completely on their expertise to get him out of this situation; that's what they were there for, after all. But Hazel was leaning forward and he smiled at her across the table, the tally of their drinking covering its surface. Had the pair of them downed as much as that? It seemed as if they'd just got here.

'Sonny,' Hazel was saying. 'Sonny, it's time. Let's go.'

He felt confused. Now, why should she want to leave, he asked himself, when they had only just arrived? And wasn't there something else, something they had to do first? He knew whatever it was, it was important, but it evaded him, he couldn't put his finger on it.

Hazel spoke again. 'They're waiting. For us. To *sing*.'

He was filled with admiration at the simple economy and, yes, even beauty of her words, when click, his brain became unscrambled and he thought, *fuck, fuck, oh fuck*. Hazel was on her feet; he didn't know if he would be able to join her, for it felt as though his blood had been transfused and the wrong type, as chill and unresponsive to his needs as tap water, had replaced it. He wanted to weep at the

190

thought of all those loyal little compounds being drained away so brutally after such sterling service on his behalf. *You may really be a junkie, after all*, he was thinking as he pressed with his palms on the table edge, willing the rest of him to follow, because it was a fact, wasn't it, that your true addict could never bring himself to blame his own particular family of stimulants?

'Sonny, everybody's waiting!'

Why did she have to keep on badgering him in this way? Already he felt that tremendous revelation of a second ago starting to lose clarity, a cloudiness creeping in, eating away at its edges.

Then she hissed, 'Your sunglasses. Put on your sunglasses, Sonny.' And the great truth disappeared for ever.

He looked at her. 'Do as I say,' she ordered and, unhesitatingly, he did so. His world went sepia-coloured as she came around the table to take his arm. He could see she was smiling, but not for him any longer. That wide, white-toothed beam was strictly for the benefit of all those strangers sitting out there now, *waiting*, to use her word. But he felt no resentment. How could he? The woman was a genius. As he picked up his guitar case Sonny vowed if ever he got out of this alive he would most definitely be proposing marriage.

Hazel said, 'Smile, Sonny,' seemingly without moving her lips and he tried, he did try. They were now moving steadily up through the tables between faces which had darkened perceptibly. Sonny was looking at a tinted world even more bizarre than the one he'd encountered when he'd first arrived in the place. He felt Hazel's hand on his arm as if willing him not to stumble, but by the time they reached the stage his new-found personality had taken over. As he mounted the short run of steps leading to the stage he appeared to falter, but it was only a tiny grace note on his part to add credence to his performance.

The one called Tank – it wasn't hard to see why – came towards them trailing a line of dark flex. Sonny let the unzipped guitar case drop away to fall at his feet like the soft discarded skin from some greenish animal. Pretending

191

to ignore it, as well as everything else around him, he stood there waiting, as if on a chalk mark, head raised in slightly patrician fashion and tilted to one side. But he mustn't go too far with this, he was thinking; more Roy Orbison than Stevie Wonder, he reckoned, would be about right. . . .

'Let me plug you in, man,' he heard Tank whisper.

There was genuine deference in his tone and Sonny smiled in his direction, showing his teeth in the same way Hazel had done earlier. This could become quite addictive, he was deciding.

'Friends, it's a real privilege to be with you all here tonight enjoying this good country music.' *Was that his own voice beating back at him?* Miraculous as it seemed, it was; the chill touch of the microphone stem now in his grasp told him so. It also felt charged in some way like an electric snake. Tightening his grip against the prickle of static – it was surely nothing more than that – he murmured huskily, 'We'd like to kick off with an old song the great Ray Price made famous. I'm sure you all know it,' and trusting to blind luck he transferred his left hand to the neck of the guitar and with the right struck a preliminary chord. The distant amplifier wailed once like a banshee, but Tank was on his knees instantly, placating it before the echo had time to die.

'I never met Ray, never had that pleasure, but it's my great wish to do so, some day, some day soon . . .' At his side Hazel sighed deeply, unhappily. He was amazed to be able to hear it so clearly. But she still kept on smiling. Those teeth, he thought, my God, what terrible damage they could do to you. . . .

He struck another chord, C this time. The progression was C-C-C-G – or was that 'Me and Bobby McGee'? Fuck it, he thought, whatever it is, we're going to find out soon enough, and he ran through the sequence, the steel strings biting into the pads of his fingers. Once more he felt the tickle of current, or was that just his nerves?

Leaning close to the microphone, he intoned, 'Some wise man once said you can take the boy out of the country, but you can never take the country out of the boy.' This time

Hazel groaned loudly. 'Just a little thought for these difficult times, folks.'

What was he saying? What was he doing? Behind the Polaroids he closed tired eyes, stamped his right foot once, two, three, four times, sang, '*Heartache number one ...*' and knew no more....

Well, not quite. Much later, when he was trying to string together impressions into some sort of order, certain images remained with him, no more than flashes, but still fixed, nonetheless. He remembered sudden small frights; Hazel walking off between two of the numbers, but only to pick up a tambourine; the fearsome Tank – his shaved dome was covered with a tattooed spider web – watching him from the wings, with dawning suspicion, it seemed to him; someone at the back of the hall drunkenly guffawing, but then being quickly shushed. He also felt convinced he must be standing directly under those antlers, which were certain to be suspended from a single, trembling nail. And he had the impression he forgot the words half-way through one of the songs in the tribute to Hank Williams. But the details of such a memory as that were just too horrific to submit themselves to any clear recall.

Dear, dear Hank, towards the end they say you were too drunk, drugged, or both, to get through a performance. That terrible night in Toronto when the crowd was in the mood for a lynching and you turned out to be the target of their wrath? But then your career was almost over; yours truly hasn't even started yet....

Something else. As they were taking their applause – it did appear to be heartfelt and Tank, he noted, was joining in – Hazel said, 'Oh Sonny, Sonny, what are we doing here?' without moving her lips.

Smiling straight ahead into the gale of handclaps and boot-stamping, he replied, 'It's only a start. We need more rehearsal time,' surprised to discover in himself a similar talent for ventriloquism.

Then they were coming off stage and down the steps – were there two, or was it three of those? For he wasn't playing a part any more, he was genuinely blinded after the dazzle of light trained on them. A hand reached up out of the shadows, taking his arm in a giant's grip. It was Hoss looking serious.

'Terrific,' he said. 'Terrific,' but it was impossible to tell whether the words meant good news or bad, for they came out as if played at the wrong speed. 'Pilgrim would like both of you to join him. At his table over here.'

Sonny's eyes had adjusted by now. Looking down at the fist encircling his forearm he could just decipher the message spanning the beefy knuckles. LOVE. The omens seemed good.

'Why not?' he replied jauntily. 'Why not? Lead on, friend,' and they began threading their way through the crush.

He anticipated some extension of their ovation to follow them, a smiling face or two, at least, a hand reaching out in congratulation, perhaps even a passing request for an autograph, it wasn't an unreasonable expectation but, no, no, these people had reverted to stone. They sat as though rooted, staring straight ahead, the drink in them turned sour. Sonny suddenly felt very angry at being denied his tiny moment of triumph, even if he couldn't quite remember if he deserved it or not. He knew these people couldn't help the way they were, but did they ever try to be different? Did they fuck!

Just before they got to the far table – Sonny could make out three people different from the rest of the regulars who were watching them – he tapped Hoss on the shoulder. 'Hey, old buddy,' he said with a smile. 'Me and this good lady here, we'd like us a quick li'l ole pow-wow before we join you and your friends. Strictly family business, you understand. Here, could you handle this?'

He held out the guitar in its quilted green case and the big one took it from him without a word. Sonny watched him until he reached the table where the men sat waiting, then he turned to face Hazel. She had halted by a pillar, her arms folded across her beautiful chest. Her expression plainly said, *come on, convince me, but I have to tell you now, your chances look remarkably slim.*

194

'First things first,' he said in his normal voice. 'Give me that number you were trying to ring.'

She looked at him in amazement. 'Nine, oh, two, three, seven, four, seven,' she said. 'Why?' The information had come out against her better judgement, that was clearly obvious.

'Good,' he replied. 'Good. That sounds easy enough to remember,' briskly repeating the sequence. What a laugh, he thought to himself, considering his chronic amnesia over the past quarter of an hour or so. Now he removed his dark glasses with more of that same vigour so that she could spot the sincerity in his eyes.

'Listen,' he said, 'I know you're worried. I can see it won't let you rest, whatever it is between you and the girl. Now, I know I didn't get a proper chance to meet her and I regret that, for I really would like to talk to her, even if it is only over the phone. Even if only for a few minutes. I know this is family business, but anything that concerns you, Hazel, makes *me* feel concerned. I can't help that. Trust me. You can shout me down if I'm stepping out of line here, but I had to say it.'

He had her clasped about the waist by now; they looked like a couple of would-be smoochers standing there up against the pillar, eyes locked, breathing in each other's air.

She said despairingly, 'Sonny, how can you, *could* you?'

Bringing up his hand, he laid a finger on her lips. 'Don't say it. Do not say it. Please. All I ask is for you to trust me. Okay? Leave the matter with old Sonny here until morning. Just trust him. Where did you say the phone was?'

'Back there,' she said helplessly, motioning towards the blue sign that said TOILETS.

'That's all I need to know. Future reference.'

Then they kissed. He told himself to let instinct follow its course, no planning ahead, even though he did feel if he could charm the mother in this way he might be able to do the same to the daughter. Natalie, Natalie, he told himself. Remember that. Just think of that lovely drowned namesake of hers with the beautiful dark eyes that had the power to turn men to jelly.

195

Keeping his hands about her waist, he moved her on gently before him towards the far table. It was like steering some heavy and unresponsive craft but then, of course, the woman's mind was on other things. As they conga-ed onwards he buried his mouth in her sweet smelling neck.

'Tell me,' he whispered. 'The truth now. Just how *did* we do back there?' He couldn't help himself, but if she did say anything he certainly didn't catch it.

Hoss was standing up when they arrived. So were two of his companions, a tough looking man in a combat jacket and a youngish guy in fringed suede. His hair was the same length as Sonny's, only darker and more lustrous, and he had a smile to charm at thirty paces.

'Hey,' he said, hand outstretched. 'I'm Choctaw. He's Bomber and this is Pilgrim.'

The third man, who kept his seat throughout, looked familiar, somehow. He wore a baseball hat braided like an American admiral's and a black, shiny, zipped jacket and he seemed tired and, at a guess, older than his true years. His eyes took them in without showing emotion of any kind.

Hazel, Sonny noticed, seemed nervous, for some reason, under that calm scrutiny but the one called Choctaw – *these names*, Sonny thought, *did anyone around here go by the one on their birth certificate?* – went into immediate top gear. With expert motions he arranged seating, ordered drinks, produced cigarettes, as well as lights, all the while keeping up an unbroken flow of small talk. Recognising a fellow professional at work, after his own little performance of a moment ago, Sonny studied him carefully. It was easy behind the dark glasses, which he decided now to stay with on a full-time basis.

'You two were *sensational*!' enthused Choctaw. 'Truly knockout. Tell me, are you appearing anywhere? Concerts? A tour?'

Sonny beamed back at him with just as many kilowatts. 'Our trip is purely vacational. With a li'l old touch of sentimental pilgrimage thrown in. You see we both come from a long, long line of Britishers. More exact, Scotch-Irish. Dunbar and Kinney? You can't come more authentic

196

than that. The good old boys from Ulster, they did open up the West, you know. But say, look here, you good people don't want to be bored with all that sort of stuff, do you, now?'

Allowing modesty to colour his expression, he raised the large whiskey which Choctaw had set before him and drank deeply. Choctaw – he did have more than a passing resemblance to an extra in a John Wayne movie, come to think of it – protested strongly. On the contrary, he insisted, they were all of them deeply fascinated by the subject, especially Pilgrim here, who, he said, happened to be something of an authority, in his own right, when it came to Americana.

'You know something?' The whites of his eyes had a bluish tinge, whiter than white, like the washing-powder ad. 'I bet Pilgrim here knows more about your country's history than you'll ever do, man.'

Sonny smiled broadly at that, for it was obviously meant in a nice way. Choctaw was the type who would find it difficult to be unpleasant to anyone. 'Reckon you could be right there, friend.'

But this young brave with his single earring and collection of junk jewellery about his neck wasn't going to be deflected that easily. 'How about a shoot-out? You against Pilgrim. What do you say, man? Question number one coming up. Are you ready? Name all the participants at the OK Corral.'

The man in the baseball hat and black silk pilot's jacket rose stiffly to his feet, 'That's enough, Ashley,' he said in a calm, deep voice. Then, to Sonny and Hazel, 'I hope you'll be able to come back to the house a little later on. Ashley here will see to it. If there is anything in the way of hospitality we can offer both of you, please don't hesitate to let us know. There's something I think *you* might be interested in.'

He was talking directly to Sonny now, his tones flat and colourless, in the same way as Hoss had sounded earlier, like a faulty recording, or as if the batteries had started to run down.

'That's sure right neighbourly of you, Mr ... er ...' said Sonny, deliberately hesitating over the name.

'Pilgrim. Everybody calls me Pilgrim.' He straightened up; he had the arms and torso of a weight-lifter, the shiny stuff of his jacket stretching alarmingly as they stared.

'Bomber,' he commanded and the tall, silent one in army surplus rose dutifully. They moved slowly off together towards a curtained doorway Sonny hadn't noticed before. Something was seriously the matter with Pilgrim's legs. Cruelly outlined by the jeans he wore, they had a weak and wasted look compared with the rest of that magnificent gladiatorial frame. As they watched he took hold of his companion's arm to give himself support and Ashley – or was it Choctaw? – mused, 'Not a day without pain. Anyone else would be in a wheelchair.'

For some reason this seemed to enrage Hoss. 'OK Corral!' he roared. 'Bullshit! They should put you in one and keep you there, *Ashley*.'

'Don't call me that! Only *he* calls me that – and only when he's vexed with me!'

'Well, I'm fucking well vexed with you, too. Right? With you *and* your fucking great mouth!' And, reverting to his marauding Hell's Angel image, he went storming off through the tables bumping into people and spilling their drinks.

Choctaw – *now remember that*, Sonny made a mental note – whistled sadly. 'There goes someone with one almighty chip on his shoulder. Poor old Hoss. What a mess. He worries me sometimes. He really does. Now, you two good people, on the other hand, I can relate to. I saw that as soon as I set eyes on you.' The radiance of his charm was on full beam again; it seemed fitting that Sonny had protection against all that dazzle of teeth and eyes in the form of tinted glass.

Glancing across at Hazel to see how she was taking the sunlamp treatment, he realised she wasn't. 'Got a pen?' he asked and Choctaw produced a ball-point with alacrity from inside his tan suede jacket. Nice jacket. On his palm Sonny wrote the telephone number Hazel had given him earlier, then he showed it to her, even though, to her, it was upside down. Choctaw averted his own gaze with great delicacy while all this was taking place. What an artist, thought Sonny; truly a prodigy, for he couldn't be much more than twenty – twenty-one, if that.

'I have a suggestion,' this young wiz announced. 'Why don't we all get smashed. I mean, seriously,' and his hand was already in the air to spirit yet another grinning young waitress out of nowhere. While she bent to take the order only Sonny noticed that that same hand had climbed up under her very short skirt. Was I ever like that at that age, Sonny couldn't help pondering. Sadly, the answer had to be no.

Hazel excused herself for the second time and seeing Sonny's look she shook her head as if to say, *I made a promise, didn't I?* But how could he be certain of that?

After she'd left Choctaw said, 'One classy lady,' and they raised their glasses in silent tribute. 'One thing – her accent – '

Sonny, picking up the query in the voice, said, 'She's got a lot of Irish in her, still. Born over there, you know.'

'Oh?' replied the other with a smile. 'I didn't know.'

'Yeah, some people never seem to lose the brogue, no matter how long they've been in a place. Tell me, old buddy, where do you hail from, if it's not a rude question?'

Choctaw opened his mouth wide to laugh. He had the most amazing teeth, not a single filling in his head. 'Oh, a little one-horse place you've never ever heard of. Barely on the map.'

'Join the club, friend,' Sonny said. 'We're all just good ole country boys' now ain't that a fact?' touching the other's glass a second time. For some reason he didn't care if this young fraudster could see through him or not. Why should he? After all, it takes one to know one.

'Looks as if the party's breaking up,' he said, for now there seemed to be signs of a low-keyed exodus. God, he thought, what a mirthless crew. Just look at those faces. For the life of him he found it hard to comprehend why people would go to so much time and trouble dressing up like this just to sit staring morosely at each other across a crowded room. For fuck's sake, where was all that enchantment, if the song was to be believed? Not all the disguises in the world could save them, could mask what lay beneath the hats, the boots, the chaps, the shirts, belts, and face-furniture. But why restrict it to western gear? All over the country, at this very minute, ordinary, middle-aged men were delving secretly into their wives' underwear drawers, if the Sunday papers were to be believed. Was anybody out there what they seemed?

Across the table from him right at this moment there sat a replica Redskin. And himself? *Come on, Sonny, own up, for aren't you just as mixed up as any of them? A grown man in pretend costume, putting on a pretend voice?*

Hazel came back and her eyes looked swollen. So, he thought, pretending not to notice, you went and reneged on our promise after all, did you, about leaving that phonecall to me? Got an earful for your pains, did you, from little Miss Delinquent back in Fulham, or wherever it is. Didn't I tell you so? But he found it hard to harbour blame. How could she resist, he told himself? Inked across his palm was a reminder of his own part of the bargain which Hazel had broken. But that didn't mean that he still wouldn't have to keep his side of it. Later, he thought, for right now their young friend with the headband and the frontiers-man's jacket wanted them to accompany him to where the action was.

Hazel allowed herself to be manoeuvred like some stately, sweet-smelling barge out into the mainstream of cowhands and their consorts making for the exit doors. Sonny felt someone put a hand on his sleeve. It was one of the women, a Loretta Lynn look-alike, and, miracle of miracles, she was asking for an autograph. Borrowing the grinning Choctaw's pen a second time he wrote, 'For the good times, Sonny and Hazel,' and smiled at her, continuing on his way. Perhaps these people weren't quite the hopeless cases he'd imagined them to be, after all. Some of them, indeed, actually appeared now to be showing signs of animation.

In the car park there was laughter, shouted farewells and the usual country cat-calling above the revving of engines. The CB aerials twitched as if in readiness as the car doors slammed. Sonny had a moment of rare poetic insight as he thought of the local airwaves being criss-crossed on the way home by drunken messages. He felt he had been granted a stunning truth concerning this race and their intricate social habits. For a moment or two, as he stood there in that open field, its vegetation beaten flat by traffic, loneliness welled up unexpectedly. For no apparent reason he was aware of suddenly he ached to be part of that tribe and their rituals, even though in his heart he knew he heartily despised them.

Putting his arms about Hazel, he buried his face in her hair. They were right beside the camper by now, and Choctaw said, 'Want me to drive, man? No problem.' In the light from the other cars his face gleamed with robust young health. Sonny handed the keys over without a word. Why fight it? And Choctaw took charge, as if everything on four wheels for him was naturally child's play.

Moving off, he slid through the gears like silk, with barely a bump or sideways motion to distract the two of them in the back. Huddled close on one of the bunk-beds in the dark, they consoled one another, at first silently, then in whispers. He felt her breath in his ear.

'What am I going to do about her, Sonny? She's only sixteen and I feel I've lost her already, failed her in some terrible way.'

He sat there like a father-confessor with a hard-on – now, why hadn't that one ever occurred to him before? – trying to keep his mind on the problem, not just Hazel's problem any more, but his, as well. That he recognised.

'When her Dad and I split up, that's when it all started. I think she blamed me for it, but I couldn't stay with him, Sonny, I just couldn't. It was all a mistake, right from the beginning. I only stuck it out because of her, no other reason. Then, when she had her first period – forgive me – I thought, now she's growing up, she'll understand, and I got a place for the two of us. He didn't seem to care and, at the time, neither did she. At least that's what I believed, but then we started having rows and arguments ...'

Did he really want to know all of this? And who ever

heard of a father-confessor with a name like Sonny?

She wept. 'I just can't get through to her, Sonny,' and he knew it wasn't a connection by phone she was talking about.

By this time they were speeding along country roads, black as pitch, and Choctaw had slid in a cassette, George Jones and ex-wife Tammy; slow, sad songs of marital heart-break, a little too close to present realities for comfort. Sonny pulled Hazel closer, her cheek against his shoulder, but he knew she was listening to the words. He felt as if it was an ambulance he was travelling in, instead of a holiday camper. Would they be in time to save the patient?

Then Choctaw turned off the tape and called out to them, 'We've arrived! Pilgrim's place!'

They felt the slow judder of a cattle grid, followed by the birdshot of gravel under them and, inching the curtains apart, Sonny saw they were heading along a wide, tree-lined avenue. The moon had come out, a fat, dimpled, slow-moving balloon, the sort to get lyrical about. He could smell new-mown hay and, as they swept up and around in a wide luxurious curve, he saw, blanched by the moonlight, a great white house set on a hill. Lights were on in every room, music travelled down to meet them, parked cars glittered on the expanse in front of the steps.

'Some spread, eh?' Choctaw, by now, had pulled back his own stretch of curtain. They could make out his wolfish grin in the green glow of the dash. 'And every bit of it his own handiwork. I mean, every brick, man, every stone, every stick of wood. Our Pilgrim is one very special individual, let me tell you. Remind me to fill you in about him some time.'

In Sonny's ear, Hazel whispered, 'Would you mind very much if I didn't go in with you? I don't think I'm in the mood for parties. Not tonight.'

'I don't like leaving you on your own. I mean out in the middle of all these cars.'

'Who's to know?' he heard her murmur. And she was right, of course. With curtains drawn, it would look like just another parked and empty vehicle sitting dark and unattended, waiting for a driver.

He had to admit, also, a certain attraction to the idea of the faithful little woman waiting for her man to come rolling home to that warm, sleeping body. Of course, Choctaw would have to be party to the plan, Choctaw, with that grin of his, and those roving hands. Sonny realised that he was becoming possessive in a way previously he would have found ridiculous, imagining would-be rapists and God knows what else, when it came to this woman snuffling into his best shirt. *To fuck with all this Mister Nice Guy stuff*, he told himself. *Tonight, just for once, I want to be a real bastard, out for number one, just like the old days.*

He craved another drink, another pill, another anything, and Choctaw (oh, what a fixer he was) as though smoothing his path for him, murmured sweetly, 'Why don't you good people stay here for the night? I know just the spot where you won't be disturbed.'

Without stopping for an answer he turned the wheel and drove off at right angles along a narrow track set aside from the house. Only a short distance away he stopped, switching off lights and engine, and waited for their appreciation of his fine judgement. 'Well?' he asked when it didn't appear to be forthcoming. 'You can see half the county from here. It's Pilgrim's favourite view. He paid enough for it.'

They'd parked on a knoll overlooking a lake and beyond the reflected silver of flat water the landscape fell away with nothing to break the descent but chequered pasture-land punctuated by inky daubs of copse and woodland. It was magical in every sense and seemingly unpopulated, too, for not a light was to be seen. Sonny felt something tightening inside, some unknown yearning for another time, another place, just such a territory as this, from which he had been banished, oh, a long, long time ago. Perhaps before he had been born.

Climbing out past Choctaw, he stood there, letting his ache flow out, down and across all that enchantment. For a moment he saw himself down there, a part of that world, a tiny dot-like figure, like one of those hunters or harvesters in a Flemish landscape painting. Above his head the moon sailed on, or appeared to, according to its habit. It made him want to throw back his head and howl. *Oh, Sonny, Sonny, what are you doing up here with all these people, when your true place is down there creeping along to some little homestead with a bundle on your back?*

'Pretty spectacular, eh?' Choctaw stood at his side. 'I thought you'd go for it.' He passed across the joint he had in his hand and Sonny put the flattened wet teat to his lips, filling his lungs with the pure stuff of dreams. A couple more puffs and he would be able to change places with that tiny toiler far below, after all.

'As far as the eye can see. Owns it all.'

'Some sort of lord of the manor, is he?'

Choctaw laughed. 'No rich daddy for him, although his old man did land him with a real fancy name. Pilgrim. Pilgrim Paine.'

'Oh,' said Sonny as the mists suddenly cleared.

'Yeah – oh,' replied the other, mocking his tone. Then he started to giggle. 'Ain't life jest wonderful?'

'Swell, pardner, simply swell.' And Sonny meant it, too. They stood there on the short, damp grass together, passing the slowly dwindling reefer back and forth between them, slowly, slowly, two high priests at their rites. Oh, the simple, sweet and uncomplicated pleasures of men with each other, thought Sonny. Certain things were beyond the power of words or explanation.

'Why don't you head on up to the house, old buddy, and I'll catch you up?'

Choctaw sucked the last breath of life out of the joint, tossing it away and down to the slopes far below where that mythical little rustic figure still had domain. 'Don't be long now, do you hear?' He gave a V sign and started off up and along the track to where the lights blazed, music played and enjoyment beckoned in the big white house that Pilgrim built.

Hazel had drawn the curtains across by the time Sonny climbed back inside.

'Where are you?' But she made no reply. Feeling his way

in the dark, his outstretched hand met a familiar outline beneath the blankets.

'Hey,' he said. 'You okay?' He put his hand out to feel her brow as if she were ill. She murmured something he couldn't catch. 'Sure you don't want to come out and play?' No reply, but still he kept on going – *now why was he like this?* 'We can just drive off, you know. Nobody will be any the wiser. Just say the word.' But he was talking to a mummy, Egyptian-style, that was plain.

Women, he thought, as he slid out the ignition keys, they really can make you feel bad about having a good time. He said, 'I'm locking you in. Okay?' And left her there with her problems.

Outside in the night air with the harvest moon pulsing gently overhead it was as if he had managed to narrowly escape from something. His head swam. Breathing in deeply, he felt the companionable coils of the cannabis reassert themselves. 'Goodbye, little friend,' he heard himself murmur to the spread landscape far below. 'I hope you make it home all right, you and your little bundle. And I also hope, for your sake, that the little woman doesn't give you a bad time. But then, what's new, eh?'

Choctaw was waiting for him half-way up the track. He was seated on an outcrop of rock and had lit up another one of his hand-rolled specials. He didn't show the slightest surprise at seeing Sonny on his own.

'The night is still young, friend. Allow me to fill you in a little concerning the great man himself before we go up to enjoy his hospitality. I guarantee you'll find it interesting.'

Sonny joined him on the cool stone, preparing to listen. Choctaw squinted through the rising cigarette smoke at a point somewhere in the far distance.

'The man's a mystery,' he began. 'That's the first thing. And likes to keep it that way. That's the second. It's hard to get a word out of him for days on end sometimes, but then, with the sort of assets he has, he doesn't have to talk to anybody unless he wants to. Most of the time, as I say, he doesn't want to. Period. He's in bad pain much of the time, because of his legs, which you may have noticed. The

legs, I mean. No, not an accident, as a lot of people believe
around these parts, nothing like that, from what I can make
out. It just came on gradually. Some sort of thing where
the actual muscles just waste away. People I've talked to
who knew him in the old days say it's on account of the
work he used to do. I don't suppose you've ever heard of
him; but there's a guy in this country the papers call Super
Hod. You know, on a building-site? He can carry more
bricks than any ten normal men in a single working day;
he's in the Guinness Book of Records, all that shit. Well,
Pilgrim did all of that first, long before anyone else ever
even thought of it. And like this other bloke I'm telling you
about, he made one helluva lot of money at it. Not enough
to allow him to buy up all this land and build that big house
up there, but enough to get him started on the way to a
fortune. He could still do it tomorrow – the work, I mean,
all that hard graft – but his legs just wouldn't allow him.
That's the really sad part. Some things are just too sick, I
mean, *sick*, man, too sick to contemplate.'

After a pause, Sonny said, 'Life is certainly mysterious, I
grant you that.' And he meant it, too. He was convinced if
he sat out here on this piece of ancient wall under that moon
long enough, genuinely mysterious things would happen to
him. Without having to lift a finger.

Choctaw said, 'Let's go to the man's shindig.'

They rose together and Sonny's head felt loose as though
it might slip its moorings at any moment to go floating off
as easily as that other great silver noddle high above them.

'Wow!' he said. 'Where do you get this shit? Sure is high
grade shit all right.'

'All home-grown. Under glass. But that's highly con-
fidential. You dig?'

'Cross my heart.'

The other held him by the wrists and they swayed trying
to focus on one another's expression.

'That other stuff about Pilgrim, that's classified as well.
Not a word to anyone. Especially him. I love the guy. He's
been like a father to me.' Were those real tears?

Sonny said, 'A legend in his time,' and he sang a line or

two of the song just to lighten the atmosphere. They continued on their way, a couple of ploughboys now, returning after a long hard day, limbs numbed like their wits. Sonny knew there was something he had to do but just what he couldn't get quite clear. He still wore his dark glasses, which was just as well, because when the house suddenly loomed up dazzlingly white like some great spotlit iceberg out of the surrounding night, it seemed just too much for him to take in properly.

Choctaw stopped. He was wheezing like an old man. Many cars were parked on the gravel sweep in front of the steps, quite a few of which hadn't been at the club earlier. They were recognisably much more expensive, several sleek Jaguars, BMWs, solid Volvos and Range Rovers, a crimson Porsche or two, and they stood out among the Fords and pick-ups with the drooping CB aerials like a bunch of polo ponies in a stable of dray-horses.

Choctaw muttered bitterly, 'I see the Rotary Club has arrived. Fucking freeloaders.'

Sonny ignored the comment, his brain in no fit state to decipher implications, and, anyway, the great house reminded him of something, some deeply buried image that came from another time and place. Those fluted pillars, like delicately iced confectionary, for instance, the classical pediment, the great glass doors thrown open to the night air, none of such details belonged in this landscape. It was the architecture of much hotter climes. The scent of bougainvillaea should have been heavy in their nostrils, the dry rasp of innumerable and unseen insects filling the night with sound. He turned to the man by his side as if for reassurance and met his look of amusement.

'When Pilgrim bought it he called it "Tara". Still does.'

'You're kidding.'

'I'm not.'

And, laughing together, they began climbing the wide, pale stone steps leading upwards to this replica of perhaps the most famous film set in history. In spite of himself, Sonny couldn't help feeling dwarfed by the sheer scope of this man's fantasy, almost as much as by the size of the colonial style mansion he was about to enter. He felt like taking off his hat, dark glasses, too, but caught himself in time for he, too, had his dream, perhaps not quite so fully realised as this, or on such a scale, but to him every bit as compelling and just as obsessional.

' "Frankly, my dear, I don't give a damn", ' he quoted, and Choctaw threw back his head, laughing in appreciation.

Taking hold of Sonny's elbow, he began hustling him towards their objective. 'Welcome home, friend!' he called out. 'Welcome to Pilgrim's Plantation!'

'Mansion on the Hill'

Hazel awoke to a hot stripe of sunlight falling across her face and the screech of the dawn chorus. She had never really experienced the latter phenomenon back in London, such sustained aggression on the part of Nature, but then there wasn't a lot of Nature or bird life, come to think of it, in the area of Fulham where she lived.

The glare, she noted, flooded in through a mere inch of space between the drawn curtains. Yet it was powerful enough to dispel any doubts she might have had about her surroundings. In the instant she knew where she was and the terrible mistake she'd made in being here at all. Across from her the other narrow bed was empty, unslept in. She looked at her watch. Five thirty-ish. Flinging off the cheap and matted blanket that covered her she was surprised to discover she was still wearing her barn-dancing shirt, her bra and pants. Only a mirror would be able to reveal whether she had become a total hobo or not, but she didn't have time, even, for that. A terrible dread of being surprised or thwarted in her desire to get away, now, this instant, made her pull on her jeans and boots with urgency. She broke one of her long and beautiful, blood-red nails and thought, this is what this business has done to me, this crazy, doomed adventure. Only, it's over now, finished with, if, *if*, I can just get dressed, out of here and off.

Her mouth felt dry, her lungs ached for a cigarette, but coffee and a smoke would have to wait. She saw herself at a table in a spotless roadside café somewhere with her hair and face repaired, alone and herself again; in a little while she would go to that phone over there in the corner and, laying out her change in a row on its metal shelf . . . It was just like a mirage and it sustained her as she threw her belongings into her old plaid Samsonite, the one that Mandy Rice-Davies had professed to despise so much.

209

For a moment she felt like dropping down and weeping for her past again, her innocent past, but then she told herself, don't think, you haven't got time, and she did as she ordered herself until, looking around to check if anything had been left behind, she saw a pair of Sonny's rolled-up socks tucked into the corner of his untouched bed. Of course that practically finished her. She groaned aloud.

Opening her black leather bag she found an eyebrow liner and, on a double tissue, wrote, 'Dear Sonny, I don't know how to –' Her hands were shaking, tears were close, she couldn't continue. She climbed over into the front, hauling her joke of a suitcase after her. Both window buttons were flat on the frame, she nearly finished off another nail prising herself free, but somehow she managed it and the door swung open.

The instant her feet touched the ground the birds ceased their racket and she froze, certain she had been discovered. But they started up again and she looked about her. It was like the dawn of the world, a clean, fresh vista of trees heavy with dew, glinting grass and a citrus-coloured sun throbbing away over distant cut-out hills. She felt soiled in the middle of it all. Her clothes smelt of stale tobacco, her eyes felt tight and gritty, the suitcase in her hand was only fit for the dump. Now she did weep, but softly, so as not to disturb the innocence all around. Even the camper seemed to have been transformed. It had a showroom sheen, a perfection of form, its metal trim the finest silver work. She felt she just couldn't walk away from all of this without a backward look. There would be days in Milton Road when the rain outside turned the London brick the colour of death. She thought of Lester, poor Lester, for the first time. She would be taking him in his little box, inside her suitcase, back to that over-populated sooty tomb.

Water was near, some sort of lake. She remembered a glimpse of its flat gleam through trees from last night. She left the suitcase forming its imprint in the damp grass and moved in the direction her instincts led her. A smell too, unmistakably marshy, exerted its pull. It was a beautiful stretch of water, no doubt about it, in the English fashion,

210

the shape of a perfectly outlined fat tear. There were coots and ducks and similar wildfowl, and a solitary heron, far out, fishing one-legged in the unruffled depths.

But there was another presence as well, standing half submerged, as still as the heron on its single stilt. This human presence had its back to her and was naked except for a black hat with a band stitched with a continuous ribbon of silver medallions. Hazel recognised that hat; she'd also seen that snowy bum before, and the dark torso above, result of many long afternoons spent lying in London's parks. She made a move to back away. If she could get to the suitcase, retrieving it on the run, and then on at a continuing trot down that curving drive to escape . . . She saw herself miles away already, magically transported, sipping coffee, inhaling smoke from that accompanying cigarette.

But Sonny turned then, and taking off his dark glasses – she hadn't noticed those – looked up and called out, 'Hazel! Is that you, Hazel?'

At the same time he also removed his hat, covering his genitals, but whether because he thought she might be a stranger or simply because of modesty – he did have quite a lot of that, even with her – there was no way of telling. It was the business with the hat, of course, that finished her. *Oh, why, why do you have to go and do things like that, Sonny?*

'Hazel?' he called again, raising a hand to his eyes. He began to wade for shore setting up twin creamy streaks of turbulence in the dark water. The heron went flapping off never to return. *You see, you see*, she told herself, but what that sudden flight was supposed to signify, or what she was meant to see, she couldn't quite make out.

He came up to her shaking moisture off himself like a tall, thin tan and white dog. The hat had been placed carefully by this time on top of a heap of his clothes, yet still he managed to keep his private parts covered. How consistent men were, it struck her, when it came to their precious tackle. All those footballers cupping themselves with such serious expressions whenever a free kick had to be taken.

211

Sonny grinned and said, 'It's a terrible hour to be coming back, I know. Just what time is it, anyway?' looking around him as if noting the advanced state of daylight for the first time.

'Half past five – a little after,' she said, then something made her add, 'No need to apologise. I'm not your wife, you know.'

Silly bitch, she thought. Just tell him it's over. Through. Do it, then walk away without a backward look. You did it to quite a few others in the past, remember, so what's got into you now at this late stage in your life?

'All dressed up, I see,' he said slyly, dabbing at himself with his spotted bandanna. 'With nowhere to go, I hope?'

Now why are you so pleased with yourself, she thought, for it must be obvious what she'd been intending to do. She knew he knew and it made her angry.

'So long, Sonny,' she said and turned to walk away, for suddenly he had made it easy for her.

He allowed her to get about a dozen paces up the slight grassy incline, her heels furiously denting the turf, when he called out lazily – this was a new Sonny all right, ahead of the game – 'What about Natalie, then?'

She swung about to face him, but he had his dark glasses back on again as if to deny her the chance of seeing what he really was up to. Standing there in his pale blue underpants with the navy waistband, he looked good, his dark wetted hair drawn back from his face. He had the appearance of someone healthy, tanned, confident. Somehow Sonny, the Sonny she thought she knew, had pulled a fast one on her. For the first time she wondered just what he'd been up to while she slept.

'I thought we had a pact, you and me,' he called out. 'Two against the world, remember?'

'It's too late for that, Sonny.'

'No, it's not,' he replied. 'No, it's not.'

He was up close now. She could smell the brackish depths on him, had a close-up of his goose-pimpled flesh. He looked just like one of the young boys back home after they had been swimming in the weir near the village where she used to live. They, too, seemed to draw assurance from the water, showing off and larking about on the bank afterwards for the benefit of her and her friends, who just *happened* to be passing that way on the long, lazy, Irish summer evenings.

Sonny put his hands on her shoulders. He was shivering, but his voice was firm. 'Listen. If you go off now you'll only miss her, that's all I'm saying. She's coming down. Here. Today.' He shook her as if to reinforce the message. 'It's all arranged. I talked to her last night. Didn't I tell you I would? Didn't I?'

She felt suddenly ready to fall, only held in place by his still wet body. A damp, soft dog's nose further down seemed to be eagerly pressing against her lower stomach. Or, a button mushroom? *To be thinking such things at a time like this. Jesus Christ, she really was turning into one of those women she'd been singing about earlier, helpless, hapless, a victim. But, oh, he was telling her things she wanted so much to hear.*

He hauled her gently back with him to where his clothes lay, still talking. She watched him hop barefoot into his jeans.

'You wouldn't lie to me about this, would you, Sonny? It's too important, you know that, don't you?'

'Come up to the house and get some breakfast. Take a bath, if you like.'

Hazel looked at him.

'Sure,' he said. 'No problem. Pilgrim's a mate. We had a great night. You should have been there.'

'How do you feel?' she asked and, in reply, he dipped a hand into his shirt pocket.

'See?'

Nestling in his outstretched palm was a small selection of capsules, white and crimson. She didn't recognise them.

'I recommend the reds,' he said. 'Highly. Want one?'

Hazel shook her head. 'Tell me about the arrangements. Again.'

He popped a pill into his mouth and crunched it like a Smartie. The sound made her nervous. Now she knew why he was so conscientious about keeping his glasses on; no one could disguise that tell-tale look in the eyes, or the size of the pupils.

'Let's go,' he said taking her arm. 'You're gonna love our mansion on the hill, I'm telling you.'

They walked together back up the track and she listened as he talked. His accent had settled into a definite mid-Atlantic twang. It may have been the pills doing the talking, but she thought not. So avid was she for details, details, she no longer cared. She was like a child making him go over and over the miraculous new turn of events again and again, until he cried, 'Look, we'll pick her up at the nearest bus station. She'll come down on one of those Rapides, just like a Greyhound. Great, eh?'

But she wanted to know more, more. What had he actually said on the phone to her? What had *she* said? Did she really want to come? Of her own accord? And what about money for the trip?

Laughing, he closed her lips with a long wet kiss, positioning her at the foot of the run of steps leading up to the great stuccoed house. Over his shoulder it rose, a slab of architectural icing, pale pink in colour, because of the flooding sun, like something in a dream, and as she climbed with him up to the wide open door she felt everything that was happening to her right now had somehow taken a sideways slip into unreality. Guarding the portals were twin painted figures, waist-high, jockeys in racing colours with boots, caps, whips. They had grinning black faces, a couple of carved Sambos sharing a joke, obviously antiques, but what were they doing here adorning the entrance to an English country house? But was it that?

She began to notice other things as well, more details that didn't add up. Two of the doors had been ripped clean from their hinges, were merely propped against the stonework. Neglect in other areas became quickly apparent – flaking paintwork, missing panes, deep, snaking cracks underfoot, as well as overhead; they had moved inside by now. The great resounding hallway reeked of damp, stale tobacco, spilt drink. Empty wine bottles and beer cans lined the walls and a motor-cycle was parked in the middle of the marble floor, yes, a motor-bike, huge, gleaming and cared for, in contrast to all the decay surrounding it.

Sonny said, 'The kitchen's this way. *If* I remember right.' He laughed as if at some private joke.

They passed through a series of high-ceilinged chambers stripped of furniture except for the most basic kind. Floor cushions were strewn about, there were more and more empties, piled paper plates and ashtrays, all testifying to a party on a wildly grand scale. One of the rooms they entered had its curtains drawn and a great television squatted there still flickering and sizzling.

The kitchen, when they reached it, was equally unreal, a vast stone-flagged cavern chill as Christmas, with a row of dangling bells high on one wall to summon up non-existent meals. The fridge was filled with cans of Budweiser, nothing else, and on the scrubbed table sat a single loaf with a bread knife embedded in it, violently, Hazel thought, as though someone had finally been angered out of all reason by those bells. She couldn't keep her eyes away from them in case she missed the slightest hint of a tremor in their mechanism.

Sonny said, 'Mother Hubbard's cupboard. Sorry.'

Hazel sat down on a chair. 'All that food upstairs, too.'

'Takeaway. Pilgrim orders everything. Sorry, again. I'd forgotten about that. Look,' he said, 'why don't you soak yourself in a nice hot bath while I rustle up some grub. There's bound to be something.'

'Vindaloo? Kebab? Chili? No thanks.'

He laughed. 'Don't forget the Kentucky Fried.'

They sat facing one another across the great, fissured pine table, that bizarre still-life of granary loaf and downward thrusting breadknife between them. Not a sound from the world outside reached their ears. They could have been in a mausoleum – the walls looked thick enough, bare stone like the floor, save for some faint evidence of a very ancient coat of eau de nil distemper.

'Well, you can't say we're not seeing life,' said Sonny, taking off his glasses for the first time. His eyes did seem normal. 'Terrific news about Natalie, eh?'

215

Hazel looked at him closely. 'Sonny,' she said, reaching out to take hold of his wrists. 'I'm trusting you, you do know that, don't you? This is too important to have messed up. I'd never forgive you if you did that to me. You wouldn't, would you?'

And Sonny, feeling his pulse being monitored, thought, look how easy it is to beat that old lie-detector test after all. But it wasn't really lying, was it, on his part? More playing for time. Which sounded like yet another of those song titles he kept storing up for posterity – 'Playing For Time, 'cause I've got no time for playing around, when it comes to our love, babee ...'

He said, 'A hot tub will soothe and smooth away all your cares, believe me,' removing her grip, so he was doctor now. She allowed him to lift her to her feet and, together, they went back up the winding stone steps to the rooms above.

They climbed the main staircase; even though its carpet was missing the long slender brass rods remained in place. The mahogany curve of the rail felt sticky to the touch with God knows what substances after the night's excesses, but Sonny determined not to even think about any of that until he'd got Hazel safely under a blanket of suds.

'If you want company,' he offered, 'just say the word. Old Sonny's at your disposal,' but with a sigh she pushed him out of the salon-sized bathroom.

He listened at the lock as she bolted the door, then on until he heard the roar of the ancient, wide-mouthed taps pumping out their load. The water, he decided, would almost certainly be the colour of tea, like that in the lake, but as long as it wasn't as cold ...

But he had vowed to stop worrying about situations over which he had no control, so he made his way downstairs murmuring, *if it happens, it happens, if it happens, it happens*, until his brain started feeling muzzy again.

Somehow, somewhere, he had lost his watch, but he knew it had to be still very early. The house slept soundly, as did all the spent wife-swappers in some other distant room or rooms. Outside, their cars gathered dew. Sonny had counted them on his way back from his morning dip, five top-of-the-range models scattered carelessly across the gravel like expensive toys, as if their owners couldn't wait to get at the action inside. In the back seats of three of them fur coats were lying. That redhead with the Caesarean, she almost certainly must own one. Her scent, musky and over-ripe like herself, was one he always associated with furs for some reason. It brought to mind those expensive women leaving perfumed trails in Bond Street, showing legs like Cyd Charisse, as they swung elegantly out of big black chauffeur-driven limousines ...

The redhead – 'Call me Monica, and that's Ted over there with Sue, or is it Paula, or, again, it might well be Beverley' (her little joke) – had risen from the jolly scrum around the VCR to take him by the hand. 'You look interesting. Join the sewing circle.'

He didn't see a great deal of the video, an epic called 'She Couldn't Let A Dago By', one action-packed stop-over in the life of a blonde air hostess in some Mediterranean resort or other. 'Fly me, I'm Hildegarde,' seemed to be her single line of dialogue and a succession of bellboys, waiters, plumbers, TV repair men and airline stewards happily obliged. On one occasion all at once. Sonny felt as though he had been here before, even though it must certainly have been his first serious orgy. Yet that word seemed too professional for so much awkward heaving and pummelling of middle-aged flesh. On the screen the situation was very different – prodigies of performance were being enacted up there with non-stop soundtrack.

Managing to slip away eventually was not easy; even harder was getting his clothes together. His watch must still be in there, he realised. On Monica of the flaming locks and Caesarean section he seemed to have made a deep impression. In every sense.

'Don't be long, cowboy,' she whispered when he said he must take a desperately needed leak.

He said, 'Don't start without me,' leaving her there with Debbie, or it may have been Sue, or perhaps even the well-developed and frolicsome Paula.

Sonny decided not to revisit the scene of the crime, even if it meant saying farewell to his watch. He would find another way to the outside air he decided, but how and where he had no idea. Last night the geography of the place seemed boundless, yet somehow manageable, as he moved in a happy daze from room to room, each with its own intense circle of devotees. Quite early on he and Choctaw had lost contact, but no harm done. He remembered catching a glimpse of that mocking, vulpine face just before it disappeared in a blur of other more serious faces where a poker game was in progress. There was music in the room next door, serious drinking in its neighbour, arm-wrestling somewhere else and, most mysterious of all, at one point he blundered into what seemed to be a business meeting, men in shirt-sleeves around a table covered with computer print-outs, endless looping scrolls of invisible figures piling up about their ankles. The men turned a look of deadly hatred on him as he backed out.

But rougher elements were abroad as well, it became apparent. A bunch of CB types, he remembered from the Country Club drinking joylessly, now roamed the corridors in surprisingly merry mood. He found himself caught in cross-fire as they pelted one another with scraps of food. Scotch eggs were flying as he ducked into the nearest doorway which happened to lead to a darkened place where someone almost immediately reached out to him to murmur, 'I'm Monica and that's my better half Ted, you might just be able to make out over there . . .'

Sonny remembered a Russian film he'd once seen set in a great stripped palace after the Revolution. Commandeered by the masses, it resembled nothing more than a human hive, where families ate, slept, sang, squabbled and fornicated under one roof across a dozen or so ruinous floors. The noise was unremitting, there was no respite from the presence of other people, and this place he had found himself in could well have been its English equivalent, if it weren't for the absence of poverty and all those weird and wonderful Slavic faces. The camera in the film roamed continuously – another detail he recalled – and he'd felt a bit like that himself peeping and peering, advancing, then retreating.

Of all the encounters of that night – not all that so long ago really, when he thought about it, as he wandered now past devastated and silent rooms – the strangest had taken place behind an unusual door which he was searching for, but couldn't find. The door was reinforced with sheet metal and appeared to possess neither locks nor handles of any kind. Choctaw was leaning up against its chill bulk as he came drifting up the corridor in a state of dreamy shock.

'Meet the man,' were his words of greeting and the door opened inwards, seemingly at his touch. 'He's waiting for you.'

There was a short, dimly-lit passageway beyond and Sonny stumbled its length until he reached another door similarly proofed against fire, theft or just plain trespassers like himself. The dope he had been feeding into his system seemed to be losing its potency. Any second now he felt certain he would feel that tap on his shoulder and hear a voice informing him that his time was up, he had been rumbled.

Instead, a voice did sound. It said, 'Come in,' and the second door opened before him with a click followed by a brief burst of electronic noise. Pilgrim, as he was known, was sitting in what looked like a film director's chair, although it had to be a lot older than that, recognisably antique with its dark wood and leather instead of the usual canvas.

He said, 'I'm glad you were able to make it.'

Sonny stood looking about him. Compared with what he'd seen earlier throughout the rest of the house, this was positively sumptuous. There were display cases lining the walls, their contents made mysterious by the firelight setting up reflections. The only other illumination came from a green shaded lamp set on an enormous open roll-top desk and, in an alcove, was the biggest jukebox Sonny had ever seen, coruscating like a living altar, rainbows and rivers of colour coming and going in sequence, silently devouring electricity. Over the open fireplace – real burning logs – hung a framed Confederate flag, faded and gossamer thin.

'Have a drink, help yourself.'

Sonny did as he was told, pouring whiskey from a cut-glass decanter. Pilgrim cradled a can of beer, a slightly jarring detail, but then he was still wearing his old jeans, trainers, his shiny aviator's jacket and, of course, that baseball hat.

'I thought you might like to see some of this stuff,' he said, describing a listless sweep of the arm. His hands looked more like those of an aesthete than of someone who'd once toiled so prodigiously on countless building sites, for Sonny was remembering what he had been told about the manner in which he'd gathered his fortune. The shoulders were immense, certainly, as were the arms, but surely such a life must have left similar traces on a man's hands. But the notion melted from Sonny's mind as quickly as it had arrived, for the man in the chair was talking again.

'Everything here has a history. Are you interested in history? It struck me you might be. This chair I'm sitting on, for instance, happens to be Robert E. Lee's campaign chair. And that flag up there's the one he fought under at Gettysburg. The desk belonged to Roosevelt – Teddy Roosevelt – and in the cases there's a lot of other smaller stuff, Doc Holliday's waistcoat, Custer's spurs. More modern things, as well. Only two Wurlitzers of that particular model over there were ever made – the other's in Graceland. In the far case over by the door I've got quite a few music items – a guitar signed by Jimmie Rodgers, Tex Ritter's cowboy boots, Patsy Cline's kewpie doll – she carried it everywhere with her, did you know that? To bring her luck. It went down with her in the plane crash. Care to see it?'

Sonny felt himself tremble. His mouth had gone dry. 'By any chance,' he heard himself croak, 'would you have anything belonging to – Hank? Hank Williams?'

The man in the legendary General's chair took a key from a bunch on his belt and said, 'Here, see if you can guess what it is,' and tossed it across to him.

Sonny took the catch and went to the case. Through the gleaming glass he could see a miscellany of objects such as Pilgrim had described. For the most part they looked ordinary in the extreme, the sort of cast-off items you might notice in any junk shop window, but on a low shelf he spotted what had to be the most priceless relic in the whole room, as far as he was concerned. His fingers shook as he slid in the tiny key, turning it in the lock. The door opened with a faint smell of beeswax and ancient dust.

'Is it all right if I – ?' he said, turning.

'Sure, sure, it isn't sacred.'

But to Sonny, it was. Tears sprang to his eyes as, tenderly, he cradled that article of personal attire which had once belonged to his idol. Turning it over in his hands he read the inscription – Sy Beckman, Outfitter To The Famous, Beverly Hills, Hollywood, California, printed in gold script on the encircling leather band. He sniffed deeply – how could he help himself – and for a tiny space he really did believe that there was something there, some faint and bygone odour of a forgotten brand of brilliantine mixed with human sweat.

'Put it on,' commanded Pilgrim and Sonny looked at him, startled. 'Go on. Let's see it.'

He did so, and from the cabinet's glass there stared back at him the face of the dead country genius in his big white Stetson hat.

Pilgrim motioned towards the only other chair in the room, an early Shaker-style rocker, and Sonny slid it forward so that they faced one another in the firelight, two reflective forty-year-olds sipping their drinks. Pilgrim's voice was slow and almost without inflection, just as his eyes, poker-player's eyes, appeared to give little or nothing away of what he might be thinking. Yet Sonny felt at ease, at home here in this room, more so than he had been for a very long time. The chair he sat in had a well-worn and comforting familiarity about it. Under his weight it set up a barely perceptible rocking.

He might have been on a porch and back in time a thousand miles away, listening to the katydids and other night creatures and planning that career that was to take him from the Alabama bars and honky-tonks to fame in

Nashville and finally to wasteful oblivion. *Oh, Hank, Hank, why did you have to die that way?*

Pilgrim said, 'This is my bunker. If anything bad ever happens out there I've all the supplies I need for a long stay behind you.' He jerked a thumb towards a door draped with a faded red and tan Indian blanket. Beside it, a second door stayed slightly ajar and Sonny could make out a bed, a chair and a table with a lamp on it.

'The past seems a much safer place to be than the present, in these times. Do you share my theory?'

'Oh, yes, yes, indeed, yes,' agreed Sonny, nodding his head sagely under the pale, wide-brimmed hat with the curl in its brim. It felt a perfect fit as if it had been made for him and the longer he sat here gently rocking the greater plausibility such an idea took on.

Pilgrim said, 'I hope you can spend some time with us. It's not often I get the chance to talk with someone I can feel I relate to in these parts.' Sonny felt a sudden surge of sentiment for the big man.

He blurted out, 'I'd like nothing better, believe me, but –' halting in mid flow. And then he thought, to hell with it, and he began telling the other all about Hazel and Natalie, the difficult daughter, and how he'd foolishly said how he'd act as middleman. Until then he hadn't realised what he'd be letting himself in for; man in the middle would shortly become pig in the middle in that situation, any fool could see that.

Pilgrim heard him out with a hint of that same smile Sonny thought he'd detected when he'd first arrived. 'Ah, women,' he said, 'a necessary evil. In my case, these days, of course,' – he winced, touching his leg – 'an unnecessary one. You must get her to come down, that's the solution. I should have thought someone of her age would enjoy what we have on offer. Make it sound like an adventure. You *can* do that, can't you?'

And Sonny felt confident, in that moment, that he could. Later, of course, when it was time to make the phone call, it did strike him that the little number he had seen on that one occasion up in London was long past the *Swallows and Amazons* stage, that's if she'd ever gone through it.

'Tomorrow,' said Pilgrim, 'I'd like to show you something. A pet project of mine. Your advice would be appreciated. That is, if you've no other plans.'

Sonny assured him that he was free as a bird, his wish was his command, and a few other suchlike flourishes, for he found himself affected by the other's manner of speaking.

Certainly he sounded less like any ex-labourer Sonny had ever met. But, then, the old class thing in this country was dying on its feet, everyone knew that. Everyone, that is, except for a few polytechnic weirdos and left-wing romantics. Sonny had never had any time for politics, for the simple reason that politics had never had any time for him. But all that was deep stuff, much too deep for the reincarnated Hank, rocking and passing the time with a kindred spirit. It was a very special moment for him; he only hoped he would be able to remember all the details in the morning.

'My friend, it's getting late,' murmured Pilgrim. He was massaging his thigh as he spoke and Sonny felt immediate concern. The man was in pain, he told himself; it never left him, day or night, according to Choctaw. Rising and taking off the white felt hat, he went to the display case and returned it to its place on the shelf. He closed the cabinet doors and turned to the man in General Lee's chair and, thinking of that, he debated whether this really was happening to him or not.

'Tomorrow,' he said.

Pilgrim repeated the word. Then the metal-sheathed door swung inwards to signal the end of the visit as mysteriously and silently as it had opened to receive him. On the point of leaving Sonny managed to see further into the bedroom than he had been able to before. On the night table he couldn't help noticing a blue-rimmed bowl with what looked like a syringe in it.

Outside, the passageway felt like a no man's land and when he reached the further door and found it closed against him for a terrible moment he half-believed he might end up being trapped there between double barriers of armoured plate. He laid his palm on the cold metal in a sort of placatory gesture and, magically, it trembled once, twice, before allowing him his freedom with a soft click.

In one of the blitzed rooms he found a phone. A single digit had somehow been rubbed off his palm where he had written Hazel's number. It was either four or six. He dialled six and after the complete sequence had rung out a sleepy voice enquired, 'Yeah?'

He said, 'Natalie?' and the teenager on the other end whined, 'She's asleep. Do you happen to know what time it is, man?'

'Get her. Now!' Sonny rapped. 'This happens to be important. It concerns her mother,' and there was about twenty seconds or so of bumps and moaning in the background before another voice, reassuringly apprehensive, whispered, 'What about my mother? Where is she? What's wrong?'

He said, 'Listen carefully and please do not interrupt. If you care for your mother and I believe you do, Natalie – we both do – I think it would be advisable that you get down here to be with her at this time.' He continued at his most silky and avuncular. 'Natalie, as you know, your mum left London to take a much needed break. I don't have to tell you how hard she works – and for you, Natalie, all for you, remember that. Well, her holiday, I have to report, is doing her a power of good. You really should see her. But then, I'm forgetting you will, and very soon, too. Now, here's the crucial part. You must promise never, ever to breathe a word to her about what I'm about to tell you. Do I have that promise? I do? Good. Let me put it this way. Natalie, your lovely mum, who we both care for so much, happens to be a lot more seriously run down than she realises.'

He allowed the words to sink home, primed and loaded. 'That's all I'm prepared to say at this stage. But I will say, hold yourself in readiness like a good girl, because I'll be ringing you back within the next few hours or so with the necessary travel arrangements. Have you got all that? Good.

224

Go back to bed now, get your beauty sleep, for I want you to be looking your best tomorrow for your mother's sake. Mine, too, for I really am looking forward very much to meeting you. *My* name? Oh, just call me Sonny, everyone does. Just plain old Sonny.' He rang off.

That little bitch, he thought, she doesn't know what's hit her yet. He hadn't the slightest guilt, not the slightest, about what he'd done. Why should he? It came down to simple self-preservation and the way to manage that was by keeping one jump ahead, or – as his new song put it – 'playing for time'.

He remembered sitting there in that empty room thinking of some more words to add to what he'd already written in his head. The silent phone was in his lap – he realised it was a little off-balance because he seemed to have a hard-on. Now, wasn't that weird, he told himself, to be entertaining such thoughts? But he was, no doubt about it. *Two* half-clad women, now – one ripe, the other not nearly so – scampered through his fantasies. With closed eyes, he pictured himself deliciously spoiled for choice.

But by then he must have lost his nerve, for the next thing he remembered was heading outside and down to the artificial lake to wash off any traces of the redhead's scent in case Hazel should rumble him.

All of that he was going over now, in his head, as he sought a way out of the house for the second time that night.

Or was it morning? His footsteps echoed along empty corridors, bare boards cracking like rifle fire; every door he passed seemed to open on yet another naked room. And no sign anywhere of the special door that had been reinforced with bare metal, like the entrance to a tomb. Had he imagined all of that, then?

One of the rooms overlooked a terrace littered with broken pots and beyond that, an overgrown lawn, and then, further still, a greenhouse in an equally picturesque state of ruin. Stopping to look out at all of this, Sonny saw there was a french window. The catch was open or, more likely, broken, so he stepped out at last into the real world of

225

birdsong, early morning dew and the heavy scents of summer.

He breathed it in like an escapee giving thanks. Then he set off, jogging unsteadily for the camper, to catch up on his sleep and to be in shape for the momentous events which he felt certain lay ahead.

—THREE—

'Deep Water'

'Remember, when you were a kid, how the summer holidays just seemed to go on and on and on?'

'Like now, you mean?'

'Something like that.'

They were stretched on a rug close to the water's edge, a couple of beached bums lazily browning. He had on a pair of old denim cut-offs and she was wearing a halter top and snug, matching shorts. Moments earlier, at her bidding, he'd undone the top to rub on some more tanning lotion. His palms felt oily. He wiped them now on the warm wool by his sides like the slob he'd always suspected he might turn out to be.

'Is today *really* Sunday?'

'Listen,' he said, raising himself on a bare elbow, and the sound of bells, continuous and closely connected, came flooding on the air from some invisible and distant steeple.

'We're a couple of pagans,' she sighed.

'Feels marvellous, doesn't it?'

It was his day of rest, but then so were all the other days now slipping past as easily as beads on a string. Closing his eyes against the hot sun he saw floating red-gold motes and, as with his necklace of days – nights too – felt too lazy to bother to count. All was well with his world. At last. Natalie was in her tent listening to her head-banger music, as ashen-faced as when they first picked her up at Taunton, but if all of that kept her happy, which meant mother as well, why should he worry? Pilgrim, too, was hiding from the light, deep in his underground retreat, brooding amongst his relics; Choctaw had taken the Buick off to pick up something an hour or more earlier. Which left our two love-birds down by the lakeside working on their tans.

Hazel said, 'I can feel my back burning. Do you mind, Sonny?' And, dutifully, he straddled that perfect, globed ass to unhook the clasp holding her halter in place. The thick, coconut-smelling cream slaked the broad expanse of hot flesh as he slid his hands around and under to where the skin was cool and milky pale.

'How's that?'

'Nice,' he heard her murmur.

It was hard to keep the groan out of his voice then, as he said, 'Why don't you take this damn thing off? You're only going to get a white stripe.'

'That's all right,' she replied, her voice muffled in the plaid of the rug, but it wasn't, was it? Since Natalie had arrived with her belongings in a single Miss Selfridge carrier bag – the tent was something Choctaw had provided – Sonny's sex life had been a beautiful memory.

'Be patient, please,' Hazel kept telling him in whispered tones. 'Please, not with Natalie out th_._.'

Out there being a site a good forty yards away and one which the young camper had agonised over until even Choctaw's grin had shown signs of strain. Now she spent her days stretched in the khaki gloom of the little army pup tent tuned into Heavy Metal, refining her graveyard looks. Perhaps she only came out at night, Sonny conjectured.

At the bus station he hadn't recognised the young Gothic, as she now called herself, waiting for them. Hazel seemed to have much the same difficulty, but put a brave face on things. It could have been much worse, she confided to Sonny and, after all, she had travelled all this way down to see them, which must mean something...

Driving back in the big white car Sonny was grateful for Choctaw's unrelenting good humour. Behind, silently sat mother and daughter – reunited, thanks to Sonny. Not a word had passed between himself and Natalie on that score since, and that was the way he wanted to keep it. Anyway, life was a funny thing, he decided, and something good might well arise yet from his endeavours, even if he was to lose his balls if the truth were ever to come out. But, fuck it, wasn't he now a born-again optimist, thanks to this life of ease here deep in the heart of the heart of the country? He felt healthier than he had been for months, years, even.

230

If only Hazel would just loosen up a little, forget her scruples about that little Miss Living-Dead of hers back there under her canvas shroud. He looked down at the deep, glistening rivulet below him, curving oh so sweetly to the cleft of the buttocks, and he groaned again. Couldn't help himself.

Hazel murmured lazily, 'You all right, Sonny?' and he lied, 'Fine, just fine.' Sometimes he was far too nice for his own good.

He rose then, leaving her spread among the Sunday papers and went down to the lake to cool off. The brown waters rose up, up, over his shins, then his knees, then on until they covered the bump of his ardour. Standing there, waist-deep, he felt like one of those Highland cattle in one of those really bad paintings, but it was a *good* feeling. He knew just what must have been going on behind those great swatches of mane covering those big, dull eyes. Moo, he thought, life really is good. I could stand here like this for ever with my hocks deep in mud and the sun on my shoulders.

It must have been like this once upon a time back home, he told himself, yet he couldn't remember it. But then, the landscapes of his own country had never really appealed, not totally. Always, there was some imperfection, some mis-shape of hill or pasture or river bank to spoil it for him. He wanted what he saw to be like the plates in the books he read, magical realisations of thicket and sward and distant turrets and above all, a winding white track with one tiny figure – himself – toiling upwards on his solitary quest. The artist who illustrated those pages must have been thinking of places such as this. The water surrounding him rippled like silver mesh, while the foliage of the trees on the far shore seemed to smoke in the heat. The sleeping heart of England, the imagined England, of all those books he'd read, enclosed him.

High above, the vapour trail of a fighter plane unravelled impossibly slowly against an unblemished backdrop of blue. The eye of the needle, the jet, was invisible. A man was up there stitching a seam across the curve of the heavens. And, as if to remind him of that other world the pilot had come from, literally seconds ago, a sonic boom arrived to crack the silence open. Sonny thought of the famous airfield with its protesting women camped like squaws about the perimeter fence. That was England, too. It was out there beyond those encircling hills, a place where people awoke each morning, seemingly a fraction crazier than the day before. Now they were poisoning food on the supermarket shelves for ransom; a mother who was being raped sang nursery rhymes to her little child in its cot and, afterwards, her attacker, a soldier on leave, asked her if she'd enjoyed it and made a date to meet her at a McDonald's the following day.

It was all in those papers lying back there. They'd gorged themselves on the details all morning. At Marlow a crowd of gypsies had blocked off the A404 bypass and staged a horse and buggy race over a mile and a half of its length, and at Welling a pitched battle had raged for nearly two hours between members of a returning Civil War Association and a pub full of locals who had jeered at their costumes. One of the combatants had been run through by a Cavalier's sword and the mob then tore a brick wall down with their bare hands in retaliation.

The tide of all that midsummer madness it seemed was lapping further and further afield. For the first time Sonny thought of the goings-on in Pilgrim's house on the night he and Hazel had arrived.

With the imagined baying of the barbarians in his ears, he dived deep into the lake and began to strike out at a leisurely crawl. After a dozen strokes he headed off parallel to the shingly shore for he had always been something of a coward when it came to fresh water. Back home, bodies were always being fished from rivers, pools and weirs in the swimming months. The darkness of the water, it seemed to him, helped conceal twice as many perils as the clean-coloured sea, yet he continued to love the soft, and silken pull of it. Leaving barely a ripple behind on the calm surface, he settled into a steady, efficient rhythm. His head he kept raised from the water, in a style which everyone seemed to use at home as if, unconsciously, the model derived from the otters and other animals which shared the same rivers. So, swimming like the country boy he still was, Sonny made his way around the man-made curve of this perfect English lake, a little figure in a story-book setting.

Presently he came to a promontory overgrown with alder and dog rose and there, on its highest point, in keeping with his fantasy, crouched a picturesque ruin, windowless and open to the sky. He swam ashore and found his footing on washed gravel which gave way to a winding path through the thorns. Rabbits had nibbled the grass down to a fine and springy carpet, their droppings scattered like liquorice pellets.

He was enjoying the feel of the warm turf beneath his soles when suddenly he heard music played at low level. He stopped to concentrate, but there were no clues in the faint throb of the beat. Picnickers? But, if so, what were they doing on Pilgrim's land? For a second or two he felt an irrational resentment. Not only were they trespassing on his host's private and well-protected domain but, in another and more curious way, it was as though they had invaded the territory of his dream of a moment ago. Then the music gave way to an announcer's soft tones and he thought, they've brought along a radio with them to cheapen all of this even further.

Crouching down, he crept the last few yards prepared for the ultimate in vulgarity – a beach umbrella perhaps, or how about a couple of those folding aluminium chairs in bright primary colours? But it was something pale and large, catching the light through the foliage, slab-sided like an expanse of fridge door, that halted him. What could it be? And how had it got here? But then he realised that it had travelled on four fat white-walled tyres – imported Firestones – for hadn't he himself remarked on their very sumptuousness each time he'd been driven in it? Parked just ahead in a clearing in front of the Gothic-looking heap was Pilgrim's big Buick. Now, this changed everything and he was about to retreat to the water leaving the man to his own private and very personal devices when someone laughed from inside the walls, a light, young and feminine

233

laugh. Sonny couldn't help himself: *Pilgrim? With a woman?*

Curiosity inflamed, he crept closer to where the fallen masonry formed a scree about the base of the ivy-covered ruin. Now he could see straight through the shell of the building, for two casement-sized gaps in the stone were suddenly perfectly aligned. Framed in the far opening was a rose bush long since returned to its wild state, great fistfuls of pink blossom detaching themselves even as he looked. A perfect backdrop for dalliance, more stuff from his book of fairy tales...

Sonny squatted on the shifting bed of debris and waited. Presently his stealth and patience were rewarded, if that were the right word, for what he witnessed next was not at all what he expected or hoped to see. Choctaw's head, in profile, came up over the nearest sill, followed by Natalie's dyed and shaved poll. They made an interesting contrast in styles, the teenager with the look of someone straight from a crypt, and the brave with his lank locks held in place by a strip of some red stuff. Choctaw put two cigarettes in his mouth and lit them, passing one across to Natalie, and Sonny's blood chilled, for there was no mistaking that post-coital gesture.

Shit, he thought, there goes my idyll for what it's worth, as he started backtracking rapidly away from the scene of the crime. For he had no doubt in his mind that crime was what Choctaw had been involved in with little Miss Jail Bait up there.

Until he reached the water he didn't dare consider the consequences of that bout of open air, under-age fucking and, indeed, he kept his head free of it until he had stroked his way well clear of the promontory and its heap of stones. He turned over on to his back then, to face the blue above, the better to think, as he floated home to Hazel. For there lay the real problem – Hazel. If she were ever to find out ... But then she didn't have to, did she? That little bitch – he'd switched from mother to daughter now – who would have believed she had it in her? Certainly not him, even though he had to admit he did have certain vague ambitions in that direction, for it seemed reasonable at the start that

234

the three of them would end up sharing the camper. But, of course, it was she who had insisted on the tent and again, of course, Choctaw was the one who had provided it. No, no, no, the time-scale on this was all wrong, because she had showed a supreme lack of interest in Choctaw and his charm right from their first meeting. So, getting into her good books, as well as her pants, must have taken place some time later.

Sonny groaned loud and long, then, as he kicked his way through the soft brown waters. He was thinking of the two of them in the tent, under cover of darkness, making up for lost time while he and the mother slept celibate, a stone's throw away, to spare the daughter's delicate young feelings.

Oh, why do you continue to care so much for these people, Sonny, he asked himself. He supposed he must still be in love, that had to be the simple answer, or maybe it was plain stubbornness on his part, a determination not to give up on his great plan of keeping this woman and himself together for as long as he could. He really hated that young London street-brat now, with her spiked hair and clown's make-up. She had brought a whiff of something stale and ugly from that old life of his and its setting that he dearly wished to forget.

But if she were such an enemy, then why couldn't he get these fantasies concerning her out of his head? Proof was there facing him in the bulge in his shorts as he sculled along on his back, like a submarine with its periscope in the raised position. Oh, hell, he thought, you must be crazy if you think all this isn't going to end up in total fucking disaster, Sonny.

Then he submerged and, with the cool waters breaking across his brow, he swam back to face what ever next little surprise fate might hold in store for him.

'Listen: "Police in the Home Counties have accidentally uncovered a gang of car thieves with their centre of operations in a Surrey copse only a short distance away from one of the county's busiest main roads. The gang, five men and a woman, specialised in stealing Fords in the surrounding radius of twenty miles or more. The cars were then driven to the secluded woodland site where they were stripped for spare parts. The police believe the gang had been operating for at least a year before being detected." And the headline? "Car Cannibals In Carshalton"!'

More bulletins from the mad, mad, mad world outside. Sonny couldn't help himself. Now he was reading them out to the others over breakfast.

Hazel slid another rasher on to his plate. She was wearing an old Fleetwood Mac sweatshirt of his as an apron over her shorts, and a blue and white bandanna on her head. She looked as if she'd been living the life of a gypsy for months past, freckled, fit, free from care. In total contrast – certainly, there was no family resemblance, Sonny had been made aware of – Natalie sat in the shade of a nearby tree protecting her pallor. This was the only hour of the day she deigned to join them and then only to nibble an oblong of toast. The rest of the time she appeared to exist on a diet of Bounty Bars, for her tent had a thick and rustling carpet of wrappers. Sonny had glanced in once when he knew she had slouched off somewhere; now, of course, he knew where and with whom.

Hazel said, 'Why don't we go for a drive today? Wouldn't it be nice to see some of the countryside for a change? We're not far from the coast, you know.'

She never addressed Natalie directly, Sonny noticed, although it was quite obvious that this overture certainly was not aimed at him. He kept his mouth filled with bacon wondering just how long these two could keep this up. Life together back in Fulham, he thought bitterly, must be one ceaseless round of girlish gaiety. So what the fuck had happened to allow things to get to such a pitch? He would never forget Hazel weeping in that way, such despair, blaming herself over and over. At the time he told himself, stay out of it, Sonny, stay clear, or at least as long as you can.

Now, putting that advice to continued good use, he observed winningly, 'Wow, you can cook this man here breakfast any old time. Terrific, really terrific.'

Hazel obliged with another sizzling egg, sunny side up. 'The water will be just about hot enough by the time you're ready to wash up.'

'Terrific,' he said again, 'terrific,' clasping the back of that firm and lightly oiled thigh. Delightful tendrils of pubic hair – the merest hint of the bounty in concealment – were just visible where the shorts bit into the flesh. *Hazel, Hazel,* he felt like groaning, *a man can only stand so much, you do know that, don't you?*

At the same time he couldn't help stealing a sly glance across at the Alien under the tree. She must really hate stuff like this between the two of them, he suspected, but that chalk-white mask gave nothing away. Today she was wearing a black string vest under a leather waistcoat, a matching mini, artfully holed tights, and a pair of jackboots. Her bare arms – quite pretty, really, in a plump, girlish way – were weighted by all manner of bracelets, chains and spiked and studded straps, the favourite motif, throughout, being the human skull. Hunkered there in the shade, mittened hands clasping her workhouse knees, she looked in that setting like someone who had got her party invitations mixed up. Or spare prick at a wedding, he thought, with renewed spite.

And, talking of pricks, who should stroll up at that very moment but Young Chief Snake In The Grass with a wide grin for all. He said, 'Hi. I see you folks are having some chow.'

Hazel gestured with the frying pan but he declined the invitation with a charming sweep of his hand. He turned his beam on Sonny. 'I bring a message from the great man back yonder.'

'Speak, oh, fleet one,' replied Sonny. 'What does the mighty chief in his big white tepee on the hill desire of this humble foot-soldier?'

Choctaw continued smiling but with a touch of unease now. Don't try it on with me, you young bastard, thought Sonny. I know where you've been dipping your wick, even though you haven't looked at her once, not once, since you got here.

237

'Pilgrim wanted me to ask you if you'd care to go with him somewhere in the car today. He didn't tell me where.'

'You mean the great pale wagon with many, many horses under its bonnet?'

'He'd like you to drive him. Is that okay?'

'Our tepee sits on the mighty chief's hunting-grounds. His wish is our command. Go, fleet one, and make ready the great wagon whose roof comes down like the walls of a wigwam.'

Choctaw dithered. There was something else. 'Why don't you go along, too?' he said, looking sideways at Hazel.

'Maybe. I'll see,' she said, busy with the breakfast things.

Then, finally, he turned on his heel and walked off up the hill. Sonny stared at his retreating shoulder blades certain he could detect nervousness there. Or guilt, perhaps? *No. Guile, guile.*

Hazel said, 'You're as bad as he is. Two grown men,' and clicked her tongue, but he knew she was in a good mood. Which was all that mattered.

The Alien still sat crouched under the tree. She was inspecting her long silver nails now, one by one, minutely. She was like one of those deadpan capuchin monkeys in the zoo obsessively grooming themselves to no apparent purpose. For a tiny moment he felt something like compassion; poor little ape, it could have been so good, the three of them on the road together. Something on the lines of Johnny Cash and his family – singing for their supper. But, alas, there seemed little hope of a miracle of that sort now, after what he'd seen yesterday around by the lake shore. More of the same seemed to be on the agenda for later, if he could read Choctaw's mind correctly. Chief Worm In The Apple. Just suppose he got her in the family way? Just suppose. Should he be concerned? Perhaps he did have a duty to warn Hazel.

He said, 'You *will* come along, won't you? For the ride? After I've washed up,' and Hazel laid her hand on his cheek, almost as if by accident, as she took his plate away. Sonny knew she didn't want the Alien to see, but he didn't care, for he felt close to danger point with sudden, exploding love.

238

'Dreams of the Everyday Housewife'

The sea. She couldn't stop thinking about the sea for some reason. All morning and now in the back of the convertible, as she rode, the sound and salty odour of it, the most amazing thing. Would they drive her there? She hadn't the courage to ask. No mention yet had been made of any destination. Sonny merely followed Pilgrim's murmured instructions, left, right, take this turn or the next, as he steered the big American car along the country roads away from traffic. The wheel, black and knobbed under his hands, looked enormous. He gripped it tightly, she noted, the way a little boy might do who has been entrusted with something very grown up and valuable. She remained unimpressed. When she'd been younger she quite liked being seen in snazzy cars. Snazzy. Christine had taught her that.

She remembered ... The two of them off for a dirty weekend with a couple of Warren Street fly-boys driving someone else's Lancia. And the sea came into it, for wasn't it Brighton? Closing her eyes, Hazel lay back against the cream leather upholstery. At night the bedroom windows of the hotel – it may have been the Grand – had been flung wide to the Channel and the rush and roar of its race up the beach. All night long that eerie scrabbling out there, as if some amphibian kept trying to get ashore, only to end up each time being sucked back down the slope of the shingle.

She and Christine had met up over breakfast to compare notes. Something of a wash-out, in both cases. The gleaming car parked on the front in the morning sun had retained its glamour, but its two drivers, alas, had not. Christine suggested they ditch them and that's what they did, sneaking out of the hotel with their vanity-cases like a couple of giggling schoolgirls. They found a bed and breakfast place and, for the rest of that week-end, became sisters on a seaside jaunt, doing all the things two country-bred girls might do

239

in such a situation. Wearing Kiss Me Quick hats and linking arms, they sauntered along the promenade with all the other trippers, eating whelks, fish and chips, rock and candyfloss; had funny photographs taken; shrieked from the top of the Big Wheel, then later out of the deep black maw of the Ghost Train. She would never forget that time, never.

Strange to realise how strong a pull salt water should continue to have on her.

Again she remembered as she travelled in the back of this great, low, growling car that when she'd been expecting Natalie she'd dreamed constantly of dulse. Which on the Beaverbrook Estate, Ealing at that time was like craving reindeer steak or truffles. Come to that, it might have been easier to obtain such items, given that she'd never, ever seen the local delicacy away from home. She saw it now, smelt, tasted the salt from the sea still on it, the red and brown edible weed. Dulse. It was part of her childhood. She wanted to call out to Sonny right now, involving him in her past. *Remember the way it used to cling to your teeth. Remember? And people always telling you it was full of iodine. Iodine? Could you ever understand that?*

But, of course, she didn't utter a word. The two in front were so serious, so preoccupied with men's matters, had been from the word go. She looked carefully at the backs of their heads. Two pigtails, one prematurely grey, the other vaguely chestnut, both held in place so neatly with rubber bands. Men, she thought. Their vanity. The image they have of themselves always based on some fantasy, as if dressing for the part could somehow make it all come true. But Sonny was all right, she could put up with him, his particular brand of conceit. Harmless, like herself.

She felt a sudden burst of affection for him and his hippy hair-do. After all, he had brought Natalie and her together. She'd no idea what he'd said on the phone that time, but whatever it was it had worked. In some sort of odd, almost superstitious way, she didn't even want to know, because for the first time in a very long time she felt she and her daughter might be able to get things straightened out between them. Certainly there had been no miraculous change in her manner, she continued to mooch in that same old, sullen, street-wise way and the clothes and the make-up were a constant shock to her, but only last night she had asked her if she, Hazel, was all right. It came out in a curious, half-reluctant fashion. They were alone at the time, Sonny had sloped off somewhere, and she had been so overcome at what she took to be concern that she'd hugged her to her and cried, 'I've never been better! Can't you see it for yourself? Look!'

She drew back seeking confirmation in the other's eyes, the truest mirror of them all. But Natalie had gone stiff again and it was like holding a total stranger who avoided her scrutiny. She smelt more than a little sweaty as well, mixed with the patchouli, but all of that she put aside, still holding on to the concern she felt certain she detected. And, as she continued to ride with her thoughts for company in the back of the car, nothing could shake that belief. A mother, she told herself, could always recognise such things, no matter how far the two people concerned had drifted apart.

She must have fallen asleep, because when she came to with a start they were passing slowly through empty, sunlit streets, a town of sorts. Crazy as it sounded, she knew they were nowhere near the sea, for there was something airless and land-locked about the place. A bell tolled softly as the car idled past tiny, old-fashioned shops closed for lunch, an Oxfam, a greengrocer's with tired looking produce behind the glass, a hairdresser's with a dozen dead driers inside in the gloom. Its window had pictures of outdated perms, the paper turned blue by the chemical action of the sunlight. You could get like one of those photographs, she told herself, if you lived long enough in such a setting.

Her mouth felt dry from her nap; she badly needed to stop somewhere to freshen up. Soon she hoped they might glide clear of these back streets and once more be able to feel the play of moving air. The leather on either side of her felt hot to the touch.

And then she saw Pilgrim lay a hand on Sonny's arm. With his other hand he gestured a little way ahead and the

241

beat of the engine slowed even further until Sonny brought the car to a halt outside what looked like a derelict cinema. Peeling signs advertising Bingo nights overlaid the remnants of an ancient *Carry On* film poster, Sid James leering down at her, the only woman in the vicinity. They sat there in silence gazing out at the padlocked, double doors and the flanking display cases stripped of their stills, until Sonny said, 'Well, here it is!' and Hazel began to realise that these two pig-tailed heroes had somehow become conspirators in something she knew little or nothing about.

Pilgrim began climbing out and Sonny, with surprising speed, moved around to the passenger side to steady and support him. He saw Hazel looking at him as he did so and flashed her a rueful smile, but again why should she concern herself with what went on between the two of them?

She had decided she would take Natalie to the sea for a few days, perhaps more, just themselves, as soon as possible, no expense spared, for she had succeeded in convincing herself that ozone possessed magical properties. Breathing in lungfuls of the stuff together would somehow hasten the healing of that rift between them. A process which had already begun, she now told herself, if last evening's little episode were to be believed, and she did, oh, she did ...

'Hazel!' Sonny was calling out to her from the steps leading to the ancient picture-house.

For the first time she saw its name ASTOR picked out across the front in faded thirties script. Hard to visualise the place as ever being spankingly modern, yet it certainly must have been, once upon a time, confounding the rustics. She remembered the country flea-pit she herself used to go to on Saturday nights. It had a green-painted corrugated iron roof and whenever there was a downpour, which wasn't rare, the clamour drowned the soundtrack, so it was like being transported back in time to an earlier silent era.

'Hazel!'

Before he could summon her a third time she scrambled out of the burning back seat. Pilgrim had handed Sonny a bunch of keys and stood swaying a little on his stick watching him fiddle with the padlock and its chain. For a moment

Sonny sweated, the eager pupil trying hard not to fail at his allotted task, but then the key did turn and the chain slid freely to the ground. The doors opened before him and Sonny led the way into the stale-smelling gloom.

They were in the foyer, unmistakably so, despite the ravages of neglect. The carpet, faintly geometric in pattern, felt spongy underfoot, for water dripped steadily and invisibly in one dark corner. But there was the ticket booth with its horseshoe opening, and over there a counter where someone must have stood bored in front of shelves of popcorn, soft drinks and souvenir programmes. A flight of stairs, almost certainly, led to an unseen balcony overhead, while to the right of where the three of them were positioned, double doors still were clearly marked STALLS. Pointing with his stick Pilgrim directed Sonny to the cashier's den.

Hazel looked at him as he followed Sonny's progress with that fierce, unblinking stare of his. Some preoccupation of enormous proportion seemed to dog him without rest. But Sonny saved her from further speculation by pulling the correct switch, and the lights sprang on.

The twin port-holes in the doors leading to the cinema proper also took on brightness and the two men headed straight through leaving her to trail behind. Inside, most of the seating had been ripped out leaving great ragged tears in the sloping floor, but she found a place to sit near the back on the aisle – old habits dying hard. Her companions had headed towards the front rows and were looking up at the curtains. The screen had also been plundered, leaving a bare expanse of brick back wall. Then Sonny climbed up on to the stage. She couldn't make out what he was saying to Pilgrim down below, but he was expressing enthusiasm, she could clearly see that. His arms went out and up, he laughed, and she thought, I know that old line, impressing others with his own fervour again.

She had a sudden desire to observe from an even more remote and private vantage point so, without fuss, she left her seat and slipped out the way she'd come. The stairs leading to the balcony (or was it the circle?) were dark and threatening but she felt stubborn and kept on going. At the

243

top the doors were missing and she did feel nervous then at the sight of that brutal, gaping opening but the lights were on inside so she went through.

Everything remained untouched, not a seat missing; there were even a few of those old double divans, reserved for courting couples, she hadn't seen since she was a child. She took her place on one – again, beside the aisle – and beyond the dusty plush of the balustrade where the girl with torch and tray would rest her behind, she had a clear view of Sonny on the stage below. He couldn't see her, at least she hoped not, and she watched his continuing performance. Now he stamped on the bare boards with his heel, listening raptly to the detonation as it echoed in the stillness. With hand cupped to an ear and a serious look on his face, he gave the impression of someone professional, knowing what they were about.

Hazel sat up there under the faded pink roof not really caring. The lighting struggled dimly down from crescent-shaped openings recessed in the curving plaster, the ancient dust of this upper place all about her. She visualised it dropping silently, invisibly, stirred up for the first time in perhaps a decade and there she sat at the heart of its gentle precipitation along with her memories. But not for long. Sonny was staring out now from the stage, a hand shading his eyes.

She heard him say, 'She must have gone back to the car. I'll get her,' and immediately felt guilty.

She called out, 'I'm up here!' making her way to the front of the balcony to show herself.

'Juliet!' he cried out, 'Come down! Romeo has need of you!'

He was waiting for her by the time she had retraced her route down the evil-smelling stairs through the foyer and back into the body of the cinema.

'Let's have a canoodle,' he said, taking her by the arm and planting her in a seat next to his.

She could see Pilgrim in the front row just like one of those solitary fanatics from her childhood. Always there would be a figure of that type taking up his position dead centre and closest to the screen. And no one would ever go near him.

'He bought it a little over a year ago,' confided Sonny, lowering his voice and putting an arm about her. 'But not to show movies in. No, the man has other plans. A dream, if you like. And, believe me, this is a guy who makes dreams come true. Hazel, sweetheart, it's all very much still in the early stages but, you and me, well, we could get involved. The two of us.'

He paused and Hazel knew he was waiting for her to say something, but what could she say? She looked at the lonely figure sitting with his 'dreams' down below them and she thought, yes, you're the one all right, the same one everyone steered clear off, even the boldest and bravest of the matinée roughs who came only to create disturbance in the front rows.

'The West Country's answer to Nashville,' Sonny was saying. 'Can't you just see it? And that man there has the vision to carry it out. As well as the wherewithal, believe me.'

She heard herself ask, 'This old flea-pit?'

'Hazel, Hazel,' Sonny gently chided her. 'Just where do you think the original Grand Old Opry had its first real home? In a place called the Hillsboro Theatre, a disused movie-house, that's where.'

He sighed expansively as if already history was repeating itself and he, Sonny, was in at the rebirth.

Hazel said, 'You mentioned something about you and me being involved in some way.'

'He needs people with vision like himself. Allies. Take it from me, there is a place for us if we really want it.'

Hazel looked at him. His eyes were shining. God, he *is* genuine, she thought, he actually means all of this. As for that other one down there with his back to them, she had no way of telling what his true motives might be. Frankly, she didn't want to, very much. What she had seen of his set-up so far – the big empty house on the lake and that eerie club full of western freaks who only came out after dark – made her wary of involvement.

'Sonny,' she said in a low voice, 'don't you think it's time we moved on? I mean all of this – ' her moving hand took in the dusty shell in which they sat – 'it's not really us, is it? I mean this wasn't the idea when we set out. Or was it? I'm confused.'

'Will you do me one favour? Just one.'

She looked at him. He still had that look in his eyes. She was wasting her breath, she could see that. 'Only if we can get out of here. All this is beginning to give me the creeps.'

And her skin did seem to her to be crawling. Flea-pit, she thought. Why did I have to mention that?

'Okay. Okay.'

He was on his feet enthusiastically dragging her up and out of her place. She could smell the dust of decades, worse things as well now, too, in her imagination. Old men in filthy raincoats haunted such places. The imprint of their lusts lingered on every seat, it suddenly occurred to her.

'Pilgrim wants to sound out the acoustics. Will you sing with me? One teeny weeny number? A chorus? Please. For me.'

Hazel sighed. For you, you great deluded dope, yes; but no way, never, for you, hunched up down there on your sick and solitary throne. For the first time she did think of the man in the black bomber jacket and the baseball cap as crippled, but that's what he was, wasn't he? And suddenly it also struck her that, yes, that other lonely outcast from her childhood had also dragged one of his legs.

'Terrific,' Sonny said, taking her assent for granted and, her hand tightly in his, half-raced her down the incline towards the front of the stalls where he helped her up on to the stage.

She felt like an idiot standing there but she managed to keep her eyes fixed firmly on the projectionist's slits away up there at the rear of the balcony, not once allowing them to drop in the direction of that other figure below.

And so that's how it came about that she found herself duetting on stage in a filthy wreck of a picture-house in some dead town or other whose name she later never even bothered to find out. By then, of course, she had other much more deadly concerns to contend with.

She and Sonny sang together, 'I Beg Your Pardon, I Never Promised You A Rose Garden', while their audience of one looked on in the half light never for an instant taking his deep, unsettling eyes off her.

'I'll Never Get Out of this World Alive'

When Sonny got back he drifted down to Pilgrim's lake, taking his guitar with him. On a flat, still warm stone close to the water's edge he ran through a few standards, surprising himself at just how much his chording seemed to have improved. As soon as he could arrange it he was going to part-exchange this old box for a newer model, he promised himself, something with class and a deeper, richer tone. His mouth watered at the prospect. All those gleaming ox-blood beauties hanging by the neck like so many prime cuts of beef. Already he saw himself fondling and sniffing, senses running riot in some music shop.

Softly he crooned:

> *Woke up this morning, Chevy wouldn't go,*
> *Just like its owner, battery low ...*

His very own song 'Depreciation Blues'. The one he still hadn't quite got around to finishing. But who could feel any urgency in such a setting?

He looked across the flat expanse of water to the far reaches of the lake fringed by its margin of rushes. A coot, *en famille*, came sailing out fussily between the stalks tug-boat fashion, and he followed its progress until it bobbed back out of sight again. The time was about four thirty, a sad sort of time, Sunday sadness. The dying sun seemed to quiver. It hurt the eyes just looking at it. Sonny threw a stone, then another, and finally one more for luck. He started taking his boots off preparatory to a gentle paddle in the lapping waters when he heard Hazel screaming.

The sound had a hard, cruel urgency about it that made his heart and stomach leap, as he did himself, hopping back into his discarded right boot. He started off up the slope at

248

a gallop, guitar under his arm, but if he'd known it at the time he might just as well have hurled it out into the lake as far as it would go. Or, better still, flogged it to ribbons on the stones, because all of those plans he'd been making were now null and void.

If he'd only known. *Poor Sonny*, he was later to commiserate with himself, *someone certainly does seem to have it in for you, all right*, and that cry echoing out in the stillness, he, somehow knew, marked the beginning of the really bad news for him.

As he ran he kept repeating, 'Fuck, fuck, *fuck*,' over and over as if lamenting his own rotten luck.

When he got to the camper Hazel couldn't be seen, but he heard her wailing some way off in the direction of the little green tent. He unloaded the guitar and raced towards the sound of those animal cries. She was stumbling about the trodden grass with a piece of paper in her hand. There was no sign of Natalie. He must still have been blaming her for his own looming misfortune because he took her roughly by the shoulders. Her face was a mess, eyes all sooty streaks and mouth a purple stain, and the instant he touched her she crumpled on to the grass at his feet. He tried lifting her but she seemed to have put on an alarming amount of weight. He took the paper from her hand.

The note – it was barely more than that – said, 'By the time you find this I'll be far away. I can't go on like this. People are always lying to me. I've got to live my own life. Don't try to find us. Natalie.'

Oh, shit, he thought. Even with your bad luck, Sonny, you couldn't have invented this one. Standing there with that little perfumed bombshell in his hand he felt as if someone had dumped a tipper load of sewage all over him from a very great height. Thank you, oh, thank you, he murmured to that great old Trucker in the Sky, thank you so very much ...

He went to the tent then, mainly to give himself more time to think. Inside nothing seemed to have altered very much. There was the same drift of sweet-shop wrappers with the addition now of several cigarette packets, four, presumably dead, batteries, and an empty Tampax carton. Little slut, he thought, good riddance, but he knew that such a hope was self-delusion. A faint residue of perfume still lingered among the bedclothes similar to that on the sheet of pink notepaper he was holding. You've done for me, you little cow, he thought, and I've got the death warrant here in my hand to prove it.

When he dropped the flap of the tent and turned, he saw that Hazel was now hunkered and rocking back and forth on her heels, hands clasped before her as if in prayer.

'*Us*,' she said. 'What does she mean by *us*? And, *lying*, Sonny. She wrote, people *lying* to me. What people, Sonny? Who?'

Surreptitiously he crumpled the note in his fist as if hoping to get rid of the evidence, but he was already convicted, he knew that. She was rising from the grass unsteadily, but getting stronger by the minute, eyes fixed on him and he suddenly thought, I'm afraid of this woman, I really am.

She got in two really good whacks at him before he made any move. And I'm a fucking masochist, to boot, he was thinking. Then the side of his jaw began to sting and he grabbed her. She was burning up, a damp, infecting animal heat he could feel as they wrestled back and forth over the flattened grass. Crazily he started getting an erection, and again he thought, is this for real? The two of them were panting hard, exhausting each other, but finally all fight seemed to leave her in a rush and she collapsed sobbing in his arms. Staggering under the dead weight of her, he lowered her to the ground and she lay there staring up at the sky. Her shirt had lost its top buttons in the struggle and one of her nipples, hard and surprisingly dark, stood out in full view.

He said, 'This does not help. Not one bit. Now, calm down,' even though it was clearly obvious she had.

'Just tell me what you said to her,' she murmured, sounding like someone under sedation.

'What does it matter?' he started to yell. 'She's fucking well not here, that's the point. Okay?' Striding up and down he was beginning to savour this new-found indignation on his part.

'I just want to know, that's all. Please.'

'Okay! Okay!' he shouted. His jaw was bloody sore by this time and the ache served to stiffen his resolve. No chickening out, he told himself, you can do it, and so he started telling her about the telephone call he had made that night in the small hours.

'You said I was *ill*? You told her *that* to get her down here?'

'Not in so many words. She was the one who put that construction on it.'

Hazel lay stretched full-length there at the centre of their little war-zone of a moment ago. The hot rich colour was leaving her face now and, as he watched, she adjusted her shirt to cover her bared breast. Pity, he thought.

'What did she say? At the time.'

'Barely a word. Just – can I bring someone with me?'

'If she had, this might never have happened.'

'You think so?' he yelled. 'Really? No kidding?'

She covered her eyes, moaning. 'It's all my fault. Deep, deep down, I know it is.'

'No way,' he said, dropping to his knees beside her. 'No way. There's someone else with a hand in this. A certain someone, a certain snake in the grass.'

'Who?' She was sitting up now, her arms rigid with concern. 'Tell me! You must! Who's she with?'

'Take it easy. I need to check something out. Go back to the camper and wait for me there.'

'Oh, Sonny,' she cried, 'we must go to the police. Right away. The sooner the better.'

He looked at her and for the first time considered washing his hands of this whole crazy business. Police, he thought, sweet Jesus Christ! He felt like socking her one. She'd done it to him, remember?

'Look,' he said, rising to his feet. 'We might still be able to get to them if we do it *my* way. Involve the boys in blue if that's the way you feel about it, but count me out, I tell you now.'

251

She looked up at him with tear-filled eyes. He knew the contest was at an end.

'Get packed,' he commanded. 'Five minutes,' holding up his spread hand and leaving her there unmoving on the trampled grass.

Up at the house the car was parked where he'd left it, on the grand sweep close by the steps so that Pilgrim could get inside more easily. They'd walked quickly away without a backward glance sensing he might prefer it that way, but the sound of that laboured ascent punctuated by the crack, crack, of the downward stabbing stick had followed them. Sonny halted now by the car. He leaned against one of its fat chromium fins looking up at Pilgrim's folly. The doors were open to the weather and the interior, as ever, had that terrible dead stillness about it.

Taking his courage in his hands Sonny started the climb, feeling, as he always did on entering this place, like the first man to board the *Marie Celeste*. Inside, dried leaves, other wind-borne debris, as well, lay in drifts along the skirting boards and his soles left long, parallel tracks in the grit underfoot. He looked into a bare room where a trapped bird started up in a frenzy at his passing. Heart beating like the bird's, he gently closed the door on it, then carried on with his pointless quest.

Some sort of confirmation was what he was after, he supposed, as he walked these corridors for the last time, that the dream was over. Somewhere deep in the heart of this mausoleum its owner had by now gone to ground. Remembering that syringe steeping in its bowl, he conjured up an image of him drifting into unconsciousness in his famous general's chair, a chair to dream in. Earlier today on the stage of that old cinema, for a brief moment, he, Sonny, had convinced himself that he might be able to share in those dreams. But how could he have deluded himself, even for the space of a single chorus of a song?

He felt a terrible coldness now, inside as well as out, as he moved along these abandoned passages. Hazel had tried to warn him in her own careful way early on; he wa remembering that now. Not to become involved. Not to get his dreams mixed up with someone else's. Those weren't the words she used, but that's what it came down to. And that other grinning one, as well, with his hippy headband and Apache good looks, he'd known the score right from the start. He had, hadn't he? The memory of those soulful brown eyes going from serious to sad and back again, always so boyish and oh, so disarming, hardened his resolve now to seek him out wherever he might be, for a tiny secret seed of intuition was growing in the dark of Sonny's mind. All it needed was a single ray of confirmation for it to flower into certainty. So he travelled upstairs, remembering vaguely that Choctaw had once mentioned he had a room on the premises on one of the upper floors. He may well have pointed to a high window when they were in the grounds together. When it came to certain details, his memory was seriously at fault these days.

But his instincts were not, because a room there was, the only one not in a completely empty state, and one that looked and smelt like his quarry's lair. The door was open and Sonny went in. On the floor a stripped mattress lay pulled out at an angle from the wall. It had a ragged and yellow-edged stain dead centre and, with malice, Sonny thought, so young Chief Piss The Bed did sleep here after all. A pile of magazines in a corner had been kicked about the floor, some of them open at the centre-folds to show various Playmates of the Month. Interpersed with these were others, catering for motor-cycling tastes, as well as a scattering of what looked like old newspaper cuttings.

As he peered more closely – he was a detective now – he saw that the walls had countless perforations. Some of the pin-ups on the floor must have once hung there, but a few tattered strips still remained of posters not entirely torn away. Sonny recognised enough of the parts of the whole of Hendrix, Zappa, Jim Morrison of The Doors, Janis Joplin and Co. to make him draw a deep breath. *He'd stumbled on to the pad of a crypto hippy.* New wave, of course, for Choctaw had to be too young to ever be part of the original move-ment.

Turning about to face the door, he saw, for the first time, on a bare stretch of wall to its right, a brutal message of defiance rawly printed in blood-red felt tip. EAT THE RICH, it howled and, underneath, THAT MEANS YOU PILGRIM. An abusive postscript read JUNKIE CRIPPLE, punctuated by peace signs. Charming, thought Sonny.

He'd seen enough – or not quite – for he bent and picked from the paper harvest on the floor a handful of the newspaper clippings. All seemed to be taken up with the Convoy, its progress and daily whereabouts as it snaked its mediaeval way across this green, but latterly not so pleasant land. Sonny folded the reports into a hard wad and stuffed them in his hip pocket. Then he closed the door behind him and went back downstairs and out into the early evening air without a backward glance.

When he got to the camper Hazel was sitting in the front looking suicidal. She managed to croak, 'Well? Well?' but he started up the engine without a word, leaving nothing but a gently dropping skein of oily blue exhaust smoke as a memento of their stay. He was in a hard, determined mood. He hoped her view of his profile would make that clear to her and after a little while she did seem to take the hint, for she climbed back over the seat into the dark of the interior. Behind him he heard her moaning to herself and bumping into things. Then there was a muffled thudding sound followed by a breathy sigh and he reckoned she'd flung herself down fully clothed on to one of the bunks. It seemed the best course for her to take in the circumstances.

He headed east, then north on the A361, and at a Texaco station outside Frome stopped to fill up. As the fuel raced through the hose in his hand a feeling of lethargy came over him, a sudden weariness. He should follow Hazel's example, it occurred to him. Why not pull into the next lay-by and wipe out everything that had happened on the bunk across from hers? But, no, that could not be.

He went into the washroom feeling like someone about to embark on a hazardous quest, and he supposed that what he was about could be termed a rescue mission of sorts. But the face reflected in the mirror was certainly no hero's and

254

when he stripped off above the waist for a quick scrub it was equally apparent that the body was hardly that of a knight errant either ...

Paying for the petrol, he bought a newspaper – the *Guardian* was the only one to have news of the Peace Convoy on its front page. A plane hijack in Athens had driven it from the headlines, but it was dying anyway, the long cruel summer having taken its toll.

Hazel was fast asleep when he climbed back into the driving seat, he could tell by her soft and measured breathing, and he felt thankful for that, at least.

On the outskirts of Chippenham the light was fading fast and he stopped to study the map. By his present reckoning he would not be able to reach his destination until well after dark and the last thing he wanted was to go blundering into a blacked-out encampment crawling with unforeseen dangers. Especially dogs. Something he'd read said that dogs figured strongly in the life of these people. The article said that the roaming packs of canines looked better fed than their owners, but he found that hard to believe.

He sat looking out at the occasional car, bus, lorry roaring past. The buses, in particular, left a brief displacement of air in their wake that rocked the camper. A Rapide went by with a painted sign across its rump saying LONDON RETURN £12.50. He watched it disappear in the direction of the M4. Why not, he thought? Just ride away from all of this in upholstered ease, no farewells, no explanations, not a backward look. People did it all the time, one of those great and universal urges, cutting loose, dropping out. John Stonehouse left his clothes behind in a tiny heap on an Australian foreshore like a cast-off skin and people went on naïvely believing that he'd actually swum away from it all, simply because it was something they all wanted to do themselves at one time or another. Deep down.

The dust on the windscreen seemed to be pocked suddenly by tiny spores. At first he couldn't decide what they might be, because no rain had fallen for weeks. It may have been months, but then the storm broke overhead and the glass looked now as if it had reached melting-point, while the taut metal boomed beneath the percussion of the downpour. Hazel slept through it all as he drove on steadily north, even though his head still teemed with escape plans. He'd done it once, remember, not really so long ago, either, when he baled out from the flat in Maida Vale, so why not a second time? Then he thought how much of the reason, then, had been because of the woman now stretched and deeply unconscious just a few feet away. Perhaps when the rain cleared. Or at the next decent-sized town. But the windscreen dried to a dry and sparkling finish and he kept on going through Malmesbury, then Cirencester and beyond.

Eventually he did pull over. The time was 10.15 and the place a stretch of grass verge on a back road not too far from the now famous and ancient airfield he'd read about in the newspapers.

Sonny switched off the lights and waited and watched for the trees and hedgerows to gradually reassert their shapes beyond the glass. He felt like the loneliest being on the planet. He also felt like a man the night before he goes into battle and now, seemingly, with no choice in the matter. And so, like every other poor sod in the same situation who thinks to himself – how did I get myself into this mess, he did what comes naturally, and what came naturally to his hand was a bottle of Bell's he had stowed away in one of the deep drawers under the vacant bunk for just such a contingency.

Legs outstretched, he sat there seriously getting drunk across from the sleeping figure on the other bed. Hazel lay in shadow, curled up facing the wall and with her thumb in her mouth, he felt certain, somehow. As the whisky snaked its way comfortingly through his system he began by feeling relaxed which, of course, led to a slow and spreading flush of sentiment. His eyes began misting at the thought of his feelings for the slumbering woman, her vulnerability, as she slept there so trustingly. And he was the man to earn that trust, he told himself. At daylight he would do what a man had to do. It all seemed so clear-cut.

He thought of an old and favourite movie, *The Searchers*.

The two great Johns, Wayne and Ford, at their finest. Now, why hadn't that come to him before? He almost laughed out loud in the semi-darkness – the moon had risen by now and, slicing through a crack in the curtains, silvered his left boot in its narrow, concentrated beam. And, my God, the girl in that, the one they went after, was actually played by *Natalie Wood*. He took another controlled slug of the whiskey and water. This was amazing, truly amazing! He was starting to feel a little tipsy by now, but he concentrated on the scenario. Young white girl is kidnapped by the Sioux or was it the Apache – what the fuck? – anyway, John Wayne and Jeffrey Hunter, taking the part of the brother, go in search of her right into the very heart of Indian territory, braving everything along the way. Girl doesn't want to go home with them, but true grit triumphs, girl gets rescued, end of movie ...

Sonny fell back on to the foam-covered cushions in the hot grip of fantasy. Already he was seeing himself carrying that other Natalie off pillioned behind him on an imaginary palomino. Oh, boy, oh, boy. He felt like rousing Hazel to acquaint her with such a stunning coincidence and surely an amazing omen as well, eh? But, then, he thought, who am I fooling, who cares? For the whisky had started changing tactics about this time. Yes, who gives a damn? Who? Go on, tell me.

Self-pity was in full flood now making his eyes water for the second time since he'd uncorked the bottle. He poured himself some more. One-way traffic. He was sick and tired of it, everything going out from him, give, give, give. I mean, just look at her, he harangued silently, lying there steeped in her own concerns, oblivious. I need, too, you know. I *need*, damn you! The bottle went over and he dived after it in half-cocked fashion but still managing to save the last third from the carpet.

The noise woke Hazel and she started up shouting, 'Where? Where?'

He made an obscene reply, loud enough for her to hear, and that marked the onset of a very ugly scene between them. The whiskey started talking in earnest and the more she retreated into herself – this was a Hazel who frightened him with her dead, despairing eyes – the crueller he became. His accusations got wilder, anything to hurt. He called her a slag, a whore; hadn't she served her apprenticeship with those other two sixties sluts? For he remembered every single thing she'd ever told him – it was all in here. He beat his temples with the bottle, then put it to his lips. And Lester. Did she take him for a total fool, there, as well? Did she? What was it like screwing an old bloke? Or did he just need a *touch*? In his inflamed state terrible images now swamped him. Lester on a bed in that flat of his, being serviced. His pensioner's body white as a corpse. Eyes closed, gasping, then going limp and death-like as if in rehearsal for the real thing. The unspeakable worked its way up into his brain. Had that in fact been the actual way of it, when it did come? That grief of hers at the funeral? My God, he could see it all so clearly!

'*Where is it? Where?*' He was yelling, out of control. He pulled her plaid suitcase from under the bunk. Even that was a target for his fury. 'All packed up, eh? Ready to go, eh? Skelter, skelter, scurry, scurry, eh? Let's see the famous remains, then. Last of the red-hot geriatric lovers.'

Digging like a crazed terrier, he was flinging her things all over the floor now until his fingers found it. The Holy Grail. He held it aloft and, God forgive him, he actually did shake it close to his ear, that sad, sealed little box of tricks. She sat on the rumpled narrow bed opposite watching all of this madness, biting her hands, and somehow it only made him worse seeing her like that, for he knew just how powerless she must feel. He knew and she knew that he, Sonny, was the only hope she'd got if she wanted her daughter returned to her. No matter what he said or did, all she could do was chew on her fists and put up with it. It seemed to him, at that moment, that he had an infinite capacity for retribution, yet nothing he could do or say, no matter how heinous, could ever hope to even the score; he felt as if he might choke on his accumulated resentment.

In a final spasm of panic he imagined that the place he was in was much too dangerously small to contain all the spite he had in him, and he lurched out into the night, clutching the by now empty bottle and hugging Lester's ashes in their foreign-made cigar box. He broke through a hedge into a field and stumbled around for a bit, arguing loudly at times with himself, at others with soft reasonableness. There was so much he had to explain, *explain*. The moon looked down, neutral as ever, on this human insect below exhausting itself.

At some stage he must have reached just such a state, dropping down where he stood, because when he came to, it was light. The grass was soaking wet, as were his clothes, and the birds kept up an unfeeling chorus that sawed at his brain. The bottle was gone. For some weird reason that threw him into a panic. He started searching feverishly, when it hit him with a hammer blow that the box was missing also. *Lester*, he thought, *for you to end up in some corner of a foreign field. Oh, my God!* He began by quartering the grass, spreading out methodically from the trampled den where he'd lain then, growing more desperate, making panicky runs to outlying parts of the field. A herd of black and white cows stood watching his antics in innocent wonder from across the hedge. In the middle of it all he thought, I could never explain this to anybody, not ever, and nobody would believe me even if I were to try. His whole life appeared to be like that in that moment, a tale told by a lunatic. But he was saved from further insanity, for there, hidden by a tussock of grass, lay the missing box, agleam with dew. Wiping it carefully he placed it inside his shirt for safe keeping, then made his way back to the camper.

Hazel was in a deep and catatonic slumber when he opened the door. He was glad of that. Without a sound he found his guitar and hat and quietly slipped back outside again. In the mirror attached to the driving door he gave himself a quick examination. He had a couple of severe looking scratches and there was a smear of dried mud on one cheek and across his brow. Soaking his bandanna in dew from the windscreen he applied it to his face and hands and then finished his gypsy's toilet by rubbing down the

259

front of his jeans and shirt. He still smelt like some creature of the wild, but then that would hardly be held against him where he was heading.

Well, Sonny, he told himself, time to do what a man's got to do. But any inspiration derived from John Wayne and his mythic quest seemed to have disappeared with that last inch at the bottom of the whiskey bottle. He set off walking, guitar slung across his shoulder, and wearing his hangover like a badge for all to see.

The line of dark blue police vans began about a mile up the road. There was also a mobile caterer's with its shutters down and the driver in his whites asleep in the cab, head under a copy of the *Sun*, which seemed appropriate, seeing that that particular paper had it in for the Convoy more than most. Sonny found himself moving past the column of parked vehicles on the balls of his feet, as if by some stroke of extreme good fortune he might just be able to slip through without being noticed.

But, up ahead, a group of about a dozen were gathered around a brazier. A dozen uniforms. They seemed in high spirits, quite a few had their helmets off and, as he came closer, he saw a couple having a stand-up wrestling bout like two overgrown schoolboys. They both had fairish moustaches and ruddy red cheeks. There was a single black constable, buttoned strictly, unlike most of the others, and with his helmet set square on his head. He was the first to spot Sonny and his attention never wavered from him as he approached. Then they all started to eye him in that professional way of theirs. Sonny felt cold and shaky and his mouth tasted like the bottom of a kiln. Certainly he was in no shape to give a good account of himself or, more to the point, 'account for his movements', to use one of their favourite expressions.

No one uttered a word until he had run the gauntlet of these short-haired, cold-eyed young guardians of the law, all of them, incidentally, making a fortune in overtime. No wonder they seemed so happy in their work. Then one of them called out, 'Come far, have we?' A plumpish rustic, his accent was pure mummerset.

Sonny idled to a halt. 'A fair bit,' he said.

Another chipped in with, 'On the road early, friend, eh?'

Sonny looked him in the eye. 'Got the time, mate?' He tapped his bare wrist in what he hoped was a disarming gesture.

The man who had spoken turned away and a fresh interrogator lazily took his place. 'Should have saved yourself the trouble – if you've travelled far. We'll be going in there in under an hour. All change. Tell your friends that, Pat, won't you?'

Sonny started to move away. 'I'll do that,' he said with the utmost politeness.

They watched in silence as he walked off. Just as he thought he'd got clear, a new voice cried, 'Hey, you! Michael!'

He turned. It was the black policeman. He was unbuttoning his tunic pocket and coming towards him. Sonny waited. The birds had stopped singing. He stood there on that bone-dry Wiltshire road smelling his own sweat with his heart doing double time, because he knew if he were to be searched now he was a goner. Shreds of dope in his pocket he wasn't concerned about, oddly enough, but the box he could feel next to his skin did cause him alarm. No way could he ever hope to explain the like of that away, particularly its sealed state, to this black tormentor now approaching, notebook out and at the ready. If there was a God anywhere and one with a sense of humour surely he must make this man recognise the irony of the situation, someone white like him about to be frisked by a black man here in Thatcher's England.

But there was no hint of humour in that face, none at all. 'Name?' the face said, uncocking his ball-point, although both knew that was merely a cynical prelude to those pale, coffee-coloured hands sliding up and down and over his body.

They confronted one another in the middle of the country road, Sonny actually praying for a divine intervention –

261

what a believer he was turning out to be – and then it actually seemed to arrive, for one of the other coppers called, 'Leave it out, Nelson!' followed by a colleague, 'Yeah, leave it out! Breakfast time! Grub up! Chop-chop!' And the black PC slowly put his pen and notebook away.

'I'll see you in about an hour's time – Paddy,' he said. 'We're going to trash you scum, then, once and for all.'

Sonny nodded humbly in reply and the other walked off in the direction of his mates.

About fifty yards beyond the route took a fork, but there were arrows painted on the tarred surface of the sort he remembered from home employed on treasure hunts over country back roads. Strips of rags had also been tied to various trees at intervals. Sonny followed all of these make-shift signs and presently he came to another turning, this time surmounted by an arch formed of saplings and crowned by the horned, bleached skull of some animal. A sign said, WELCUM TO SLEEPY HOLLOW and below it another one read, ABANDON HOPE ALL YE WHO ENTER HERE. Some joker had put a cross through HOPE and substituted SOAP. Sonny smiled in spite of himself and passed through the rustic arch.

He found himself looking over a flat and derelict expanse dotted by a crazy collection of ancient vehicles of all ages and sizes – lorries, vans, campers, cars and caravans and a sprinkling of period touring coaches, most of which bore signs of habitation. Many had smokestacks and tattered drawn curtains, as well as lines of washing. No evidence of external life appeared to exist, for nothing stirred and nothing could be heard save the birds.

Sonny stood surveying the scene, convinced he had made a massive miscalculation. He felt like an alien visitor on some remote and undreamt-of planet, while at the same time recognising that his means of escape had been cut off. The guitar on his back weighed a ton. He'd only brought the damn thing in the hope it might help to make him less conspicuous, lending credence to his presence. So, he thought.

He decided to go forward. There were indications that the site once had echoed to the roar of Spitfires and Hurricanes. A brick-built stump in the distance could well have been a control-tower and, underfoot, were the remains of what he took to be ancient runways. The imprint of their archaeology carried him in a straight line right to the heart of the encampment. Among the buses and vans he now saw low shelters covered in tarpaulin which he understood were called 'benders' by the sleepers within. A smell of wood smoke hung in the air, yet he could see no rising trails anywhere across the site. His nose led him on to an almost dead campfire and he prodded the ashes with a length of pipe for a bit before dropping down on to an old bus seat nearby.

He must have dozed off because the next thing he knew he was encircled by a cluster of grubby urchins, one of whom must have reached out to touch him. They observed him silently with the utmost seriousness, like little ragged old men. Sonny smiled but it was something useless he'd carried with him from the outer world where children were supposed to react positively and pleasantly to such overtures.

'Play us something,' the eldest one said in a hoarse voice, pointing to the guitar. 'Do you know "Pigs In Blue"?'

'Afraid not, son. What's your name?'

'I'm not a son, I'm a girl, and my name is Rainbow. This is Ziggy and he's Zack, and that's Plum, my sister.'

'Ah,' said Sonny feeling even more of an alien.

Signs of activity were now becoming apparent to him. One or two bedraggled figures wrapped in blankets were wandering around stretching and yawning. A girl staggered along under a yoke made out of two petrol cans, and fingers of smoke could be seen climbing lazily from several of the chimneys.

'I'm looking for a friend of mine,' he said. 'His name's Choctaw and he's only been here a little while. He came last night with his friend. She's a punk girl called Natalie. They came on his motor-bike. I tell you what, if you tell me where I can find them, I'll sing you a song. How's that?'

The one called Rainbow fixed him with a beady blue eye. 'You're not a *real* traveller, are you? You don't look

263

like one. He doesn't look like one, does he?' The others shook their matted little heads and Sonny suddenly recalled that painful Western sequence where the captured white man gets handed over to the tender mercies of the young fry and squaws of the tribe.

Hurriedly he said, 'Here, why don't you buy yourself some sweeties,' pulling out a handful of change, most of which were pound coins.

Little Miss Tormentor In Chief looked into his cupped palm and then up at him. 'Sweets are bad for you, didn't you know that? They're not pure, they're not natural.' Then, with chilling disdain, 'You must go and talk to Baz, not us. We're only children. Baz is our leader. He lives over there,' and she pointed to a large white truck with PURITAN MAID painted on its side.

Sonny graciously thanked her but she dismissed all of that with another of her deadly stares. 'Let's go and keep a look out for the pigs,' she said to the others and she marched her little band of ragamuffins off in the direction of the arch with its totem of the unknown animal skull.

While they had been talking the encampment had come to life. Radios were warming up, more and more figures were emerging from their sleeping quarters and a great deal of communal foraging for firewood seemed to be taking place. Roaming dogs, as well, were now in evidence and a nervous Sonny mentally measured the distance between himself and the big white truck. He decided to make a dash for it. Well, not exactly a *dash*, for that would have implied nervous haste and drawn even further attention to himself. More a brisk, strolling action was closer to the truth.

Half-way across the expanse of grass a pack of gambolling curs caught up with him and swarmed about him in playful fashion with open jaws. They also threw a deadly stink which he tried hard to keep at bay. It was like stumbling through a living, moving, knee-high carpet but somehow he managed to stay upright. Then they darted away as quickly and as silently as they had come, and he found himself trembling. He felt as if he had been mugged by one of those gangs of 'steamers' who pass through the London

Underground like a sudden and malevolent gale.

The hippy leader's truck had a door cut into its offside, balanced by a couple of normal-sized, curtained windows. The famous Maid herself, with her kerchief and modest gown, still beamed reassuringly down from her painted vantage point, despite having two of her front teeth blacked out. The effect was more akin to a leer and Sonny hesitated a shade because of it. Then he saw a bell and a sign, obviously purloined, that read SURGERY HOURS 10.00–12.00. He pressed the bell and stepped back. For the first time he became aware of a faint droning sound coming from within, which he couldn't place. He thumbed the white, domed push again and the droning ceased.

Some little distance away a group of young New Age Travellers had gathered to watch. They conferred together and seemed to be on the point of taking some action regarding him, so Sonny shoved hard on the door which unexpectedly gave way before him.

The dimly lit interior he found himself in had its floor and walls thickly covered with rugs of the *kelim* variety, and an incense burner was choking the atmosphere with a smoky blue haze. On a mattress facing him, a plump middle-aged man, naked except for a skull cap, squatted in the lotus position. He had his eyes tightly closed and it was obvious now to Sonny he had been interrupted in the middle of his first mantra of the day. Sonny coughed loudly from a combination of the jitters and the heavy fumes and the man with the Buddha-like breasts, returning to the earthly plane, said wearily, 'I hope you're not some creature from the media, some press jackal or other, for I'm picking up a set of extremely bad vibes.' Accent and delivery were pure public school and, screwing up his eyes against the reeking joss, Sonny realised that the thing on his shaved head was, in reality, a tasselled cricket cap turned back to front.

'I come in peace,' he croaked. 'On an errand of mercy,' feeling like an idiot as he spoke.

The man called Baz sighed wearily. 'They all say that.'

He closed his heavy, glossed eyelids once more and Sonny cried, 'Please, please, just hear me out! *I* used to be a hippy, too. It never leaves you.' And he launched into an incoherent retelling of his quest. It was a humiliating performance, certainly one that John Wayne would never have understood or tolerated, even in script form, but Sonny was past caring.

When he'd finished, passion spent and all of his narrative seemingly wasted, like water disappearing into sand, he heard the man on the mattress murmur, 'Karma is all. All is Karma.' Then – 'Travellers such as you describe come and go constantly through our Rainbow Valley. Every single soul in transit, after all, must seek his own Heavenly Way. No one keeps track here, my friend. It is our way. However, if you yourself are a genuine seeker after the Truthful Path, give up your possessions and join us. You may make a small beginning by donating something to our Fighting Fund.' With a long, pale hand he languidly indicated a plastic replica of a policeman's helmet sitting open-ended in the shadows. Looking inside Sonny saw it was a little more than half full of cash, notes as well as coins. He took out his wallet from his back pocket hardly noticing how thin it had become over the past days – or was it weeks? – and let drop two tenners. Then he stood there on the soft, rich thickness of the rugs, dazed as well as dumb, until the spiritual leader in his cricket cap began humming through his nose again.

Outside in the open, Sonny felt even more of a displaced person. But, if so, where had he come from? It was a question posed in a foreign language, as far as he was concerned. Aimlessly he wandered across the tract of burnt and beaten turf, ignored now by everyone, it seemed, even the dogs. At some stage he found himself standing by a roaring fire fuelled by what appeared to be bright new fencing posts. Someone handed him a mug of tea and he swallowed the sweet brown liquid gratefully. By some strange alchemy he had achieved the same look as all the others. His face hung like meat, heavy and unresponsive; even his clothes felt as if they had been thickened and 'distressed' in some way by a life in the open.

A bearded giant in a RAF greatcoat asked politely if

he could possibly spare just a single cigarette. Sonny felt ridiculous tears of gratitude spring to his eyes for, indeed, he did happen to have one. Just one. Revived and emboldened, he asked the young giant if, by any remote chance, he'd come across a youngish guy on a motor-cycle with a bird on the back. 'Calls himself by a Red Indian name and rides a pretty powerful set of wheels.'

The tall youth in the greatcoat pondered for a moment. 'Come to think of it, I did hear a great ole chopper. Around three, four in the morning.' He looked around him. 'Did anyone else notice that?'

'Oi did,' said someone nondescript and hairy. 'Oi'd say it were a Harley Davidson. Nothing sounds quite like your good ole Harley.'

Keeping his voice calm and level, Sonny enquired, 'Do you think they might still be here?'

The one puffing on his last cigarette blew a thin lance of smoke out into the early morning air. 'More'n likely. If they didn't head off bright and earlyish. Which hardly makes much sense, does it? If they're travelling on the light side I'd say they'd have kipped down over there.' He pointed to the remains of the old brick control-tower at the far end of the man-made steppe they were now standing on. 'That's where the one-nighters usually have their squat-downs. Ain't that so, lads?'

But Sonny didn't wait for confirmation. Already he was travelling across the summer-scorched earth in a parody of one of those scrawny men in shorts and singlet who jerkily race at walking speed, his intention, of course, being not to attract the dogs a second time by any show of excessive movement. The young travellers at the fire laughed loudly at the sight, but he was immune by now, attention fixed firmly on the ruins ahead.

When he got to about a dozen yards from the place he slowed down. His heart was pumping but his head felt clear. He began to creep closer. Any signs of life appeared extinct; possibly since the early forties, it came to him. Men in flying jackets and handlebar moustaches once had 'scrambled' here, now there were sheep droppings and spider webs. He looked through the corroded metal window bars into a museum of decay, then he made his way around to the back. Bushes were growing there in rich profusion; he recognised currant and possibly gooseberry, too, gone back to the wild. It seemed odd to think of someone cultivating such plants between sorties over the Channel.

The thorns clawed at his clothes as he edged close to the walls. He saw what appeared at first like the tail of some animal poking out through a window opening. He moved nearer. The striped fur seemed to be attached to a tapering metal rod, an aerial, he realised, and when he peered closer he saw that it extended from the rear end of a high-powered motor-cycle inside, perhaps as much as 1000 cc.

His eyes were getting accustomed to the gloom. In a far corner lay a heap of bedding and, as he watched, he detected movement and a naked arm extended itself, the arm of a healthy young male. But even if one arm was much like another, Sonny recognised the sleeping-bag. He had last seen it in the little green tent.

Drawing back from the window, he deliberated. The scenario which had sustained him this far was beginning to show signs of stress, because it was clearly obvious that the situation did not call for any bursting in with six-guns blazing. But, then, he thought, I'm getting my movies mixed up again, and he went off foraging until he found a thin, springy shoot long enough for his purpose. Feeding it through the opening of the window, he slid it across the floor close to the sleeper's bare arm and then very gently made contact. It took some little time to get a response but finally Choctaw's head emerged from its nest. Scratching his bared arm, he stretched, yawned, opened his eyes and looked straight away across at the motor-cycle. Then he saw Sonny and, to the latter's great surprise, he beamed a slow, welcoming grin of recognition that lit up his face. Sonny put his finger to his lips, the other nodded and, withdrawing from the window out of decency's sake, Sonny made his way around to the front to wait for him.

'Hey, if it ain't old Hank Williams himself,' were Choctaw's first words as he came across the grass to where Sonny was sitting on a rusty oil drum. 'What brings you to these parts, man? Great minds think alike, eh?'

'Time for a pow-wow, Ashley.'

Choctaw lowered himself to the ground. Putting his hand into the pocket of his unbuttoned shirt he brought out a fat virgin joint, shreds spilling from either end. 'You've got the name wrong, but I won't hold it against you. I like you, man. By the way, what happened to the accent?'

'It's too late for all of that. This is serious. You know why I'm here.'

The other sighed as he busied himself with the ritual of lighting up. He blew softly on the reddening tip until it achieved the correct glow. Closing his eyes he took a long and pleasurable drag. 'Peace-pipe time. Have a pull.'

Sonny joined him on the grass and they squatted like a couple of celebrants passing the sacred weed back and forth, back and forth, until Sonny felt his resolve unravel.

Choctaw said, 'Come with us, man. We're heading for Happy Valley in the Brecons. Teepee territory. Dream-time. Just the three of us.'

'The girl isn't going anywhere,' said Sonny.

'It's a free country.'

'Not for her, it isn't. She belongs with her mother. More importantly, she happens to be under age.'

Choctaw sighed heavily. 'And the little darlin' told me she'd just turned seventeen.'

'Fifteen, chief, fifteen. A schoolgirl.'

'What's wrong with schoolgirls?'

Sonny got to his feet. This had been a mistake, he could see that now, jaw instead of war. He felt fuddled but not too far gone to pile on one final ounce of pressure. 'You know what's on the far side of that gate back there?' he said, pointing to the rustic arch in the distance.

'The big bad world?'

'No, half of Hampshire's fucking police force, that's what. I've just walked past them. They're gearing up to come in here and, when they do, they'll be checking out every poor sod they can get their maulers on. I suppose you realise what you can get for screwing a minor.'

Choctaw said, 'What if I were to tell you we were in love?'

'One – I wouldn't believe you. Two – you'll never make it to Gretna Green.'

The man on the grass laughed loudly at that. 'You're quite a bullshitter yourself, old Hank, in your own way. That's why I like you so much. All that country and western crap. Still, it was pretty good while it lasted.'

Sonny looked down at him with something akin to affection. 'I fooled your pal Pilgrim, though,' he said. 'I did, didn't I?'

Choctaw rose a trifle unsteadily. 'Wow,' he said, shaking his head. 'Afghan Black. Only the best for me and my blood-brother here.' Circling about on the grass he did an impromptu little tribal dance.

'Pilgrim, you say,' he grinned. 'Now that is the daddy of them all when we're talking fantasy, man. What an artist. You didn't believe all that stuff of his, did you? And that junk he has downstairs? Pure counterfeit, just like the man himself. He collects people as well as fakes. Didn't you know that? That's why I got out when I did. I could see you might be next in line. He's like that. He has to have a rapid turnover. This is a man who deals in dreams, my friend, as well as other stuff you really don't want to know too much about. Like white powder you put up your nose or maybe stick into your arm? Bad medicine, heap bad medicine, believe me.' He came close and put both hands on Sonny's shoulders, giving him a little shake. 'Come to Wales, man. Just the two of us. It's beautiful this time of year.'

'This has to be sorted out first. Unfinished business. Between the mother and me.'

'They're not into dreams like you and me. Don't you know that? No woman ever is. They have to *get on* with things. Don't you understand that?'

Sonny looked at him with sadness, for the first time realising that he could be his own son in terms of age difference. 'Just send the girl out, Choctaw, before the pigs get here. Okay?'

The other turned away and Sonny watched him walk back to the ruined building. He felt old and tired, for that could have been himself an age ago, young and resilient and gathering resolve with each step. He dropped down on to the oil drum again, his rusty throne. The mist was clearing rapidly. He could see distant farmsteads and their silver silos catching the sun. Copses appeared to quiver gently, almost navy blue in places. On a far-off hill a tiny figure toiled upwards with his own very personal thoughts. Sonny ached at the beauty of this country. All of it. It was a hurt he could never, ever put into words just as, in the same way, he and his kind would never be able to make an impact, or imprint, on any part of it. Seated there, it was as if he didn't exist, had never existed, for that matter . . .

He thought of that final thing he'd done after he'd closed the door of the flat in London for the last time, all his bridges burned at his back. He'd prised off the painted-over *mezuza* from the jamb just to see what was inside, hoping for some clue to all those generations who'd gone before in that dark and underground place. And when he'd got it away from the wood, what did he find there? Nothing but an empty socket. No trace, none, of those other outsiders like himself with their Old World habits of keeping their noses clean, never making waves.

He took out Lester's little box from where he'd stowed it next to his skin. Like himself, it was beginning to show signs of wear and tear. This journey together had taken its toll on both of them. Lester, he thought, this isn't the resting place for you, I see that now. I'll find you somewhere else, God knows where, but not here, not in this country where you never belonged.

And then he heard the coughing roar of the motor-cycle and Choctaw came riding straight out through an opening in the walls of the old ruin. He was helmeted and leaning back in the saddle, Easy Rider fashion, for it was that kind of machine. The long, fur-tailed aerial waved like a pennant at his back. The machine bumped over the rough expanse in Sonny's direction and came to a halt a few feet away.

'Jump on, man!' cried Choctaw with a flash of teeth.

271

'We'll conquer the West together!'

But Sonny just shook his head. 'Go in peace, brother,' he said.

Choctaw twisted back the throttle, the engine roared. 'See you in Wales!' Then he sped off across the grass.

Sonny watched him until he disappeared from view among the drift of distant vehicles. He waited for the girl. Everything seemed to be falling into place as though it had been planned a very long time ago. Even when the minutes passed, three, four, five – he'd no means of knowing – it never entered his head that she still might be fast asleep in there, that Choctaw might well have played the rat, leaving explanations to him. He sat cradling the box in his lap as if even that, somehow, was part of the predetermined pattern. Then she came out of the ruins, just as he'd first seen her when she stepped down from that long-distance bus with nothing to her name but her tattered Miss Selfridge bag. She came towards him with her head lowered, seemingly scanning the grass, and Sonny, for the first time, felt something close to compassion for the clown-like figure with the painted features and haystack hair.

He said to her, 'Your mum's waiting for us up the road a piece, Natalie. Everything's cool, believe me. But before we go and meet her, let me try and explain something. You see, when she was your age she was a lot like you, maybe even wilder in her own way. That's why she gets in such a state. You've just got to be patient with her, that's all. Mothers tend to be that way, so they tell me. I know you think I'm something of a prize arsehole, okay, so do a lot of other people, but as that good old song puts it:

> *Cowboys are special,*
> *With their own brand of misery,*
> *From being alone too long . . .*

And, unbelievably, he continued singing to her as they stood together in the middle of that ancient airfield. He could see she was cruelly embarrassed but he kept on, regardless.

When he'd finished he said, 'Let's go find your mum,' and the two of them set off, the country crooning asshole and the little city punkette, towards the mêlée in the distance, for, by now, a phalanx of running figures in blue, riot shields at the ready, had trampled down the arch and were streaming on to the site to enforce the law of the land on people like themselves.

—FOUR—

'After the Fire is Gone'

'I'm sorry I said all those things. About you and Lester. I didn't mean any of them.'

Far below through the glass of the cafeteria wall Hazel could make out the solitary figure in a black one-piece at the edge of the deep end, hair in rats' tails. A single swimmer, a snorting, bald man in goggles, had the pool to himself. Already he had covered a dozen painful, ploughing lengths, for she couldn't help keeping count sensing Natalie would be doing the same, waiting patiently for him to complete his early morning session.

'Hazel?'

Poor Sonny, she was neglecting her other chick.

'He was only an old man,' she said. 'There was no harm in what I did for him.' Then as she saw the hurt flooding those spaniel eyes, she added softly, 'I love you, too, you know, Sonny.'

'Yeah,' he said with a sigh. 'Split three ways,' and she knew he was thinking of that lonely hunched teenager down below them with those blanched city limbs of hers.

'Guess we've come through a lot,' he went on. 'Our little family.'

'I feel like the Wreck of the Hesperus,' she sighed.

'You don't look like the Wreck of the Hesperus.'

'*You* certainly do.'

And he laughed, a glimpse of the old Sonny briefly lighting up across the coffee cups at her. *Oh, keep it like that, please, please,* Hazel prayed, *because that's the way I want to remember you.*

The swimmer was rising now out of the water, purple-faced and more than a shade shaky on the short length of upright metal ladder. Standing on the flooded tiles he blew out his cheeks and slapped colour into his torso. As he settled his trunks more becomingly over his womanly hips Hazel

277

realised suddenly all of this was for the benefit of her daughter at the far end of the pool staring morosely into its blue depths. God, she thought, does it – will it – never end?

Then Sonny said quietly, 'Is she all right?' the first time he'd made any mention of past events, just as in the same way some strange and frozen reticence on her part had kept her away from the subject.

She looked at him. 'I don't know, I really do not know.'

The two of them continued to gaze down at the by now lone figure sitting at the edge of the slowly settling pool.

It was still very early. They had been the first arrivals, beating the bald man to it by a matter of seconds. He hadn't taken kindly to that, Hazel had noticed, one of those people whose lives are structured to a T. His dog, beefy and bad-tempered like its owner, kept up a steady snarling where he'd left it in the car park.

The journey here had been her idea, for her immediate thought had been to get Natalie into a shower as soon as possible. Some sort of cleansing ritual must have been at the back of her mind, she supposed, but she didn't consider any of that at the time, acting purely on instinct. And Sonny and Natalie allowed themselves to be swept along by that impulse without protest or comment of any kind.

At the nearest town she got Sonny to stop outside the first clothing shop they came to, where she bought jeans, underwear, a pair of plimsolls and the simplest bathing suit they could provide. Then she directed Sonny to follow the signs to the municipal swimming pool and, in its changing-room, she made Natalie put all her old clothes into a plastic rubbish sack she had brought with her and then get into the new black one-piece. She watched and waited as she did so and it was as if they had both returned in time to an earlier and innocent age when she would supervise her nine-year old in the old enamelled bath in that council flat in Ealing.

Sitting there on the slatted bench in the high humidity, it came to Hazel that this was the first time she'd seen her own daughter, flesh of her flesh, naked like this since that time. She sat there holding back her tears.

Sonny said, 'Remember the Rainbow Room? There's lots more of those out there just waiting to be discovered. Natalie needs her own Rainbow Room too, you know, Hazel.'

'Maybe it never existed,' she said sadly. 'That old dance-hall of ours by the sea. I just don't know any more.'

He took her hands in his. 'Don't say that.'

But she could tell that he knew, in his heart of hearts, that the old magic had almost run out for both of them. 'You're being very, very nice to us, Sonny,' she said.

'I know,' he replied. 'And it's bloody well killing me, if you must know.'

They both laughed at that. Far below, as if the sound had somehow penetrated the glass, Natalie turned her face, pale and scrubbed, seemingly, of expression, and for the first time, in spite of herself, Hazel allowed conjecture to gnaw at her. The cruellest part of this whole affair, she told herself, was knowing that she would never ever find out the truth of what really had taken place. For who was going to tell her if she did ask. But then, did she really want to hear *details*?

Sonny twisted his cup in its saucer. The knuckles of his right hand were scraped raw and dark blue crescents showed beneath the nails. A distinct gypsy-like odour also clung to him and she felt herself tugged by love once more for this man and what he had undergone on her behalf. Again, the exact details of that, too, were something she would never know about.

'Look,' he said, 'about last night . . .'

Stop him now before it's too late, she told herself, but something self-punishing within made her hold her tongue.

'I don't think anything *serious* occurred. I had a talk with this Choctaw character and he – '

'*Talk!*' she cried. 'You had a *talk* with him!' He bowed his head before the onslaught. 'That animal, that viper who took advantage of that child down there – you *talked* with him!'

She was thinking of that night she'd heard the pair of them laughing together outside the camper before heading off, stoned, to Pilgrim's party, two male conspirators, buddy-buddying.

He said, 'What did you want me to do, Hazel? Beat the shit out of him?'

'*I* would have, if it had been me.'

'Yeah,' he said sighing, 'you probably would – if you could. But, then, it wasn't that sort of situation, and you're not me, are you?'

He rose looking down at her and she felt suddenly very confused.

'I didn't mean, it, truly I didn't.'

'Sure you did,' he said. 'Why pretend? A couple of great pretenders, that's you and me. Another good old oldie, eh, Hazel?'

She felt her eyes go moist. 'You never really finished your own song, did you?'

'Guess I must have just run out of time. We both did.'

'Oh, Sonny,' she cried reaching out to him across the table, and he met her half way, hands clasping hers above the crockery. Natalie was forgotten in that moment, as was the yawning young waitress at the far counter pretending not to notice or stare. Exerting a steady pressure, Hazel pulled him back down into his seat and Sonny, being Sonny, put up little resistance.

'I'll never forget you,' she said. 'You do know that, don't you?' Now she was weeping unrestrainedly, an additional bonus for the waitress in the distance.

'Hey,' he said, 'you know, as well as I do, cowgirls don't cry,' and he wrenched a handful of paper napkins from the dispenser on the table, reaching them across. She dabbed at her eyes.

'Please don't look too closely at the Wreck of the Hesperus.' Then, 'Just who or what the hell was that, anyway? A ship?'

Sonny grinned.

> '*It was the schooner Hesperus,*
> *That sailed the wintry sea.*
> *And the skipper had taken his little daughter,*
> *To bear him company.*

280

'Just like you and me, Hazel. Our very own Hesperus out there in the car-park at this very moment.'

'You're such an idiot, Sonny,' she said. 'You really are.'

'Henry Wadsworth Longfellow. We had it hammered into us at school. By this one teacher. Didn't I ever tell you about him? I thought I had. He was the joker who gave yours truly this handle.'

They sat there holding hands like a couple of teenagers completely engrossed in whatever nonsense might flow across the table between them next. Only it wasn't that, was it, she was suddenly telling herself. It was part of something the two of them had shared together, something precious which could never be explained or made significant to another single soul. She had a moment of panic then, anticipating her own future, the one she'd mapped out for herself like a sentence. That slumped and deadened teenager below; both of them locked tight into their shells incapable of sharing any of their innermost feelings or even something as corny as this.

'Where will you go?' she asked, turning serious again.

'Wales, most likely. I've heard it can be pretty spectacular up there around this time of year. The Brecons. All those magic mushrooms, you know?' He grinned at her. 'No need to worry about this kiddo. He's a survivor.'

But both of them knew that might well be just another of those old and secondhand sentiments lifted from any of a dozen songs they'd been singing together over the past weeks.

Then he said, 'How about you?'

She hesitated before answering. 'I thought we might spend a little time by the sea together. The South coast.'

She could see the hurt in his eyes for the second time as he realised that she'd been making her plans for some little time, plans which hadn't included him. But what about his own Welsh trip, she thought. That hadn't arrived in his head out of nowhere a minute earlier, either.

In silence they sat there as the implication of what they'd just said spread like the ripples on that pool below. Two depth charges stirring the depths. She wanted to weep again.

A bleached blonde arrived with a trio of noisy kids in tow and plumped herself down at a table further along close to the glass. After she'd seen her brood off she took a paperback out of her beach bag and lit up a cigarette. They both stared at her, dully, like a couple of heavy-eyed tourists. She might have been a slab of stone as far as they were concerned. Sonny spoke first.

He said, 'She's going to get a chill sitting down there like that,' and she looked at him sharply, but there was no trace of irony in his voice, on his face, either, for that matter.

'I'd better get her, then.'

'Good idea,' he said.

'Are you coming?'

'Not right away.' For some reason he seemed embarrassed. 'I just need to calm down a bit first.'

'Oh, Sonny, I'm sorry, so sorry,' she blurted, feeling suddenly contrite. What a hard and unfeeling cow she really was.

'No, no, no,' he said. 'It's nothing like that. I'm afraid I've just got a little excited, that's all. Down – ' He left it unfinished and she stared at him. 'I know it sounds sick, but I can't help it.'

His face was a picture as he sat there. She began to laugh. 'Oh, Sonny, Sonny,' she gasped. 'There's never been anyone quite like you. Never.' And without thought for what the waitress or the chain-smoking housewife with the dog-eared Jackie Collins might see and think, she reached out shamelessly to him under the table.

Why couldn't life be like the movies, she was speculating. If it was, the two of them would be all over one another in seconds across the coffee things, or on the floor throwing off their clothes, and to hell with appearances. But instead, they continued to sit there feeling aroused and nostalgic at the same time, like two old flames, while she fondled him just for old time's sake.

'You were the best, Sonny,' she said.

'I was?'

'No doubt about it.' Giving one final farewell squeeze she slowly got to her feet. 'See you in the car-park?'

He grinned up at her. 'Highway is my home. Remember?'

And so she left him there with that old, sad, Sonny half-smile on his face, the one she knew would be there to haunt her on those bad days in Fulham when she would be feeling low and in the mood for recollection.

Oblivious to the wash about her ankles, for the three children had set up a considerable swell in the shallows, Natalie continued to stare down into the deep end of the pool. For an instant Hazel stood watching from the doorway. In her hand she had a lime and orange coloured bath towel, another purchase she'd made in that shop this morning. Like the black one-piece, it, too, was meant for their trip to the sea together. She smelt its newness, its rich factory odour, pressing it to her cheek for the briefest of moments, then she moved forward holding it before her.

Natalie didn't stir or look up, even when its folds fell about her and Hazel had to hoist her wrapped and unresponsive weight up off the wet tiles until she stood by her side. Nothing was said, not a look passed between them as they made their way back to the changing-room, away from the chlorine-scented, slapping waves. All the while Hazel kept her arm about the other's shoulders and, taking a corner of the thick, fleecy material, she suddenly found herself gently towelling her daughter's hair. The action was purely instinctive on her part but Natalie's reaction seemed equally spontaneous for she submitted herself as if what was happening to her was the most natural thing in the world. Which it was, Hazel addressed herself fiercely, it was, for suddenly, for the first time in a very long time, she felt genuinely hopeful about the future.

High above, behind the glass of the cafeteria, Sonny, she knew, was watching, but there was nothing she could do about it, she told herself. A part of her went out to him and what he must be feeling seeing the two of them like this, but in her heart she knew the rest of her had already moved on, even as she and Natalie passed out of view and into the heat and steam of the changing-room.

'Take Me Home, Country Roads'

The garage man in Abergavenny shook his head pityingly, like all his kind, and said, 'It's a wonder you're still in one piece. You've been driving a time-bomb, if you don't mind me saying so.'

All of which Sonny took to mean expense, a considerable amount of expense.

'How long to have it fixed?' he asked.

The man removed his cap and looked inside as if some primitive form of calculator lurked there. Sonny meanwhile stared at a pin-up on the wall advertising spark-plugs. The man went into a long, lilting monologue about parts and labour, while the rain drummed down on the corrugated iron roof. The girl on the calendar, it seemed to Sonny, had every solitary sexual hormone air-brushed out of her. She looked edible like a wet and glistening dessert.

Sonny said, 'I'll throw in fifty for yourself, if I can drive out of here in under two hours,' adding, 'I've got a boat to catch. Holyhead. The first sailing in the morning.'

He'd no idea why he'd said it, for it was a lie, at least it had been a lie up until then. The plan had been to motor leisurely to Brecon. Where else, after Hazel had loved him and left him at the bus station.

They'd wept together while outside Natalie crouched down in the waiting express with its reclining seats, toilet, the two hostesses to serve coffee and light refreshments and the video over the driver's head. For thirty miles up the motorway the two of them watched it while pretending not to notice him driving demented, nose to tail behind their coach. That blue flicker mocking him until, finally, he felt the madness leave him. The next turnoff said MONMOUTH AND GWENT and sucked him in and he took the curve like someone under sedation.

Now, leaving the garage, he went outside to kill time in

284

some dark, cheerless Welsh pub. The fruit machine sang intermittently to the emptiness while the rain coursed down the window panes, for the heatwave had finally broken. He drank steadily until closing time, not feeling a thing, then he got up and went back down the street to the garage again.

The light from a welding torch lent an infernal quality now to the interior. The little man in the greasy cap cast the shadow of a deformed giant in a helmet, while the camper's guts lay strewn in crude disarray about the floor. Even the pin-up looked like a vampire. Sonny sat on a pile of tyres and switched off, something he seemed to be getting quite good at just recently. The sparks flew while the gauge on the cylinders patiently measured out the burning gas. There seemed to be no urgency about anything.

At one in the morning the bonnet came down finally, and the two men faced one another in the still shed. Money changed hands. The garage owner, sighing, went back to his midnight accounting in his tiny office and Sonny drove out into dead, wet streets.

He kept going without a break right up through the Border counties, then across wilder country towards Anglesey, blackness abounding. The wipers beat strongly; he hadn't a thought or opinion in his head any more, for he was on automatic pilot, as he had been since early that morning.

At some point he crested the final hill and saw, ahead and below, a paler mass. He smelt sea-wrack through the open window, then there were lights and the port appeared. Past darkened, sleeping houses he took the camper until the great, illuminated, white ship loomed up with its open cargo doors and engine hum. All the arrangements that had to be made to secure passage he accomplished seemingly by instinct, for not once did he have to ask for directions or instructions of any kind. Then, after he'd cut the camper's engines on the car deck and stepped out into the haze of fumes that hung there, he climbed up the wet stairway as far as it was possible for him to go.

The rain had stopped when he reached the air and he

found a bench on the empty deck. A knife-thin, reddening line of demarcation between land and sky had begun to form in the east and he watched it spread with fascination. He found he couldn't take his eyes off it, greedily, selfishly, even, for suddenly it was as if he wanted no one else to share it with him.

When all was carnation pink, as high as the radar mast, Sonny rose and gripped the rail, but his attention was still held by that angry glow, low on the horizon. It looked like a fire back there, it seemed to him, a big fire, something burning on a very large scale indeed, and as he stood there he began to laugh at his own private joke.

Now, see what you've gone and done, he said to the gulls. *No going back now for you, old son.*

He was still laughing when the *Saint Columba*'s great invisible screws began to turn and, in a welter of foam and bobbing kitchen waste, she commenced coming round. The seagulls cried, various chains rattled and thumped into place and, finally, they were thrusting out towards the open sea.

When Sonny felt convinced in his own inexplicable way that finally they might well be beyond the tidal pull of the mainland, he unbuttoned his shirt and carefully, reverently, brought out the little carved box. He held it for a moment or two and, unable to help himself, examined it one last time to see if there was an opening or join in the construction he might have missed, but it still held on to its secrets to the last. Then he threw it out as far as his strength would allow and he watched it bob off in the grey-green wake of the ship until it was gone from sight.

'Sweet dreams, Lester, old buddy,' he murmured. '*Hasta la vista.*'

Someone coughed close by, a man in a buttoned rainproof and fisherman's tweed hat. He was leaning on the rail looking lonely, retired, middle-class, obviously desperate for someone to talk to. He said, 'Excuse me, but are you American?' His accent Sonny detected instantly was Northern like his own, possibly Belfast.

He said, 'How did you guess?'

The man laughed, they both laughed, at the idiocy of the question.

Emboldened by this, the stranger asked, 'Forgive me, but was that a wee box of some description I happened to see you throw over the side?'

Sonny looked at him. 'Just casting my dead upon the waters, friend,' and the stranger laughed uncomprehendingly. Then, 'Tell me, friend, does country music appeal to you, by any chance? Because that just so happens to be my professional line of business. I've got a major tour lined up with first class supporting acts. I did have a singing partner at one time, but that's all water under the bridge. Strictly solo from now on. Ain't it always the best?'

And as the gulls wheeled, dived and foraged in the foaming wake he began to sing.

> *Woke up this mornin', Chevy wouldn't go,*
> *Just like its owner, battery low.*
> *Bodywork all shot to hell, power and steering, too,*
> *Ain't just trucks an' cars, you know, that end up runnin' slow.*
> *Depreciation, depreciation, depreci-ation blues,*
> *When nature's tow-truck gets you, ain't nothin' left to lose.*

A Selection of Arrow Books

☐ No Enemy But Time	Evelyn Anthony	£2.95
☐ The Lilac Bus	Maeve Binchy	£2.99
☐ Rates of Exchange	Malcolm Bradbury	£3.50
☐ Prime Time	Joan Collins	£3.50
☐ Rosemary Conley's Complete Hip and Thigh Diet	Rosemary Conley	£2.99
☐ Staying Off the Beaten Track	Elizabeth Gundrey	£6.99
☐ Duncton Wood	William Horwood	£4.50
☐ Duncton Quest	William Horwood	£4.50
☐ A World Apart	Marie Joseph	£3.50
☐ Erin's Child	Sheelagh Kelly	£3.99
☐ Colours Aloft	Alexander Kent	£2.99
☐ Gondar	Nicholas Luard	£4.50
☐ The Ladies of Missalonghi	Colleen McCullough	£2.50
☐ The Veiled One	Ruth Rendell	£3.50
☐ Sarum	Edward Rutherfurd	£4.99
☐ Communion	Whitley Strieber	£3.99

Prices and other details are liable to change

ARROW BOOKS, BOOKSERVICE BY POST, PO BOX 29, DOUGLAS, ISLE OF MAN, BRITISH ISLES

NAME...

ADDRESS...

....

....

Please enclose a cheque or postal order made out to Arrow Books Ltd. for the amount due and allow the following for postage and packing.

U.K. CUSTOMERS: Please allow 22p per book to a maximum of £3.00.

B.F.P.O. & EIRE: Please allow 22p per book to a maximum of £3.00.

OVERSEAS CUSTOMERS: Please allow 22p per book.

Whilst every effort is made to keep prices low it is sometimes necessary to increase cover prices at short notice. Arrow Books reserve the right to show new retail prices on covers which may differ from those previously advertised in the text or elsewhere.

Bestselling Fiction

☐ No Enemy But Time	Evelyn Anthony	£2.95
☐ The Lilac Bus	Maeve Binchy	£2.99
☐ Prime Time	Joan Collins	£3.50
☐ A World Apart	Marie Joseph	£3.50
☐ Erin's Child	Sheelagh Kelly	£3.99
☐ Colours Aloft	Alexander Kent	£2.99
☐ Gondar	Nicholas Luard	£4.50
☐ The Ladies of Missalonghi	Colleen McCullough	£2.50
☐ Lily Golightly	Pamela Oldfield	£3.50
☐ Talking to Strange Men	Ruth Rendell	£2.99
☐ The Veiled One	Ruth Rendell	£3.50
☐ Sarum	Edward Rutherfurd	£4.99
☐ The Heart of the Country	Fay Weldon	£2.50

Prices and other details are liable to change

ARROW BOOKS, BOOKSERVICE BY POST, PO BOX 29, DOUGLAS, ISLE
OF MAN, BRITISH ISLES

NAME..

ADDRESS..

....

....

Please enclose a cheque or postal order made out to Arrow Books Ltd. for the amount
due and allow the following for postage and packing.

U.K. CUSTOMERS: Please allow 22p per book to a maximum of £3.00.

B.F.P.O. & EIRE: Please allow 22p per book to a maximum of £3.00.

OVERSEAS CUSTOMERS: Please allow 22p per book.

Whilst every effort is made to keep prices low it is sometimes necessary to increase cover
prices at short notice. Arrow Books reserve the right to show new retail prices on covers
which may differ from those previously advertised in the text or elsewhere.

Bestselling General Fiction

☐	No Enemy But Time	Evelyn Anthony	£2.95
☐	Skydancer	Geoffrey Archer	£3.50
☐	The Sisters	Pat Booth	£3.50
☐	Captives of Time	Malcolm Bosse	£2.99
☐	Saudi	Laurie Devine	£2.95
☐	Duncton Wood	William Horwood	£4.50
☐	Aztec	Gary Jennings	£3.95
☐	A World Apart	Marie Joseph	£3.50
☐	The Ladies of Missalonghi	Colleen McCullough	£2.50
☐	Lily Golightly	Pamela Oldfield	£3.50
☐	Sarum	Edward Rutherfurd	£4.99
☐	Communion	Whitley Strieber	£3.99

Prices and other details are liable to change

ARROW BOOKS, BOOKSERVICE BY POST, PO BOX 29, DOUGLAS, ISLE
OF MAN, BRITISH ISLES

NAME...

ADDRESS ....

....

....

Please enclose a cheque or postal order made out to Arrow Books Ltd. for the amount
due and allow the following for postage and packing.

U.K. CUSTOMERS: Please allow 22p per book to a maximum of £3.00.

B.F.P.O. & EIRE: Please allow 22p per book to a maximum of £3.00.

OVERSEAS CUSTOMERS: Please allow 22p per book.

Whilst every effort is made to keep prices low it is sometimes necessary to increase cover
prices at short notice. Arrow Books reserve the right to show new retail prices on covers
which may differ from those previously advertised in the text or elsewhere.

Arena

☐ The Gooseboy	A L Barker	£3.99
☐ The History Man	Malcolm Bradbury	£3.50
☐ Rates of Exchange	Malcolm Bradbury	£3.50
☐ Albert's Memorial	David Cook	£3.99
☐ Another Little Drink	Jane Ellison	£3.99
☐ Mother's Girl	Elaine Feinstein	£3.99
☐ Roots	Alex Haley	£5.95
☐ The March of the Long Shadows	Norman Lewis	£3.99
☐ After a Fashion	Stanley Middleton	£3.50
☐ Kiss of the Spiderwoman	Manuel Puig	£2.95
☐ Second Sight	Anne Redmon	£3.99
☐ Season of Anomy	Wole Soyinka	£3.99
☐ Nairn in Darkness and Light	David Thomson	£3.99
☐ The Clock Winder	Anne Tyler	£2.95
☐ The Rules of Life	Fay Weldon	£2.50

Prices and other details are liable to change

ARROW BOOKS, BOOKSERVICE BY POST, PO BOX 29, DOUGLAS, ISLE
OF MAN, BRITISH ISLES

NAME..

ADDRESS..

....

....

Please enclose a cheque or postal order made out to Arrow Books Ltd. for the amount
due and allow the following for postage and packing.

U.K. CUSTOMERS: Please allow 22p per book to a maximum of £3.00.

B.F.P.O. & EIRE: Please allow 22p per book to a maximum of £3.00.

OVERSEAS CUSTOMERS: Please allow 22p per book.

Whilst every effort is made to keep prices low it is sometimes necessary to increase cover
prices at short notice. Arrow Books reserve the right to show new retail prices on covers
which may differ from those previously advertised in the text or elsewhere.